JACK SHEPPARD.

LIFE AND ADVENTURES

OF

JACK SHEPPARD.

NEW EDITION.

LONDON. JAMES COCHRANE

THE

LIFE AND ADVENTURES

OF

JACK SHEPPARD.

BY

LINCOLN FORTESCUE, ESQ.

———

NEW EDITION,

WITH NUMEROUS ADDITIONS.

———

ILLUSTRATED WITH TWELVE PLATES.

" Truth is stranger than Fiction."—BYRON.

LONDON:

JAMES COCHRANE, 128, CHANCERY LANE.

———

1845.

PREFACE.

A NEW and improved edition of the following popular work, in a more convenient and economical form, having long imperatively been called for by the public, the Author and Publisher, in compliance with this general request, have now the pleasure of presenting it to their patrons, greatly extended in matter, and as greatly reduced in cost. In fact, stimulated by the encouragement extended to former endeavours, at least one-third of the present edition will be found to be entirely original, while another third has been nearly re-written, and the remaining third so carefully revised and corrected as to render the whole, to all intents and purposes, an entirely new work.

Much outcry has been raised against the, so-called, Jack Sheppardism, and Tom and Jerryism, of our literature, by the pseudo moralists of the day, the pharasaitical scribes and elders of the age, who proclaim their benefactions through the voice of the public crier, and by the medium of the parish bell-man in our different market places, together with the affectors of fine writing, and those precious noodles who draw their ideas of *vulgarity* from the common words of dictionaries. The very same yell was raised by the Mohocks of Gay's time against that writer's inimitable " Beggars' Opera :" it was pronounced to be " low—*demn'd low !*" What will the exquisite censors of the present age say, when they are informed that the refined Italians have of late days forsaken the " Pastor Fido" of their own elegant Guarini to pour over the unpastoral adventures of the Giovanni Pastor of our Newgate Calendar? Yet such is the fact ! Sterne might well have added the cant of *refinement* to the different cants he has so admirably gibbetted in his " Tristram Shandy." Those sensitive persons that rail so pathetically against the slang and debasement of certain writers, must remind the reader of the bear leader in Goldsmith's delightful comedy " She Stoops to Conquer," who liked the squire, Tony Lumpkin, because he hated " all as vas low, and who wished the glass he vas a taking might be his *pison* if his bear ever danced to any but the genteelestest of tunes — ' Vater parted,' and the ' Minnyvit,' in ' Harry Adne.' "

The most perfect lines of slang ever written occur in a poem by Byron*—the sublime Byron ! and it should not be forgotten that the prince of

* Who in a row like Tom could lead the van,
   Booze the ken, or at the Spell-ken hustle?
 Who queer a flat ? Who ('spite of Bow-street ban)
   On the high toby-spice so flash the muzzle?

Spanish painters, Murillo, whose beggar boys and vagabonds are immortal, was equally successful in innumerable sacred compositions of the loftiest conception, and the most exalted character, while one of the most fanciful of modern poets has often left Anacreon, and the Greeks of the old time, to dally with the modern Greeks of the town and turf, and revel with the fancy of the ring.*

The humanity of many of our first writers becomes the more noble and refined in proportion to the humility of their subject, but those who can find no other fault with the life-like creations of an Eugene Sue, that master spirit of our times, can comfortably wrap themselves up in their own assumed superiority, with the sweeping condemnation that he is low—cursedly low !   The assumed

> " Who, on a lark, with black-eyed Sal (his Blowing),
>   So prime, so swell, so nutty, and so knowing?"
>   *Don Juan*, canto xi. stanza 19.

To these lines Byron adds, in a note, the following stanza of a song, which was very popular in my early days:—

> " On the high toby-spice flash the muzzle,
>   In spite of each gallows old scout ;
> If you at the spell-ken can't hustle,
>   You'll be hobbled in making a clout :
> Then your Blowing will wax gallows haughty,
>   When she hears of your scaly mistake,
> She'll surely turn snitch for the forty,
>   That her Jack may be regular weight."

* Moore, ' Memorial to Congress,' &c. &c.

refinement of these individuals, and the morbid
sensibility of those sickly persons who shrink from
and denounce as immoral and improper all subjects
having their foundation in the annals of crime, will,
we think, be fully answered by some remarks of
an able and eloquent writer, occurring in a powerful article on a work entitled ' Causes Criminelles
Célèbres du dix-Neuvième Siècle, Paris, 1828.'—
an article which appeared in No. VII. of *The
Foreign Quarterly Review for April*, 1829. In
some preliminary observations on criminal trials,
speaking of the absorbing interest so universally
felt by all classes in the details of crime, the writer
makes the following striking and very convincing
observations, a sufficient answer, we should presume, to all the eminent twaddle of those who,
from a false affectation of morality, a squeamish
fear of excitement, have prated so largely of the
non-legitimacy of criminal subjects for the purposes
of the poet and romancist, the novelist, the dramatist, &c.

" Four thousand years after the birth of crime,"
says the writer we have named, " it may well be
imagined that people have become critical and
fastidious on this subject. Taste as well as in-
stinct enters into the question : we weep by rule
as much as by sympathy. This is not to be wondered at. The only remarkable thing is, that

after mankind have been committing crimes of all sorts and sizes for forty centuries, our attention should be vehemently stirred by any act of guilt whatever. It is a perversity to call the uncontrollable and mysterious feeling which impels us to read and listen, when the subject is of this nature—and to gloat, as it were, upon the *loathsome details of misery and guilt—a vulgar passion.* It is a human passion. In this the learned and the ignorant, and the coarse-minded and the intellectual, are alike. Our attraction is twofold—a sympathy with the injured, and a sympathy with the guilty. There is something in the purest bosom which acknowledges an awful fellowship of humanity even with those who are held, by their deeds, to outrage human nature—a still small voice within, which says in a moral as well as a physical sense, ' to corruption thou art my father —to the worm, thou art my brother and my sister.' This is the essence of human nature, and the internal evidence of the great truths of religion. Crime is within us, and around us; its seeds are in our hearts; its blossoms and bitter fruits hang above our path; it is—

> ' That deadly Upas—that all blasting tree,
> Whose root is earth, whose leaves and branches be
> The skies, that rain their plagues on men like dew.'

It is the business of our thoughts, the stimulant of our wishes, the subject of our prayers, the theme of our studies, the life of our amusement; it is the very *body of history*; it is THE VERY SOUL OF ROMANCE."

To these remarks nothing need be added as they can receive no denial—Jack Sheppard, with all his improvements and imperfections on his head, is therefore confidently committed to the protection of the considerate reader. No pains nor expense have been spared either by Author or Publisher to render this edition worthy of the patronage now solicited for it.

Jack Sheppard's own account of his Life, written by himself, while he was confined in Newgate, and much curious memoranda from the newspapers of the period, relating to the different persons and events forming the subject matter of the Text, has been subjoined in an Appendix, that the reader may have an opportunity of judging how far the Author has deviated from recorded facts. It will be found that no startling improbability has been set forth with the view of merely creating an effect, that the House-breaker has not been exalted into a Hero for the dangerous example of others; but that, on the contrary, only such deviations have been made, as were absolutely necessary, and are sanctioned in such cases, by the best writers.

128, CHANCERY LANE,
May 1st, 1845.

INTRODUCTION.

NEWGATE IN THE OLDEN TIME.

THE turnkeys bowed as a visiter entered the lodge
of Old Newgate, Tuesday, November the 17th,
1724, the morning after the memorable execution
of Jack Sheppard; and slipping a two-guinea piece
into the hand of the head gaoler, Mr. Austin, requested to know if he could not be indulged with
the sight of the building, particularly those portions of it that had been the scene of the wonderful
escapes of this notorious and daring individual.

"Certainly, Sir," answered that officer, respect-
fully touching his hat, and pocketing the money:
"ve don't show Newgate to every body that don't
come here exactly on *business* and purfeshonal;
but vith a gemman like you, Sir, as vants to inform
your mind, or vhat not, vhy the case is different—
it's alvays a pleasure then. Ve vere just going
our rounds, to see that our flock arn't in vant of
any thing, so you can't have a better opportunity."

"You have lost your most remarkable lodger?"
said the visiter.

"Oh! vhat? Captain Sheppard!" answered the
gaoler; "yes, he's gone, poor fellow, to our loss

B

and his own, too —vhy, ve used to take a matter
of thirty pound a day, sometimes, by the quality
coming to see him !—Jack vas an astonishing fellow, Sir, a wery astonishing fellow, that's the truth
on't—he played me two or three scurvy tricks, certainly, plague on him ; but I can't help being sorry
ve vere obliged to part vith him. It vas in this
wery lodge that he made his first escape from these
valls, before our identical eyes.—Newgate lost her
inwincibility that day, if she never did afore. Yes,
our honour received a tarnish then, that vill re-
quvire all our future wigilance to rub off."

"I am acquainted with the circumstance," said
the visiter, "and am not sorry to have an opportunity of actually observing the scene of this remarkable proof of hardihood and dexterity."

He made a minute survey of the place, and wrote
down some memoranda in a small pocket-book
which he had brought for that purpose. After
having been shown the relics usually exhibited in
the lodge to visiters at that period, such as the
spike which Sheppard had broken off the hatch
when he forced his way through it ; the knife with
which Blueskin had attempted to cut the throat of
Mr. Jonathan Wild ; a nosegay which had been
given by a duchess to Claude Du Val, and the irons
of the far-famed Captain Hinde, &c., he proceeded,
with Mr. Austin and the two turnkeys, Langley and
Revel, to the condemned hold. Here he satisfied
his curiosity with the complete inspection of this

last abode of crime, and read the names its different tenants had, at various times, scratched on
its dreary walls.

"There are some fine bold hands there, Sir,"
remarked Mr. Austin, alluding to the writing,
" and some wery curious ones, too: that name you
are looking at now, vhich is in German text, or
some other outlandish lingo, vas written there by
its owner, Jack Meff, the veawer, the wery last
morning he left us. Poor Jack vas a striking proof
of the truth of the old proverb, that he who is
born to be hanged vill never be drowned."

" How was that?" inquired the visiter, a tall
thin man, dressed in black, with high boots, a somewhat small cocked hat, a two-tailed wig, a rather
stiffly starched neckcloth, and a very investigating
look.—" I shall be thankful to be informed of any
remarkable particulars not generally known, that
may have happened to have come under your cog-
nizance."

" Bless your soul, Sir," said the gaoler, " I'm a
man as is full of remarkable particulars. Meff
vas first ordered to be hanged for milling a ken,
that is, breaking open a house; but as he vas a
going to Tyburn, just as they vere stopping to
give him his last draught out of St. Giles's bowl,
hang me if Jack Ketch vasn't arrested for debt.
It vas said it vas a sham arrest, and that Meff vas
at the bottom of it; but be that as it may, they
vere obliged to bring him back again here; and,

to make amends for his disappointment, his majesty ordered him to be lagged to Wirginny : vell, on their woyage there a terrible storm arose, the ship vas run bump ashore, and more than von half of the crew vent to glory ; but, as I said, those as is born to be hanged von't never be drowned.   Meff escaped, and some years arterwards took the liberty of returning vithout leave to the Hundreds of Drury again, vhere he carried on business as brisk as ever ; but, as the devil vould have it, hang me if he vasn't cotched von fine day by a fellow vot know'd him, and brought back to his old quarters ; in course, he was tried for returning from transportation, and took a second airing in the cart. Jack Ketch didn't happen to have any debts to pay this time, so poor Meff —— "

" Paid the last debt of nature, I suppose," said the stranger, faintly smiling.

" Just so, Sir ; he was topped at Tyburn, arter all his escapes.—That name you are looking at there, Sir, is the writing of Lewis Houssart, the French barber, a sad fellow, Sir—cut his vife's throat vith von of his master's razors.   He vas the favourite companion of Jack Sheppard, during the time they vere confined together here, before Jack's first escape."

" Ha !" said the visiter, eagerly, " how so ?"

" Lord bless you, Sir," returned Mr. Austin, " there's no telling you the rigs they put upon the other prisoners."

" Sheppard was a lively fellow, then ?"

"Lively !" said Mr. Austin—" hang me if I ever saw his like—vhy, before his second escape, just because I happened to observe to him, as I vas stapling him down in the castle-room vith three hundred veight of iron, that I'd give him leave to get avay if he could, hang me if he didn't take me at my vord; and then had the impudence to send me a letter, through Mr. Applebee, the publisher of the dying speeches, vhich he took there himself, dressed as a porter, and in vhich he begged my pardon for not stopping to take leave of me, and also apologised for taking the irons vith him, vhich he said he should not have done if I hadn't *given* them to him; assuring me he vould wery gladly have left them behind him, if it hadn't been extremely inconwenient to him." The fellow then concluded vith some poetry—" perhaps you don't deal much in poetry, Sir; it aint to your taste ?"

" A little," drily returned the visiter; " but, I must confess, I am not over fond of it—I find it rather a drug."

" Vell, Jack's is not wery good, Sir, as far as I'm a judge, so I von't trouble you vith it. I should have told you, that, along vith my letter, he sent a wery jeering one to Mr. Applebee himself—to be sure I believe these publishers, as they calls themselves, are wery queer gentry, and deals in all manner of lies;" the visiter winced a little; " but

I don't think Jack ought to have served Muster Applebee in that vay—but come, Sir, I'll now conduct you to the castle, our great show room."

" I am anxious to see it," said the visiter.

Passing across the lodge at the end of a long passage, there advanced from one of the wards, in which there were several untried prisoners, a man whose remarkable appearance caught the visiter's attention ; his throat was enveloped in a huge roll of neckcloth, and his frontispiece seemed to have been much battered.

" That's the celebrated Mr. Vild," whispered the gaoler, observing his companion's attention drawn towards him ; " an extraordinary character, Sir, a wery extraordinary character ; it is to him that the country is indebted for getting rid of Jack Sheppard and Blueskin."

" I have heard as much," significantly answered the other.

" Yes, Sir, he has hung as many men as Jack Ketch himself: it vas he that brought Thurland, Dun, Ray, and the other rogues, to the nubbing cheat* for the murder of Mrs. Knapp ; and lagged Bob Parrot for speaking to† the Bishop of Norwich's Crib ; and lifted Bill Rigglesden and Bess Shirley for breaking into the Banqueting House, Vhitehall, and holding communion vith the sacrament plate vithout being ordained ; he's a fearful

* The gallows. † Robbing.

man—hang me if I care to speak of him vithin his hearing; nobody's life ain't safe with him; but he's gone now. You saw those marks on his canister: they are cracks he got in capturing his different wictims; vas forced to get trepanned himself through trepanning others, ha! ha! But if I vas to tell you von half of the terrible stories that are told of him, vhy they'd fill up a wolum, and turn you into calf's foot jelly."

" I should be glad to hear them, nevertheless," quickly returned the visiter, " and will pay handsomely for the information."

" Then, I'm just the man to furnish you vith it," returned the gaoler; " and if your honour vill only step down here to the lodge any von of these hevenings arter locking-up time, hang me, if, over a bowl of punch, you shan't be made acquvainted with all I've known and heard, and that's not saying a little."

" Agreed," said the visiter, " I'll take you at your word; but let us onwards to the castle."

To this place, then, they repaired; on their way they passed a cell that seemed fitted up in rather a superior style to the others.

" You sees that apartment, Sir?" said Mr. Austin to his companion, pointing to it, " that vas vhere Sally Salisbury vas caged; she served her time there.—A fine spanky wench, Madam Sally, sir, and I varrant she paid like a princess; she vas here for cutting and maiming ve von't say who, because he vas von of the nobs, cousin to government—some little bit of jealousy, Sir.—Gemmen oughtn't to mind a little slashing of their ribs over their vine vhen it's all for love.—We made her so werry comfortable, that, blow me, if I don't think she took it to heart vhen she vent avay, for she died three months arterwards.

In the castle, a strong room, the scene of Jack Sheppard's far-famed last escape, the party were joined by the Reverend Mr. Thomas Wagstaff, at that time the Ordinary of Newgate. The massive staple and enormous padlock by which Jack had been fastened to the floor, together with his feetlocks and handcuffs, were here exhibited; but out of respect to the presence of the Ordinary, and in compliment to the gentlemanlike appearance and liberality of the visiter, the usual waggery of persuading the curious stranger to suffer the irons to be fastened on him in order to see if *he* could release himself from them, and then making him pay a considerable sum for his liberation, was omitted. The old nail with which Jack had picked the padlock, the iron bar he had wrested from the chimney, and the chimney itself, were all objects of keen investigation.

" You seem greatly interested," observed the Ordinary to the visiter, " in the transactions and fate of that unfortunate criminal, Sheppard !"

" I am more than ordinarily so," returned the visiter.

" He was, indeed, a striking example of the folly of men," observed the Ordinary gravely, "as I had occasion to remark in a late sermon. What a melancholy consideration it is that men should show so much regard for the preservation of a poor perishing body, that can remain at most but a few years, and at the same time be so unaccountably negligent of a precious soul which must continue through the ages of eternity. What amazing difficulties did the notorious malefactor, Jack Sheppard, overcome! Oh, that mankind were all Jack Sheppards!"

The visiter started.

" Don't mistake me!" exclaimed the reverend gentleman, " I don't mean in a bodily, but in a spiritual sense. I would exhort the world to open the locks of their hearts with the nail of repentance; burst asunder the fetters of their lusts; mount the chimney of hope, take from thence the bar of good resolution, break through the stone wall of despair, and all the strongholds of the dark entry of the valley of the shadow of death; raise themselves to the leads of divine meditation; fix the blanket of faith with the spike of the church; let themselves down to the turner's house of resignation, and descend the stairs of humility, so that they may come to the door of deliverance from the prison of iniquity, and escape the clutches of that old executioner, the devil."

Here the reverend gentleman had entirely ex-

hausted himself by the force of his own eloquence,
and suddenly stopped.

"I am given to understand that the world has
been much misled concerning the true history of
this daring offender, Jack Sheppard," remarked
the visiter. after a pause: "his parentage has, I
am told, been grossly mis-stated, and he himself
associated with many persons that never had any
existence; so that the public have been led to form
very erroneous ideas of him: I would fain, if I
could, obtain a true history of his eventful life and
transactions."

"That, Sir," answered the Ordinary, confiden-
tially, "can only be obtained from myself. In
addition to the criminal's own confession, which I
obtained by virtue of my holy office, I have procured many particulars, equally as worthy of notice
as they are veracious, and which, I am persuaded,
would be very acceptable to the world at large;
but the cares of my flock do not allow me leisure
to bestow on these memoranda the necessary form
of a continuous narrative. I should be happy to
commit my materials into the hands of any ingenious gentleman, whose talents and time might
permit of his rendering to the actions of this
great criminal that justice, after death, which,
in his life-time, so signally conducted him to the
halter."

"If you would entrust these manuscripts to my
care," said the visiter, eagerly, his eyes glistening

with pleasure and satisfaction, " I would take care that an 'eminent hand,' whom I have in my pay, should render them their full literary deserts. It was in search of such documents and testimonies that I came hither; my gratitude shall evince itself beyond bare words. Fifty guineas—I speak without offence, Reverend Sir,—shall gladly be at your disposal for their use."

" Inasmuch as they will enable me to do, I trust, a considerable worldly good," gravely answered the Ordinary, " I will accept your offer. My narrative attends the wretched sufferer from his very cradle, through all the events of his boyhood, to his last solemn exit. Many circumstances have come to my knowledge which have escaped all others, the truth of which will be borne out, in all their more important points, by the various imperfect accounts that have hitherto been published. The narrative will, indeed, be as interesting as it will be authentic and complete."

" Ah, Sir ! let the idle and frivolous seek for excitement in the pages of the poet, and the wild fictions of the romance writer, as they will; if they would really stir up their jaded feelings, they should resort to the terrible realities so often to be found within these walls : all that imagination can conceive to interest the fancy, and hold attention breathless, will fall short compared with the every-day occurrences it is but too constantly my painful duty to witness."

" I doubt it not, Reverend Sir ; I doubt it not," replied the visiter ; " the eagerness the public have ever manifested to become acquainted with those whose crimes have rendered them notorious, the sympathy that is extended to their sufferings, the varied feelings and emotions, their exploits, escapes, and ultimate fate awaken, strikingly attest the truth of your observations. The adventures of the desperado have ever possessed more charms for the multitude than those even of the hero. In all ages, the lives of the rogue, the pirate, the burglar, the highwayman, and the murderer, have had their attractions for the general reader. The most gentle natures are often those that peruse, with the greatest avidity, the actions of the most daring and ferocious ; their appetite becoming greater in proportion to the amount of turpitude presented for its digestion."

" Exactly so," said the Ordinary," else, where-fore the throngs of the weaker sex that invariably crowd our courts to catch a glimpse of any criminal of more than ordinary hardihood ; would not one naturally suppose they would shrink with abhorrence from such exhibitions ? but no, the greater the offender the greater is their—what shall I term it ?—I will give it its mildest name, *curiosity.*"

" It is a thorough knowledge of this fact that has led me here this day," remarked the visiter. " I despair not to see the time, Reverend Sir, when the poet, the dramatist, the romance-writer, and the novelist, shall all draw the materials of their various works from the calendar of crime recorded within these walls; when genius, as priestcraft has done before it, shall canonise the memory of the malefactor, and make the saint the greater the more he has been the sinner. Punishment will appear martyrdom when a halo is thrown round the guilt for which it was endured."

The Ordinary winced slightly at the observation of the stranger reflecting on the priesthood; he, however, said nothing in answer to it, comforting himself with the idea that the priestcraft alluded to did not belong to *his* church; though he could not help remarking, with much seriousness, that he hoped the time would never come when genius would so far prostitute its noble powers, as, for the sake of effect, to invest the worthless and dissolute with factitious interest, and distort, or misrepresent those facts which, in every age and time, so signally manifest the justice of Providence, and prove to uninstructed man that the certain wages of sin is death; while, *vice versa*, the paths of righteousness and virtue ever prove the paths of pleasantness and peace. The reverend gentleman drew a long breath. Mr. Austin put on a penitential air, and tried to look devout. There was a few moments' silence, which was at length broken by the visiter.

" I will take an early opportunity of calling on you for the manuscripts, Reverend Sir," said he, " and will not, at the same time, forget the coin."

It may here be mentioned that the speaker was a distinguished bookseller and publisher of that day.

He kept his word : a day or two afterwards he paid his promised visit to the reverend Ordinary, and obtained the precious memoranda in question. From the Ordinary he proceeded to Mr. Austin in the lodge, from whom he gained much information of the most astounding and exciting nature relative to Mr. Jonathan Wild, &c. &c. It is from these combined materials the eminent hand alluded to by the publisher, and who was a poor author whom he occasionally employed, prepared the narrative, which, for reasons not now necessary to explain, will here, for the first time, be given to the world, and which will form its own comment. Nothing has been extenuated nor ought set down in malice. The Housebreaker and Footpad has not been turned into a Hero, nor held up as an example to the admiration and imitation of the ignorant and unpractised. No veil has been thrown over the certain consequences of crime— the end of the malefactor is shewn to be the gibbet; and the gains of Sin, inquietude, infamy, and destruction. In fact, this Work will be found to be the only correct detail hitherto published, among the many that have appeared, of the Life, Adventures, and Escapes of the renowned House and Prison breaker, the redoubtable JACK SHEP-PARD.

JACK SHEPPARD.

CHAPTER I.

INFANCY OF JACK SHEPPARD.

HOW OUR HERO HAPPENED TO BE BORN.—LOVE IN THE
CRADLE.—THE GIPSY'S PREDICTION.

It was the month of March, in the year of our
Lord, 1702. The time-honoured bells of Stepney old church, celebrated for its monumental
"𝔉𝔶𝔰𝔥𝔢 𝔞𝔫𝔡 𝔎𝔶𝔫𝔤𝔢," were ringing one of their
merriest peals. A bullock, given to the populace
by the liberal authorities of that no less liberal
parish, which, as it is well known, extends its
guardian registration to all such offspring of wayfaring English subjects as may have the misfortune
to be born on, or beyond, the seas, was roasting
whole upon the village green, where an immense
bonfire had been kindled, in the ashes of which
several sacks of potatoes were embedded, to form
an appropriate addition in the mastication of the

noble animal then undergoing the established process of the culinary art.   Several barrels of strong
beer, the joint benefaction of the just mentioned
generous churchwardens, and Messrs. Tapmen and
Hopkins of the " Crown," and " Marlborough's
Head," two worthy publicans and sinners, who
had grown rich by administering to the necessities
of the draught-loving topers of Stepney, were ju-
diciously placed under the care of Mr. Burley,
the respectable beadle of the parish, in order to
be ready for distribution to the loyal inhabitants
of Stepney, when the completion of the cookery
should require their accompaniment.   Mr. Burley was assisted in his important and arduous
trust, by a strong body-guard of stout paupers, with
pitchforks, or it might have proved no easy task
to have kept off the thirsty and eager crowd.
The royal standard of England was proudly floating on the ancient church tower, courteously waving to the vibrations of the joyous bells beneath
it.   The moon, which had risen full and high in
the heavens immediately above, was brightly and
complacently shining, as if in approbation of what
was passing within its view ; pouring a rich flood
of splendour on all around, its calm and silvery
beams contrasting strikingly with the fierce and
glaring flames of the bonfire.   Squibs were flying,
and crackers bursting, in all directions.   Men were
hurrahing, boys were hallooing, and children were
screaming, all half frantic with delight and ex-

pectation; nearly the whole population of Stepney were assembled, from helpless infancy to tottering age. The auspicious event which had congregated this multitude, and called forth these rejoicings, was no other than the accession to the throne of merry England of Anne of Denmark, afterwards called " Good Queen Anne," though she is now more generally remembered for the supposed rarity of her farthings, than for any recorded virtue, or authenticated public good. Nevertheless, at this period her accession had inspired the whole nation with universal joy; all parties, Whig, Tory, and intermediate, coalesced together to hail the commencement of a reign, under which they expected to see the power of France humbled still more effectually abroad, and the Protestant religion established still more firmly at home.

It was at this precise juncture that, in a neat, though poor cottage in one of the bye-lanes of that then picturesque village, tenanted by one Robert Sheppard, a rural carpenter, the front part of which served as his workshop, while the room behind formed the dormitory and general meeting place of the family, that the renowned hero of this memorable history first saw the light.

The worthy carpenter, not dreaming that an addition to his family was so suddenly to have been made, for Mrs. Sheppard's calculations, and the received period for the occurrence of such

events had not led them to look for it, for at least
two months to come, had gone to join the general
throng that rushed forth to hail the happy advent
of the time, and partake of the good cheer provided, as has been premised, on the green, leaving
his helpmate, whose interesting situation, and rather delicate health just then, did not make it
seem prudent that she should accompany him,
under the surveillance of their eldest daughter, a
child of about ten or twelve years of age. Some
time had elapsed since his departure when the sudden firing of several old pieces of musketry, joined
to the loud clamour of the rustic crowd, and the
glaring light from the huge bonfire that made its
way through the lattice of their little dwelling, so
alarmed the good matron, that her cries speedily
drove the child into the lane to look for assistance;
but their few neighbours, the inhabitants of the
scattered hovels that here and there rose above
the hedges that skirted the lane on either side,
had departed for the general festivity, and the
little girl was perfectly in despair, when, to her
great joy, she saw emerging from a clump of hazels, towards the top of the lane, a female, whose
garb and manners at once pointed her out as one
of that wandering race, known in this country by
the name of gipsy. With one arm she supported
an infant, while, with the other, she guided her
steps by the assistance of a long, thin, straggling
wand or stick, cleft at the top, formed of the strip-

ped branch of a tree; her figure was tall, erect, and commanding, even though she was partially in tatters, and strongly reminded the spectator of that mixture of masculine strength and feminine beauty, which is found in the females of many of the southern parts of Ireland. Her features were earnest, but somewhat stern, and careworn; she was enveloped in a long mantle, or cloak: a species of wallet-bag was fastened to her waist; her only head-dress, which was partially covered by the hood of her mantle, was a sort of toque, formed of a twisted handkerchief, similar to that worn by the French peasantry, beneath which her long raven hair hung wildly over her shoulders; the usual gay 'kerchief of the gipsy females covered her neck, nor were their customary profusion of rings and broaches wanting. To her the little girl made known her story—she was a gipsy, outcast, and wandering, hunted and lawless, scorned and revengeful—but she was a woman! To hasten to the cottage was the work of a moment; she laid the infant she bore in a cradle, which stood in one part of the room, and speedily rendered to the suffering matron those attentions which only woman best can, or ought to render. Her skill and care, made familiar to her by the practice of her tribe, soon enabled her to relieve, at once, all Mrs. Sheppard's pains and fears, by bringing safely into the world a healthy boy. At the moment of his birth a still merrier peal than before burst from

the village bells. " This should be an omen," muttered the gipsy, in the wild Romanee jargon of
her nation, " but whether of future private joy or
public notoriety I know not." The infant was
soon completely wrapped in some clothes that had
not been provided for him, but which had served
the same office for two or three brothers and sisters
before him. As he seemed inclined to sleep, the
gipsy laid him down in the cradle by the side of
the infant she had previously placed there, whose
exceeding fairness, so greatly at variance with her
own swarthy hue, forbade any one for a moment
supposing it was her's ; for in her arms it, indeed,
seemed like some pure pearl upon an Ethiope's
breast ; while she turned to administer some necessary cordial to the now happy mother. Gaining strength, Mrs. Sheppard proceeded to return
her grateful thanks to the gipsy for the timely
aid she had rendered her, and to express her surprise that she should have been found absent from
the festivities then going forward. "What is the
new queen to me?" muttered the gipsy. "I owe
her no allegiance, and what are these rejoicings?
I cannot sympathise in their wild tumult : my
thoughts should rather be of one as highly born,
as justly, too, entitled to dominion,—one fugitive
and beggared—her only canopy the forest bough,
her only roof the spaceless sky above her,—one
from the burning East—one to whom, albeit born
of the royal race of Pharoah, and mated with the

dukes of Lesser Egypt, no one now bends the knee—her sceptre but this worthless hazel wand, her realms but those all may at pleasure drive her from." The gipsy's dark eye flashed as she spoke these words, which, had they not been uttered in the mystic language of her race, would in any other have been equally unintelligible to the wondering matron. "Yes," continued the gipsy, " but Zara shall avenge her wrongs. Ring on, ring on, ye empty, senseless flatterers! the homage of the world, e'en when not less loud, is not less hollow, nor less fleeting!—ring on, ring on! I'll war upon the world—the base, the ingrate world, that so has wronged, despoiled, and scorned me; already my first hostage has been taken, this poor child Bess!" At this instant the bells suddenly ceased their jovial clamour, and for a few moments a dead silence pervaded the air, when the iron tongue of midnight slowly knelled forth that witching hour. The gipsy started—again a deafening shout in the distance rent the sky, and a fiercer glare gleamed in at the casement window, and streamed full upon the cradle, in which, side by side, lay reposing the two infants. The cradle was placed immediately under the casement which looked into the cottage garden; the head of it touched the wall at that side of the apartment, on which, just above it, was pasted a favourite ballad of that period, describing the life and exploits of the " Ladies' highwayman," the celebrated CLAUDE DU

VAL. On the top of this ballad was a rude wood-
cut of a gibbet, to which the handsome gallant
was seen suspended. As the gipsy's eye fell. on
turning round, upon the cradle, she started at perceiving that the infant she had borne had moved
from the position in which she had placed it, and
nestling itself more closely to the new-born boy,
had thrown its little arm in fondness round his
neck, but so tightly as almost to strangle him.

" Mighty Pharoah !" she exclaimed, extricating
the poor babe from the unconscious jeopardy in
which the tenderness of his companion had placed
him ; " what dread portent is this? Ah ! that
blood-red glare—how fierce it gleams upon that
picture gibbet, this mark of love akin to death,
too. Quick ! let me examine the firmament, my
only horoscope." As swift as lightning her eagle-
eye was turned to the heavens. " What is this I
see ?" she shrieked, gazing with painful earnestness on two planets that shone brightly out from
amidst the myriad of stars that twinkled round
them. " VENUS and SATURN in conjunction—
strange ! Venus ! it is her natal star—poor Bess,
yes, luckless wench ! fair as that orb, thy lot
will own its sway, thy fate will feel its influence.
Love ! love ! will be thine all, thy joy, thy sorrow. Saturn—ah ! 'tis a fearful planet, moody
and malignant. Why hurried this poor babe to
life to own its influence ? It rose upon him at his
birth ; I marked its aspect ; it is his natal, ruling

star! what will be their fate? my Art impels me
—I must, although I fain would not, foretell it."
The gipsy then in a wild and low, but solemn
chant, muttered in a species of ROMANEE dog-
gerel some lines, of which the following is the sub-
stance :—

The Prediction.

By the power to me that's given,
What matters if from hell or heaven,
From star or planet, charm or spell,
  From card or omen, angel fiend,
The fates of mortals to foretell,
  And trace their course, and point their end,
As through this vale of tears they go,
Their pains and pleasures, weal and woe?
I must, though fain I would be dumb,
Their fortune show, for it *will* come!
Yes, yes! I feel within me burning
Words, that for utterance are yearning;
A secret knowledge that *will* speak,
Howe'er the prophecy I'd check.
Yes, I the fortunes *must* unfold—
Sad secret! but it will be told!
Of those who lie unconscious here
Of all but life—who hope, and fear,
And joy and woe know not as yet,
Nor nurse the sad wish to forget!
The baleful light through the casement pane
That redly glares on the infant twain—
What does that baleful light proclaim
But guilt and anguish, sin and shame?
Dim SATURN sadly shines afar,
This new-born infant's *natal star*!

VENUS, the loveliest gem of eve,
Seems o'er her subject-babe to grieve—
What does their strange *conjunction* mean ?
In vain I would the knowledge skreen :—
That arm around the new-born thrown !—
What of their destiny is shown ?
A fatal love allied to death :
Through her, alas ! he'll yield his breath !
Closer than sister's to a brother
Their fates are wound with one another :
Howe'er removed, they still will join—
In rapture, and in anguish twine.
The POWER impels me, I must on,
Ere yet the witching hour is gone !
The GIBBET that now frowns above,
Sad emblem of their end will prove !
I'll read no more ;—unhappy mother !
'Twere well for thee, though thou'dst no other,
Thy babe in birth had breath'd its last,
The words are said—the power has pass'd !

The gipsy ceased. It was fortunate the good matron had all this time been in a sound but gentle slumber, or the wild exclamations of the sibyl might have alarmed her more than might have been safe for one in her peculiar situation. The little girl who had been ministering to her mother, as occasion required, affrighted by the mysterious gestures and deep tones of her strange companion, had cowered fearfully behind the bed-curtains, from which at intervals, as her courage permitted her, she anxiously watched all that was going on. Recovering herself after a short pause, the gipsy resumed her mutterings. " Their destinies linked unto each other, there then should be within their

palms the line of marriage ;—let me convince myself ; yes," taking up, and examining the hand of
the infant girl, " 'tis here parallel with the line of
life.—Now for the boy." The hand of the new-
born infant was here subjected to a similiar scrutiny. " Plagues of Egypt !" exclaimed the fortune-
teller, " the palm is smooth ! he'll die unwedded ;
so much the worse for thee, poor girl, so much the
worse ;—but here's a line, the line of death,—
where does it run to ? I trace it from the hand
across the palm, and up the arm, until it joins
this vein, and here it is lost.—What vein is this ?
Powers of darkness ! again the omen—the fatal
one, the *jugular*." Here the door of the humble apartment was suddenly opened, and honest
Robert Sheppard, the owner of the mansion, in a
most happy state of intoxication, was led in by
Mr. Burley, the beadle. " Huzzah ! Long live
the Queen ! Long live her Majesty," hiccupped
the carpenter. The gipsy started ; but honest
Sheppard, though he saw double, did not at the
moment see her. " Huzza ! dam'me if ever she
shall want money to buy a pot of strong drink
while Bob Sheppard has got sixpence left in the
world. But where's my better half, Kate ?" calling her. His boisterous vociferation here awakened the sleeping infant, who set up a loud cry,
which in turn awoke the mother. " Halloo !"
said the carpenter, almost sobered with surprise,
" why, what the devil's this ? My wife in the

straw, and a couple of children in the basket ?"
" No, only one child, dear Robert," murmured
Mrs. Sheppard, affectionately. " Then I must be
seeing double, as you say, Mr. Burley, for curse
me if there aint two ; but how comes it all about,
Mrs. Sheppard, and why did'nt you wait till I
came home, before you suffered this to happen ?"

" The event certainly was rather unexpected,"
said Mrs. Sheppard, smiling, perceiving the condition of her husband ; " and but for this good
woman's timely skill and solicitude, I know not
what would have been the result." Here the attention both of the carpenter and the beadle was
turned to the gipsy. " Eh ! This good woman ?"
hiccupped the carpenter. " Ah ! a gipsy !" roared
the beadle, as his eyes encountered hers. " Oh !
the baggage—the witch—the vagrant ! See that
you have your spoons safe, Master Sheppard, and
that none of the poultry's necks have been twisted
off in the hen-roost. I must exercise my official
authority here—this woman must go to the cage."
" Mercy !" shrieked the gipsy, catching up the
child she had brought with her, and pressing it
to her bosom. " Punish me not for having been
the means, through heaven, of preserving, perhaps, two lives." " Nay, nay, touch her not—
harm her not, Mr. Burley, I entreat, I implore
you !" supplicated Mrs. Sheppard. The parish
functionary stood irresolute. " Answer me one
question, hussy," hiccupped the carpenter. " Are

you going to take that second child away with
you ?" " I am," returned the gipsy. " Is it
yours ?" " It is." " Then on that account I'll
forgive you ; but if my family had been increased,
through you, by two children instead of one, to
the cage you should have gone ; nothing should
have saved you. You must let her walk off scot-
free, Mr. Burley, though I dare say she's a terrible offender ; but if she's deprived me of a chicken
or two, she's given me another chicken, this child !
so it's tantamount—tit for tat ; therefore we must
let her go." " This is a very onerous piece of
business, Mr. Sheppard," gravely observed the
cock'd-hatted authority. " But stop, now I think
of it, this being the accession of her most gracious
Majesty, God bless her ! an act of amnesty has
passed, letting loose all felons and other prisoners;
so I think I may let her loose. But stop, stop !
what am I doing ?—the act does not extend to criminals guilty of murder ; and how do I know but
this woman has been murdering some of your
cocks and hens ?" " No, no," indignantly exclaimed the gipsy. " I will stake my life on her
innocence," said Mrs. Sheppard. " Well, well, on
that consideration, and with the understanding
that you will take all the responsibility upon
yourself, friend Sheppard, I shall even let her go
about her business ; so vanish, woman ! quick !
trudge !" Placing the lips of the infant she bore
to those of the new-born offspring of the carpenter,

and ejaculating in a sad but solemn tone, "You'll meet again, ill-starred ones! naught can resist the force of destiny. Farewell, good mistress; Heaven shield you and your offspring in your dark hour's peril—farewell!" The gipsy walked with an air, possessing much of innate dignity, out of the apartment, and plunging with her little charge into the lane, was speedily lost in its darkest shade.

No sooner was the cottage relieved from her presence, than the carpenter began to examine the new subject that had that night been born, to own the sway of good Queen Anne. The little fellow crowed, as the father, more gently than was usual with him patted his infant cheek. "Odds my life!" he exclaimed, "he'll be a fine boy!—in a devilish hurry to see the world, though—no fear of his pushing his way anywhere—nothing will stop him. Well, bless his little round poll! I shall make a carpenter of him like myself; he'll be a rare one to handle a chisel, a saw, and a centre-bit, I'll warrant him." Mr. Burley, the beadle, now in his turn advanced to examine the little stranger, but no sooner did he stoop down, than the infant manifested the utmost dislike and terror at his appearance—squalling, kicking, and struggling to get away, with all his might and main. "It must be my cocked hat and staff that frightens him," said the beadle, drawing away somewhat disconcerted: they certainly are the terror of all offenders; but this little rogue has done nothing as yet to make him alarmed at them. But come, friend Robert; I see Mrs. Sheppard can well dispense with our presence, so I'll go and get neighbour Diggin's wife to sit up the remainder of the night with her, and get you a shake down at the ' Marlborough's Head:' they will open their doors to me at any hour ; and there, over a cool tankard, I'll tell you what are the Duke's plans in the next campaign with the allies against the French. I have it official : we in authority know these things ; therefore come. Good night, or good morning rather, Mrs. Sheppard." Taking leave of his wife and new-born son and heir, the carpenter departed with the beadle, who speedily got a nurse for Mrs. Sheppard, a bed for her husband, and a foaming tankard of nut-brown ale for himself ; in the enjoyment of which we will for the present beg to leave him.

CHAPTER II.

THE CHRISTENING.

EARLY INDICATIONS.—"𝕿𝔥𝔢 𝔣𝔞𝔪𝔬𝔲𝔰 𝕭𝔞𝔩𝔩𝔞𝔡𝔢 𝔬𝔣 𝕮𝔩𝔞𝔲𝔡𝔢 𝔡𝔲 𝔙𝔞𝔩."—THE DEPARTURE FROM STEPNEY.

THE little urchin, the future hero of our history, throve, his premature birth, though it rendered him somewhat diminutive and delicate in appearance, not interfering with his future growth and strength. His mother, who had all along been, as the gossips call it, as well as could be expected, got about again earlier than usual, and in due course of time a day was fixed for our hero's christening. It was settled that he should be called JOHN; Mr. BURLEY, the beadle, who bore that name, having consented to do him the honour of standing sponsor to him; but on the day appointed, the clergyman of the parish, the Reverend Mr. Muggeridge, who was a bachelor, and a wag, and withal an Oxford man (one of the conditions on which the living is bestowed, which is in the gift of Brazen Nose College, and a very valuable one, being, that the incumbent shall in all cases be a bachelor); the aforesaid reverend gentleman, we repeat, by what spirit inspired we know not, but we will charitably set it down to his innocent desire of passing a joke on his official, the beadle ! chose to make that important functionary's intention of giving our hero his name, somewhat imperfect, by facetiously christening him JACK, instead of *John*. The gravest men will joke at times; and when they do, their inferiors are specially bound to laugh : accordingly, the whole affair was passed over as a most excellent jest, betraying a vast deal of wit in the reverend fellow from BRAZEN NOSE ; though there were times when the beadle did not scruple in private to express his opinion that our hero would come to *no good* from the *misnomer*, it sounding to him very much like an *alias!*

Little Jack was an uncommonly good-tempered child, like others, when he was pleased; but he liked to have his own way, and discovered at times a headstrong obstinacy and wilfulness that somewhat alarmed his good mother : he was also subject to gusts of passion, but was always pacified whenever his mother sang to him the good old " Ballade of Claude du Val, the Ladies' Highwayman," which had, ever since the exit of that worthy, been an especial favourite with all cantatrices in the middle and lower walks of life. As this " Ballade" may be considered, even at that early age, to have had some effect in biassing our hero's future course and character, we may be excused introducing it.

The famous Ballade of Claude du Val.*

THE LADIES' HIGHWAYMAN'

1.

OF ROBIN HOOD, that *Archer* good,
    Our Forest minstrels tell;
A gentle thief, of outlaws chief,
    He bore from all the Bell!
While GILDEROY was *Scotland's* joy,
    Though bound in prison thrall;
But all the field for fame must yield
    To gallant CLAUDE DU VAL!
Oh, rare DU VAL! oh fair DU VAL!
    Since first the world began,
On plain or green unmatched in mien—
    The Ladies' Highwayman!

2.

From sunny France, with song and dance
    He came and stole all hearts;
His graceful air won all the fair;
    His eyes were Cupid's darts!
So blythe and bold, no fair proved cold,
    But freely yielded all;
With ruin pleased, if he but seized,—
    The gallant CLAUDE DU VAL!
Oh, rare DU VAL! oh, bold DU VAL!
    To rifle was his plan,
Both young and old, of love, and gold,—
    The Ladies' Highwayman!

---

* In plain prose, this celebrated highwayman was by birth a Frenchman, having been born at Domfront, in Normandy, in the year 1643. His father was a miller, and he himself having ran away from his home, was for some time a footman in Paris. He came to England on the restoration of Charles the Second, in 1660. Being very gay and extravagant, his excesses soon forced him to take to the highway, where he became so celebrated, that he had the honour of being named first in a proclamation for the capture of several notorious malefactors; on which he decamped to France for safety, but soon returned and resumed his lawless practices. The anecdotes recorded of him in the ballad, are, with many others of a similar nature, detailed by most of his biographers. He was the most accomplished, polished, handsome, and well dressed thief, gallant, and gambler, of which we have

3.

One day a coach he saw approach,
　In which a lady sat,
Who sweetly played;—he smiled and said.
　While doffing low his hat:—
" My country, France, with me but dance.
　I'll seek no other *Ball!*"
" Thanks, sir," said she, " I'll partner be
　To gallant, gay Du Val!
Oh, rare Du Val! Oh, gay Du Val!
　Thy equal find who can?
All, joy'd to be—robb'd, if by *thee,*
　The Ladies' Highwayman!"

4,

He took her hand, a Saraband
　They danced upon the heath;
Her spouse, the knight, gaz'd with delight,
　And laugh'd till out of breath.
Said Claude, " Fair May you'll not, to pay
　The music, surely, fail?"
When soon was found a hundred pound
　For gallant, gay Du Val.

any record; and was a prodigious favourite, as might be expected, with the ladies. His career, after some years, was at length cut short by his being arrested, while drunk, at the "Hole-in-the-Wall" Tavern, Chandos Street, Covent Garden. While he lay in the condemned hold in Newgate, he was visited by myriads of ladies of the first quality, all anxious to have a *safe* peep at the handsome highwayman; though they by no means grudged to *pay* for peeping, such was his attraction. Great intercession was made to save him, but in vain; he was executed at Tyburn on the 21st of January, 1670, when he had barely reached the age of twenty-seven, amidst the universal tears of crowds of handsome females. The immortal author of Hudibras honored his memory with some lines on that occasion. A house called Du Val's house, situated in Du Val's Lane, or Devil's Lane, as it has been popularly vulgarized, at Islington, leading to Hornsey Wood, is still pointed out to the curious as having been the comely highwayman's retreat. Full accounts of Du Val are to be found in the Harleian Miscellany, his Life by Dr. Pope, Johnson's Lives of the Highwaymen, Leigh Hunt's Indicator, and Chambers's Edinburgh Journal for 1838.

D

Oh, brave Du Val! polite Du Val!
  Still first in Cupid's van;
Who danc'd so gay a purse away,—
  The Ladies' Highwayman!

5.

In France, 'tis told, a Jesuit old
  Could not his arts resist;
But gave his gold, to have tenfold
  Chang'd by our *Alchymist!*
This he in *lead*, through the old fool's head,
  Return'd with a pistol ball!
" I've oft, of old, turn'd *lead* to gold!
  Quoth the gallant, gay Du Val.
Oh, rare Du Val! jocose Du Val!
  In the flashing of a pan
The money came, and went the same,
  With the Ladies' Highwayman!

6.

A comrade once, an arrant dunce,
  From a *child* its coral bore;
The mother fair, with many a prayer,
  Begg'd he'd the toy restore,
In vain; till Claude, at point of sword,
  Cried, " Yield it fool you shall!
You're not *wean'd* yet, thus to forget
  The *manners* of Du Val!"
Oh, rare du Val! genteel Du Val!
  No chariot or sedan
More gallant load took on the road
  Than the Ladies' Highwayman!

7.

But wine did what—the world could not;
  Du Val was snar'd at last;
Was seiz'd and tried, and, till he died,
  In Newgate's cells was cast.

At *Tyburn*, he—grac'd the triple tree,
  And none in park or mall
Dimm'd more bright eyes, woke more fond sighs
  Than the gallant CLAUDE DU VAL !
Oh, rare DU VAL ! ill-starr'd DU VAL !
  Such race none else e'er ran,
Bewept his fall, and lov'd—by all,—
  The Ladies' Highwayman.

Speech, which is but action in sound, or, as the Chinese call it, vocal painting, was the last of the two great gifts of childhood which little Jack acquired in full perfection.

Nothing more had been seen nor heard of the mysterious gipsy, and her little charge, whose fate, according to the prediction, was so strangely mixed up with that of our hero. The worthy carpenter, or honest Bob Sheppard, as he was generally called by his neighbours and acquaintances, unfortunately about this time possessed himself with a very good excuse for visiting the public-house, by acquiring a taste for politics. The fact was, Bob was a very sociable, well-meaning fellow; but strong drinks had strong attractions for him, and so, as he fancied, by the attention he paid to it, had the policy of the then existing government; and accordingly at the " Marlborough's Head," he regularly twice a day, with the assistance of the *Farthing Post*, conned over all the measures of the then ministers GODOLPHIN and NOTTINGHAM, and examined into the expediency of the military movements of the great duke and his allies against the GRANDE MONARQUE! But a working man can seldom attend much to public without neglecting his own private, affairs; and poor Sheppard soon began to complain that he found his business deserting him: whereas, the truth was, 'twas he that was deserting his business; but, be this as it may, the result was a determination on the part of honest Bob to quit Stepney, where he had resided for so many years, and to take up his quarters in London, where he imagined he should not only get more business, but have a better opportunity of exercising his political talents. Accordingly, about five years after the commencement of this history, just before little Jack had achieved that first and most anxious honour of boyhood—the being breeched, the family left the cottage in which they had passed so many happy hours, and took their departure for a small house and shop in one of the by-streets of the then populous and thriving neighbourhood of Spitalfields, which the kind advances of a patron had enabled them to take: this person was a Mr. WILLIAM KNEEBONE, a substantial woollen draper living in the Strand, at the sign of *The Fleece and Shears*, near St. Clement's Church. In his family Mrs. Sheppard had passed her early years, more as a companion than a servant, having been god-daughter to the woollen draper's mother, and married her first love, honest Robert (whom she met at a tea gardens in Clerkenwell), from the woollen draper's house.

As the matron, with little Jack hanging by her gown, turned at the top of the lane to quit the village, she cast one last glance at the home of her love. The little cottage had been erected on a shelving bank on one side of the lane, between a profusion of wild briar bushes, hazels, and woodbine. The ascent to it was by the means of some rude stones, intended for steps, which the care of the matron had rendered of dazzling whiteness; its neatly thatched roof, 'neath which two or three robins had found a refuge; its clean whitewashed front, covered with honeysuckles; the little casement in which had been exhibited the emblems of the carpenter's occupation,—all awoke remembrances, now more sad, in proportion as the sources of them had formerly been pleasing. The good-natured carpenter witnessed the evident heaviness of heart with which his spouse surveyed the scene; and gently taking her arm to remove her from the spot, endeavoured to cheer her, by jokingly remarking that, in leaving Stepney for Spitalfields they were getting a *step* nearer to the object of their ambition,—a humble but comfortable independence. Yielding to his wishes, she wiped the tear from her eye, and taking little Jack by one hand, while her husband led him by the other, followed by their daughter, they quitted White Thorn Lane—for so the place of their residence was named—for ever.

CHAPTER III.

JACK'S FIRST SCHOOLING.

MR. GARRET THE SCHOOLMASTER.——TEACHING " THE
YOUNG IDEAS HOW TO SHOOT" IN 1708.—MASTER BLAKE.
—INITIATORY PILFERING.

No sooner were the carpenter and his family settled in their new habitation, in Spitalfields, than
Mrs. Sheppard turned her thoughts to the education of her son, little Jack, which honest Bob said
must be particularly attended to, inasmuch as he
meant to bring him up to his own honourable trade
of a carpenter, which, he affirmed, was one of the
most ancient and important of all, belonging to the
three originally practised by our general ancestor,
Adam, on his departure from Eden, maintaining,
that the first master-crafts in the world were the
primeval ones of tailor, carpenter, and gardener:
Adam having first made himself clothes of the fig-
leaves, then constructed a habitation, and then cul-
tivated the earth for sustenance. Accordingly,
Mrs. Sheppard selected a day-school, in some repute, in St. Helen's, Bishopsgate, the master of
which was a Mr. Garret.

Jack proved an apt scholar, thanks to the attractions of his first Christmas-piece, which portrayed,

in a series of glaringly-coloured cuts, " THE
NOTABLE AND MERRY EXPLOITS OF ROBIN HOOD
AND HIS MEN," including his " slaying the fifteen
foresters," his robbing " the proud bishop and his
company," his " cozening the sheriff of Nottingham, in Sherwood Forest," his " rescuing the three
squires from Nottingham gallows," and other
memorable feats of this celebrated outlaw,—all
which served still further to sway Jack's future
progress.

Among the scholars with whom our hero early
formed a friendship, were Masters William Blewit
and Joseph Blake, though they were considerably older than himself. School friendships do not
usually survive till manhood ; but as in this case
they continued till death, and as the latter young
gentleman is destined to cut a very conspicuous
figure in these pages, the reader must pardon us if
we record, somewhat minutely, the progress of this
intimacy. Master William Blewit was a dogged.
sullen, mischievous boy, one of those still streams
that run deepest ; while Master Joseph Blake, or
Blueskin,* as he was nicknamed by the other boys,

* Blueness of skin, amounting in some cases almost to the
darkness of a mulatto, is not of such rare occurrence as may be
imagined ; it is sometimes born with persons, as in the case of
Master *Blake*, and then is caused, as we have been assured by
an eminent surgeon and anatomist, by some interior disor-
ganisation of the blood-vessels. In other cases it is owing to a
sudden revulsion of the blood, arising from fright or other
strong excitement ; while, in other cases, it may arise from an

rom the peculiar purple hue of his complexion,—
a nickname he retained, and by which he acquired
such an unenviable notoriety in after-life,—was of
a more lively turn. He was a stout-built thick-set
lad of about twelve years of age, with hard, but not
unpleasant, features ; a spice of cunning roguery
continually mingling with the sterner expression.
He first won Jack's unqualified admiration by the
dexterity with which—having committed some
fault that required punishment, upon being ordered by Mr. Garret to hold out his hand to receive certain cuts with a leathern strap which the
pedagogue always carried in his coat pocket for
that purpose—he managed to pick the master's
pocket of the aforesaid leathern strap, with one
hand, and pass it to Blewit, while, with apparent
fear and trembling, he held out the other. This
trait of genius tickled Jack amazingly : genius is
always acquisitive in its outset. A predilection for
taking that which does not belong to it, being
almost the first impulse that developes itself in the
infant mind ; though what is vulgarly called
thieving in some, through a different manifesta-
tion, is often termed a thirst for knowledge—a
praiseworthy ambition—a daring love of enter-

over-dose of some mineral poison, such as nitrate of silver, as
in the instance of a lady at Highgate, known by the name of
the *Blue Lady*, whose discoloration proceeded from her taking
poison, happily ineffectually, on being disappointed in a love
affair: also in the person of a popular comic actress, whose
good looks, however, were not materially spoiled by it.

prise, with a hundred similar fine names in others; but, however they may be diverted in after life, their original source is the same,—an innate love of acquisitiveness. We all know those learned *phrenologists*, Messrs. Gall and Spurzheim, have declared the organ of forming good dramatic plots, and that of acquisitiveness, or plunder, to be one and the same,—a fact strikingly proved in our own day, most of the present race of playwrights, from Bulwer to Moncrieff, doing nothing but steal! steal! steal!

To Master Blake and his companion William Blewit, though in a lesser degree to the latter, little Jack very soon attached himself; and it was not long before an incident occurred, which had the effect of cementing his connexion with the former young gentleman, more or less, during the rest of his life. One day, after their school hours, Master Blake—having a very fine collection of "taws" and "alleys," which, with other inferior marbles, he had, Elgin-like, acquired, wherever he had found them, without being at all particular about the means, was indulging in the well-known game of "Lagging out." When little Jack came up and began to gaze very wistfully at his stores, and the manner in which he was increasing them; Master Blake immediately invited him to join in their game.

" I cannot," answered our hero, in a disconcerted tone. " I have no marbles."

" That's one reason, certainly," answered his companion ; " but you've got some money to buy some, haven't you?" Our hero reluctantly confessed that he had not. " Neither money nor marbles!" continued Master Blake; " that is a blue look out, certainly ; I'm thinking little ARTHUR CHAMBERS* wouldn't have been long without money, or marbles either, before he was half your age, if he'd been in your situation." " And who was little Arthur Chambers?" asked little Jack. " Not know who Arthur Chambers was!" exclaimed Master Blake in surprise ; " well, that is a go! why, Arthur Chambers was the very prince of prigs ; the downiest diver, the rummest pad, the kiddiest scamp, the prettiest cheat, and the most dexterous filch upon town ; but I'll tell

---

* This prince of prigs was the most dexterous pickpocket of his own or any other day. He was of low extraction, and, according to Captain Charles Johnson, commenced pilfering even while he was in petticoats. He was a perfect master of slang in all its varieties, from the maunders, or beggars, cant, to the *Romance*, or gipsy patter, and Newgate flash of the light-fingered gentry. Many curious stories are related by Johnson of Arthur's proficiency as a cheat: one in which he got himself conveyed into his own lodgings as a dead man, and, in the character of a ghost, contrived, during the night, to rifle the house, is really dramatic, and might almost form a farce. After a long career of roguery in all the lower walks of his profession, for Arthur never aspired to the dignity of a house-breaker or highwayman, and being confined in Bridewell and many other prisons, he was detected in a street robbery, found guilty, and, some time before the birth of our hero, suffered the usual fate of such offenders at Tyburn.

you what Arthur Chambers was, my blade, ay, and in his own words, too."

Here he began singing a well known song, which had formerly been a great favourite with little Arthur, and was generally supposed to have been composed by that hero himself. It ran as follows :—

The Song of the Young Prig.*

My mother she dwelt in Dyott's isle,[a]
    One of the canting crew,[b] sirs;
And if you'd know my father's style,
    He was the Lord *Knows-who*, sirs!
I first held horses in the street,
    But being found defaulter,
Turned rumbler's flunky[c] for my meat,
    So was brought up to the halter,
Frisk the cly,[d] and fork the rag,[e]
    Draw the fogles plummy,[f]
Speak to the tattler,[g] bag the swag,[h]
    And finely hunt the dummy. [i]

* The name of the particular tune to which this "most choice chant," was originally sung. The tune was composed for the purpose, was long used as an old English morris dance, and is known in our own time by being associated with the words of a popular comic song called the " Literary Dustman," written by that son of mirth—not Dusty Bob—but BOB GLINDON.

a " Dyott's isle :" St. Giles's; so called from Sir Edward Dyott, a celebrated judge, having a mansion there in a street named after him—Dyott street; and which was afterwards desecrated to the purposes of a twopenny lodging-house, better known by the name of the Rookery, it has lately been pulled down to make way for the improvements in that quarter.

b " Canting crew :" beggars.

c " Rumbler's flunky :" a cad, or *footman*, to hackney coaches, to water the horses, &c.

d " Frisk the cly :" to pick a pocket.

e " Fork the rag :" lay hold of the notes or money.

f " Fogles plummy :" draw out the handkerchiefs dexterously.

g " Speak to the tattler :" steal a watch.

h " Bag the swag :" pocket the chain and seals.

i " Finely hunt the dummy :" adroitly search for a pocket-book.

2.

My name they say is young BIRDLIME,
   My fingers are fish-hooks, sirs;
And I my reading learnt betime,
   From studying pocket-books,[a] sirs.
I have a sweet eye for a plant,[b]
   And graceful as I amble,
Fine-draw a coat—tail sure I can't,
   So Kiddy is my famble.[c]
      Frisk the cly, &c.

3.

A night bird[d] oft I'm in the cage,[e]
   But my rum chants ne'er fail, sirs,
The dubsman's[f] senses to engage,
   While I tip him leg-bail,[g] sirs.
There's not, for picking, to be had,
   A lad so light and larky,[h]
The cleanest angler on the pad,[i]
   In daylight or the darky.[k]
      Frisk the cly, &c.

4.

And though I don't work capital,[l]
   And do not weigh my weight,[m] sirs,
Who knows but that in time I shall,
   For there's no queering fate, sirs.
If I'm not lagged to Virgin-nee,[n]
   I may a Tyburn show be,[o]
Perhaps a tip-top cracksman be,[p]
   Or go on the high toby.[q]

a "Pocket books are called "readers."
b "Plant:" an intended robbery.
c "Kiddy famble:" having a practical and skilful hand.
d "A disorderly vagabond.   e The round-house.
f Gaoler.   g Running away.
h Frolicsome.   i Expert street robber.
k The night.
l Commit any offence punishable with death.
m The 40l. payable on capital conviction.
n Transported.   o Hanged.   p House-breaker.
q Turn highwayman.

Frisk the cly, and fork the rag,
Draw the fogles plummy,
Speak to the tatler, bag the swag,
And finely hunt the dummy.

The greater part of this pious chanson being perfect Greek to Jack, Master Joseph Blake, who was thoroughly initiated in the language of the modern Greeks, or slang, as it is termed, undertook to explain it to him, which he did to Jack's great edification, making him wish most devoutly that he could emulate the accomplishments of "young Birdlime," to get him out of the dilemma in which he was at that moment placed.

"That you can easily do," said Master Joseph Blake. "Has your mother got any jewels?" Jack had never heard the word. "Well, that is a rum start! Here, Bill Blewit, here's this young kid, Jack Sheppard, don't know what jewels is! Well, then, has she got any trinkets?" Jack was equally as ignorant in this particular. "Well, then, has she got any rings, or brooches, or pins —— ?"

"Yes, she's got some pins," said Jack, very innocently; "I bought her a ha'p'orth this morning."

"Psha!" said his companion, laughing at his simplicity; "I mean has she got any lockets—things with sparkling stones set in gold, with a tongue at the back to fasten them to the breast, that we could speak to, or a gold chain to hang them round the neck with? —though hanging round the neck ain't exactly the rabbit."

" Mother had a good many rings and them sort of things once," said Jack ; " but since father has had so little work, and has been so busy with the political club down at the " Blue Posts," I arn't seen any of them ; they have all disappeared ; she never wears them now : there's only one,—it's a white glass heart, with father's name at the back ; it's got gold all round it, and a pretty chain that it is fastened to. I know where she keeps it ; it's in one of her drawers: it's locked up, but I can easily push back the lock with a knife."

" That will do capitally," exclaimed Master Blake, rubbing his hands with much satisfaction. " Only you get that, without anybody seeing you, and bring it to me, without anybody knowing it, and I'll take it to my friend Levy Laurence, the Jew, who keeps a fence in Mop Alley, Rosemary Lane, and you shall soon have marbles, and money too, my trump. Lipey arn't particular ; he'll take anything."

Jack promised to comply with his wishes, and returning home, committed his first robbery that very evening, by skilfully forcing open the lock of his mother's drawer, and taking out the only ornament that remained to her of her former days of prosperity. It was a treasured one ; she had struggled hard to retain it, had wrestled sorely with want and necessity, but she had kept it— kept it to be stolen by her child, her darling, to whom she looked for future comfort and support.

The next morning Jack conveyed his ill-gotten spoil to Master Blake, who conveyed it equally as speedily to honest Levy, or Lipey, as he was more usually called. The worthy Israelite declared upon his conscience that the heart, which was of the purest crystal, was only composed of imitation glass, while the setting and chain, both which were virgin gold, was, he affirmed, "coppersh, vasht over vith a little Dutch gilt, and not vorth more, at the outside, than a shilling." Master Blake doubting the veracity of this statement, the Jew conjured several solemn evidences, not to be treated lightly, to bear witness to his truth and integrity; Master Blake therefore told him to hand over the bob, which, in less than half an hour afterwards was expended in sweetmeats, marbles, &c., and divided equally between the two juvenile culprits.

Some days elapsed before Mrs. Sheppard missed her locket; when she did, and found her drawer had been forced open, her suspicions immediately rested on our hero, who had for some time before manifested an extreme degree of ingenuity and perseverance, in getting corks and stopples out of bottles, untying difficult knots, and other works of handicraft. She had only been led very reluctantly to seek the ornament, to extricate her from a situation of urgent need; and her disappointment at its non-appearance was doubly bitter. She immediately taxed her son, for she knew no one

else could have taken it, with the theft, threatening to punish him in the most dreadful way if he
did not instantly make a full confession.

It is amazing how very terrible the threats of
really fond mothers are; their anger always appearing more violent than that of others. Mrs.
Sheppard assured her son that if he did not immediately tell her what he had done with the locket,
she would tear him limb from limb, be the death
of him—with many other dreadful denunciations
of vengeance of a similar kind;—to all which Jack,
after giving a determined denial of any knowledge
of the theft, listened with sullen silence. After
many other equally fruitless efforts to extort the
truth, the poor woman gave up the attempt in despair.

"It was the last of my ornaments," she exclaimed, with bitter sadness; "the last remembrance of my former days of happiness and comfort. I had preserved it through every exigence
—poverty had sought to deprive me of it in vain.
I had resisted even the sharp promptings of hunger; and now to lose it thus!" The tears stole
into her eyes. "My poor misguided husband!"
she continued; "it was his first and dearest gift—
that with which he declared his passion for me:
never shall I forget that time! It was a lovely
summer's eve—we left the busy town at Clerkenwell, and wandered through the pleasant meadows
towards Islington by the banks of the rapid Fleet,

which then flowed brightly onwards: all nature seemed to welcome us. Then it was, while the evening breeze breathed wooingly, that he cast the chain around my neck, and heart met heart: a crystal heart, and set in virgin gold, bearing his name upon it, as mine still does his image—pure, precious, bright; showing—how truly!—our then happy state. Alas! what is it now? Sullied, despoiled, and wretched! the last link of my former happiness is gone, and only misery and anguish now remain." Here she burst into an agony of grief, and gave vent to her feelings in a flood of tears.

Jack, who had heard all this with an apparent apathy, could resist no longer. "Mother, dear mother!" he exclaimed, "I don't want not to be punished, but I can't bear to see you cry: I did take the locket; I did force open the drawer, and I'll tell you who I gave it to, and where it is. I gave it to Joe Blake, my schoolfellow, and he sold it to Levy Laurence, the Jew; and now beat me; do what you like with me; I can bear it all."

This was a harrowing confession for a doting mother to hear; her darling son a thief, and at so tender an age too! But her anguish was somewhat alleviated by the openness of the disclosure, and the generosity of the feeling that had prompted it: then there was the prospect of recovering the cherished token. Casting a look of sad reproach at her guilty son, which touched him more

E

deeply than would have done the keenest invective, her first step was to repair to the nondescript residence of the Jew Levy, a forbidden looking dwelling, the lower part of which would have been described by an Irishman as composed of four halves, half cellar, half parlour, half shop, and half warehouse. As there was no law then in force for the punishment of the receiver of stolen goods, the conscientious Lipey immediately confessed having bought the article in question, describing it in the most frank and unblushing manner, but declaring as before that the crystal was glass, and the gold copper. He was offered ten times what he had given for its return, but this was impossible: the article, as is usual in those cases, had been broken up; but the Jew commiseratingly assured her she should have the remains for "half the monish." They were brought: the gold, and chain were gone; the name had been effaced from the crystal; and the heart was broken.

"It is my fate," said the stricken woman, with a heavy sigh. as she gazed on the fragments, "The gold and chain are gone, the name no longer dwells within the heart ; the heart is broken."

CHAPTER IV.

JACK'S SCHOOLING CONTINUED.

PRECOCIOUS EVASIVENESS.—THE PUBLIC GOOD NOT ALWAYS
PRIVATE BENEFIT.—DEATH OF ROBERT SHEPPARD.

ON the discovery of the robbery of Mrs. Sheppard's locket being made known at the school the next day, the discipline of the birch was, by particular desire of Master Blake's parents, administered to that exemplary young gentleman, for his participation in it, by Mr. Garret himself, and had the effect of materially changing the colour of his skin, during the sittings, for some time afterwards, though, in the progress of its infliction, he had only thrust his tongue in his cheek, and made other unseemly grimaces. Mrs. Sheppard's tenderness would not suffer her to expose her son to the corporal mercies of the preceptor; she therefore determined on taking his punishment into her own hands. Accordingly, conveying him to a garret at the top of the house, she locked him up in a large spare closet which happened to be empty, expressing her intention of keeping him prisoner there, without victuals, during the whole of the day. Our hero neither expressed contrition, nor besought pardon, but yielded to his fate with a passive unconcern that awakened in his mother's breast many a sad foreboding. Not content with locking him up in the cupboard, she, for greater security, bolted, on the outside, the door of the garret in which the cupboard was situated. She was no sooner out of hearing, than Jack began to whistle the well-known tune of " Lillibullero," and instantly set his little wits to work to devise some means of escape. Searching the shelves of the closet in which he was confined, he found an old broken fork with only one prong ; with this prong he very soon managed to force back the lock of his prison door, and was the next moment at liberty in the middle of the room. He had then the outer door to force : with the same implement, by working the prong through the crevice of the door, which was an old, and consequently a crazy one, he managed to shoot back the bolt, and was in an instant on the landing-place. As he did not dare to venture down stairs, the only access to the street being through the two lower apartments—for the luxury of a passage was then rarely known in the houses of mechanics,— and he must inevitably have been seen by, at least, one of his parents, he boldly passed through the garret staircase window into a gutter, skirting a small parapet that ran along the roof of the whole of the houses on that side the street. He crawled along this gutter like a cat, at the imminent hazard of his neck, till he came to a house, the inhabitants of which he knew would, at that time, be absent; and procuring an entrance from the roof through a small trap-door into a species of cockloft, made his way down the various stories, and through the different rooms, securely into the street, committing no other offence in his progress than the entire destruction of a whole pot of preserves, which a maiden lady had with great pains prepared for the purpose of furnishing the contents of a series of roll puddings, during the ensuing winter. This was Jack's first escape—a precocious one, certainly, but strongly foretelling what might afterwards be expected of him.

Mrs. Sheppard had, meanwhile, with much heaviness of heart, proceeded to Spitalfields market to provide the dinner of the day; but though she had mentally resolved that her son should not dine with her, but rather with Duke Humphry, and might have dispensed with at least half a pound of the meat she usually provided, she had somehow contrived, by accident of course, to buy half a pound more. Returning homewards, her maternal bosom filled with a thousand anxious visions of the dismal situation in which she had placed her peccant son; what was her surprise, in crossing Spitalfield's Square, to behold the supposed prisoner so very zealously engaged, playing at " knuckle down," with a parcel of other boys.

She could scarcely believe her eyes. " Why,
good gracious ! you little villain !" she exclaimed, " who can possibly have let you out ? tell me
this moment, or I'll tear you to pieces, I will !
your father, I dare say---for since he's taken to
drinking that strong bubb, and puzzling his poor
weak head with politics, he's grown foolish enough
for any thing."

" Nobody didn't let me out," said Jack, boldly.

" Then how did you get out ?"

" I let myself out," coolly returned the boy.

" What, when I locked and bolted you in ?"
said his mother.

" Yes," Jack replied sturdily, " and would if
you had locked and bolted me in ten times as
much."

" Why, you incorrigible little scoundrel !"
screamed his mother, almost choking with rage.

" I don't care," said Jack ; " no locks nor bolts,
neither, shall keep me in. I won't be shut up for
anybody, and so I tell you."

" I am petrified !" said his mother.

" Well, no more I won't," repeated Jack in a
still louder and firmer tone.

" Can I believe my ears ?" ejaculated the astonished Mrs. Sheppard. " Jack, Jack ! you'll come
to no good ; I can plainly perceive that ; but if
there's a stick to be had for love or money, your
back shall pay for this, Sir. Only wait till I get
you home."

"Only wait till you catch me," said Jack, with a laugh, snatching up his marbles, and running off with a celerity that took him out of sight in a minute, leaving his astonished mother perfectly thunderstruck at his hardihood and audacity.

"He is lost!" she exclaimed, "ruined—hardened! punishment will have no effect on him; I must try and reclaim him by kindness.—Yes! I will not let any one know of this dissolute conduct of his, lest they should suppose that he is past mending. I will reason with him by ourselves. Ah! if his father—if Robert Sheppard were but true to himself—to his family—to me, how easily might all this be remedied; but that fatal 'Blue Posts,'—those endless politics! No, no! there is no hope."

It must now be premised, that from the moment the Sheppards settled in Spitalfields, honest Bob had plunged more deeply into politics, and porter, or strong bubb, as it was then called, than ever. Some parish *quid nuncs* had, a short time previously to Bob's arrival there, formed themselves into a sort of political club, or society, at the "Blue Posts," a house noted for the strength of its liquors, into which he got immediately admitted. One of the overseers of Spitalfields, a somewhat wealthy weaver, with the parish clerk— who also held the office of sexton, which he underlet—a jobbing attorney, the exciseman of the district, and a disbanded lieutenant, advocated the

Tory cause, and were of the high-church and state party, vigorously supporting the pretensions of Harley, afterwards Earl of Oxford, and Mr. St. John, who subsequently became Lord Boling-broke, lauding the influence of Mrs. Masham with the Queen, and speaking with greater respect than became good subjects of the Pretender, the Duke of Berwick, or James the Third, as he styled himself; Bob, on the contrary, backed by the fore-man of a silk manufactory, a distiller's clerk, a rider to a Manchester house in the City, and a half crazy barber, were of the Whig party, as strenuously espoused the Marlborough administra-tion, regularly regulating the plan of attack for the Duke and his allies at the opening of every fresh campaign in Flanders. Great were the cal-culations in the financial department, that Bob made for the ministers Somers and Godolphin, to-tally regardless, poor fellow! of his own finances; but while he was busy in voting fifty thousand here, and raising a hundred thousand there, how could he be expected to cast a thought upon such paltry considerations as shillings and sixpences at home? His rejoicings at every fresh victory of the great Duke were unbounded: he had foreseen them—he had marked them out. The Duke was not more indebted to the confederation of Prince Eugene and the States, than to him (Bob), for the zeal with which he backed all his movements in Spitalfields; and as the Tory faction now began

to gain ground to the prejudice of the hero of
Blenheim and Ramillies,—the idol of Holland and
glory of England,—fervently did Bob execrate
Mrs. Masham as a meddling, underhanded ——,
we must not mention what, to " ears polite."

As the star of his hero waned in the ascendant,
and the Court faction became more powerful, Bob's
indignation increased. The names of the great
men of the age were as familiar in his mouth as
" household words," and nothing was to be heard
from morning to night but Marshal Villars, the
Elector of Bavaria, the Emperor of Austria, the
King of Spain, &c. Continued talking produced
continued thirst, and the butts of the landlord of
the " Blue Posts," were in constant requisition.

To public difficulties now began to be added pe-
cuniary embarrassments at home. The critical position of national affairs from the intrigues of the
opposition party, the rapidly increasing decline of
the Duke's power and favour, with the necessity of
checking the triumph of the weaving overseer and
parish clerk, and their party so preyed upon poor
Bob's weak mind, joined to his own personal trou-
bles, that he began at last to sink under them.
Vainly were his *ebbing* spirits attempted to be rallied by the eloquence of his friend the barber, and
the strong drinks of the potentate of the " Blue
Posts :"—Bob took to his bed. A distress was, unfortunately at this period, put into his house for
rent ; the tide of adversity flowed in full upon

him ; Mrs. Sheppard courageouly strove to stem
it, and might have succeeded, but for a public
event which just then occurred, and not only settled the destinies of Europe for the time being,
but sealed the fate of poor Bob for ever.

We have said that he was reduced to his bed :
a distress for rent was in his house. The man in
possession sat like an evil genius—a goule—a night-
mare, in the little room at the back of the shop,
in which the family lived. They had let the other
part of the house, with the exception of the aforesaid garret in which little Jack slept. An order
had just been received for the shell of some parish
pauper. The overseer at the " Blue Posts," though
opposed to Bob in politics, honouring the zeal he
evinced for his party, and anxious to assist him, the
order was given to be executed to Bob's only journeyman, who was then busily engaged upon it.

Mrs. Sheppard had procured the daily Journal
for her husband, the more to amuse his mind,
which, to say the truth, had for some time previously betrayed symptoms of being wandering, and
unsettled. She was speaking to him of the expediency of paying their unwelcome and ill-boding
inmate his daily half-crown, that their goods might
not be sold, until at least they had made an effort
to save them.

" Yes," faintly murmured Bob, " we must pay
him—we must pay him. Ah ! what is this ?" he
said, his eye catching a paragraph in the paper,

announcing the signing the memorable treaty of Utrecht. "What is this?" glancing his eye rapidly over it; "the Tories have triumphed! our queen has been betrayed—sold! The lustre of England's crown is sullied!"

"But the man, dear Robert, the man," whispered Mrs. Sheppard, seeing how much he had become excited, and wishing to divert his attention.

"True, true," groaned Bob, much agitated; "pay him the half-crown; we must get rid of him. There are villains in the cabinet—the confederation is broken up—they must not sell our goods, you will go to our landlord, love?—the French king has been too much for us—we are lost —the balance of power—the distress—what am I talking of? my senses wander—they must not turn you out into the streets, poor wench!—the troops—the taxes—ruin!—I could have saved all —strong measure—no, no—would I had never gone to that fatal public-house!—but all shall be well yet.—I grow weaker—give me your hand, Kate—God bless old England!—take care of our boy—watch over little Jack—let him be a carpenter.—The cabinet will be broken up—the duke— the queen—my eyes grow dim—let Thomas finish the shell—good-bye—good——"

Poor Bob let the fatal paper fall from his grasp and sank upon his pillow. The martyr to public good, for private ill, had fallen to rise no more! The nation still went on as usual—but Mrs. Sheppard was a widow, and little Jack was fatherless.

CHAPTER V.

JACK'S SCHOOLING COMPLETED.

JACK ADOPTED BY MR. KNEEBONE.—THE OLD BAILEY SESSIONS OF 1712.—THE GIPSY'S WARNING.

THE death of Robert Sheppard soon brought all his friends and acquaintances around his widow: —death is a stern and uncompromising moralist, and often teaches their duty to many, who would listen to no other schoolmaster. We fear him, and dare not treat him with disrespect. Numbers who had for months preceding deserted Bob in his poverty, now that he no longer needed their aid, came to offer their assistance—it is remarkable how ostentatious and gratuitous is one half of the charity of the world—but their attendance had the effect of procuring the poor carpenter a respectable funeral. The political club, his attention to which had cost him so dear, paid him the last mark of respect, both parties mingling in peace and good will together at his grave. But amongst all the friends this calamity had rallied round her, none were more sympathising, more serviceable to the poor widow, than her old acquaintance Mr. Knee-

bone, the woollen-draper, the son, it may be remembered, of her former protectress, when she
was happy and unmarried. Now that poor Bob
is dead, we may venture to disclose a secret which,
during his lifetime, might have savoured somewhat
of scandal. The worthy woollen-draper had early
felt a very ardent passion for his mother's comely
god-daughter—for comely she then was: she was
the first love of his heart; and he had earnestly
looked forward to an union, but the Fates had
ordered it otherwise—the connubial angel, whose
gentle task it is, according to received belief, to
make marriages in Heaven, having been induced
by poor Bob's apparent fervour and sincerity in
his addresses to Kate to link their fates together.
We may wonder at the number of mistakes committed by this sweet spirit in paring mortals together; but when the thousand arts and " per-
juries of lovers, at which Jove laughs," are considered, we can easily conceive why he should be
so often deceived in the course of his delicate and
important registration.

Mr. Kneebone's first step was to clear the poor
widow's house of every species of *distress*, save
that caused by her bereavement, by kicking out
the man in possession, and satisfying the various
claims on poor Bob's insolvent estate. As there
was a very considerable custom attached to the
shop, which would be easily attended to by a fore-
man, and was capable of providing a very com-

fortable subsistence for Mrs. Sheppard, it was agreed that she should still carry on the business. As for little Jack, Mr. Kneebone declared his intention of wholly taking the future care of providing for him upon himself. It is almost needless to remark how grateful the poor widow was for all this real kindness. Jack was immediately removed from Mr. Garret's, where he had learnt little but roguery,—for Mr. Garret had not much to teach: he invariably, when his acquirements were brought to a stand still, got out of the dilemma by flogging the boy whose superior knowledge had got him into it,—an approved method with London Orbiliuses even to this day. Little Jack left Mr. Garret without regret.

Master Joseph Blake had previously been expelled the school for having, in concert with Master William Blewit, stolen the pedagogue's best silver snuff-box, and got it converted into a white soup* for their joint benefit, by worthy Lipey Laurence. Accordingly, leaving the widow as comfortable as she could be, under the circumstances, Mr. Kneebone conveyed little Jack to his own residence in the Strand, which, as mentioned before, was at the sign of the " Fleece and Shears," situated near the Old Angel Inn, in a row of houses long since pulled down, and which faced one side of St. Clement's Church, looking into the church-

---

* Melted.

yard, according to the strange fancy at that period
of mingling the living and the dead in the closest
neighbourhood.

Mr. Kneebone had, it would seem, proved constant to his first love, for he was still unmarried,
his domestic arrangements being superintended by
a dear, good, unconscious old creature, a widow of
the name of Partington. Mrs. Partington, without
being deficient in common sense, natural shrewdness, and even judgment, was the most simple soul
imaginable. She had passed through life smoothly,
and had experienced none of those trials, which,
like the rough stones of the cutler, serve to sharpen
us as we are brought in contact with them. She
had never known the want of money, and could
not, therefore, have any idea of the struggles required in its acquisition, or of its real value; for
the value given to money in the common arithme-
tical tables of our ciphering books, that twelve
pence make a shilling, and twenty shillings a
pound, but little conveys an idea of its real worth
when wanted. How different is the pound acquired by inheritance, gift, or the labours of others,
to that which has to be borrowed or worked for!
The offspring of parents in comfortable circumstances, with an easy temper, and perpetual good
humour, she had been married early in life without
experiencing any of the pangs of previous passion,
to a thriving suitor, who, after some years of child-
less wedlock, died, leaving her a widow with what,

if well managed, would have proved a snug com-
petency for her life.   But poor Mrs. Partington,
guileless herself, never suspected guile in others :
she took every thing literally, and thought all she
heard was what it purported to be—all she saw
what it appeared to be ; and it was only when she
had got rid of almost all that had been left her,
that she found out her mistake.   Luckily for her,
the death of Mr. Kneebone's mother at this juncture, by rendering it necessary that he should have
some one to preside over his domestic arrangements, one neither too young to excite scandal,
nor too old to prevent the duly attending to his
comforts provided her with a home not inferior
to either of those she had enjoyed with her parents
and with her husband.   Poor Mrs. Partington !—
so long as she did not know the want of a shilling,
she was perfectly ready to believe the streets were
paved with gold ; and yet she was notable in her
occupations, and an admirable manager in all that
required her superintendence.   But extreme simplicity is very often to be found united to the very
highest qualities of the mind.   Fontaine, Gay, and
our inimitable Goldsmith, all, in wit were men.
but children in simplicity.   She received Jack very
kindly, and when Mr. Kneebone told her she must
be a mother to him, earnestly promised to be so,
and in a short time really almost imagined that she
was so.   Mr. Kneebone's house was substantial,
and well furnished ; he had a flourishing business,

and but for an habitual gravity, the cause of which, whether it arose from the disappointment in his early love affair, a natural tendency, or any other source, was quite a mystery, might have been considered a completely happy man : his temper was equable, his habits regular, and his wishes moderate. Faithful to the trust he had taken upon himself, he immediately commenced completing Jack's education ; he sent him, as our hero afterwards gratefully confessed, copies with his own hand, and took a delight in hearing him read from any book or printed paper that presented itself.

One day as they were sitting behind the counter, the beadle of St. Clement's entered with a jury paper, in which Mr. Kneebone was summoned to attend the sessions then holding in the Old Bailey. Little Jack was very curious to know all the particulars of this duty, asking many questions touching the functions of the judge, and what juries were for, and what was the meaning of counsel, with other pertinent interrogatories ; also what sort of a place Newgate was, and how persons fared who were transported either to Virginia, or Maryland, —to which colonies convicts were usually transported at that period,—whether they were nice places or not ;—to all which questions the good-natured Mr. Kneebone, seeing the deep interest Jack took in them, answered as well as he could, promising further particulars the first opportunity. When the day arrived for Mr. Kneebone's attend-

ance at the court, Jack was very eager, on his
return, to know all that had passed ; and Mr.
Kneebone could only get rid of some very puzzling importunities, by promising at the end of the
sessions he would bring him a printed " report of
all the trials, with the sentences of the prisoners,
&c." and would hear him read out of that, instead
of the family Bible, which they had then nearly got
halfway through.   The sessions soon terminated,
and Mr. Kneebone proved as good as his word: he
brought Jack the official account of the various
trials that had taken place, which Jack immediately proceeded to spell out with great avidity.
The principal trial was that of a highwayman !
one John Hawkins, who subsequently became very
notorious, and was some years afterwards executed
at Tyburn for robbing the Bristol mail.*   He was
accused of stopping Justice Blenkinsop in his carriage on Hounslow Heath, and taking from his
person twenty guineas, a silk nightgown, a new
tie-wig, a pinchbeck family watch, and a shagreen
spectacle case.   Thomas Biddlecomb, the coachman, a Mr. Whiffin, who was in the carriage at
the time, and several other witnesses swore positively to the fact.   Hawkins' defence was an *alibi.*
He brought one Solomon Shabner, who kept a
lodging-house in Knave's Acre, London, to swear

* He was hung with his accomplice, James Simpson, after
an extraordinary career of villany, on the 21st of May, 1722.

that he was at his house at the very time the robbery was committed, in proof of which Shabner produced a receipt of thirty shillings for a pair of leather breeches, which he affirmed had been given him at that very time by Hawkins; but the judge having examined the receipt, and finding that the body of it was written with ink of a different colour to that with which the name at the bottom was signed, told the jury, he did not think Shabner's evidence was entitled to any credit, and they were about to bring in a verdict of guilty, when an acquaintance of the prisoner, who said his name was Stephen Quigley, happening to look over the notes of Mr. Cuttlemuck, the short hand-writer to the court, perceived, that by dipping his pen into an inkstand, the ink in which was thick and muddy at the bottom, and watery at the top, part of his writing was pale, while the other was more than usually dark, snatched it out of his possession, and handed it to the foreman of the jury, a Mr. Puddledock, who, with his brother jurors, was so staggered by this testimony to the truth of Shabner's evidence, that in spite of all the other witnesses, they immediately allowed the *alibi*, and acquitted the prisoner.

Jack was overjoyed at this result, declared that he thought an *alibi* was a capital thing, and was what he should always procure if ever he was tried; and when told by Mr. Kneebone that in a case of doubtful evidence, where he wished to acquit the offender, he had remained locked up with his brother jurors for more than two hours past his dinner time, until fairly worn out by famine— having had only his usual lunch—he was obliged to give in, Jack expressed his determination, if ever he was on a jury, to die of hunger before he'd find a single prisoner guilty. Mr. Kneebone good-naturedly set down these sentiments as proofs of the simplicity and tenderness of Jack's heart. The next trial which attracted Jack's attention was of one Thomas Donnikin, for housebreaking. It appeared this prisoner had burglariously attempted to enter the dwelling-house of a Mr. Lammiman, a ladies' tailor, and had been caught in the fact, through the bungling manner in which he had gone to work. In forcing open a shutter he had awkwardly broken a window, which had alarmed a cat that was asleep in the room, who suddenly jumping up, had in her fright overturned a large glass globe, filled with gold and silver fish; this had aroused Mrs. Lammiman's poodle, who having aroused Mr. Lammiman, he immediately awakened his wife, she in her turn summoned the apprentices, and they called the attention of the watch. Donnikin was taken in the act of running away; he was found guilty, and sentenced to be transported. This, Jack said, he was very glad of, for that Donnikin quite deserved it; that he ought to have taken a centre-bit and a knife, or a small saw, and cut a pannel of the shutter out, when he could have put in his hand, slipped back the bolts, opened the window, and got in without any noise.

Mr. Kneebone admired the love of justice manifested in his *protégé's* approbation at the conviction of this man, and was also pleased at the workman-like knowledge displayed in his pointing out the *proper* way by which the shutters ought to have been opened.

" Jack must be a carpenter," he exclaimed ; " his poor father was right ; and however much I may wish to bring him up to my own trade of a woollen-draper, his natural genius must have its way.

The last trial of the sessions was one which, when he came to it, so surprised and confused our little hero, as to render him perfectly unintelligible when he attempted to read it. It was the trial of William Blewit and Joseph Blake, two youths about fifteen years of age, for picking the pocket of the Rev. Ebenezer Spooner, a dissenting minister, of a silver tobacco-stopper, a gilt toothpick, an old linen handkerchief, a leathern pocket-book, containing some valuable notes for an intended charity sermon, a list of subscriptions for the New Bethesda Chapel, together with four-pence in copper. A Mrs. Ogle and one Peter Winks, two passers-by, with several other respectable witnesses, deposed to seeing the prisoners—who appeared very hardened—hustle the reverend pro-

secutor, though they managed by their audacity
to escape at the time; but Mr. Jonathan Wild
coming forward, stated that, being employed to
restore the stolen property by the reverend gentleman's congregation, he had occasion to know
that it was taken by one Tit Blundell, who was
then out of the way. He further spoke to the
good character of the two prisoners; and it appearing, on his cross-examination, that the two
guineas reward paid for the recovery of the property being all swallowed up in expenses, he would
only accept of the prayers of his pious employer,
as he was actuated solely for the public good,
the prisoners were acquitted, though the judge expressed very strong doubts of their innocence.

"And well he might," said Mr. Kneebone, " I
never saw two such ill-looking young scoundrels in
my life; they must have been brought up in a
very bad school."

Here Jack, who had a tender recollection at his
back of sundry visitations of Mr. Garret's cane
said he was certain it *was* a very bad school; and
immediately began making some inquiries respecting Mr. Jonathan Wild, through whose evidence
the prisoners had so fortunately got off.

" Whoso toucheth pitch shall be defiled," answered Mr. Kneebone; " all I know of him is,
that he keeps an office in the Old Bailey for restoring stolen goods to their proper owners, on
consideration of an adequate reward being given,

and ' no questions asked ;' and from his success in his vocation he must be acquainted with almost every thief in London. He passes for a person of probity and credit; but there's an old saying, ' birds of a feather flock together;' and for my part," continued Mr. Kneebone, " the saints preserve me from his coop, say I. I should expect to be pretty well plucked if ever I got in his clutches, as my opinion is, that he rather encourages and protects the thieves by his proceedings than any thing else."

Jack greedily swallowed this information. "They must have been my old schoolfellows, Will Blewit and Joe Blake," thought he to himself—" the names and age are the same ;" but all doubt was removed from his mind by his protector's next observation.

" If they'd had a grain of modesty in their compositions," said Mr. Kneebone, " they must have been moved when the reverend prosecutor so pathetically admonished them to restore his manuscript notes, which it appeared had not been recovered with the other valuables ;—but I forgot —it was impossible to make one of them blush, for his face was as blue as a bilberry ; indeed, one of the constables deposed that he was well known among the young prigs of Moorfields by the nickname of Blueskin."

This was enough ; Jack did not venture to betray his acquaintance with them by any further remarks, but dropped the subject;—still the memory of this occurrence incessantly haunted his imagination: in his sleep he was with his former companions lightening the Reverend Ebenezer of his wordly load, and sharing with them the worthy minister's four-pence in copper, under the protection of the charitable Mr. Wild. Some time after this, our hero, discovering that it was rather inconvenient at times to be without a supply of ready cash to purchase cakes, fruit, and other luxuries that might occasionally present themselves, bethought himself of Levy Laurence, as a probable banker; but as it was necessary honest Levy should have assets in hand, ere he would answer any demands upon him, Jack looked about to see if there was any valuable that had not been properly put away. He was not long before he discovered a piece of negligence that he thought required being made an example of. Mrs. Partington had a large gold seal-ring, which had belonged to her grandfather, and which she prized very much, and only wore on high days and holidays. It was of amazing consistency, and bore, on a large red cornelian that stood out like a nutmeg, the very original device of a pair of scissors, with a motto, "We only part to meet again." This ring she had taken off, one summer's evening, and placed on her prayer-book in the window-seat of the dining-room, which was deeply embayed, intending to carry it up stairs with her, when she should retire to bed. This ring Jack found next morning, though she did not,—albeit she searched diligently for it, which was more than he had done. The suspicion that any one in the house had taken it, much less that little Jack had done so, never entered Mrs. Partington's innocent imagination; she only knew that she had lost it; and as she set great store by it, she determined to employ every means in her power to recover it.

Before Jack had an opportunity of visiting his friend Lipey, in Houndsditch, her resolution was taken. " If I could but see the dumb man at Westminster, that answers all sorts of difficult questions," she exclaimed, " he would tell me in a moment; but unfortunately he is in Bridewell for breaking the peace in a night-brawl. Then there's Mrs. Bunce, the cunning woman of the maze in Southwark, that tells fortunes by teacups, but she's picking oakum in the New Prison for not being able to account for a pair of sheets and some silver spoons that was to be used by her as a charm. Never mind, I shall find somebody."

Mrs. Partington was not wrong in her supposition: that very afternoon, a wandering gipsy, who was going about from house to house, covertly soliciting the females to become acquainted with the secrets of futurity, peeped in at Mr. Kneebone's door. To convey her, unobserved, to the kitchen where little Jack was most unconsciously

sitting, was the work of only a few moments.
Jack was humming to himself the burden of Arthur Chambers's " Lay of the Prince of Prigs,"
—which our readers will remember had been sung
to him by Master Blake previously to the robbery
of his mother's locket—and which he had represented to Mrs. Partington, when she inquired its
meaning, to be *Latin ;* an assertion the good
woman firmly believed.   As the gipsy's dark
shadow fell upon him, on her entrance, he started
up in some surprise. Her appearance was in truth
somewhat wild and striking ; which the reader
will readily believe, when informed she was the
very identical gipsy who had some years previously assisted at Jack's birth in the little cottage
at Stepney. Jack's surprise almost changed to
terror, when he heard Mrs. Partington immediately afterwards proceed to explain to the gipsy
the business on which she wanted her.

" I know, my good woman," said the worthy
dame, " that you gipsies can tell every thing, discover hidden treasures, point out the thief, when
any robbery has been committed, and reveal the
place where any thing that is lost may be found."

Jack's colour changed at these words—the gipsy
fixed her piercing eye full upon him, which had
not the effect of materially lessening his apprehensions.

" I *can* point out the thief," said she, in a deep

but hollow tone, " I *can* reveal where the lost property may be found. Nothing is unknown to me—nothing can be concealed from me: the planets are my servants, and the stars hold secret council with me."

Jack trembled in every limb.

" Ay, ay, I know that," rejoined Mrs. Partington, " I know that very well. Why, I've heard that you gipsies can read the stars as easily as we do our A B C—Lord bless me! that you are as intimate with Venus and Mercury, and Gemini, and Jupiter, and all the other planets, as if you had been brought up with them—that you are visited at night by the Great Bear and the Dogstar; and that you can ride on the Dragon's tail. Now, you must understand, that I have lost a very valuable ring. There is no occasion to describe it to you, for I dare say you are perfectly well acquainted with it, though you have never seen it, mercy on me!"

" I am well acquainted with it," said the gipsy confidently, glancing at the same time very significantly at Jack. " It was lost ——"

" In this house," said Mrs. Partington.

" I knew it," returned the gipsy. " You must cross my hand with a piece of silver, and then leave me. Do not be alarmed," she continued, observing the good dame's hesitating look; "leave me with this boy—he will be my guarantee, that while your ring is found, nothing shall be missing; the owner of the lost property must not be present during the potent incantations necessary to be performed in order to effect its restoration."

Jack felt a strange species of fear and awe steal over him at the prospect of being left alone with the mysterious stranger. We have remarked the singleness and simplicity of Mrs. Partington's character—though superstition was no predominant feature in her nature, for superstition implies a degree of fear and weakness which did not exactly belong to her—yet she implicitly believed in fortune-tellers, dreams, charms, prognostics, &c. ; accordingly, she without hesitation crossed the gipsy's hand with a shilling ; and saying that she would wait in the back kitchen during the performance of the mystic ceremonies, and that the gipsy was to cry " hem !" when she had finished, as a signal for her return, she retired in full confidence as to the result, promising the further reward of a silver crown if it should prove to be a successful one.

" Never fear," cried the gipsy, as she closed the door after her ; " my art has never failed me yet." She then advanced slowly towards Jack, and stopping directly before him, gazed at him full in the face with a searching look under which he quailed, while she muttered the following lines, probably part of the formula of her profession :—

The Gipsy's Chant

1.

THINK'ST thou the gipsy's art is vain,
And does but dwell in Fancy's brain;
That o'er the earth a wanderer driven,
No mystic power to her is given
The secrets of the past to read,
And tell the present's hidden deed,
With all, the future shall bestow,
Of good and bad, of joy and woe?
   False is thy thought, by sign and spell
   The gipsy every thing can tell.

2.

Think'st thou the spheres exist alone;
That earth and sky no kindred own;
That 'tween the stars which people heaven
And man, no sympathy is given;
That planets roll above our earth,
And beam upon each infant's birth;
Nor own an influence o'er its fate,
To sway its future love and hate?
   False is thy thought, by their weird spell,
   The gipsy every thing can tell.

3.

Sprung from the East, where wisdom reign'd,
Why is the gipsy's skill disdain'd?
Her power is in her being shown,—
Unmix'd she lives—apart—alone.
Seek, if in others thou canst trace,
One feature of the gipsy race;
Mark the dark words she, only, speaks;
See the warm glow that stains her cheeks;
   And slight her not! By sign and spell,
   The gipsy every thing can tell.

4.

To her each hidden secret's known ;
To her the future still is shown ;
She in the teacup's dregs can read
Whate'er the Fates may have decreed :
Can in the lines which cross the palm,
Trace future welfare, future harm ;
The hidden and the lost unfold ;
Point out the thief, yield back the gold.
    Scorn not her words, but mark them well—
    The gipsy every thing can tell.

Absolutely terrified at the solemnity of the gipsy's tones, the mystic import of her words, and the angry glaring of her eye, without staying for any question, Jack's hand instinctively sought his breeches pocket, from which he tremblingly drew forth the lost ring.

" I found it, ma'am," he faltered forth, " and was going to give it back, only I didn't know exactly who it belonged to.   Indeed I did not steal it : I only *took* it.   Pray don't tell Mrs. Partington,—she'll give you twice as much if she thinks you found it all of yourself, and nobody told you."

" Peace, boy !" said the gipsy, sternly, taking the ring ; " you begin by times.—Your hand— let me peruse its palm—your left hand, imp !— the lines run deepest there—ah ! what is this ? What see I on the plain of Mars ?—a crooked line, crossing the table line :—that should betoken sudden death.—The sister line is broken too,— the line of fate !—that looks not well ; this line

which runs across the wrist, and there is lost in
blood—have I not read this palm before? Let
me regard thee—that mole upon the neck, on the
left side—ah! I remember now, when I removed
her infant hand which shadowed it—then first I
saw it.—Thy name, boy?"

" Sheppard, Jack Sheppard," faltered Jack.

" Thy parents came from Stepney?"—" Yes."

" It is the hand of fate that brought me here!"
exclaimed the gipsy; and immediately set herself
about drawing a planetary configuration on the
floor with the bi-forked hazel wand she had in
her hand, and with which she guided her steps.
" Strange, strange!" she continued, as she gazed
on the figures, and began to cast their relative
positions to each other. " This house which seeming chance has brought me to, has reference to
both their future fates; there's a dark secret wound
with it in which they both have part. What has
this house to do with *her* nativity? Strange that
I should meet this boy again, and here!" She
fell into a deep and sad abstraction. After a few
moments, recovering from her musing, she turned
to Jack, and with looks and words that partook
more of sorrow than of anger, thus addressed him:
—" Listen to me, boy!—a baleful star gleams
over thee, betokening a shameful end: if thou'dst
not die a felon's death, withdraw thee from its
influence—forsake thy present course; I'll not
betray thy confidence, moved by some previous
knowledge; but beware! and let this present

mercy induce repentance, where punishment per-
chance had hardened.—Shun evil ways—theft,
and the council of the wicked; but, above all,
should there e'er cross thy path one fair as morning, with eyes mild as the unclouded blue that
veils the heaven of a summer's eve, and tresses
golden as the grain that ripens in autumnal suns,
one wearing thine own age, and bearing on her
neck a spot impressed by art, a counterpart of that
which nature, for thy warning, so ominously hath
planted upon thine;—should such e'er cross thee,
avoid her—fly her, ay, as thou would'st a scorpion,
or aught more foul. Though promising elysium,
she'll prove destruction to thee: thy seeming bliss
will be thy certain bane. Treasure my words—
how shall I show thee farther?"

Here she began again to make various planetary
and zodiacal signs upon the floor. "What's this?
Ah! Leo—the LION! Though gentle as the
breath of noon in spring, far better 'twere that
thou should'st meet a *lioness*: her love will be
thy doom—avoid her—fly her—she bears a royal
virgin's name. I may not tell thee more—avoid
her—fly her, ay, as thou would'st the hangman:
but should'st thou disregard me—ah! what then?
—aid me my art!—In thy dark hour of peril,"—
and she again resorted to her mystic characters on
the floor—" once may'st thou escape, twice may'st
thou escape—ay, when the doom is said, the coffin
made, and the grave dug, and—Magi! what see
I? By the twelve plagues that overspread our

land, by the ensanguined sea that overwhelmed
our might, e'en though the hemp be twined, the
beam be raised, the priest be ready, *thrice*, THRICE,
shalt thou escape ; but then—ah ! there's a blank :
all's dark—dark as eternity. I've warned thee,
boy : beware the third time—beware the temp-
tress.—Let me away !—but first this ring." She
hemmed thrice.

Jack was mute and motionless with terror. He
understood but half of what had been addressed
to him, but that half was enough : his spirit was
checked, his blood ran cold in his veins, and a
determined resolution of future honesty took full
possession of his mind. All expectation and apprehension, Mrs. Partington was not long in making her appearance.

" Well, my good mother," she asked, with
much eagerness, " have your conjurations proved
successful."—" They have, mistress," said the gipsy, solemnly.

" Shall I recover my ring ?"—" You will."

Mrs. Partington was overjoyed.

" Bring hither a Bible and a key, a plate of salt,
and a clean napkin, together with one of the garters
you wore the day on which the article was lost."

" Mercy on me !" said Mrs. Partington, " this
is wonderful ; but I have heard of such things before :" and, retiring for a minute or two, she returned, bringing with her all that the gipsy had
required.

" 'Tis well," said the sibyl, beginning to mutter some unintelligible words, which Mrs. Partington had no difficulty in believing was a very powerful charm ; she then placed a portion of the salt in the napkin, which she folded up in a very peculiar and mystic manner, very much after the fashion of what are called 'puzzle purses ;' then binding the key and Bible together with the garter, she suspended them from her fore-finger over the cloth, making them perform a number of gyrations, muttering all the time a variety of uncouth sentences in an unknown tongue, which had the effect of greatly adding to the imposing nature of the proceedings. The ceremonies being at length concluded, and apparently to her satisfaction, " It is enough," she said. " Take this napkin, bury it where no living eye can see—no human voice can tell ; let it remain inurned three days : on the morning of the fourth day go, fasting and in secret, dig it up, repeating thrice the words, ' In the name of Egypt, I charge thee, O ring, appear !' and the bauble will be restored to you."

" Wonderful !" exclaimed the unsuspecting matron, at the same time gratefully thrusting a five shilling piece into the gipsy's hand. " I'll not fail, depend upon it."

" Good. Farewell mistress," returned the gipsy. —" Remember ! And you, boy," she added, casting an expressive glance at Jack, " do not *you* forget :" saying which, she mysteriously departed.

CHAPTER VI.

JACK'S APPRENTICESHIP.

MR. WOOD, THE CARPENTER.—JACK'S APPRENTICESHIP.—
MADAM WOOD.—JACK'S WELCOME.

IT is almost needless to observe that Mrs. Partington most religiously obeyed the gipsy's injunctions. Secretly digging up the buried napkin
on the morning of the fourth day, in the manner
directed, she had the inexpressible satisfaction, on
pronouncing the mystic words, of finding her lost
ring duly preserved in the salt. " It is really
astonishing," she exclaimed ; " but I knew it would
be so. What disinterested and praiseworthy creatures these gipsies must be, not to find every thing
that is lost for themselves ! Well, I shall never
be at any trouble for any thing that is missing
after this."

As for Jack, he had received so complete a
lesson by the narrow escape from detection which
he had experienced, that he thought it best to say
as little as possible on the subject. He resolved
to think no more about his former companion,
Master Blake, nor of honest Levy Laurence, but

to keep his fingers to himself.   The gipsy's warning had made a deep impression upon him—perhaps the more so from the greater part being
unintelligible to him.   He was confirmed in his
belief of her supernatural powers by a conversation
with Mrs. Partington, some time afterwards, to
which he artfully led, and in which that good
lady, in answer to Jack's remarks on the credi-
bility of the gipsy's skill, took occasion to observe,
that the restoration of the ring was nothing ; that
she had known many things much more remarkable ; particularly one, where some plate having
been mislaid, by a gentlewoman of her acquaintance, a gipsy was called in, who. with nothing
more than a pack of cards, found out that the
whole of the plate had been sent away, by mistake, of course, along with some foul linen to the
butler's own mother.   She also related another
circumstance, where a second gentlewoman of her
acquaintance, in order to obtain a prize in the
lottery, had consulted a celebrated fortune-teller,
who advised her, by way of charm, to bury a
silver teapot, with a snail in it, in her garden for
nine days, when she would find the *lucky number*,
traced by the snail at the bottom of the pot ; but
that forgetting one of the many ceremonies she
was enjoined to observe during this transaction,
when she came to dig up the pot, she only found
a brickbat buried in its place ; consequently, instead of getting the 20,000*l.* prize, when she

bought a ticket, she only drew a blank, which
Mrs. Partington thought a very proper punishment for her negligence in omitting any one of
the ceremonies. These instances made a deep
impression on Jack's mind; and it is but justice
to say, that for the two years afterwards—the
period of time which he spent at Mr. Kneebone's
house before he was apprenticed—his honesty was
perfectly unimpeachable. But becoming now a
well-grown boy, having reached the age of thir-
teen, and having learned as much in the way of
reading, writing, and arithmetic, from Mr. Kneebone's tuition, as it seemed probable he ever would
learn—for we have before observed Jack's parts
were not remarkably bright in these particulars
—the worthy woollen-draper looked about to find
some proper person, following the profitable trade
of carpenter, with whom he could apprentice Jack,
agreeably to poor Bob Sheppard's last request,
and the boy's own express wish on the subject.
He was not long before an eligible opportunity
presented itself, in the person of a Mr. Owen
Wood, a substantial carpenter, residing at the
sign of " The Ark," in Wych-street, Drury-lane.
Mr. Kneebone had formed an acquaintance with
this individual in his occasional evening visits to
a tavern in the neighbourhood of Clare Market,
known by the name of the " Black Jack," from the
ale drank there being usually served up in large leathern measures called jacks, or, from their colour,

black jacks. Mr. Kneebone was accustomed to visit this house of an evening, to recreate himself after the labours of the day with the company of some of his brother tradesmen in the immediate neighbourhood, amongst whom was Mr. Wood. The house had also the additional recommendation of being frequented by Mr. Joseph Miller, the well known comedian, who at that time performed at the Theatre Royal, Drury Lane, and who was more distinguished by a certain taciturnity and dryness of manner, than by any remarkable brilliancy of wit, though a collection of jests was, after his death, appositely enough, printed under his name, for the benefit of his widow, by a Mr. Motley, a wag about town at that period, which has since formed a foundling hospital for every stray witticism and fatherless joke that has been uttered for the last century; nevertheless, as his tombstone in the adjacent parish burial ground informs us, Mr. Miller was an honest man; to which we may add, he was certainly a very dry, and consequently a convivial one.

Mr. Owen Wood was by birth a Cambro-Briton, being a native of Caernarvon. He was an honest but somewhat irascible man, like most of the descendants of St. David. He was about the middle stature, strongly built, but not over bulky; his features had rather a frosty and puckered appearance, wearing somewhat of an expression of fretful pettishness, not at all compromised by a very sober bob-wig. He wore a waistcoat of grey stuff with large flaps; a stiff skirted coat of brown cloth, with figured brass buttons about the size of a crown-piece; black velvet breeches, the knees of which were concealed by the grey ribbed hose which rolled over them, according to the fashion of the time, and very high shoes with enormous silver buckles.

It so happened that about this time an acquaintance and customer of Mr. Kneebone had commenced building a house at Hampstead, being a gentleman of independent fortune.—He had contracted for the brickwork and masonry, but had not settled with any one to execute the woodwork of the intended edifice. This Mr. Kneebone knew; and, as he had great interest with the gentleman, it struck him as affording him a favourable opportunity for accomplishing his wishes as respected Jack; he therefore proposed at once to the honest Cambro-Briton to procure him the contract for the carpenters' work of the building, which could not fail to prove highly lucrative, on condition that he, Mr. Wood, should take Jack as his apprentice for the term of seven years, without requiring any other premium. This was gladly agreed to; and accordingly, very soon afterwards, on a day fixed, Mr. Kneebone and Mr. Wood took little Jack before the Chamberlain at Guildhall, where the indentures were formally signed and sealed; Mr. Kneebone contracting, on his part, that little Jack should not, during his apprenticeship, commit matrimony, or any other improper act; while Mr. Wood, on the other hand, agreed to supply him for the said term with all proper and necessary food, lodging, and raiment; and, further, to induct him completely into the noble art and mystery of his own trade of a carpenter.

Apprenticeships were treated at that time as much more solemn, important, and binding engagements, than they are now. After a suitable discourse from the Chamberlain, embracing much conventional advice and admonition, the parties retired to partake of an entertainment provided by Mrs. Partington at Mr. Kneebone's house, previously to Jack's leaving it in the afternoon for his new quarters. The plum-pudding, and other delicacies, somewhat reconciled Jack to entering upon his noviciate; for his master had taken him without trial on the strength of the contract.

A copious supply of the strongest ale had been procured for the occasion from the " Black Jack," with which Mr. Wood indulged himself until a genial flush had completely thawed the usual frostiness of his furrowed features; and he descanted to Jack very largely on the dignity and utility of the master-craft to which he was about to be brought up, which he described as first having been brought to perfection by the patriarch Noah, in the construction of the ark, the sign of his shop. He spoke of the handiworks of Hiram the builder ; of the rare joinery and precious wood employed by Solomon to augment the magnificence of his temple, with much other edifying matter of a like nature. He then went on to descant on the virtues of the rule and compasses, the plane and line, and the difficulties that might be accomplished by the judicious use of the centre-bit, the chisel, the saw, together with the hammer and gimlet, and other implements of the trade. Jack knew already what might be done with some of these tools, perhaps even better than the worthy carpenter himself ; for though he had scrupulously abstained for some time from all dishonest courses, yet when Mr. Kneebone had innocently exchanged the Bible for the Old Bailey Calendar in Jack's reading lesson, from that moment, unfortunately, did that fatal calendar become Jack's only gospel.

After the honest Cambro-Briton had taken as much ale as he could conveniently carry, and was becoming, if the truth must be spoken, somewhat quarrelsome, Mr. Kneebone thought it advisable Jack should depart to his new home. A new prayer-book, bought for the occasion, in which his name was written, and a large plum cake, was given to him, with some tears and a quantity of goodly advice, by the kind-hearted Mrs. Partington, to which Mr. Kneebone added a complete change of new wearing apparel, and a handsomely bound copy of " The Carpenter's Guide and Joiner's Assistant," with a bran span new half-crown, with some hearty wishes that he might turn out a good boy, mind what his master said to him, and make a bright man. A shake of the hand from Mr. Kneebone, a few motherly kisses from Mrs. Partington, and taking his little bundles under his arm, Jack, conducted by **Mr. Wood**, commenced his journey from his kind protector's house, adjoining " The Angel," to his master's shop in the adjacent Wych-street—a short journey, certainly ; but how important a one to Jack !

Arriving at the door of Mr. Wood's shop, which was by this time shut up, a resolute though rather staggering knock of its master summoned to their admittance a dirty servant girl. Ascertaining from this handmaid that Mrs. Wood was up stairs in the best room. the carpenter was about to conduct Jack thither to introduce him to his future mistress, when, with a prodigious rustle and sweep of silk and brocade, Mrs. Wood encountered them at the foot of the stairs. She was a lady of what is usually termed " a certain age," which, by the bye, is generally the most uncertain age we know of. A prodigious high cap. embellished with a profusion of ribands. and having long lappets, was stuck upon a large mass of turned up hair thickly powdered ; her stomacher, which was high and ample, as well as particularly low, was liberally ornamented with lace and jewellery ; added to these were a stiffly starched muslin apron, a festooned hoop petticoat. a large flowered damask silk gown. with a negative species of train ;—she had worked mittens on her hands, and wore an embroidered kerchief over her shoulders, pinned carefully down; a large mock pearl necklace encircled her throat, two or three beauty spots of black Taffeta, or *mouches*, as they were called, diversified her face, which from excitement or some other cause, very strongly, at that moment, resembled a full blown peony; a large fan, on which was represented the various scenes in Mr. Dryden's improvement of Shakspeare's Tempest, " The Enchanted Island," at that time a very popular subject, hung suspended from her right wrist; a shagreen cased watch, about the diameter of a saucer, and almost the consistency of a turnip, dangled from her girdle at the left side: high red-heeled shoes with paste buckles, completed the picture.

" A pretty hour this is to come home," she exclaimed, looking fiercely at Mr. Wood, and then casting a disdainful glance at Jack, " when you knew I wished to visit the Duke's Theatre. Every person of any consideration has been to see Mr. Otway's new tragedy of ' Venice Preserved ;' and how could I posssibly go to Lincoln's Inn Fields without having somebody to walk by the side of my chair. You know, independently of other respects, there has been a great many robberies in that quarter, lately."

" Very true, Mrs. Woot, my lofe," answered the carpenter in a rather conciliatory tone; " ferry true; but what could I do? You know I was opliged to stay out; I had to pind the poy."

" And I suppose the chamberlain kept you till this time," answered Mrs. Wood disdainfully, " and that you have been entertained in the Guild-hall with spiced wines and other potations, instead of swilling your ale at that filthy Black Jack ;— a likely matter indeed !—If I had gone, such a thing might have happened. The city authorities would have known how to have paid a proper re-spect to one whose cousin has passed the chair, and who has received the honour of knighthood from her Majesty's own gracious hands."

It must here be remarked that Mrs. Wood, or Madam Wood as she was universally called by the neighbours, on account of her lofty deport-ment and high pretensions, was originally a small city heiress, a distant relation of an eminent tallow chandler who had arrived at the dignity of mayor, and having to carry up an address of congratula-tion on one of Marlborough's victories to good Queen Anne, in St. James's palace, had received the honour of knighthood with Prince George's own sword. By one of those mistakes which the amiable angel we have before alluded to so often makes, the heiress had early in life been destined for Mr. Wood, then only a journeyman carpenter ; though no one could discover the reasons for this match, except that there was no very great dispa-rity of age between them, nor overpowering pre-dominance of beauty on either side :—to be sure Mr. Wood traced his pedigree through the line of Cadwallader considerably beyond Caractacus, which assimilated in some measure with the gentility of Mrs. Wood's condition, and her relationship to the ex-mayor before alluded to, Sir Timothy Gutteridge. Then Mrs. Wood's money had helped to set Mr. Wood up in business on his own account. Thus far they seemed suited to each other, but in no other respect. Mr. Wood was choleric and Mrs. Wood was haughty; and that peculiar variety of married life, known by the name of " cat and dog," was the continual and perpetual consequence.

" I say, Sir," said Mrs. Wood after a short pause, in which the carpenter was either trying to keep his spirit down or to work himself up, it was not very clear or material which,—" I say, Sir," she exclaimed in a louder tone, " it is shameful that an heiress in her own right, as I was before I had the misfortune to marry you, one with the offers that I had—there was the bridgemaster's son and the city remembrancer's nephew—should be neglected in the manner I am. If my cousin Sir Timothy——"

Here the worthy Cambro-Briton could contain himself no longer—his anger burst out with full force. " Look you, Mrs. Woot, Got's pody! hur will hafe no more of this. What if you had a thousant pounts from your uncle, the tidewaiter, tid'nt you marry a gentleman by pirth and blood? When you think of your city rememprancers, look you, do not forget that. What though your cousin Sir Timothy, the tallow chantler, fas Lort

Mayor, when hur father the squires fas married, look you, hur had no less than twelve cooks at her fedding, though that fag, Mr. Joseph Millers, said it fas because every man toasted his own cheese; but it fas not: hur has not tallow in hur veins, though hur has lights in her podies, look you Mrs. Woot; do not forget that, I pray you."

" Why, you pitiful, ignorant, leek-eating fellow!" said Mrs. Wood, growing greatly enraged; " wouldn't you have been running bare-legged over the mountains, after your own ill-savoured goats, at this very time, if it hadn't been for me? Would you ever have tasted anything beyond the luxury of the toasted cheese you speak of, but for my money? I that demeaned myself, by marrying such an uncultivated barbarian; but I am rightly served." Here she thought proper to go into hysterics, which Mr. Wood seemed to regard as a matter of course, though Jack was very frightened.

" Let her alone, poy," said the choleric carpenter; " she fill gife ofer fen she's tired. Get to your garrets, look you; you fill find it fen you hafe cot to the top of the house as far as you can go. See that you are up early in the mornings, that hur may set you to work. You fill not fant a light—there is the moons, look you. Your mistress fill hafe plenty of times to come to her senses, while hur is taking her onion and salt in the kitchens fith the mait."

" I shall not wait for that, you wretch!" said

Mrs. Wood, suddenly recovering. " You'll eat no onion to-night if you mean to come near me, I can tell you that.   What are you standing staring for there, boy?" turning to Jack, who was gazing at her, with his eyes and mouth open to their utmost extent.   " I'll make *you* treat me with respect, at all events, if other people don't.   Take that, and get to bed directly, sirrah! leave your pretty master to sober himself as he can." Here, giving Jack a hearty slap of the face by way of supper, she flounced into her bed-room, the door of which she immediately locked after her, resorting for consolation to an ample flask of *rosa solis*, which she invariably kept filled for such occasions.   " Tam her for a cantankerous tefel!" muttered Mr. Wood, as she departed;   " but hur is glad she is gone. Get to ped, poy, get to ped.   Here, Taffleen!" calling to the servant girl, " get hur onions and salt reaty, and go to the White Lions for a quart of ale, look you.   Hur will be comfortable yet, py the plessings of Got, though she is one great pig primstone Jezepel;   tat is the fact, and hur does not care if she knows it." With these words he staggered down stairs, and Jack crawled his way up, not over-elated at the prospect that had opened itself before him;   but a slice of his plum cake, which he fortunately had with him, reconciled him to his bare garret, and the hard truckle bed he found in it, and he soon fell asleep to awake on the morrow to a new life.

CHAPTER VII.

_____

JACK'S APPRENTICESHIP CONTINUED.

MR. WOOD'S FAMILY.— THE WRITING ON THE BEAM.—
MEETING AN OLD ACQUAINTANCE.—THE WHITE LION.

'New brooms sweep clean,' says the old Proverb.
' and new servants rise early;' Jack was up betimes
to commence his apprenticeship. He found Mr.
Wood somewhat clouded from the events of the
previous day. Madam Wood did not show herself till the afternoon. Mr. Wood soon set Jack to
work, and was both surprised and pleased with
the quickness and aptitude he evinced.

The carpenter had no family of his own, which
was to be lamented, as the want of those conjugal
peace-makers, children, rather augmented that tendency to cat-and-dogism so evident in him and
his sleeping partner. His household consisted of
Taffleen, a Welsh orphan girl, who officiated in
the character of servant of all work, and Griffith
Thomas, also a native of the Principality, the fellow apprentice to Jack. Taffleen was a slatternly,
fiery, but not ill-tempered wench : the misfortune
of having a fine mistress greatly contributed to

her being so untidy a maid. Griffith Thomas, or
Thomas, as he was always called,—for Griffith is
an awkward word in any but a Welsh mouth—
was a wooden-headed youth, well suited for the
performance of the practical part of the trade to
which he was bound: he did what he was put to
with a staid punctuality that rendered him very
dependable. Had steam machines been in fashion
in those days, and the carpenter had had one in
human shape to perform certain duties, it would
have been much of the same value. Thomas could
do nothing without being duly fed, no more than
a steam engine can; and a certain portion of received morality, that had been early implanted in
him, served as a sort of safety valve to prevent
mischievous explosions. Jack was very different;
there was no regulating him: he worked by impulse, very frequently with six-boy power, though
often, when the steam was not up, he would not
work at all,—he either wanted no telling, or
telling ten times over. Yet he suited very well
with Thomas, supplying mind to his body and
skill to his labour; and Mr. Wood was well
pleased. If there was a fault to be found with
Jack's new situation, it was that he had rather too
much his own way. Madam Wood was too fine
a lady to trouble herself with her husband's apprentices, and poor Mr. Wood was too glad to get
out of the sound of his wife's 'larum, to remain
longer at home at any time than was absolutely

necessary. The worthy Cambro-Briton was very much addicted to the practice of pennillion singing*, according to the custom of his country, and in which, by the bye, he was very skilful; this he pursued with the greater gusto, as it gave him frequent opportunities of indulging in invectives against the sex, those pleasant compositions being by no means sparing in their sarcasms at married life, and the frailties of the weaker vessel.

It was Mr. Wood's wont to resort, two or three times a week, to the different houses in the metropolis where his countrymen congregated, to pursue, with the assistance of a native harper, this national pastime. Though Madam and Mr. Wood

---

* Pennillion singing is a convivial custom of some antiquity practised by the Welsh, which, after having long fallen into disuse, is now again being brought into fashion. It consists of a party meeting together, attended by a harper, when *Pennills* —a name given to a variety of stanzas on different subjects in the ancient Welsh tongue, handed down by oral record from father to son—are sung, either attached or detached, and of different lengths of metre, to any tune the harper may happen to play! for it is irregular, and, in fact, not allowable for any particular one to be chosen. One person commences, after two or three bars have been played, with as many pennills as will fill out the melody; adapting them to the air as he goes on; he is joined, as he proceeds, by as many others as may choose, which has a very social and inspiring effect, as the company can sing or not as they please. The pennills are mostly in praise of the harp, Wales, the Welsh tongue, and other national subjects. Among other societies existing now in London, that of the "UNDEB CYMRU," or ' United Welshmen,' is the most prominent.

regularly attended church every Sunday,—Madam Wood for the real purpose of showing off the fashions of St. James's in her own person, to the envying gaze of the congregation, and Mr. Wood for the no less praiseworthy motive of gaining the character of a worshipful tradesman with the parishioners and his neighbours,—they cared little how the Lord's day was passed by their household. The domestic drudge, Taffleen, employed the day in the exercise of the dishclout, and other equally commendable services : Thomas, on the contrary, sought the organ-loft at St. Clement's Danes, where he carefully noted down the text, and slept during the whole of its commentary. Jack, under pretext of visiting Mr. Kneebone, listlessly lounged away the day in rambling about the metropolis, joining whatever idle boys he met, and indulging in all sorts of desultory ways of passing the time, never omitting, however, to give the worthy Mrs. Partington a call some time before he went home at night, for the double purpose of keeping up appearances, and getting the solid lumps of pudding and other tit-bits she had stored up for him during the week,—he relishing these much more than the good advice with which they were accompanied.

Bitterly did Jack regret, in after-life, this too great laxity. " I am far from presuming to say," he observed in his last sad confession, when speaking of his apprenticeship to Mr. Wood, " that I was one of the best of servants ; but I believe, if less liberty had been allowed me then, I should scarce have had so much sorrow and confinement after."*   In truth, this unrestrained liberty paved the way for a host of future evils; Jack acquired habits he could not shake off, and made acquaintances he could not forget.

When the contract for the carpenter's work of the house at Hampstead, which had led to his apprenticeship, was required to be executed, the proficiency Jack had then made, though the period of time had been so short, rendered him of the greatest service to his master : the pannelling, flooring, doors, windows, &c., all engaged his especial attention, and were much indebted for their completeness to his adroitness and handi-work.   His skill was rewarded by his master even more liberally than was prudent.   It is as bad for a boy to have too much money, as it is for him to have too little : excess is encouraged by the one, while temptation gains force by the other.

Thus two or three years passed away. Jack became an able but self-willed workman. No serious quarrel, however, had as yet arisen between him and his master, who, though naturally choleric and testy, had, to say the truth, sufficient to employ him in the way of dispute with Madam Wood, to allow of his being over anxious for any contest with other people. With Madam Wood herself the case was somewhat different. Jack

* Vide ' Confession,' APPENDIX.

could never bring himself to pay her the homage
she required; execrating her in his heart as a
fantastical and affected old duchess, he took a delight in slighting her injunctions. To take madam
down a peg, as he called it, was to him the height
of gratification; and in this, as candid historians,
we are bound to confess, he was often secretly encouraged by Mr. Wood himself. But the period
was approaching when this good understanding
between master and man—for man Jack now began
to think himself—was to be materially disturbed.

One day, having taken a holiday on his own
account, which was not unusual with him when
business happened to be rather slack, Jack paid
a visit to the Tower of London for the purpose of
seeing the curiosities there. He was first shown the
LIONS, after the customary joke had been passed
on him of being asked if he would not rather stay
and see them *washed*. The presence of these noble
animals did not excite such admiration in Jack as
might have been expected—in fact, he rather expressed a contempt for them, that, with their
strength and powers of offence, they should suffer
themselves to remain in such insignificant cages as
those within which they were shut up. Passing
over the horse and foot armoury, he then visited
the Jewel Office. The sight of the Regalia perfectly made his mouth water; and he listened with
breathless attention to the warden's account of Colo-
nel Blood's daring attempt to steal the crown, &c.,

during the reign of Charles II., greatly lamenting the unexpected arrival of the then keeper's nephew from sea. which had had the effect of detecting and frustrating the plot. His last step was to visit the different dungeons and apartments, &c., reserved for the reception of state prisoners, all of which he examined very minutely. In the room which had so long served as the prison of the illustrious Sir Walter Raleigh, he was shown the name of that celebrated man scratched by himself on one of the walls. He surveyed it with deep interest; a noble ambition seemed to inspire him.

"I will do something," he mentally resolved, "to make my name memorable. Yes! I won't be a common man—I won't die and be forgotten: people shall think of me after I am dead; and I'll carve *my* name, the first thing when I go home on one of the beams in old Wood's shop, that the world may hereafter have a record, under his own hand, to gaze at of Jack Sheppard." Filled with this heroic determination he immediately returned to Wych Street, and, the coast being clear, entered the workshop, where, with a large clasp knife he proceeded to cut his name in very legible characters on one of the principal beams, as may be seen to this day, the autograph being much more durable than elegant. He was interrupted in this choice employment by the entrance of Mr. Wood.

"Cot's poty!" exclaimed the Cambrian, "fhat

toings is here? 'Tis your pusiness, look you, to repair the woot works of puildings, and not testroy them. Fhat the tefil are you cutting your name up there for?"

" Nobody has a better right," answered Jack rather surlily. "for nobody does so much business here as I do."

" Pusiness, pusiness! you hafe no pusiness to do tat, you idle tog!" said Mr. Wood getting greatly incensed.

" Well, I have done it, at all events," said Jack; and as I don't see what particular harm there is in it, I should like to see who will dare to deface it. My name is as good as any body else's."

" Fhat is tat you say?" exclaimed the angry Welshman. " Do you presume to say tat your name is as goot as mine, sirrah! dat has descentet through fifty generations, look you, from the Ap Shenkinses to the Ap Watkinses, and from the Ap Watkinses to the Griffithes, the Tavises, the Williamses, the Thomases, the Philipses, the Lloyds, the Llewellyns, the Wynnes, and the Woots, look you? Passion of our pody! what intignities is this! Put hur will get you sent to Pridewell to teach you petter manners, sirrah! The champerlain shall learn you how to pehave to your master, Owen Woot. Do you forget that Matan Woot is cousin to Sir Timothy Cutteridge, dat was Lort Mayor, and kissed the Queen's own hant."

" If I do," muttered Jack, " there's no fear that you'll forget it ; you have it dinned into your ears too often for that."

" Passion of hur heart!" spluttered Mr. Wood almost choking with rage, " fhat to you mean by fat, you young fillains? Hur will teach you dat hur has no occasion to look to Madam Woot's for hur respectability, tat hur own father was a squire, tat hur own grantfather hat a harper, and tat hur own self in hur own country is a shentle-mans porn, and hur will not have hur work ne-glected and hur timper wastet. Hur toes not feet and clothe you to testroy hur property : the Ty-purn peam will preserve your name petter than any peam here, and so I tells you,—you will tie like a tog."

" So long as I am not forgotten like a dog," said Jack sturdily, " I should not much care for that ; but there's no occasion to make such a fuss about your paltry rafter. A day may come when you may be proud to have my name there, when it may be more famous than all your pedigree put together—with old St. David at the head of it."

Mr. Wood could contain no longer ; this de-preciation of his patron saint, and his illustrious ancestors was not to be borne with. Seizing Jack by the leg, and getting his heel in his mouth for his pains, to the dislodgment of a couple of his front teeth, he pulled him from off the bench on which he had been standing, for the better execution of his autograph, he began to cuff him about his head and ears with all his might and main—uttering at the same time a profusion of maledictions in Welsh.

Jack did not venture to fight again though his wrath had risen to a height very nearly equal to his master's: he however, extricated himself as swiftly as he could, and made his escape into the street.

The offended Welshman, who had beat himself with his own passion, was glad to sit down and attempt the recovery of his lost breath. " Plessings on hur forpearance!" he muttered; "it is Cot's mercies that hur has not killed the fillain. Compare himself with St. Tavit, and hur ancestor Catwallader!—it was not to be entured! Hur is only glat hur has not quite peat his prains out. Hur must get some salt and try to fasten hur two teeth in again, or what will become of hur penillion singing? Here, Taffleen, Taffleen! pring the salt-box. Hur is glat no one fas here to see hur,—Mercy of Cot! if hur has not swallowed one of hur own teeth! Hur is ruined! Here, Taffleen, Taffleen!"

The poor carpenter ran into the kitchen to concert measures for the recovery of his lost tooth, where we will for the present leave him, and proceed to Jack, who was making his way up Wych Street in no very enviable mood of mind, smarting under the blows he had received, and burning with indignation at the injustice of them.

He was going blindly along, too much occupied with his own thoughts to regard any thing else, when, passing the entrance of White Lion Court, (a very short distance from his master's shop) a murky and ominous-looking passage conducting to the White Lion, a substantial building of some antiquity, erected at the back of the houses in Wych Street, and the alehouse we have before mentioned, he ran violently against a person who was at that moment rather hastily about to enter it, a concussion which had the effect of sending one party sprawling into the kennel, and the other against a young woman who was just then issuing from it, holding in her hand a foaming tankard of strong bubb, which was immediately precipitated to the ground, to the total loss of the precious liquor.

" Oh, goodness gracious ! goodness gracious !" said the girl, wringing her hands, " What shall I do, what will missus say ?"

Disregarding the distress of the girl, and turning, somewhat alarmed for the consequences, to help up the person he had so unceremoniously consigned to the kennel, Jack was greatly astonished at recognizing his old schoolfellow, Master Joseph Blake, or Blueskin, as we shall henceforth call him, now presenting the appearance of a sturdy young man.

" What, Jack—Johnny Sheppard !" roared out that exemplary youth, recognizing Jack.—" Well, strike me lucky! but this *is* a go. Who'd have thought of meeting you in this manner? Is this the way you welcome your old acquaintance— Knocking them down, while you are tossing off a tankard?"

"Here, the girl continuing her lamentations for the loss of her liquor, the outcry brought out the landlord, Mr. Nightingale. "Halloa, my covies," said he, "What's this? you are not going to frisk the young woman on the run, are you?"

"All right, Master Nightingale," said Blueskin, "merely an accidental spill, I'll shell out the pewter.—Don't be afraid, my girl, you shall have some bub with your grub, yet, never fear—there, take that bob and bolt, my queen of Sheba."

The girl gladly picked up her pot, and immediately disappeared to replenish it, and pocket the change. That done,—"Master Nightingale," said Blueskin, "do you go and get us your best punch bowl filled with a quart of the reg'lar, do you hear, and we'll be with you in a jiffy, I'll stand the damage."

"Oh! what, you are breeched!" returned the landlord.

"Yes, in Tip Street, thanks to a bunch of onions* I grabbed last night, which Mr. Wild has been so kind as to say he'll get made into a brown gravy, and has advanced a quid upon."

* Watch, chain, and seals.

"Oh, that's another thing," returned Mr. Night-ingale, beginning to sing part of an old song.—

> "Punch cures the gout, the cholic, and the phthisic,
> And is for all men the very best of physic."

I'll get you your rum slim* ready directly, gentlemen."

"Do, and let it be stiffish,—do you hear?" returned Blueskin. "This kinchen's an old pal."

"A young one, I should rather think," muttered Mr. Nightingale in a low tone. "Why, blow me, if it isn't one of old Wood the carpenter's lads, down the street! Well, this is a turn up. You shall have your suck before you know where you are." So saying, Mr. Nightingale disappeared up the avenue, and entered his premises to prepare the punch as ordered.

The White Lion† had the reputation, at this

---

* Punch.

† This house must not be confounded with another of a nearly similar sign and character—the *Black Lion*, in Drury Lane, mentioned and denounced by Jack in his confession, and stated by him to have been kept by a very dissolute character, Joseph Hind, a button moulder, who came to a miserable end—as that was a lion of another colour. The "Black Lion" is still extant, though it has been converted into a modern gin palace; the "White Lion," on the contrary, though the building is still standing, has long lost its license, and is now converted into one of the very lowest species of lodging-houses. Of Jack's visits to this den, there can be no doubt; some idea may be formed of the substantial manner in which this house was built, from the following fact:—In the year 1815, one Pym, an entrepreneur in private theatricals, and amateur low

time, of being a low species of flash ken, and general receptacle for loose characters, for which pur-

comedian, took the attics of this building, and converted them
into a private theatre. The writer of this note was one of the
audience the first night this theatre was opened to the public,
or the *private*, rather, having obtained a ticket from a musical
friend who acted as leader of the band on the occasion. Ascending the spacious staircase, on one side the bar entrance of
the house, with its carved massive balustrades, so infinitely
superior to the fragile and shabby bannisters of the present day,
he found, on the third story, a very neat little theatre; there
was a very compact stage and orchestra, while the audience
part comprised a comfortable pit, and a snug tier of boxes.
Favoured with a seat in the boxes, between a comely old lady
and her daughter, the writer prepared to enjoy the promised
treat. The play announced was *The Mountaineers*, in which the
great PYM himself was to personate the character of *Lope Tocho*;
it was to be followed by the well-known private theatrical
farce, par excellence, *All at Coventry*. The writer's Orphean
friend flourished his fiddlestick in one of Romberg's old-fashioned lumbering overtures to admiration; and, at length, the
curtain drew up. BULCASIN MULEY was enacted by an Irish
gentleman, with a very rich Munster brogue; the Irish Count,
however, was not so fortunate, being supported by a Scotch
young gentleman; but, the Octavian—the Octavian—the love-
sick, distraught Octavian—Ah! that was the treat! Octavian was supported by an amateur from Yorkshire, who, as
Ducrow would have said, delivered the *dialect* with singular
correctness; but, alas! something else proved to be cracked
as well as Octavian. In one of his most impassioned speeches,
uttered according to the peculiar notions of the North Riding,
awful sounds of fracture announced there was something rotten
in the state of Denmark; and, in a moment, the boxes, with
the whole of their contents, found their way into the pit—
great was the shrieking, the consternation, and the dust—the
writer fell on the old lady, where he lay embedded comfortably
enough, her ample front affording him a very pleasant cushion,

pose it seemed admirably adapted from its covert
and retired situation behind the houses in the front
the fair form of her daughter covering him above like a virgin
sheet. Fully satisfied that the whole building was giving way,
the writer felicitated himself on having got down one story so
well, wondering whether he should have equal luck in his
descent to the second floor, and hoping the line wouldn't quite
stretch to the crack of doom. Warmly embracing the old
lady, he determined to maintain his position, but it soon appeared he had got to his journey's end, that the flooring of the
theatre was to be his ultimate ground-floor—nothing further
gave way. Raising herself, the young lady proceeded to do
the same kind office for the writer:—" I hope you are not
killed, Sir," said she, commiseratingly. " I don't know, but I
think not," was the reply. The giving way of the boxes,
which had been very slightly erected, appeared to be the only
mischief that had taken place, with the exception of some serious fractures in two or three hats, the loss of some caps, and
a few *wounds* inflicted on sundry gowns and petticoats. The
play was, however, put a stop to, and the writer repaired,
with his companions, to the lower story of the " White Lion,"
where they recruited their exhausted spirits with a glass of
brandy-and-water, and with this we will close our story. The
boxes were afterwards re-erected more strongly—many were
the ludicrous scenes that subsequently occurred in this place,
but the congregation of both sexes, and the dissolute conduct occasioned by this contiguity of the drama to the dram, at length,
lost this celebrated house its license, and occasioned its degradation to its present state. Jack Sheppard's name is now the only
spell by which its former existence is remembered. The sign
of Leo, would seem to have been a fatal one in Jack's zodiac—
when Jack once had his fortune told by that celebrated sooth-
sayer, the Dumb Man of Shoreditch, the seer foretold that
Jack would be destroyed by three lions and a lioness, at which
every body laughed—the prediction was, however, singularly
verified—in fact, it was through his intimacy with the White
Lion of Wych-street, the Black Lion of Drury-lane, and the no

street, offering a snug place of concealment, as it were, from the eye of the general passenger.

After a few hasty greetings, Blueskin conducted our wondering hero into a little back parlour of this snug retreat, which happened, at that time, to have no one in it. Sitting down, Jack was about to ask half a hundred questions, when he was stopped by his companion.

Wait till we get the booze *, Jack, and then I will tell you all about it." The liquor was not long before it made its appearance, Mr. Nightingale bringing it in, humming part of Iago's song to Cassio :—

> " Let us the cannikin clink, brave boys,
> And let us the cannikin clink."

It must be observed that Mr. Nightingale, or Mr. Nightingal as he was more commonly termed, was an universal vocalist, and accompanied every thing he did with a snatch of some appropriate ditty, always singing most intently when any mischief was going on. Filling himself a glass, in order to ascertain whether it was brewed *secundem artem*, and drinking to our hero's better acquaintance, Mr. Nightingale tossed it off, and, declaring it imperial, left the room humming part of the old catch,—

less infamous Red Lion of Chick-lane, together with his betrayal by his companion, Edgeworth Bess (Elizabeth Lyon), the lioness, that he ultimately came to his untimely end.

> " There are more things in Heaven and earth, Horatio,
> Than are dreamt of in your philosophy."

* Punch.

" Nose, nose, and who gave thee that jolly red nose ?
     Nutmeg, and ginger, and cinnamon, and cloves ;
     And they gave me this jolly red nose."

The moment his back was turned, the two young gentlemen, after ascertaining that he had spoken the truth, by each draining a brimming glass of the generous fluid to the bottom, proceeded to relate their various adventures since they last met. Mr. Blueskin intimated, that finding he had no genius for the trade to which his father had destined him, he had one night suddenly left that revered person, and had set up in business on his own account, having become acquainted with Mr. Jonathan Wild, by whose advice, and under whose patronage, he had chosen a very light and lucrative profession. He did not exactly mention the precise nature of his employment, but Jack was at no loss to understand it. Jack, in his turn, recounted the circumstances of his adoption by Mr. Kneebone, together with his apprenticeship to Mr. Wood, finishing by detailing the particulars of the affray that had that day occurred between them.

Mr. Blueskin pathetically damned Mr. Wood for an old hunks ; and grasping Jack's hand with great fervour and sincerity, swore by the living jingo, that it should go hard if they didn't, before long, make the old Welshman skip like one of his own goats, and smoke him as they would a piece of toasted cheese. This declaration, which was pledged bumper deep, afforded Jack great satisfaction.

As they penetrated deeper into the contents of the bowl, the two friends became more confidential. Jack hinted at his knowledge of that transaction in the Old Bailey Calendar, in which his schoolfellow's name had appeared conjointly with that of Master William Blewitt, and made many inquiries respecting Mr. Wild.

"He's the primest trump in town," exclaimed Blueskin, with enthusiasm, " and will glory in doing a good turn for a lad of spirit like you."

"Jack said he should be happy to make his acquaintance."

"You shall," said Blueskin energetically; I'll introduce you myself." The bowl was drained on this assurance; and Blueskin having settled the reckoning, and paid the damage which had caused their meeting, which Mr. Nightingal received, humming the appropriate song of—

" Sing tantarantara rogues all, rogues all,"

the *nobile fratrum* parted,—Mr. Blueskin to attend a little appointment he had in the dusk on the pavement in Fleet Street, and Jack, punch valiant, to encounter his master, Mr. Wood. The worthy Cambrian had, however, fortunately gone to join in a penillion meeting at the " Goat in Boots," in Little Britain. Our hero, therefore, retired to his truckle bed without any farther quarrel, and passed the night in dreaming of the promised meeting with Mr. Wild.

CHAPTER VIII.

———

JACK'S APPRENTICESHIP, CONTINUED.

SAINT DAVID'S DAY IN 1715.—WELSH PENNILLS. — JACK
SHEPPARD'S FIRST MEETING WITH JONATHAN WILD.

WHEN Jack and his master met the next morning, their meeting, as may be imagined, was any
thing but a cordial one. Mr. Wood was alternately short, sharp, morose, and silent ; though he
had swallowed his own tooth, he could not swallow
the affront that had been put upon his ancestors,
and his patron saint, St. David, by Jack's hinting
at the probability of his name one day eclipsing
their's. Jack was, on the other hand, dogged, sullen, and gloomy, brooding over the blows he had received, and, in fancy, planning, with the assistance
of his former schoolfellow, Mr. Blueskin, a variety
of schemes to revenge his wrongs. Mr. Wood, at
times, gave vent to his feelings in sundry muttered
sentences ; but, as they all happened to be in the
Welsh tongue, Jack did not think it necessary to
notice them. Before he had left Blueskin on the
previous evening, he had made an appointment
with that exemplary youth to meet him at the

" White Lion" on the evening of the following Thursday, for the purpose of being introduced, as promised, to Mr. Wild ; when Jack determined not to stick upon niceties any longer. Since the affair of Mrs. Partington's ring, he had religiously obeyed the laws of *meum* and *tuum* ; but now that it was to avenge his own wrongs, the observance of the strict bounds of honesty appeared a very different thing ; and he determined that the carpenter should literally pay for the injuries which, as he conceived, that unlucky Cambro-Briton had inflicted upon him.

It happened that the Thursday appointed for the interview with Mr. Wild was St. David's Day, a day, which the reader need scarcely be told, is a very memorable one with all true Welshmen : then do leeks become flowers, while toasted cheese is provided as a bait in various " mousetraps of a larger growth." Every honest Cambrian skips and rejoices, like one of his own native goats ; the glories of the Principality are sung and said by a thousand tongues ; the heroic actions of that church militant, St. David, are recounted ; pedigrees are traced, and draughts of the lusty *cwrw* go round to the inspiring sounds of the harp, and the cheering sentiments of the national *Pennill.*

It was the custom of Madam Wood, who took no interest in the patriotic enthusiasm of her lord and master, on this auspicious day, to withdraw herself to the house of some friend, that she might neither sanction nor thwart, by her presence, the enjoyments in which her husband might think fit to indulge; she had accordingly set out very early in the morning to the country house at Hogsden of her great relation, Sir Timothy Gutteridge, the ex-mayor, from whence she did not propose to return till very late.

It is not to be supposed that so staunch an ancient Briton as Mr. Wood would suffer any work to be done in his house on so memorable a day as St. David's. It was his custom to make it a holiday with his whole household: he did not depart from this custom on the present occasion, but gave Jack and his fellow-apprentice, Griffith Thomas, full liberty to do what they pleased with themselves, but enjoined them very particularly to return in the afternoon, as their presence would be required on an occasion that could not be neglected. As he was always wont to make them some little present on this day, they naturally enough supposed, from his significant winks, and smirking nods, that something very agreeable was forthcoming.

Jack, having his appointment in the evening to attend to, did not stroll very far from home, and was in waiting on the carpenter very shortly after the usual dinner hour. He was somewhat surprised to find his master sitting over a spacious bowl, dressed in his best clothes, with a huge leek stuck, by way of nosegay, in his bosom; an immense two-handed sword, nearly as long as a spit, which had been formerly the property of one of his ancestors, was buckled, with a broad leathern strap round his waist, to the imminent danger of tripping him up whenever he attempted to move; a large sandy-coloured tie perriwig ornamented his sconce, in lieu of the usual bob, on the top of which, though he was in the house, was stuck a very fierce three-cornered cocked hat, bearing, by way of cockade, another large leek; a few sprigs of olive, which accompanied this latter, somewhat neutralised, by their peaceful character, the alarm this military display might otherwise have created. The good-natured Welshman (for, like all hasty people, he was at the core really good-natured), had provided from mine host of the " Black Jack," several quarts of the strongest ale, which he had spiced with his own hand. Taffleen had prepared a proportionate quantity of toast: pippins and cheese were not wanting; and, for the first time since their quarrel, Jack was re- ceived by his master, on his entrance, with a welcoming smile. Several circumstances had trans- pired to put the worthy Cambrian into a more than usual good humour. On this particular First of March, A. D. 1715, it being the birthday of the then Princess of Wales, Wilhelmina Carolina, as well as the anniversary of the Cambrian tutelar saint, the Honourable and Loyal Society of Ancient Bri- tons had been instituted, at once in compliment to the Princess and in celebration of the saint.

A dinner had been given in Haberdashers' Hall, at which an ode, written by Hughes, the poet, and set to music by the celebrated Dr. Pepusch, was sung by Madame Margaretta and Madame Barbier. The well-known Tom Durfey, the dramatist and song writer, had also volunteered, and given one of his comical chants. This alone was cause sufficient for excitement; but there was added to it the exhilaration induced by the various tastings the worthy carpenter had had occasion to make of the spiced ale while in the process of preparing it; and, lastly, though not least, there was the absence of Madam Wood.

"Come in, Jack, you tog," said the worthy carpenter, as his eye fell on our hero, "and take a seat. This is Saint Tavit's tay, a glorious Saint Tavit's tay! ant py the plessings of Cot, we must forget all crievances; though you fas wrong, fery wrong, look you, to tisparage St. Tavit ant hur ancestors. St Tavit fas a creat saint—he could fight as well as he could pray; and he suptued the heathen as well with his sword as his pible: you must drink a cup of ale in honour of St. Tavit!" To this ceremony Jack was nothing loth, and a bumper was speedily drained.

"Wales is a great country, look you," continued the carpenter, with true national enthusiasm—"a fery great country! there is not hur equal; and hur county, Caernarfon, is the paradise of Wales! You must drink success to Wales, and hur native place, Caernarfon, Jack." Handing Jack another glass of ale, here the carpenter began to sing the well-known pennill in praise of Caernarvon, beginning with, " *Wyf ofalus* (*a phaham*) *o hiracth am Caernarfon*," to the tune of " *Anhawdd Ymadael*," or " Lotth to part;" a rude translation of which, for the further delectation of our readers, we shall here attempt :—

The Praise of Caernarbon.

1.

" My heart is sad when to my mind
Spring thoughts of sweet Caernarvon !—
What woe was Adam's, forced through Eve,
His native Paradise to leave—
Such woe is mine, to leave behind
My paradise, Caernarvon !

2.

Oh ! still in smiles, ye gentle skies,
Look down on sweet Caernarvon ;
Its pleasant vales, the rose of health,
Yields each maid's cheek her dearest wealth ;
Then still shall wake my fondest sighs
For Wales and for Caernarvon !"

They were now joined by Griffith Thomas, who was also forced by the carpenter to do honour to the two toasts which had been drank in his absence. As the ale circulated, so did the *amor patria* of Mr. Wood grow stronger. " Jack, Jack, you tog !" he burst forth, " you fas wrong, fery wrong, to say anything against hur ancestors or hur country. Caractacus was a fine prince, so fas Cadwallater,

ant Matoc, and Llewellyn, and so is the Lort Pishop
of Pangor, look you ! hur language is a fine lan-
cuage,—it fas the one spoken by Atem ant Eve
pefore their fall in the Carten of Eten, and fas
only one safet from the confusion of tongues in the
the tower of Papel—look you, it is like puttermilk
in the mouth, all eloquence and honey. Oh ! it is
a nople tongues, the Welsh !"—Here he sung to
the air of " *Yr Eos lais*," or " The Nightingale's
Voice," the well known pennill, in praise of the
Welsh language, commencing, " *Iaith wiw lan i'r
gan hib goll*," and which may be thus para-
phrased :—

The Praise of the Welsh Tongue.

1.

" As sweet as sugar in the mouth,
  Mild as the breezes of the south,
  Soft as the cooings of the dove,
  Steals on the ear the speech I love ;
  The angel-tongue, to song most dear,
  Which warrior, sage, delight to hear :
  The speech that best the heart can move.
  The words of Wales, the speech of love.

2.

" He only sings, in Welsh who sings,
  For Welsh alone the harp has strings ;
  No bard is he who cannot write
  In Welsh—the muses' best delight.
  He has no learning who's unskill'd
  In Welsh, with all of wisdom filled.
  Still shall its praise by men be sung,
  My native Welsh, my mother tongue.

3.

" Its accents, like some pleasant tune,
   Or ripplings of a brook in June,
   Dear to the throat, as mead or wine,—
   Well for its love may echo pine ;
   While there is water in the sea,
   Or air in heaven, beloved shall be
   Thy language, Wales, which still shall last,
   Till earth has into chaos passed."

The softness, sweetness, copiousness, and energy of the Welsh language celebrated in this last pennill, or rather pennills—for it was composed of a series of three—might have been more credited if delivered in any other language ; as it was, the loss of Mr. Wood's two teeth might have been very well ascribed to the force of the crack-jaw words in which the panegyric was pronounced. Warming with the subject, though he still could not help reverting to what had passed,—

" Jack, Jack, you tog!" he continued, replenishing the glasses, " you should not have said any thing in tisparagement of the ancient Pritons, look you : they are the original people of the earth, ant can trace their ancestors further pack than any other nations! I myself am tescended from a collateral pranch of Uther Pentracon ! put let that rest—it is nothings; I have seen much higher tescents tan tat, though I do not go so far as my joking friend Mr. Joseph Millers, at the " Black Jack," who says he once saw a petigree of a Welsh gentleman, in the middle of which was written,

" Apout this time the world was created." I do not go so far as to say that, put the Welsh are the original people; and py the plessings of Cot, and the great teed of this tay, we shall continue to flourish. You hafe peen wrong, Jack, fery wrong! you should have learnt wistom from the coat, look you. To you not see, when two coats meet on a narrow pridge, and neither can pass without pushing the other into the waters, that one coat will lie town, and let the other coat jump over him; so it shoult pe with you. You shoult supmit,—yes, we shoult all be coats. Ah! the coat is a wise animal; look at his peard!"

" And his *horns*," said Jack, the sullen resentment he had preserved since their quarrel gradually giving way before the good humour of his master. " But come, Sir," he continued, rather maliciously, " with your permission I will give a toast: here's the health of our mistress, Madam Wood."

Mr. Wood made a wry face, and drank it in Welsh, Jack shrewdly suspected with some variation; we shall not presume to conjecture what, but it appeared to want some washing down, as he drained two or three copious draughts after it, and rather inarticulately hiccupped out another pennill, the not very gallant one, " *Tri pheth ni saif yn llonydd*," " The Husband's Experience," which he sung to the tune of " *Ar hyd y Nos*," or " All night long," and which may be thus rendered :—

The Husband's Experience.

" Three things that ne'er stand still I sing:
A pig whose hind leg's in a string,
A snail that crawls the walls along,
And Mrs. Wood's confounded tongue.
Three things there are, most puzzling to man,
The wind, the weather, and a woman:
The wind's uncertain, so the weather,
And Mrs. W. more than either."

Having apparently relieved himself by this last
ebullition of feeling. Mr. Wood took from his
pocket two new silver crown pieces, and gave one
to each of his apprentices, requesting they might
be kept in commemoration of the day, " which,
though you have kicked out two of my teeth, Cot
help me, Jack." he said, " does creat credit to the
ancient Pritons, whom you would have tisparaged,
look you. We have this tay founded an institution py which many a poor lat shall be snatched
henceforth like a fireprant from the flame, and be
rentered an honouraple memper of society, taking
them from the paths of temptation, and teaching
them virtue and sopriety,—a great thing, look
you, for a Welshman to hafe tone—follow hur
example, poys." Here, seizing the bowl, he did
not stop till he had completely drained it of its
contents. which had such an effect upon him, that,
after attempting to sing another pennill in praise
of the maids of Merioneth, to the tune of " *Megen
a Gollodd ei gardas*," or " Peggy that lost her
Garter," the lads thought it prudent to carry him

to bed, which they did, he singing very good hu-
mouredly all the way as they were proceeding
with him up stairs, the fine old melody, "Of a
noble Race was Shenkin," leaving them in undisturbed possession of an immense pipkin of leek
porridge, which had been made for his supper.

The hour for Jack's meeting with Blueskin had
arrived ; but so much had his master's good nature,
kindness, and the few exhortations arising out of
the events of the day affected him, that he half
repented his appointment, and more than once
resolved to break it.   But on what trifling things
hinge the fate of mortals !   The thought that
Blueskin had paid for him at the previous meeting,
and that he should appear shabby, if he did not
return it on this occasion, overcame all his virtuous
resolutions, and, shutting up the shop, he slipped
out of the back door, through the yard, and was
in a few moments at the " White Lion."

Mr. Blueskin was punctual to his appointment,
and welcomed Jack with apparent delight, cordially shaking him by the hand, and assuring him
he was a trump and a half, good weight, and a
penn'orth over.   " The governor," said he, with a
significant look, " is here; all's right; he's only
settling a small account of dues and regulars for
some odd fogles and fawnies, with Okey, Simon
Jacobs, Levi, and a few other coves of the right
sort, in the *sanctum*, behind the bar ; the moment
he's done with them I'll introduce you. His usher

of the big stick, *Mr.* Quilt Arnold, *Esquire*, has been in attendance these two hours, so come along, and I'll get the governor to enter your name in his books, and take you under his own especial thumb, in no time. I have got a rare bowl of Huckle-my-butt ready for us in the parlour."

Jack had half made up his mind to back out of the association, but there was no withdrawing after this. He did venture to stammer out he was afraid he had not money enough to pay for his entrance.

" Why, you precious soft," said Mr. Blueskin, " there's nothing to tip; the governor will tip you; he always stands Sam at first : he'll give you a retaining fee, by way of earnest, and then you will consider yourself bound to him. Lord bless you, we do business on the most liberal terms imaginable." The conversation was here interrupted by the arrival of Mr. Wild's first satellite, the aforesaid Mr. Quilt Arnold, Esquire, as he was usually called by *Wild's men*, for such was the name by which the gang who flourished under Jonathan's protection styled themselves. Jack was duly introduced to this worthy, and received from him the encouraging assurance that he had no doubt he would do in time.

" Do! to be sure he will," said Blueskin ; " he's just the one to do. Look at him, why he could worm himself through a mouse hole. Then there's a hand ! why, it seems made for a pocket ! If he minds what he's at, he'll make as pretty a pad, and as kiddy a diver, as any on town. But come, where's the cove of the ken? here, landlord! Joe Nightingal, why don't you show three *gentlemen* in, Mister?

"Beg your pardon my nobles," said Nightingal, suddenly appearing. "This way;" and he began humming the, at that time, popular song,

"Come unto these yellow sands,"—

whether in allusion to the newly sanded floor of the back parlour we cannot say; but to that apartment he ushered them. Here they found a foaming bowl of Huckle-my-butt,* ready prepared, a potation composed of beer, brandy, sugar, eggs, spice, &c. which Jack insisted on paying for. After a little demur on the part of Blueskin, his wish was acceded to. Mr. Nightingal was desired to name the figure. "I am not mercenary," said he, singing the gallant Lovelace's song of

"My mind to me a kingdom is;"

"so you may tip me a crown." Mr. Wood's present in commemoration of the day was instantly put into his hand by Jack, and was as instantly conveyed into his pocket.

Mr. Nightingal was then politely entreated by Jack to give a proof of the excellence of the compound before them by taking a glass, to which

---

* Sometimes called Huckle-my-buff, see Grose's Classical Dictionary of the vulgar tongue.

he, nothing loth, consented, and further to while away the time, till Mr. Wild should have settled his business in the little bar parlour, volunteered to tip a stave in praise of his favourite beverage. The glasses were accordingly filled, and toasting their own noble selves, were duly emptied by all present, Mr. Nightingal then gave them the promised chaunt, then a very popular one, and suspected to have been written by honest Tom D'Urfey; though it certainly is not be found in his celebrated ' Pills to Purge Melancholy'—It was to the following effect :—

Song,—Huckle-my-Butt.

1.

Huckle-my-butt, Huckle-my-butt,
Come brew me a bowl of right Huckle-my-butt;
First pour in the bubb,* brisk and brown as a nut,
Brandy, eggs, sugar, spice, for that's Huckle-my-butt.
> Huckle-my-butt, &c.

2.

Huckle-my-butt, Huckle-my-butt,
Come brim me a bumper of Huckle-my-butt,
'Tis pleasant to smoke mild returns, or short-cut,
With a friend that, like us, can drink Huckle-my-butt.
> Huckle-my-butt, &c.

3.

Huckle-my-butt, Huckle-my-butt,
It improves on acquaintance, does Huckle-my-butt;
The man who'd not drink, is a fool and a put,
For there never was liquor like Huckle-my-butt.
> Huckle-my-butt, &c.

* Beer.

4.

Huckle-my-butt, Huckle-my-butt,
It is welcome alike both in palace and hut,
Should I have fifty children, each rogue and each slut,
Shall only be christened in Huckle-my-butt.
              Huckle-my-butt, &c.

5.

Huckle-my-butt, Huckle-my-butt,
Meat, drink, clothes, and lodging, is Huckle-my-butt.
I'd gladly be drowned—from existence be shut—
Provided the liquor was Huckle-my-butt.
              Huckle-my-butt, &c.

6.

Huckle-my-butt, Huckle-my-butt,
If there ever was nectar, 'tis Huckle-my-butt;
The haughty may sneer, and the swaggerer strut,
Let them keep their Tokay, give me Huckle-my-butt.
              Huckle-my-butt, &c.*

Filling a large bumper of the Huckle-my-butt, and inviting his companions to follow his example, Mr. Quilt Arnold, Esquire, pronounced a high eulogium on the liberality, power, and other good qualities of Mr. Jonathan Wild, concluding by proposing his health which was drank with enthusiasm. A door in the passage opening at this moment attracted the attention of Mr. Nightingal.

     " Hark ! hark ! the watch-dog's bark,"

sung that gentleman, " the culls are mizzling, and the governor's coming.—You're a lucky kinchin,

* Composers, publishers, music-sellers, &c., will please to take notice that this song, and the other Lyrics in this Work are Copyright, and cannot be used without the permission of the Author and Publisher.

young fellow," continued he, addressing Jack, " to be taken by the hand by Mr. Wild so early ; there's no knowing to what height he may raise you."

Mr. Nightingal's reflections were cut short by the entrance of a red-headed, blear-eyed, dirty-bearded Jew, in a loose, shambling dress, another of Mr. Wild's satellites, who came to announce his master. Abraham, or Abraham Mendez—for that was the Jew's name—dropped on one side, and the great man entered. Jack and the others rose to receive him. He was a grave-looking man, dressed in a rather sober suit, but under the assumed frankness and general benevolence of his appearance, an acute observer could not have failed to remark a determination and cunning that sufficiently explained his character. He wore a small cocked hat, and had a rather genteel sword by his side : a few ornaments of jewellery adorned his person, intended more to indicate his responsibility and rank in society than for any purpose of embellishment.

" This is the kin hen cove I spoke to you about, governor," said Mr. Blueskin, pointing to Jack; " you'll find him the thing, depend on't." Mr. Nightingal began humming Carew's song—

" Ask me why I send you here,
This *firstling* of the infant year."

" Peace, landlord !" said Mr. Wild, benevolently. " Be seated, friends ; I am right glad to

K

meet you, young gentleman ; your schoolfellow has
spoken favourably of you : you are inexperienced,
it appears, and require a guide—I love youth, and
would be a parent to you——"

"Full fathoms five, thy FATHER *lies*,"

sung Mr. Nightingal.   "Peace, landlord !" cried
Mr. Wild, rather angrily; "go, and replenish this
bowl."

   "I'm gone, Sir, but anon, Sir,
    I'll be with you in a trice,
    Like the old vice, &c.."

hummed Mr. Nightingal, vanishing. Jonathan resumed his observations.   "You will remain here,
Abraham, and you, too, Quilt," he remarked, in
order to do honour to the inauguration of our
young friend."

 "I shall do dat, governor," said the Jew, who
generally went by the name of the patriarch, "and
so will Mr. Quilt Arnold, Esquire, here."   How
this latter gentleman had acquired this form of
address, we don't know, except that it might be
from his always wearing an immense cocked hat,
very like a footman's, with broad lace, and his
being dressed in a large faded silk coat, with
huge cuffs, and vast skirts, trimmed with a quantity of tarnished gold binding, an embroidered silk
waistcoat, with extensive flaps, which was very
much soiled and worn, a singular profusion of
dirty neckcloth, a very swaggering sword, and a

quantity of mock jewellery,—the whole presenting a very tawdry appearance.

" Youths," said Mr. Wild, impressively, " are too apt to commit themselves, and get into trouble ; youth is the season of inexperience, and subject to a thousand temptations, and, more than any other, particularly requires the protection of some one, whose age and observation may render him capable of shielding it, from the consequences of those little ebullitions and extravagances, natural to that buoyant age.   For my part," continued Mr. Wild, " I'm not for checking those playful eccentricities, which lead the juvenile mind to scorn the severer restraints of society, and neglect the vulgar observance of those limits, which a musty prudence and twaddling morality may have prescribed, for the guidance of the uninformed."

" Jist my sentiments," roared out one of the satellites, the aforesaid Mr. Quilt Arnold, Esquire.

" Good, damned good," emphatically observed Mr. Blueskin; "the governor speaks like an angel!"

" I love youth, promising youth," continued Jonathan, " and willingly extend to them my protection and advice. I regard them as my children, and expect from them, in return, the obedience and reverence due to a father. A monarchy must naturally be despotic ; and having constituted myself king of the whole fraternity, from the lully prigger to the high spice toby gloak, I expect implicit obedience from my subjects."

" Exactly my sentiments," again ejaculated the satellite. " Damned good !" said Mr. Blueskin.

" Yes," said Jonathan, sentimentally, " constituted as human nature is, what is called robbery must inevitably form a part and parcel of the commonwealth ; and it is my aim to render it respectable, and put it upon an established footing."

" Jist my sentiments !" once more re-echoed the satellite ; and " Damned good !" again rejoined Mr. Blueskin.

" It is but just," continued Mr. Wild, " that people who lose their property, through carelessness, should have it restored to them on an adequate remuneration being made. I like fair play in every thing, and am a stickler to my word : honour is my foible. I would not act dishonestly, even if I were dealing with the devil himself— there is no occasion for one to behave meanly or dishonourably, even in what the world calls vice."

" Beautiful, by G— !" bellowed out the satellite, giving the table a knock with his fist that made the glasses dance again. " Oh, superfine, smother me !" said Mr. Blueskin.

" With these views then it is," said Mr. Wild, " that I am willing to take you under my protection, young gentleman," addressing Jack; " you will henceforth belong to me: I will enter you in my book, and regard you as my child ; you will form one of the great family of which I am the head and arbiter: all that I shall require from you, in return, is frankness and confidence. I shall not presume to direct your actions, but shall leave you to the free exercise of your own natural genius. You will follow the unrestrained bent of your own inclinations: no evil consequences shall accrue from any action of which there may be a full avowal made to me. Whatever is confided to my care, shall be liberally, and punctually accounted for, without fear of detection; but, I again repeat, confidence I expect—there must be no secrets: I must know every thing;—this observed, the law is impotent, and justice may pursue her efforts in vain."

" Equitable to a hair !" roared out the satellite. " The Governor could not say more, if the kinchen was his own flesh and blood."

" Oh, damned equitable—damned equitable !' said Mr. Blueskin.

" If you do any thing in the fullness of your fancy," continued Mr. Wild, not regarding the interruption, " that may expose you to awkward results, confide the evidences of your indiscretion to me: I will protect you—give you the full value of whatever you may have hazarded your liberty to obtain, and ensure you the continuance of your efforts with freedom and impunity." With this edifying assurance, which was very grateful to Jack, and which Mr. Blueskin swore, " curse him, was infernally fair, and such as no gemman could possibly object to," Jonathan concluded his harangue.

Mr. Wild then entered Jack's name in his fatal book, who on his part went through a sort of formula, attested by the attendant satellites and Blueskin, pledging himself wholly to Jonathan, and was duly admitted into the fraternity; Jonathan presenting him with a guinea as the binding part of the compact. Not more surely does the urchin who, in exchange for a halfpenny, receives from the baker in return a roll of the same value, —not more surely, we repeat, does that urchin purchase that roll, than did Jonathan Wild with that guinea purchase the life-blood of the unsuspecting victim before him. Shutting his book which he was accustomed to call his *Poll-book,* Jonathan summoned the landlord to produce the second bowl of Huckle-my-butt, in which to drink Jack's enlistment.

"Where the devil is that fellow?" said Blueskin.

"Where the bee *sucks,* there *lurk* I,"

sung Mr. Nightingal from the cellar.

"But we want you to suck here," rejoined Blueskin, violently agitating the tinkler.

"In a cowslip's bell I *lie,*"

answered Mr. Nightingal, who had by this time regained his bar. "Yes, and every where else," said Mr. Blueskin. "I'll pound you for that, Master Joe!" The bowl was brought in, and paid for by Mr. Wild, who told Jack he should be very happy to see him in the Old Bailey whenever he might come that way, and receive any little proofs he might choose to bring him of his aptitude for the profession, on the noviciate of which he was about to enter. Mr. Wild further, in reply to Jack's wish that he might one day have an opportunity of visiting Newgate, cordially assured him that his desire should be gratified. With a variety of pleasant matter of this description the bowl was emptied, and the meeting broke up: Mr. Wild and his satellites departing for the Old Bailey, Blueskin taking a dive into the hundreds of Drury, and Jack, with Jonathan Wild's guinea in his pocket, stealing cautiously to his truckle bed in the garret of Mr. Wood.

CHAPTER IX.

JACK'S APPRENTICESHIP, CONTINUED.

JACK'S FIRST PUBLIC ROBBERY.—EARLY LIFE AND TRANS-
ACTIONS OF MR. JONATHAN WILD.—JACK'S FIRST VISIT TO
NEWGATE.

ALL the next day, and for many succeeding days,
Jonathan Wild's guinea nearly burnt a hole in
Jack's breeches' pocket; he dared not spend it, and
yet felt almost afraid to keep it. At length, mustering up resolution, he laid it out in the purchase of
an old pair of pistols, which he saw exposed for sale
in the shop window of the "Four Balls," a pawn-
broker's in Holywell Street. The price of blood
was thus appropriately expended in purchasing
the instruments of destruction. Mr. Wood's good
nature, however—for he had soon totally forgotten
their quarrel—so wrought upon Jack from this
time, that, notwithstanding his compact with Jonathan Wild, he shrank from all thoughts of pre-
meditated depredation; he, however, constantly
visited the "White Lion," where his nightly association with Mr. Blueskin, and other gentlemen of
a similar stamp, sapped by degrees the few re-

maining virtuous resolutions he had managed to preserve; and at the repeated instigation of Blue-skin, who took every opportunity of reminding him that Mr. Wild would expect some proof that he had not improperly been admitted a member of the fraternity, he determined to try his skill by laying hands on the first loose articles that presented themselves. He was not long without an opportunity; very soon afterwards having to execute some jobs, in the way of his trade, at the "Rummer Tavern," Charing Cross; amongst other repairs, he was to make a cupboard secure in one of the store-rooms. Jack performed his task to a miracle; but as tinkers generally make two holes where they mend one, Jack, while making this depositary safe, managed to pick the lock of another in the same room, where he found a couple of apostle spoons, or " gossips," as they were called in the slang of the day, from a dozen, or set, of them being the received present of respectable sponsors at every christening. These spoons, which were rather larger than the dessert spoons of the present day, were formed of solid silver, and had the effigies of the Twelve Apostles chased on the tops of the handles; the bowls were generally gilt. Their ostensible purpose was, to be used in drinking that most maternal potation, caudle, though they were afterwards devoted to general service. The two spoons that so temptingly met the eyes of Jack bore the effigies of St.

Peter and St. Thomas. These two saints were very
speedily enshrined in Jack's breeches' pocket; a
species of canonisation which, in this instance, happened to go off very well, for, dexterously shooting
the lock back again, so as to leave the cupboard as
he found it, Jack got clear off with his booty. This
was his *first robbery.*

The articles were not missed for two or three
days; and then, as Jack afterwards learnt from
the columns of the " Daily Post," suspicion having
fallen on a Jew who had visited the premises in the
pursuit of his vocation, he was traced to his residence, which being searched, a quantity of broken
silver was found; this not being very satisfactorily
accounted for, the Jew was point-blank charged
with the robbery. St. Peter did not more lustily
deny his Master than did the Jew forswear all
knowledge of that saint or his spoon. The landlord, however, proved as unbelieving as St. Thomas
himself. The poor Israelite was dragged before
Mr. Justice Page, who, as the robbery could not
be clearly brought home, answered the ends of justice by mulcting the Jew, on suspicion, in three
times the value of the stolen property; in addition
to which, the descendant of Abraham was on his
way home put under the pump, to gratify the virtuous indignation of the populace, a species of
christening which, not having the Apostles' spoons,
the Jew thought very unchristianlike; he was also
otherwise much maltreated.

Making the best of his way with his plunder to the office of his patron, Jonathan Wild, in the Old Bailey, Jack found that useful and amiable member of society deeply engaged in consultation with an old lady, touching the possibility of the recovery of a snuff-box set in brilliants, that had been abstracted from her on her way to Court at the last drawing-room, and which, just at that moment, happened to be most identically contained in Mr. Wild's waistcoat pocket. Jonathan was very particular in taking down a most minute description of the article in question, with the whole of the circumstances attending its abduction, and having ascertained that Lady Noseworthy—for such was the name of its owner—would willingly give a reward of twenty guineas for its return—rather more than its full value—he, most commiseratingly, requested her ladyship would do him the favour to look in upon him again, in the course of a week, during which period he would, in consideration of its being a family relic, and the love he had of public justice, set such inquiries on foot, as he had no doubt would lead to some agreeable information as to " its whereabout." Being requested by the good old lady to name what he would expect for his disinterestedness, he very conscientiously turned up the whites of his eyes, and refused to accept a single farthing, declaring that her ladyship's prayers and his own innate satisfaction would more than repay him. After entertaining the dowager with some affecting remarks on the calumnies with which he had been assailed, both in public and in private, particularly the libels contained in a pamphlet, entitled "The Regulator; or a Discovery of Thieving and Thief-takers," written by Charles Hitchin, the city marshal, a brother thief-taker and rival in iniquity, and pointing out the injustice of supposing that the act of parliament just then passed, subjecting all persons receiving goods, knowing them to be stolen, to fourteen years transportation, was levelled at him, he drew from her ladyship five shillings as a retaining fee, took down her name and address with all the particulars in his office-book, and another customer coming in, he very politely bowed her out, Jack standing meanwhile a silent spectator of all that had passed.

The second visiter was a Mr. Obadiah Woolfree, a traveller to a manufacturing house in Birmingham, who had had his pocket picked of several samples of jewellery, with the particulars of which he had previously made Jonathan acquainted, and now came, according to direction, to know if any information had been procured.

Jonathan, assuming the most friendly look imaginable, told him that he had found out, by mere chance, that some suspected goods had been stopped by a very honest man, a broker, with whom he was acquainted, and that if the lost goods fortunately should happen to be those in the hands of his friend, restitution should be made; that of course his friend would expect to be remunerated; and that it must be perfectly understood that no evil consequences should accrue to him, from his having imprudently neglected to apprehend the offenders. This, Obadiah, rather than encounter the trouble and expense of a prosecution, readily consented to, the more especially as the goods had been lost in a place, and under circumstances, that might have savoured ill in the eyes of his employers.

The next applicant was Mr. Peter Entwistle, a gentleman who had been robbed of a pocket-book, containing a great number of very valuable memoranda, of no use to any body but the owner; he received the same answer that Obadiah had done, but was not equally satisfied with it. Being a limb of the law, Mr. Entwistle very pertina-ciously put some questions, very like cross questions, as to the particular manner in which his property had been discovered, &c. Upon this Jonathan immediately ascended the high ropes, and pretended to be very much offended that his honour should be called in question. " The only motive I have," said he, " is to afford all the service in my power to persons who may have been plundered; but since my intentions are re-ceived in so ungracious a manner, and it is thought necessary to interrogate me in so suspicious a way, I have nothing further to say on the subject. I have my own conscience to satisfy me, and that is enough; the name of Jonathan Wild need not shrink from investigation." The legal gentleman was here convinced he had been too hasty; he therefore apologised to Jonathan, and offered him an additional reward—on which the good man became somewhat pacified; and a time and place were fixed for the restoration of the property.

To a fourth party, Mr. Jonah Strugnell, a dry-salter, who had been hustled under Gray's Inn-wall, and almost stripped to the skin, Jonathan answered, he had received some information respecting his (Mr. Strugnell's) lost cocked hat, periwig, coat, sword, and silver buckles, but that the agent he had employed had informed him, that the thieves pretended they could raise more money by pawning the property, than by returning it for the proposed reward; " but," added Jonathan, " if I can by any means procure an interview with the villains, whom I earnestly implore heaven to punish, I shall, I doubt not, be able to settle matters agreeably to the terms proposed;" though he artfully insinuated that the most safe, expeditious, and prudent method, would be to make a small addition to the reward. Poor Jonah, on hearing this, eagerly agreed to give an extra ten shillings, when Jonathan, with a benevolent air, told him to call the next day at three o'clock, when his confidential assistant, Mr. Mendez, the patriarch before alluded to, should accompany him to a certain post in Kent-street, where a gentleman in a smock-frock and dustman's slouched hat would, on receiving the reward, return the lost property—" no questions being asked." Jonah departed highly delighted, fancying himself once more in his own coat, periwig, &c.

Wild next despatched his satellite, Quilt Arnold, to Miss Virginia Withers, an elderly spinster, who, by the cutting away of her pocket in the New Jerusalem Chapel, had been robbed of " The Whole Duty of Man," a large silver smelling-bottle, which by mistake had been filled with strong waters, and a silk purse containing a note of hand of the Reverend Simon Cunnington, together with some loose silver, desiring Quilt to inform the bereaved lady, that she could have her smelling-bottle, note of hand, and " Whole Duty of Man," back again, on payment of a certain sum ; but that the strong waters and loose silver were missing. Jonathan then beckoned our hero into a little back room, and, assuming a bland air, most encouragingly inquired the nature of his communication.

Previously to entering upon this, however, as Mr. Jonathan Wild will henceforth be one of the principal persons that figure in this very memorable and veracious history, it may be necessary to give the readers, for the better understanding our pages, some account of this great personage's " birth, parentage, and education," together with his " life, character, and behaviour," up to this precise period.

This extraordinary man, according to all *Ordinary* accounts, was born at Wolverhampton, in Staffordshire, about the year 1682. Posterity have to lament that the precise day of the birth of this distinguished man has not been ascertained with sufficient accuracy to allow us, as conscientious historians, to record it with any degree of confidence. His parents were somewhat humble, but extremely respectable; he was their eldest son, their firstborn, as may well be imagined from the strength of character he afterwards displayed. At a proper age they put him to an established day-school, which he continued to attend till he had gained sufficient knowledge in reading, writing, and accounts, for general purposes; his father intended to have brought him up to his own trade, but afterwards changed his mind; and when his son was about fifteen, put him apprentice for seven years to a buckle-maker in Birmingham; which, at that time, was a flourishing business. Upon the expiration of his apprenticeship, Jonathan returned to Wolverhampton, and soon feeling the soft infection of love, married a young woman possessing both virtue and comeliness, and for some time earned a tolerable livelihood, by following his business in the minor degree of journeyman. But a mechanical life possessed few charms for Jonathan: his spirit aspired to higher things; he had a soul above buckles, he could never quite buckle too; and after two years dallying with buckle-making, during which time his consort had presented him with a son and heir, he, one fine morning, to gratify his love of change, and give some scope to his wish for distinction and command, showed his beautiful wife and lovely offspring a fair pair of heels, and unceremoniously left them, and repaired to London, where he imagined his talents would meet with proper encouragement. In the great metropolis he soon procured employment, and for some time supported himself by his trade ; but being in addition to his ambition, of a very lively turn, and above prejudices, and having withal, very original ideas touching the correct disposition of property, it is not to be wondered at that he should soon have got into debt, still less so, that, getting into debt, he should have got into the hands of the lawyers, and after that, have got into gaol. The fact was, that very few months after his arrival in London he was arrested, and thrown into Wood Street compter, where he remained a prisoner for debt upwards of four years.

Prisons were then very different to what they are now ; money could do almost any thing in them, and debtors who had any means at all, led very jovial lives; in fact, prisons presented one continued scene of riot and revelry ; liquors could be obtained in any quantity, and no restraint in the way of speech or expenditure was placed on any of the prisoners ; it is well known that their inmates often left them with regret—care was ban-ished by universal consent, morality scouted, and impunity was the order of the day.

At that time, contrary to the present practice, there was no classification ; and debtors and felons mixed indiscriminately together during the day, and very often at night. Neither was the modern poor-law system of separating the sexes in vogue ; consequently Mr. Wild soon became acquainted with most of the reigning depredators of that period : he was admitted into their privy councils, —became acquainted with all the secrets of their several states,—learnt how they levied contributions on the public, imposed exactions, raised supplies, made war on their neighbours, and replenished their exhausted treasuries. The city marshal, the notorious Charles Hitchin,* was at that time, lord paramount of all the thieves in the kingdom. Jonathan soon began to envy the sway this man exercised. During his confinement, he formed an acquaintance with a fair nymph of Venus, known on the *pavé* by the name of Mary Milliner, the most redoubtable purloiner of hearts and handkerchiefs that then occasionally illumined his majesty's gaols. Naturally inflammable, Jona-

* This consummate miscreant, who was undoubtedly Jonathan Wild's master in the peculiar profession which he subsequently pursued with so much notoriety, was overtaken by the arm of justice for a gross misdemeanor, and dying soon afterwards, left Wild in undisputed possession of the field. It is hard to say which was the greatest scoundrel of the two ; but Wild was the more artful and specious.

than soon formed a tender *penchant* for this vestal and the usual *liaison* was the consequence. She had escaped the penalties attendant on sundry larcenies, but the liberality of her disposition was too great to shield her from the inexorable hands of John Doe and Richard Roe.

Obtaining their joint freedom, after a short period, this congenial pair availed themselves of the independent facility afforded by a saltatory movement over a broomstick, to appear to the world's eye as man and wife. The adroitness of the fair Mary in the way of her vocation, and the knowledge Jonathan had acquired while in " durance vile," soon enabled them to raise sufficient money to take a small public house, The Cock, in Cripplegate, where Jonathan commenced his well-known trade of restoring stolen property. For some time his house was a regular lock, or receptacle for plunder of every description; but on the passing of the act against receivers, he called all the thieves together, and constituting himself their head and arbiter, entered into a compact with them, that all articles stolen should be committed to his custody, for which he would regularly pay more than they could procure from the pawn-broker, and without any risk to them, trusting to re-imburse himself by the rewards obtained from their owners, to whom he might restore them. His success was great—he contested the palm of sovereignty with the then king of the thieves, the arch-villain Hitchin. These worthies at first attacked each other in pamphlets, and tried which could prove his rival to be the greatest rascal; but finding, that by their opposition they were cutting each other's throat, they joined in partnership together. Hitchin, who had lost his situation as marshal, acting as master, and our *ci-devant* buckle-maker, Jonathan Wild, officiating as man. This union did not long continue. The towering genius of Jonathan soon crushed all the pretensions of the ex-marshal, notwithstanding there was no act of villany, however great or daring, from which the latter shrunk. Jonathan was soon left master of the field, and reigned alone; he gave up his public house, and opened a public office, at the house of a Mrs. Sego, in the Old Bailey, where his fame became so great, that scarcely any thing was lost but application was made to him for its recovery; not a prig dared practice his profession without having first received a diploma from Wild's hands. Mill-kens§ and Bridle-culls,† alike trembled at his nod,—in a word, he reigned undisputed king of the thieves; but though terrible to his own immediate subjects, whose lives he held in his hands, to the public at large he was plausible and pious—as sleek and fair to appearance as the serpent of the desert, but not less venomous and deadly. Such was Jonathan Wild's position and history, at the time that Jack brought him

* Housebreakers.   † Highwaymen.

the first fruits of his deviation from the paths of honesty.

"What is your business with me, my son ?" said Wild, addressing Jack with an air of parental kindness. "Any little outbreak, eh?—Well, well, youth will be lively; we cannot put old heads upon young shoulders."

Jack produced the two spoons. "Ah, ha! a couple of *Godfathers!* Good, good; these give you a *name* that fully entitles you to be received among my children; no reward will be offered for these. Here, Abraham!" said he, summoning the patriarch.

"Yesh, Mishter Vild, shur," answered that worthy, suddenly appearing from behind an immensely ugly bushy beard. "Any tings de mattersh?"

"No, Nabs," answered the potentate. "Is the white broth on ?"

"Jusht on, Mr. Vild, shur."

"That's right; stir it up with those two spoons then, Nabs,"—tossing them to him. The Jew grinned horribly a ghastly smile at the thoughts of *crucibling* the good saints.

"Dey shall be in de pot directly, Mishter Vild, shur," said he; and disappeared with them in a twinkling.

"As old silver, they may fetch five shillings," said Jonathan, handing Jack the money: the value of them was at least a guinea. "Now relate to me the particulars of their capture."

Jack gave an account of the robbery with a commendable modesty. Mr. Wild bestowed much praise on the cleanness of Jack's workmanship, and assured him there was no doubt but that in time he would become a great artist, encouraging him to pursue the path on which he had so auspiciously entered. Then desiring the patriarch to step over with Jack to Newgate, and request Mr. Revel, the under turnkey, to afford him the high treat of a thorough inspection of that celebrated mansion—that last " retreat of the unfortunate *brave*," Mr. Wild shook hands with Jack, and bade him good bye, hoping very shortly to see him again.

The inspection of Newgate very deeply interested Jack; there was no part of it to which he did not, as if by some secret prescience, bestow the most minute attention, an attention which proved of singular use to him in after life. He asked Mr. Revel a thousand questions, and appeared so interested as to excite the patriarch's observation.

" Vy, you seems quite sthruck vith the plaishe, my kinchin," said that worthy. " Vell it is a nishe plaishe, certainly ; quite out of the way of the coaches : has got a very nishe pump too, peoples come far and near to drink de vatersh, dere so goot for dem. You must treat him vell, Mishter Revel if ever he comes here for a short time, as who knows vot may happen ; give him one of your best berths."

" Ay, ay, we'll accommodate him," said the dubster.

" Much obliged to you," returned Jack, I may look in upon you one of these days."

" But come," said the patriarch, " you musht make haste, youngster, for I'm in a hurry. Vhy, hang me if I don't think youl'd like to stay here altogether, you seem so fond of the plaishe."

" You *will* be hanged, then," said Jack, for I shouldn't like to stay here at all, and, what's more, I wouldn't.—What do they call these things ?" said he, examining some fetters and handcuffs that were hanging up ready for use.

" Vot the darbies and the ruffles ?" said the Jew. " Oh ! you'll know all in goot time, you may depend upon dat."

"Shall I ! I thank you for the information. They must be made a little stronger than these to last long with me. Why I should wear a suit out in no time."

" Ve shall see, ve shall see !" said the Jew. " But come, you've staid quite long enough ; so make your bow to the gentlemans, and bowl dish vay."

" I'll not detain you," said Jack nobody shall ever complain of my wanting to *stay too long*, whenever I happen to come here."

" Dat's very goot," chuckled the Jew. " But come, I've got to go to Newtoner's Lane, so I'll see you safe out here, and valk vith you as far as

Vych Street; so goot morning, Mishter Revels, goot morning, shur, thanking you vastly for gratifying my young friend here."

"Shall be happy to see him at any time," growled out Mr. Revel; " he seems a promising young bird."

"Don't you wish you may get me?" laughed Jack; " but your's are snug quarters, I must say: when I want to learn a trick or two, I don't know that I can come to a better college."

Jack and the Jew then departed, and made their way—the patriarch to Newtoner's Lane, and Jack to the shop of his master.

CHAPTER X.

JACK'S APPRENTICESHIP, CONTINUED.

MAY-DAY IN 1716. — THE MILK-MAID'S GARLAND. — JACK'S
FIRST LOVE.

A TWELVEMONTH rolled away, during the whole
of which period our hero did not once attempt to
repeat his handiwork of the spoons; though tender
inquiries how he went on were made from time to
time by Mr. Wild, through the medium of Blueskin, who assured Jack that the governor took a
great interest in him, and hoped he would'nt dis-
appoint that gentleman's expectations, nor disgrace
his, Mr. Blueskin's recommendation. Jack replied,
it was all in good time, and that he should wait
and see how things turned out.

At length time brought the first of May, 1716,
and a glorious first of May it was—bright, balmy,
warm, and inspiring—not one of the first of Mays
we have been used to have since the great M. N. S.
Murphy has meddled with the weather; but one
recalling images of joy and beauty, and awakening
thoughts of repose and love. The skies were without a cloud—the hawthorn and early fruit trees
presented, with their gay profusion of blossoms,

the appearance of gigantic nosegays—the air was
as vocal as it was fragrant : it seemed as if both
birds and flowers, in gratitude for their being,
were rendering back to heaven the sweet breath
they inhaled from it in love and honour—the one
in incense and the other in song.   The waters, as
they glittered in the sunbeams, looked bright and
pure, yielding those ideas of comfortable coolness
and grateful refreshment that only belong to the
limpid element in summer.   Jack's heart felt the
delicious exhilaration of the season, and was at-
tuned to the reception of tenderness and pleasure.

He was conveying, with a bounding step and
buoyant bosom, a packing—not a law—*case* to the
chambers of Counsellor Jay, in the Temple, when
crossing through one of the leading streets in the
Strand, his notice was attracted by the sounds of a
pipe and tabor, to what was then the usual exhibition of May-day, but which has long since given
way to a less pleasing pageant : the cleanly milk-
maid having been superseded in her appeals to the
public generosity at this vernal season by the sooty
sweep.   " Ah, ah ! the milkmaid's garland !" said
Jack.   " I must see this ; it seems one of the gayest
and grandest I have witnessed yet."   Making his
way through the crowd which had gathered round
it, Jack soon got a clear view of this, then, very
innocent and pleasing sight.   A pyramid of some
six or eight feet in height, covered with fine damask,
was erected on a sort of stand, which a couple of

bearers carried, by means of two horizontal poles, similar to those of a sedan chair. This pyramid was ornamented on each side from top to bottom, with a great number of real silver salvers, spoons, jugs, watches, tea-pots, cream ewers, dishes, &c., surmounted at the top by an elegant tea or coffee urn,—the whole borrowed for the day from the various customers of the milkman, with some occasional loans from pawnbrokers, who let out plate on security for the purpose. The various pieces were tastefully and profusely decorated with bunches of ribands of different colours, the articles being so disposed as to form many fanciful devices. A man playing on the fife and tabor headed the procession, and a number of milkmaids in their best Sunday boddices and kirtles, trimmed with bunches of ribands, and their neat straw hats, adorned with flowers, danced around the pyramid at the several places where it rested, which was generally before the doors of their customers, whose contributions they solicited as well as those of the spectators. The sight of so much valuable plate, and so many watches, considerably excited Jack's interest and awoke sundry speculations in his mind of a nature which we shall not here allude to further,—suffice it, " he looked and longed, and longed and looked again"; but all at once, his eye glancing by chance from the pyramid and its treasures, his vision fell upon an object which from that moment was never erased from his memory.

Before the pyramid, in the centre of the other maidens, he beheld a young girl dancing, whose surpassing grace and loveliness immediately made the ribands look dull, and the plate seem valueless. She appeared about fifteen years of age: the bud of girlhood was just expanding into the first blossom of woman; her skin was of a warm dazzling whiteness, exhibiting a rich purity which could only be compared with that of the water lily, and which made the milk she vended look cold and chalky, when coming in contact with it, as it would have done snow, and many other substances to which poets have delighted to compare the outward surface of their mistresses. Her eyes were of that clear blue, in which as you gaze, you seem, as when gazing on the heavens, to lose all thoughts of mortality, and only receive glimpses of peace and delight. Her mouth was small, with ripe rosy lips compressed, as if withdrawing into their own odorous bower, and gave, perhaps, a stronger promise of innocence and modesty than was conveyed even by her retiring look, and somewhat downcast lids: clusters of flaxen ringlets fell beneath her straw hat, over her shoulders, on either side her face. Her figure was *petite*, and seemingly fragile, but exquisitely moulded, and of the most perfect symmetry. A bystander might have thought it wonderful that such a world of beauty and enchantment could have been enshrined in so small a compass. Her dress was elegantly simple:

but **had** it been that of a queen, it would have obtained no regard opposed to such **attractions of** person as those with which it was united. In her hand she held a wreath, or garland of flowers, which, in conjunction with a companion with whom she danced, she was twining into a number of graceful figures. Jack stood entranced, gazing at her in stupid wonder. Though he had walked abroad all his life amid a world of female beauty, this was the first time a consciousness of its existence had crossed his mind. All the charms that he had ever individually seen, in the thousand lovely creatures he had at times beheld, were here concentrated into one, and seemed to unite their hitherto separate force to overpower and enslave him. On a sudden the maiden stopped in her dance, and curtseying to the multitude, sung, in a somewhat tremulous but unusually clear and melodious voice, the customary " *Milkmaid's May-day Carol,*" with a copy of which we have been favoured, taken down from the recitation of an old lady of our acquaintance, and which we here present to our readers.

The Milk-Maid's May-Day Carol.

1.

The skies shine bright, the meads look gay, and streams run
    soft and clear,
And bees and flowers proclaim 'tis May, the sweet time of the
    year;

And lowing kine, where hawthorns twine, the luscious draught
    supply—
A drink divine, like generous wine, fit for the gods on high.
The fount of innocence and love, it cheers both young and old;
And erst, the care of princess fair! was, in the age of gold.
Then pretty maids above, below, as you our carol hear,
Remember the poor milk-maid in the sweet time of the year.

2.

We bring our garlands to your doors, with rose and lily twin'd,
To call alike your beauty and your purity to mind.
With silver tankard, ewer, cup, your memories to rub
Of curds and whey, and custard, and the fragrant sillabub.
Without our aid, ah! what would all your foreign luxuries be?
Our milk it is gives relish to your coffee and your tea.
Then pretty maids, above, below, as you our carol hear,
Remember the poor milk-maid in the sweet time of the year.

3.

Think how, when wintry rains fall deep, and howls the dreary
    wind,
While to your cheerful fires you creep, and warmth and com-
    fort find,
Think how we go through frost and snow, ere morn begins to
    gleam,
To fold and field, to you to yield new milk and clouted cream.
Regardless both of toil and care, of anguish and of ease,
So we, our merry masters and mistresses but please.
Then pretty maids, above, below, as you our carol hear,
Remember the poor milk-maid in the sweet time of the year.

She ceased. A shower of pieces of money from
copper to silver rewarded her skill. Jack drank in
every word, as he had done every look, and was
only aroused from his dream of light and joy by a
deep voice muttering—" That Kinchen! he is
mine! I have him *now:*" when turning round, he

beheld with surprise Jonathan Wild, regarding him with sinister satisfaction. By Jonathan's side stood a gaunt-looking fellow, somewhat rudely attired, with a companion of the same stamp, significantly pointing with his finger to the various valuable articles of plate suspended on the pyramid. Jack was somewhat alarmed as well as surprised at this sudden appearance of Mr. Wild; and more so, when continuing his gaze around, he discovered the exemplary Mr. Blueskin and some gipsy friends of his of rather equivocal character, that he had met occasionally at the "White Lion." At this moment, the fair girl with whom he had been so struck suddenly rested her attention upon him. A glance was exchanged between them which seemed to have some electrical power, for a sympathetic thrill in each was its immediate result. A feeling of sadness passed for a moment over Jack's mind; his fancy conjured up a thousand images—he became once more wrapped, his eyes fixed on the enchanting vision before him; and it was not till jostled by the retiring crowd, that he discovered that he was gazing on vacancy, and that the fairy-like creature who had so deeply spelled his senses had imperceptibly glided away, and that with her had vanished the garland, Jonathan Wild, Mr. Blueskin, and his companions, with the numerous persons by which it was accompanied. Arousing himself from his reverie, though he still continued to behold in fancy the bright object of his enchantment—the mind's eye retaining the impression

of particular images long after they have departed
—Jack repaired with the case to Counsellor Jay's.

After some time, his suspicions began to direct
themselves to the motives that had brought Jonathan Wild and his friend Blueskin in attendance
upon the garland ; and he remembered, among the
plate which was affixed to the pyramid, there were
some massive salvers, bearing the well-known arms
of Mr. Kneebone, which consisted of three legs
and thighs, so connected together at the femoral
extremities as to form a species of radius ; and that
there were also the well-known Sunday tea-urn
of Madam Wood, and her set of state spoons,
which had been presented to her on her marriage
by no less a person than her distinguished relation
the ex-mayor, Sir Timothy Gutteridge himself :
there was also Mr. Wood's great family turnip-
shaped watch, with its imposing appendages ; and
it now occurred to Jack that the leader of the procession, the man who played the pipe and tabor,
and carried the money-box, was Mr. Wood's and
Mr. Kneebone's own milkman, David Lloyd, a
countryman of Mr. Wood, proprietor of the principal milk-walk in that quarter, and an extensive
cow-keeper. The truth now flashed upon him that
some mischief was intended, though he recoiled
at the idea that the fair damsel who had so intensely interested him, was, either knowingly or
willingly, a party to it. Mr. Kneebone's plate he
had no doubt had been borrowed by the milkman
of the good natured Mrs. Partington ; and national

predilection satisfactorily accounted for the possession of Mr. Wood's time-teller, and other property. He felt inclined to go and warn both his protector and his master. Jonathan Wild, Blueskin, and their associates, were, he was convinced, only lurking about the valuables for the purpose of plunder ; but he was restrained by the thought that he might, by disclosing his suspicions, unintentionally get the lovely milkmaid into trouble ; he therefore returned to his work, though not with that alacrity with which he usually pursued it : he was thoughtful and moody, and could not help reverting to the scene which had so lately passed. Again was the form of the beautiful milkmaid dancing before his eyes—again were her melodious accents ringing in his ears. He saw the malignant looks of Jonathan, the furtive glances of Blueskin and his companions, and he anxiously awaited for some intelligence. The afternoon had scarcely well set in, when his worst fears were confirmed by the sudden entrance of Mr. Wood.

"Mercies of Cot !" exclaimed that gentleman, " here is calamities, look you ! hur is ruined ! hur creat family fatch that has tescented to hur from father to son pefore fatchmaking fas known, and hat peen worn by Catwallater himself, with hur creat seal of the leek, is gone, look you ! Put that is not the worst ; Matam Woot's pest tea-urns ant all her Suntay tea-spoons tat fas given to her py her relation, Sir Timothy Cutteridge, that fas

M

lort mayor, ant which hur hat lent tat fillain Tavit Lloyt, without hur knowletge, is gone too. Some scountrels have run away with the garlant, plate and all. Hur is ruinet! hur is ruinet! That fillain, Tavit Lloyt, passion of hur heart! but he shall give hur satisfaction for hur losses, which hur shall never hear the last of from hur laty, Matam Woot."

The unfortunate Welshman here applied for consolation to a huge jug of *cwrw*, which happened, luckily, to have been just brought in by Taffleen, to be in readiness for the family supper. It produced a momentary calm, during which Jack managed, adroitly enough, to extract from his master, without exciting any suspicion, the information, that a gang of desperadoes had attacked the garland as it was proceeding through a place near the top of the Strand, then known by the name of Porridge Island, and which was of somewhat doubtful character: that after violently beating the bearers of it, knocking down, and otherwise ill treating its owner, the aforesaid David Lloyd, and frightening away the milkmaids in all directions, they had got clear off with their booty, leaving no trace behind them by which they could be discovered. Leaving Mr. Wood at one moment mourning over his loss, and the next burning with indignation at the authors of it, Jack repaired in the evening, as usual, to the " White Lion." It was some time before he was joined by any of the company that regularly resorted there; their absence did not particularly surprise him : he had long settled, in his own mind, who were the persons that had so daringly carried off the May-day treasures, and felt a proportionate degree of anxiety to learn the fate of the beautiful milkmaid. He was not long left in doubt. About ten o'clock Mr. Blueskin, with his gipsy companions before mentioned, entered the room ; they were immediately followed by Jonathan Wild.

" Cleanly done enough, that I must own," said that great man to Blueskin. " Rather unlucky, though:" and here he fixed a marked look on Jack. " rather unlucky that pretty Bess should be nabbed : the gang must shift their quarters for a while in case she should squeak." Jack's blood flew to his cheeks, and his heart throbbed violently —she was, then, a prisoner! " Where have they caged our little singing bird ?" continued Mr. Wild. " In old St. Giles's roundhouse," answered Blueskin.

" Ah, there !" said the potentate. " Not much of a ken that ; a lad of any spirit might get her out in no time. Old Guffin, the keeper, wouldn't stand the kick of a fly's leg. If the little beauty had but a *fancy man, now*——" here he fixed another glance of peculiar meaning on our hero.

Jack stopped to hear no more ; he rushed out of the " White Lion," and hastily bent his steps towards St. Giles's, resolving either to rescue the beautiful milkmaid, or remain and suffer with her.

CHAPTER XI.

JACK SHEPPARD A PRISON-BREAKER.

ST. GILES'S ROUNDHOUSE.—RESCUE OF EDGEWORTH BESS.—
VISIT TO NORWOOD.

WHIRLED along by the impetuosity of his feelings, and scarcely knowing which path he took, Jack made his way up Drury Lane, across Long Acre, and through the maze of streets that constitute the Seven Dials, till he came to St. Giles's roundhouse, then a square building of two stories, forming a sort of postern, situated on one side of St. Giles's church-yard, having the church and church-yard in its rear, with a street in front. Arriving at this official structure, Jack, without any settled purpose, or fixed plan, saving that of rescuing the pretty milkmaid by any means that presented themselves, knocked violently at the door; it was speedily opened by Mr. Hannibal Guffin, the parish beadle, and keeper of the roundhouse.

" Hey-day !" said that functionary, who had exchanged his cocked hat and official wig for a comfortable thrum cap, in which he meant to enjoy a pleasant sleep in the parochial night-chair, though he still retained the imposing blue great-coat, with its huge red collar and broad gold binding, which marked his rank and authority—" Hey-day ! what night bird have we here? why one would think the whole parish were at the door by the noise— you couldn't be in a greater hurry if you were Mr. Head Churchwarden himself."

" You have a young girl here," interrupted Jack, " unjustly charged on suspicion of being concerned in a daring robbery."

" What ! Edgeworth Bess ? for so some of the villains were heard to call her, or plain Bess, as she styled herself, though the jade is pretty enough for that matter, but that was the only name she'd give. The baggage pretended, before the justice, that she never knew she had another. What do you want with her ? If you have any thing good to give her, let me have it ; I'll take care it's properly delivered."

" I must see her," exclaimed Jack, " and that instantly ; she is innocent : I am ready to swear it—to stake my life upon it. She has been en- trapped—betrayed," he continued passionately.

" Hoity-toity !" exclaimed the dignitary of the roundhouse—" here's a young bantem, *must see her!* What, then, have you got an order from Justice Page, my fine fellow ?"

" No," said Jack, energetically ; " but I repeat, I must and will see her. Where is she ?"

" Out of your reach, young Pickle. What, I suppose you are one of the gang, are you ? Well, you're beginning betimes, at all events. But come, take yourself off, and thank your stars that I haven't my Sunday service cane at hand, or I might mark such a pretty backgammon board, of red and black stripes on your back, as you wouldn't forget in a hurry. Come, tramp, tramp !"

" Not before I have seen this poor luckless girl," returned Jack, with a determined air. " Where is she, I ask you ?"

" Halloa ! ' said the astonished functionary, " do you know who you are speaking to, scoundrel ? Do you know that I am Mr. Hannibal Guffin, the *locum tenens* of their worships the overseers, and keeper of the roundhouse ?"

" If you were ten thousand beadles," said Jack, losing all command of himself, " you *shall* let me see your ill-used victim."

" I am petrified !" roared out the astonished Mr. Hannibal. " This language to me ! St Giles's is certainly coming to a chaos ; but I'll make short work of it. The hussy you speak of is there, in that cage," pointing to the door of a small cell at the back of the apartment, " safely cooped up, and if you don't instantly show a fair pair of heels, I'll make you her companion, by clapping you into the fellow-cage to it."

" Scoundrel !" cried Jack, enraged ; " but I'll hesitate no longer : the coast is clear—I have a fair opportunity, so here goes."

With these words he snatched up a stout watch-man's bill, which happend to be lying on a table, before which the beadle had been sitting, and directed it at the functionary's skull with such good will, that not having any hat or wig as protection, it instantly stretched him senseless on the floor. Jack's next step was to force open, with the beadle's own **staff**, the door of the cell which had been pointed out as containing the fair prisoner. The poor girl was sitting on a bundle of straw, suffused in tears, and looking, if possible, even lovelier in her tears than when Jack saw her, all life and joy in the morning. She arose in surprise and alarm.

"Oh! for mercy's sake!" she exclaimed, with a faint shriek, "spare me, spare me! indeed I am innocent—I knew not what I did."

"Compose yourself, dear girl," said Jack; "I am come to save you; but we must not lose a moment—quick! let us fly, then."

"Ah, at liberty?" said the amazed girl, suddenly brightening up. "To whom do I owe my deliverance? Oh, let my thanks, my gratitude—"

"It matters not who I am," said Jack; "it is sufficient I have rescued you: hereafter we may know each other better. But come, dear damsel, let us complete your escape while we can."

It was fortunate that the respectable Mr. Hannibal Guffin and pretty Bess were the only inmates of the roundhouse at the period of Jack's visit. The nightly watch had been set, and those worthy guardians of the rest of his Majesty's subjects had departed on their several beats, and the hour had not arrived when the usual nocturnal visiters of the roundhouse were generally installed in it, or Jack's exploit might have been one of somewhat more difficulty.

Taking the fair maiden's hand, who, to say the truth, was nothing loth, and bestowing a hearty kick on the prostrate carcass of the senseless beadle as he passed him, Jack hastened with his precious prize into the street, carefully shutting the door of the roundhouse after him. Hurrying onwards in the direction of Drury Lane, neither feeling inclined, till perfectly out of danger, to indulge in conversation, they were stopped at the corner of Monmouth Street, by encountering the tall muffled figure of a woman, which Jack immediately recognised as that of the gipsy, who had discovered the pilfering of Mrs. Partington's ring at Mr. Kneebone's.

" Ah, my mother !" said the little maiden, springing joyfully towards her. " Welcome, welcome ; Why did you ever leave me ? That terrible black Martin—I have been betrayed, dear mother, accused of theft—dragged through the streets a prisoner—thrust into a dungeon, and but for this good youth——" here her emotions completely overpowered her ; her spirit, which had borne up till this moment, now suddenly appeared to fail her ; the remembrance of all she had suffered flashed across her. It was too much for one so tender, so timid ; and she sank fainting on Jack's shoulder.

" Ah!" said the gipsy, as if struck by an electric shock, and flashing her dark eye on Jack. " And is it with thee, boy, I thus meet her; is it by thy hand she's been rescued from her peril? Then I foretold too truly. Did I not warn thee to avoid her—did I not tell thee those flaxen ringlets would prove chains to thee; that beneath those now closed lids beamed fires whose brilliancy, like the lightnings, would blight thee?"

Jack was startled, and listened with silent wonder to the vehemence of the hag. " See," she continued, removing a necklace, and pointing out a counter mole on the throat of the insensible girl— " see that fatal mark, twin to the one thou bearest. Did I not name it to thee, and charge thee, boy, to fly its bearer? By Satan, we are but willing puppets of the Fates, and lend ourselves to our own destinies; then what avails our prescience—what avails the gipsy's warning—what imports the foreknowledge drawn from star and planet?"

" Indeed," said Jack, who almost quailed beneath the gipsy's hollow tones and mystic words, and vainly tried to shrink from her searching glances, which seemed to have the deadly facination of the serpent's, " indeed, I meant no harm, I thought no harm; but I couldn't bear that such a pretty creature should be shut up in prison for what I was sure she had not done. If she had really stolen the things, it wouldn't have been so bad; so I determined to get her out, and I have.

I knocked the old beadle on the head —Don't be frightened,—I did not kill him, bless you !—his skull's too thick for that ; and now where's the harm ?"

" Unconscious instrument of destiny and ill," exclaimed the gipsy, " who shall explain to thee the dark riddles of futurity ?   Time is the only certain solver—he unravels all things: let Time, then, answer thee; I cannot—will not.   But let me revive this child of revenge and misfortune. Poor wench ! this day she has turned o'er the first page of her book of woe.   How many are there ere the volume close ? 'Tis a black-lettered tome: its leaves illumined with characters of blood ;— 'twould sear mine eyeballs did I seek to read them !" She here applied a powerful essence to the senses of her *protegée* who was still enclosed in Jack's arms : it speedily revived her.

" Where am I ?" said the poor girl.   " In that horrid cell, dragged by those fearful men ?   No, no,—free, and with her I love ! Yes, I remember all."

" You must away, Bess," said the gipsy, sternly. " Take leave of thy deliverer."

" Ah !" said Jack, " must we then part so soon ? But we shall meet again—you'll surely not deny me that ?"

" Oh yes, yes !" tenderly ejaculated the poor girl, as the gipsy withdrew her from Jack's embrace, " often, very often, — that is, I hope—

perhaps — shall we not, mother?" observing the severe look of the gipsy.

"You must part, child," returned the gipsy, solemnly, "with my consent never to meet again. What the stars will, they will; I may not change their bidding: my rule is but of earth—and how brief that—how wretched! A wandering race, an outcast tribe, the thicket, and the ruin. When will the curse upon our nation leave us? But come, there's danger in our tarrying here :—night wears, the alarm ere now is doubtless given, and we may be surprised. Say farewell, Bess, to thy preserver."

"Good bye, good bye! and thank you," sobbed the poor girl, gratefully pressing Jack's hand. "I may not disobey the bidding of my mother. Good bye, God bless you! You have my thanks —my prayers."

Ere Jack could sufficiently rally his thoughts to answer her, the gipsy had withdrawn her from the spot, and both had vanished.

Recovering from the surprise of their disappearance, Jack turned his steps back again to the domicile of the tuneful Mr. Nightingal. He found the vocal landlord of the blanched monarch of the woods in close attendance on Mr. Wild, Mr. Blueskin, and the gipsy gentlemen of their acquaintance. A significant glance successively passed from one to the other of the whole of these interesting persons.

> " Drink to me only with thine eyes,
>   And I will pledge with mine,"

hummed Mr. Nightingal, emptying a glass of punch that happened to he standing just then before him, and leering with an expression of peculiar meaning from Jack to the company around him. " Or leave a kiss, tol lol de diddle doll !"— he did not conclude Ben Jonson's well known song.

For a moment there was a deep pause, which was at length broken by the bland tones of Jonathan.

" Why you left us all in a hurry, Jack," said he, encouragingly.

" Yes, there was no time to be lost," answered Jack.

"Something particular, eh ?" said Mr. Wild, in an insinuating tone.

" Yes," said Jack. " I thought the sooner the poor girl was released from her unjust confinement the better."

" What, then, is she free ?" said Wild, exultingly.—" All's safe boys," he muttered aside to his companions. " But you surely haven't committed any violence?"

" I have only broken open the door of her dungeon," said Jack, " and given old Guffin, the beadle, a rap on the mazzard—that's all."

"Your hand," said Jonathan; " you have proved yourself one of the right sort, Jack ; and whenever you choose regularly to enter the service, you shan't want a commission : I'll appoint you one of my lieutenants the very first thing."

" Ve'll drink the le-tenant's goot healths," said the patriarch, who happened to be present.

" With all my heart," returned Blueskin, " if it was a mile to the bottom. I always said Jack was a regular court card, and that whoever turned him up would find he'd turned up his nob."

" It was a lover and his lass,"

sang Mr. Nightingal.

" But where is the wench ?" inquired Jonathan of Jack.

" With one we met upon our way; one she called mother."

" Tall, and in tatters ?" asked Jonathan.

" The same," answered Jack.

" Ah! the witch, Zara," said the monarch of the thieving fraternity; " that is unlucky: the baggage, Bess, may slip through our fingers; and I have further business for her. But we will not think of that now. Landlord ! bring in a double crown bowl of punch, and let us drink to the hero of the night, the champion of love and beauty. You must all pledge me in this toast, gentlemen."

" To be sure we will," said Mr. Nightingal, singing,—

" We'll drink, and we'll never have done, boys !"

He soon produced a foaming bowl ; bumpers

were filled all round; and Jonathan proposed the health of their staunch colleague, Jack Sheppard, which, it is needless to say, was drank with loud acclamations.   Mr. Blueskin was affected even to tears at the proof Jack had given of his gallantry and courage, and hiccupped out something about his having been the first to discover his friend's great genius.   Jack returned thanks in an appropriate speech.   The health of pretty Bess was then drank — Mr. Nightingal humming Shakspeare's beautiful madrigal—

"Oh! happy, happy, fair,
    Thine eyes are lode-stars, and thy breath sweet air."

Other toasts followed in rapid succession, till one of the watchmen of St. Clement's was heard proclaiming the hour of midnight.

"Hark! the lark at heaven's gate sing,,"

sang Mr. Nightingal.

"The bowl is out, and it is time we should break up, gentlemen," said Jonathan, starting at hearing a distant cock crow.   "There is much business to be done to-morrow.   No doubt numerous applications will be made at my office for the recovery of the stolen plate.   We must be on the alert.   The girl having so fortunately effected her escape, thanks to the bravery and genius of our young friend, Sheppard, there is no clue to the authors of the abstraction; so we may expect to make a pretty market.   Let all betake themselves in peace to their retreats."

" Yes, but not before my friends GIZZARD and THORAX have accompanied me in my favorite 'Three Man's Song,' The 'Cock Crow,' said Mr. Nightingal. That Rooster, alluding to the wakeful chanticleer he had just heard, reminds me very oppor-*tune*-ly." Here in conjunction with Messrs. Gizzard and Thorax, he struck up the following reminiscence of the old song, which at that time was rather a favorite.

The Cock Crow.
THREE MAN'S SONG.

1.

Start not! 'tis but the *first* Cock crow
    That hails the break of day,
He does but sound his clarion so
    To scare foul things away ;
'Tis only ghosts and fiends should part,
    No need have we to go ;
The glass that gladdens most the heart,
    Fills at the first Cock crow.

2.

Stir not, 'tis but the *second* Cock,
    He does but rouse the air,
In sport, to mock the village clock
    And warn us to prepare ;
'Tis a fond draught, as rare as brief,
    Snatched from the grasp of woe ;
We christen pleasure, and drown grief,
    At the Cock's blithe second Crow.

3.

But, hark ! I hear the *third* Cock crow ;
    Fill up ! we must away,
That call but sounds to let us know
    That it is perfect day.

> The reign of revel now is past,
>   See morning's ruddy glow ;
> One bumper then—the fullest—last,
>   For 'tis the third Cock crow !

"Very well, very well sung, indeed, Mr. Nightingal," said Mr. Wild, " but come, it is time to be off lads, good night, good night! Come, Abraham."

" Ay, ay," said Mr. Nightingal, " good night:" and observing two or three of the company in a very blissful state of intoxication, he sung part of the witches' chorus in Macbeth, which he waggishly altered for the occasion, and which he made run thus :

" We fly by night with *lots of spirits,*"

A general leave-taking here ensued ; the party retired to their several abiding places—the major part to dream over fresh schemes of plunder, while Jack stole to his garret, to enjoy once more in sleep the vision of the enchanting milk-maid.

———

The news of Bess's escape from the roundhouse was early spread abroad the following day, and excited much surprise and chagrin. Suspicion had fallen on her, in consequence of her having been seen in frequent communication with the villains who had afterwards so severely beaten Mr. David Lloyd, and carried off the plate ; and it was ascertained, on inquiry, that the written recommendation of a lady at Norwood, upon the faith of which she had been engaged in the milkman's service, was a false one, no such lady being known

at Norwood, or in any of the adjacent villages. Fortunately for Jack, Mr. Hannibal Guffin's regard
for his own character as a man of valour and discretion did not permit him to give a very correct
version of his prisoner's escape; consequently, detection was out of the question. The beadle affirm-
ing that Bess had been rescued by at least ten or
twelve powerful men armed with bludgeons, with
whom he had held a fearful combat of nearly half
an hour, much to their damage, before he sank
under the force of numbers; he was handsomely
rewarded by the parish board for his courage and
sufferings; and there being thus no trace, the
affair of the escape speedily died away.

As Jonathan foretold, applications were immediately made at his office for the recovery of the
stolen property. Mr. Wood, Mrs. Partington, and
David Lloyd, the poor milkman, all met there at
one time; and a very ludicrous scene of lamenta-
tion and reproach was the consequence. The poor
milkman, whose cows had been impounded by the
pawnbroker, to whom he had given bond to secure
the value of the plate that had been borrowed from
him, and who had been threatened with what he
called actions " *of clover*," from the different customers who had lent their property to him, particularly his countryman Mr. Wood, and Mrs. Partington, was very nigh having the coat torn off his
back by the latter amiable persons. Jonathan, however, interfered with his usual philanthropy, and,

N

on the promise of adequate reward being paid, assured them he had but little doubt of tracing the horrid villains who had perpetrated the robbery; that Mrs. Wood should have her civic tea-pot and spoons returned; that the pawnbroker's property should be redeemed, though he did not exactly pledge himself to this; and that Mr. Kneebone's plate should be restored, without a leg having been removed from his escutcheon. This latter assurance particularly gratified Mrs. Partington, though she observed she knew very well it would be the case; for a gipsy man in her neighbourhood, whom she had accidentally met coming out· of the " White Lion," had assured her, on consulting him, that if she applied at the respectable office of Mr. Jonathan Wild, in the Old Bailey, she would be certain, through his means, of having the property restored to her; that the gipsies never told wrong.

Weeks passed away—the property was of course regained on being paid for; but from the moment that Jack saw the beautiful Bess, his value as a good and industrious apprentice was gone: he could think of nothing, pin himself down to nothing in the way of business—his mind was wholly absorbed with her image. Mr. Wood's irritability was roused by Jack's negligence, and frequent quarrels were the consequence, from which Jack invariably retired for refuge to the back parlour of the hospitable and harmonious Mr. Nightingal. Blueskin was not long in obtaining the secret of Jack's heart, and readily promised his good offices to find out, if possible, where the beautiful milkmaid had been conveyed to, after her escape with Jack. He was as good as his word. Not long after Jack had disclosed his love, this true friend one day sought him with a look of unusual exultation.

" Tip us your daddle, my covey," said he, " it's all as right as a trivet ; I've found her out."

" Who—who ?" eagerly asked Jack.

" Why the pretty bit of goods who helped us to speak to the garland last May-day."

" Ah !" exclaimed Jack, transported, " the beauteous creature I rescued from the round-house ?"

" Herself, my Trojan," returned Mr. Blueskin ; " and, what's more, all ready to jump into your arms ; I can tell you that."

" Delightful, delightful !" cried Jack, in ecstacy. " Blueskin, you are a true friend ! But where is the charmer ?"

" Ah, where is she," slily echoed Blueskin ; " that's the secret,"—and here he winked very significantly—" and a secret worth knowing, too."

" Do not trifle with an old pal, I conjure you !" earnestly exclaimed Jack. " For heaven's sake, if you really do know where she is to be found, disclose it instantly. I have never known a moment's rest since I saw her—she has been my dream by night, my thought by day."

" And now she may be your doxey by night

N 2

and your *dell* by day, if you only play your cards rightly," said Blueskin. " Listen to me ;—but you must stand a dram for my giving you the office."

" Any thing, even to my soul's salvation ;— only tell me!" exclaimed Jack, in an impassioned manner.

" Well, well," said Blueskin, apparently moved by his earnestness, " not to keep you in suspense, then, I happened to have a little business with one of our gentlemen to 'speak to a ken'[a] at Norwood the other day. It was a 'put up affair';[b] and it being rather necessary we should go cautiously to work, as the old cove of the castle was known to keep ' barking irons all ready fed'[c] in his ' snooze,'[d] and did not want for pluck to give them tongue[e] whenever there should be occasion for it, we were obliged to lie snug in the neighbourhood till the 'Johnny Raw,'[f] who was our pal, and was to go ' regulars,'[g] ' nosed'[h] to us when the coast was clear. So, by way of passing the time in a gentlemanlike manner, we thought we'd amuse ourselves with a little shooting in some of the preserves round the neighbourhood, ' bag a few short ones,'[i] and ' wire a long one,'[k] or so, for a friend in Romeville.[l] So, ram-

[a] Break open a house.
[b] A planned robbery in which the servants are concerned.
[c] Loaded pistols.
[d] Bed-room.
[e] Fire them.

[f] Footman.
[g] Share in the booty.
[h] Gave information.
[i] Partridges.
[k] Snare a hare.
[l] London.

bling about the woods, who the old one should we fall in with but Black Martin's gang of Romaners."

" Romaners !" cried Jack, not as yet wholly understanding Mr. Blueskin's mystic *cabala* ; " and who the plague are they ?"

" What ! don't you know? well you are an innocent ! Why, gipsies, to be sure—the palming tribe. Being " the season of the year," there they were, all of them, ' Ben Morts,'[m] and ' Abram men,'[n] mixed together under the bushes as gay as larks, and as merry as sand boys. Of course it was all ' Oli Compoli,'[o] with lads of the right stamp like us. 'The Dimber Dambers'[p] were as pleased as so many trouts to see us, and invited us to a boozing bout, when Oliver ' whiddled,'[q] in their leaf palace down in the three-tree dingle. You may be sure we did not fail to join company,—we'd too good a taste for the stock pot ; we knew too well what Pharaoh's lean kine was, to do that. When, never trust me, among the 'Autem Morts,'[r] and 'Dimber Dells,'[s] who should we clap our ogles on, the very first thing, but your pretty milkmaid. Yes, there she was, all amongst the tawny ones, looking for all the world like a lily among so many marigolds; and, what's more, there she is still."

Jack was overjoyed at this information ; he

[m] Fine Girls.
[n] Impostors.
[o] All right.
[p] Pretty Fellows.

[q] Moonlight.
[r] Married women.
[s] Pretty girls.

expended his last farthing in a bowl of punch on
the strength of it ; and asked a thousand questions
respecting his charmer—who she was, what she did
there, how she became mixed up with the robbery,
when he could see her, &c.; to all which Mr. Blueskin answered with becoming frankness and friendship; from which Jack gathered, that she was an
orphan, under the protection of Zara, the queen of
the gipsies, and was known among the gang by the
name of Edgeworth Bess, from her having been
born in Edgeworth;* that during the temporary
absence of the queen, Black Martin, the generalis-
simo of the tribe, and potentate, in default of Zara,
had, at the instigation of Jonathan Wild, procured
her an engagement in the service of David Lloyd,
the milkman, and had given her instructions by
which she was unconsciously made the instrument
of the robbery of that unfortunate Cambrian's
May-day garland, her participation in which had
thrown her into the confinement from whence Jack
had rescued her. In answer to Jack's further interrogatories, as to when he could visit her, Blueskin pacified his impatience with the intelligence
that they could never have a more favourable
chance than presented itself at that very juncture;
that the old queen, Zara, was then again absent,
on some state business of her people, and that
Black Martin would receive him with open arms.

"I care not for Black Martin," laughed Jack,

* Now called Edgware.

" but pretty Bess. It is too late to set off for Norwood to night, but I will procure leave of absence from old Wood ; or if he won't grant it me, take French leave, and start with you the first thing to-morrow morning."

" I am yours, to the backbone," said Mr. Blueskin. " To-morrow morning !—be it. Bess will be delighted to see you."

" I will die rather than fail," said Jack ; and with this understanding, after draining the bowl, they parted company.

CHAPTER XII.

JACK SHEPPARD, A HOUSEBREAKER.

LOVE AND DESPERATION.—THE GIPSY ENCAMPMENT.— ROBBERY OF MR. BAINS.

LONG before it was light the following morning—for he could not sleep, thinking of his charmer—Jack was up; and having procured a day's holiday from Mr. Wood, under pretence that he wanted to visit his mother, who was dangerously ill, and had sent for him, he repaired to the residence of Mr. Blueskin, which was, at that time, in the sanctuary of the Old Mint in the Borough, that gentleman honouring a back garret in the Maze with his particular sojourn, in company with another gentleman known by the name of Tom Trick Tyburn, from the dexterity with which he had, at various times, escaped conviction for capital offences. Routing out his friend, and procuring a morning dram at the flash house of the master of the Mint, Jack, with Mr. Blueskin, started for Norwood. It was a lovely summer's morning. Emerging from the murky recesses of the Mint, at that time the usual retreat of profligate debtors, suspected felons, and bad characters of every description, they were soon on the high road to their place of destination.

Jack's heart was more than usually buoyant at the thought of so soon meeting the beautiful object of his affections; he laughed, sung, jumped, and committed a thousand extravagances. Mr. Blueskin, who was more phlegmatic, proceeded with greater prudence, cautiously peeping in at the doors of the different cottages as he passed along, having determined, if he found any of them without their tenants, to make the said tenants pay for their negligence, by the abstraction of any little article that might present itself.

"There's nothing like reading people a practical lesson," said he: "words go for nothing; but the loss of their property they never forget."

This was a maxim he had learnt from the judicious Mr. Wild. They made their way across Kennington Common, and passed the gibbets where, to mark the civilisation of the country at that period, were suspended in irons the mouldering carcasses of two notorious footpads and murderers, who had been executed there some years previously, and whom they did not either of them affect to notice, till they came to the somewhat straggling village of Brixton, celebrated in our own time for the virtue of its *mill*, by which many disorders are often corrected, and old offenders comparatively ground young again. It had, then, no such blessing. Refreshing themselves with a cool tankard at a pleasant road-side alehouse, the only one Brixton then possessed, they pushed forward to the beautiful resort of Tulse Hill. Passing under the refreshing shade of its umbrageous trees, and catching glimpses as they went of two or three of those snug, comfortable looking boxes to which our wealthy citizens retire, that they may enjoy the fruits of their early industry in the pleasing leisure of age, and which seemed, as Mr. Blueskin emphatically remarked, only built on purpose to be *cracked*,* they reached at length the object of their wishes; the verdant vales, the bosky dingles, and gently rising slopes of Norwood unveiled themselves before them—we need not say to our hero's high content and gratification.

" Well, here we are at last, my Romeo," said Mr. Blueskin. " This is the favourite retreat of the sibyls; this is the spot to learn your fortunes in, and have the stars and planets read for you— the Fates can't keep any secrets here."

Jack was well aware that the secret of his destiny would be here unravelled.

" But let us look out for the gipsy's standard," continued Mr. Blueskin. " Ah! there it is waving in the air, above that clump of trees, there; I twig it."

" I see no flag," impatiently returned Jack.

" Where are your ogles, then ?" retorted Blue-

* Broken open.

skin. " Don't you see that thin spiral column of blue smoke, that's losing itself in the sky there ? That's the gipsies' flag, my boy; and see, here's one of their advanced outposts,"—pointing to a wiry-looking long-faced cur, with a peculiar significance of countenance, that was approaching towards them, his eye glistening with satisfaction as he sniffed Blueskin, while his tail was fastly wagging behind him in token of amity. " We shall not be long now before we stumble on a sentinel who will conduct us to the camp," said he, returning the dog's caress with a friendly pat. " Good boy, Fox, good boy ! It's all right—he's a friend :" seeing the animal sniffing Jack. " On with you, Fox—he'll lead us into the right path, Jack, never fear that ; but we are not on a wrong scent, if I may trust my nose—what a savoury odour ! almost makes one hungry only smelling it. Ah ! there's nothing like the flesh pots of Egypt, my boy; I am quite longing for a glass of Usquebaugh, and a dive into the general kettle; sure to bring up the thigh of a partridge, the back of a hare, or the leg of some barn-door rooster."

Jack's love had quite taken away his appetite, and he did not enjoy in perspective the promised delicacies so greatly as his companion.

The dog now bounded quickly before them, barking, and tossing his head in the air with unusual liveliness and vigour; and presently afterwards the hum of many voices was heard, and a man suddenly appeared at an opening in the thicket before them, as if to challenge their approach.

"Ah! by the Hookey, here's Black Martin himself," shouted Blueskin. "Welcome, Duke, welcome! His grace is duke of Lesser Egypt, Jack," said he in a side wind to our hero, " and a rum duke he is, too. I've brought a friend to visit you—one of the right sort—as *jannock* as steel."

"Welcome, young Sir," gruffly muttered out Black Martin, a tall bony man, of swarthy aspect, with matted black hair, and garments of very uncouth, but not unpicturesque, appearance, "You're welcome to Three-tree Dingle. Being a pal of Mr. Blueskin, you cannot but be a *Ben Cove*. This way, this way."

Jack's heart throbbed quickly as they entered into the *sanctum sanctorum* of the tribe. His eye glanced with the rapidity of lightning over the motley crew that then presented themselves, and as quickly rested its gaze, with fixed intensity, on the lovely features of his inamorato. Yes, there she stood, looking in her little straw hat, her gay 'kerchief, neat stuff petticoat, and smart red cloak, if possible, still more bewitching than when tricked out, as he had last seen her, in all her May-day finery.

"Ah!" said she, recognising him in an instant, and blushing deeply as she encountered his enamoured gaze, "my preserver! my deliverer! Welcome, welcome!"

" What !" cried Martin, " is this the *Ben Kin-chin cove* that delivered Bess from the Philistines, broke open her prison, let her out of limbo ?—Why didn't you tell me this before, Blueskin ? He shall have Freeman's key here, and no mistake." 'Encouraged by the gipsy chief's approbation of Jack's visit, Bess had by this time ventured to advance towards him, and cordially offered her hand : Jack covered it with a shower of kisses. Bess's example was followed by almost all the members of the swarthy race : men, women, and children, all greeted Jack with much warmth ; and many a sparkling black eye, and clear brown cheek, beneath which the rich blood mantled, till it assumed the ripe blush of some mellow pear, slily smiled approbation on him for his gallantry and manhood in rescuing their companion. The chief declared that in honour of Jack's visit the day should be a holiday ; and some patient donkeys that were browsing under the boughs, waiting to set forth on their usual foraging excursions, were immediately unpanniered—the fire under a huge kettle that was mystically suspended from three sticks in the centre of the hollow, or dingle, as it was termed, was replenished, a cloth of snowy whiteness was spread on the grass by Bess, cups of horn, some pewter platters, with knives and forks, and spoons, the latter of silver—probably the produce of plunder—were arranged in due order. Jack was invited to take a seat—which was assigned to him, out of compliment to his heroism—by the side of the fair creature he had rescued. It need hardly be said that he did not want to be asked twice to take it. Some flasks of usquebaugh and a keg of humming ale were produced from a leathern budget, together with some brown bread; and the kettle, from which issued a rich steam of all savoury odours—capons, partridges, pheasants, hares, rabbits, celery, onions, thyme, sweet marjoram, and a few lumps of salted pork—was unhooked from its supporters, and separately borne round to all present, that they might help themselves to as much as they chose of its contents. Bess, whose experience in angling in this palatable caldron was greater, and her dexterity more perfect than could be expected of her companion, had soon supplied his plate with a delicious knuckle of ham, the breast of a pheasant, and the wings of a fine capon, with a proportionate quantity of the rich soup and its vegetable ingredients. But half her care was thrown away; Jack could eat but little: he was too much occupied in feasting his eyes on her ever-varying beauties, and pouring into her ear, in rude but fervent terms, his admiration—his delight. Perceiving how much they were occupied with each other, the chief forbore to task Jack's attention; and the rest of the tribe, in conformity with their general rule never to spoil sport, turned their notice from the lovers —for such they had both by unconscious consent

become—and directed their cares to the usquebaugh and ale, and some nuts and apples, which
served to finish their repast. A variety of gipsy
songs, in praise of poaching, fortune-telling, and
similar subjects, then went round, during which
Jack found abundant opportunity to declare his
passion for his beautiful companion, and receive
her blushing avowal in return that he was not
indifferent to her. The afternoon advancing, an
old fellow with a white beard, who had said grace
at their banquet, and who, it appeared, was the
PATRICO, or priest, of the beggar part of the tribe,
produced from a bag a cracked fiddle. A general
shout of " A dance! a dance!" arose, the pan-
niers were stowed away, the sward was cleared,
the inspiring tones of *Money-musk* were struck
up, and every toe was immediately in action.

Jack had, of course, for his partner his charming
companion, Bess; and Mr. Blueskin was honoured
with the brown hand of Mrs. Mary Maggot, an
Amazonian Autem Mort of the tribe. Bess's grace
and fascination in dancing have been before noticed;
but on this occasion she outshone herself. As he
whirled the lovely girl over the smooth sward,
Jack's brain grew giddy with rapture, and he felt
a corresponding gloom steal over his mind, when
the advancing shades of night warned him it was
time to bend his steps back again to town. He
had enjoyed one perfect day of happiness—but
happiness has more limited bounds than misery.

There are infinite varieties of wretchedness and modes of sorrow; the pleasurable sensations are but few—love, fame, friendship, competence, parental affection, and religious contentment, make up the sum of worldly enjoyment. Jack had tasted transport and rapture, the fulfilment of hope, the nourishment of desire. He turned to bid farewell to his companions—his regret in doing so, tempered by the remembrance of the pleasure he had experienced. The tribe accompanied him and Blueskin to the limits of the thicket in which their retreat was situated, Black Martin expressing his earnest wish that they might speedily see Jack again; and pretty Bess, as she tenderly pressed his hand, bedewing it with a tear, and, with a half-choked voice, affectionately bidding him farewell.

On their way to town, Blueskin provokingly fed Jack's willing fancy by repeated eulogiums on the beauty of Bess, adroitly drawing a picture of the happiness that might be enjoyed with so rare a creature, by any young fellow of spirit, who had the means and leisure to devote himself to her society: he then contrasted this by speculating upon the little chance there was of any one, in the station of a mechanic, arriving at such a blessing. His words, which were apparently uttered without intention, made a deep impression on Jack's mind, and he fell into a fit of profound abstraction. When they at length arrived in Wych Street, he declined visiting Mr. Nightingal's house that night, and immediately retired to rest, telling Mr. Wood, as he bade him good-night, that he had found his mother better. He rose the next morning not much refreshed: his sleep had been broken and troubled; and his dreams, if the truth must be told, though chiefly occupied with the angel semblance of the lovely milkmaid, were fraught, at least, with as much of bad as good.

The employment of his trade became henceforward more irksome to Jack than ever. It has been said that idleness is the nurse of love: it certainly is as much the offspring as the nurse. Jack's passion rendered him indolent and inattentive; he thought of nothing but the beautiful Bess; and delighted to bask away the hours in alehouses, skittle-grounds, and similar retreats, musing on her image. Mr. Wood, who, not to speak it profanely, was, like a great many of his countrymen, rather wooden-headed, and knew little of his craft beyond common jobbing, had long felt and acknowledged the superiority of his apprentice, confiding to his skill and vigour all work requiring any degree of dexterity and enterprise, rewarding him with a liberal commission on the profits of his labours for his pains.

It was with no small degree of vexation and anger that Mr. Wood all at once found his main prop failing him: complaints of negligence and carelessness became the order of the day; customers grew impatient and indignant; and business

o

threatened to leave the honest Cambrian quite as quickly as it had, through Jack's exertions, increased. Frequent visits to Norwood left jobs unfinished and calls unanswered. For some time Jack accounted for the frequency of his absence, by saying it was necessary, in order to acquire a more perfect knowledge of some of the finishing branches of the art, that he should work with experienced artisans, and that therefore he undertook various jobs in the country gratuitously, in order that he might get an insight into things. This did very well for some time.

" Put, passions of hur heart, Jack," one day exclaimed honest Owen, " you neet not pe apsent all *nights:* you cannot pe at work in your sleep, though, Cot's poty, you too often sleep over your work. This must pe amentet, look you. Hur is afrait it is some very improper *joinery* you are apout when you are apsent. Charity pekins at home, Jack ; you shoult attent to hur costomers first ; as to learning the craft, Cot pless hur, hur is afrait you know too much of the craft, Jack. Hur will have hur work tone, look you, or hur will know the reasons why."

Jack took little heed of these remonstrances ; he had become a favourite guest with the gipsies, and Bess's passion soon grew as ardent as his own. This lovely creature was a singular instance of unconscious purity existing in the very circle of contagion ; from her very infancy she had been used to the details of acts of plunder and deception, till she accounted them as matters of course, as things of general practice, and listened to them without either reprobation or surprise. But though she passed over them so lightly in others, there was a certain consciousness of right and wrong within herself, that would have led her to shrink from the slightest action contrary to the strictest morality,—she was a gem, where all around was dark and worthless—a well of hidden waters in a desert, where all was blight and barrenness. As foul things shun the light, it seemed as if vice and contagion, though moving continually around her, recoiled from her contact, and left her pure and undefiled. In her communion, the hours passed with Jack as moments; their young love, as yet unstained, untroubled, was a dream of golden sunshine; but the clouds were gathering around them —the storm was lowering in the distance.

On his return from one of these sweet, but furtive, visits, he was summoned by Mr. Wood to accompany him to Ball's Pond, in the neighbourhood of Islington, to execute some repairs in the house of a customer, whose patience had been nearly exhausted by Jack's repeated procrastination, and who came now peremptorily to demand completion of his work, threatening, that if any further delay took place, he should immediately employ some other person.

Mr. Wood was in a very ill-humour, which he

oddly enough manifested by a variety of guttural sounds, which he persuaded himself was singing. He growled out, in Welsh, a pennill in favour of St. David's virtues, which he intermixed with execrations on Jack's bad conduct. Jack's conscience smote him, and, gathering his tools together, he determined to make up, by extra diligence, for his past misbehaviour. Repairing, with his master and Griffith Thomas, to Ball's Pond, he set to work in such good earnest, that, long ere the afternoon was over, to the great astonishment of the owner of the house, the whole of the repairs, which would have occupied an ordinary workman at least three days, were completed in the most masterly and finished manner. This should have been sufficient to have restored harmony—but we have said that Mr. Wood was in an ill-humour. By a strange perversity of human nature, that which should have destroyed his anger, only increased it. The exhibition of what Jack could do, did but make Mr. Wood the more angry that he had delayed doing it so long, and did not even do more. He retired, very grumpily, to a public house in Islington, kept by one Britt, and known by the name of the Rising Sun; here, as they were all in need of refreshment, he ordered Jack and Griffith Thomas a pint of small drink, and a halfpenny loaf each; while he solaced himself with a quart of the strongest ale, accompanied by some sea biscuits, which the landlord produced as a rarity, with a very respectable piece of cheese and a good sized bunch of leeks.

Jack by no means relished the lenten entertainment that had been assigned to him ; he, however, said nothing, thinking that his master would recover his good-humour in time. As for the dolt Griffith Thomas, he would have been satisfied if the small drink had only been water.

Dipping the head of a leek in some salt, and accompanying it with a large lump of cheese, Mr. Wood now commenced his meal, washing every mouthful down with a copious draught of ale, singing meanwhile, as if to cover his ill humour, the favourite pennil of the leek, which he did to the harmonious air known by the name of " Difyrwch - y - Frenhines," or " The Queen's Fancy." and which ran thus :—

The Leek.

1.

" Of all that springs from mother earth,
 Commend me to the Leek :
Nature gives nought more precious birth,
 Its praise Bards well may speak ;
In fruit, and flower, for rarer worth,
 Mankind will vainly seek.

2.

" Let England for her Red Rose shout,
 Scots o'er their Thistle grin,
Ireland her Shamrock boast about,
 The Leek the prize will win ;
For 'tis an ornament without,
 And *very good* WITHIN."

Mr. Wood suited the action to the word, by immediately engulphing one of his favourite leeks, which he did with an air of determination sufficiently marking his stifled choler. Finding nothing was to be got by silence, Jack plucked up resolution, reminded Mr. Wood that he had had a hard day's work, and that the refreshment provided for him was not of a nature greatly calculated to recruit his exhausted strength, ventured to request that he would, as usual, allow him something, by way of commission for what he had done, that he might procure some better entertainment for himself.

" Cot's ploot, you idle tog !" cried the aroused Cambrian, " allow you commissions for what you have tone ! Will you allow me commissions for what you have not tone? look you, tell me tat : you are a goot for nothing fillain, ant coes to your alehouses, your White and Plack Lions and other apominations insteat of toing hur work ; put hur will not put up with it." Here he began to sing something in praise of striking the harp, to which he added, in an under tone, something about his intention of striking Jack, if he did not mend his manners.

Jack could hold out no longer, but resolved at once to break all squares with his master. " If I do neglect my business," said Jack, " aint it your own fault ? you are not able to teach it me : I am sure I work like a horse sometimes."

" Ant like an ass, look you, at other times,"
cried the enraged Cambrian. " Not teach you
your pusiness ! Put you are right, or you woult
not talk to hur in this way, hur that is a shentle-
man porn and tescented from the great Catwallatar himself : if hur hat taught you your pusiness
properly, hur shoult have taught you petter manners, look you : put hur will speak to the Champerlain apout it ; you shall be privately whipped,
and publicly reprimanted for your insolences ant
tisrespects, look you."

" I don't care for you, nor the Chamberlain
either," growled Jack surlily, " nor old Cadwalla-
dar into the bargain,—some old Put, I dare say,
like yourself, never satisfied with any thing."

" What !" screamed Mr. Wood, almost inarti-
culate with passion, " not care for Catwallatar,—
old Putt,—hur will make you rememper these
plasphemies ; look you ; only let hur get at you !"
Here darting suddenly on Jack, he caught him by
the hair.

" Hold off," cried Jack, fiercely, " or by the
living God you shall repent it !"

" Ah ! to you tare to threaten, tog ?" roared
out the carpenter, pot-valiant ; " take that." Here
he aimed a smart cuff at Jack's dexter listener.
Disengaging himself from his master's grasp, with
the velocity of lightning, Jack, aroused to a pitch
of fury, returned the blow with a force and good
will, that immediately stretched his opponent over

the chair, on the floor, where his sconce coming in
contact with the ale-can, that had fallen in the
scuffle, he was very near showing more of his
brains than was absolutely necessary to attest his
knowledge.

" Mercy of Cot, hur is murteret—her is murteret?" cried the prostrate Welshman: " put let
the fillain pe securet ; hur will have him hanget
ant quarteret ; striking a master is petty treason,
mark tat: hur will have his heat on Temple Par.
—Knock the scountrel town, Griffith Thomas,—
ton't let the fillain escape.—Murter ! murter ?"

Doubtful of the extent of the mischief he had
occasioned, Jack here thought it prudent to de-
camp: accordingly, jumping out of the window,—
(they were in the back parlour), he made his way
across the skittle-ground, and over a ditch in the
rear of the premises, which conducted him to some
fields ; and very soon arrived, unpursued, in London. His first step was to see how the land lay in
the house of his master. It may easily be conceived, he was in no very amiable mood of mind.
The first person he met with was Madam Wood,
who received him with a volley of matronly reproaches. She had learnt from Taffleen, that a
young female had been that morning inquiring
after Jack, and demanded how he dared have any
creatures come after him in a decent respectable
house like hers.

" By your indentures, Sir," said she, " you are

bound to attend to no other female than your mistress, who, being at years of discretion, and of a proper age, knows how to treat young fellows properly."

Jack muttered something, that she might be the reverse of blessed, and proceeded to the carpenter's yard at the side of the house, when his passions were instantly aroused by the sudden appearance of Bess.

" Oh ! Jack, Jack !" she exclaimed, rushing towards him, " save me ! save me !"

" Explain yourself, dear girl," hastily cried Jack ; " what means this alarm ?"

" They will tear me from you, dear Jack !" answered the maiden. " Our Queen has sent a suitor."

" Ah ! the hag Zara ?" rejoined Jack, fiercely.

" Yes, yes, my adopted mother; she would have me wedded, Jack—wedded to another—a hateful man who follows, who pursues me. Ah ! he is here !" she shrieked, suddenly seeing some one.— " Save me ! save me !" She threw herself into Jack's arms.

Turning his eyes in the direction to which she had pointed, Jack now saw a young fellow in the undress of a foot soldier entering.

" So, I have you, Bess !" exclaimed he, exultingly ; " you won't escape me this time."

He was advancing towards the poor girl, when Jack, stung by rage and jealousy, having no other

means of stopping him, restrained as he was by
his fair burthen, hurled a small lathe, which happened to be in his hand, at the intruder with
all his force.   Unfortunately, the soldier adroitly
ducking down, the missile took effect on the portly
person of Madam Wood, who was at that moment
entering to see what was the matter, and grazing
her left cheek in its passage, gave occasion for the
application of a beauty spot of rather more unseemly dimensions than those she usually wore.
She hastily screamed out murder, at the very top
of her voice, till the entrance of Taffleen allowed
of her fainting in that maiden's arms, in a safe and
dignified manner.   Bess had extricated herself from
Jack's embrace on the first alarm, and, with the
swiftness of the affrighted dove, had made good
her escape, while her lover and his rival were most
affectionately engaged in ascertaining the exact
diameter of each other's wind-pipes.   It was not
until there was some doubt which was the black-
est, the face or the hat of the intruding soldier,
that Jack unlocked his loving grasp, and suffered
his foe to beat a retreat ; an example which he himself immediately followed, leaving Taffleen busily
engaged in singeing Madam Wood's nose with
sundry fumigations of burnt feathers, brown
paper, &c.

Unable to obtain any trace of the route of his
fair enslaver, Jack bent his steps in search of
his staunch friend and counsellor, Blueskin, and

fortunately found him taking his siesta in Mr. Nightingal's back parlour. From Blueskin Jack obtained confirmation of pretty Bess's tidings, that a suitor had been sent by Zara, in the person of the soldier, with a mandate to Black Martin, that he should be received as her future husband : the arrival of her Majesty herself to witness the consummation of the nuptials was daily expected.

"Things are all as queer as Dick's hatband, Jack," continued Blueskin, "and, strike me funny, if the wench won't slip through your fingers, if you don't mind. You have only one chance, and that is, to try the effect of a little oil of palm* with the gang—make the girl your own at once: fifteen or twenty quid† now might do the trick; but where's that to be got?—I haven't a mag."‡

Jack's brain was all on fire, his senses in a whirl.

"Say no more," said he; something shall be done; but where is Bess?—Where can she have fled to?"

"Oh! she's safe enough, never fear that. Poll Maggot was waiting for her, and she'll take care of her—Poll's a match for half a dozen such swaddies§ as that rival of yours—no doubt they have returned to the camp."

"No doubt, no doubt!" said Jack, wildly; "will you promise me one thing, Blueskin?"

"What is it?" asked that worthy.

"That you will be ready to start with me to Norwood by day-break to-morrow morning.

* Bribery.   † Guinea.   ‡ Halfpenny.   § Foot soldiers.

" Why, what then have you resolved upon ?"
said Blueskin, with an air of affected carelessness.

" Ask me not, I know not !" answered Jack,
desperately, " only say that you will meet me."

" I will—in the Mint," coolly replied Blueskin.

" Enough !" said Jack, gratefully squeezing
his hand. " Bess shall be mine to-morrow, if I
swing for it the day afterwards."

With these words Jack rushed out of the room.

" Wheugh ! Tol lol de diddle doll !" sung
Blueskin.

" Buz quoth the blue fly, hum quoth the bee,"
sung Mr. Nightingal, entering at the moment ; if
that young fellow don't show his indentures a fair
pair of heels, before he's four and twenty hours
older, I'm no conjuror." The gentlemen emptied
a jug, on the strength of the prophecy, and parted.

Unable to resolve on any settled course, Jack
wandered about till he found himself in White
Horse Yard, in Drury Lane, a narrow turning,
secluded enough from observation, and chiefly
occupied, as it is to this day, by piece-brokers,
persons who deal in remnants of cloth, stuff, &c.
Here it occurred to him, that he had a job to
finish in the house of Mr. Baines, one of this fraternity ; and without any precise intention he entered that gentleman's shop, and proceeded to
accomplish his task : among other things he had
to repair the shutters of the shop ; whilst engaged
in this employment, seeing the quantity of rolls

of fustian, and other property scattered about the shop, and perceiving, on Mr. Baines casually unlocking the till, that it contained a quantity of money, the thought all at once flashed across him, that here would be an easy opportunity of effecting all his wishes. His resolution was immediately taken: minutely inspecting the premises, he soon saw in what way an entrance was best to be effected; all the bars and fastenings of Mr. Baines s shop he purposely made more secure than ever, to that gentleman's great satisfaction.

" I'll defy any scoundrel to break into my shop now, said that gentleman, " thanks to your skill and pains, my honest lad; there's a shilling for you to drink.

Jack's plan was soon laid. Leaving the piece-broker, he loitered about the neighbourhood till twelve o'clock at night; during his rambles, he, unnoticed, heard some of the neighbours talking of the desperate attempt he had made to murder his master and mistress; he had the satisfaction, however, of finding that Mr. Wood had walked home, and retired to rest, and that Mrs. Wood had required nothing more from the doctor than a large piece of sticking-plaster and an extra bottle of sal volatile.

It was the night of the first of August, 1716!— we like to be particular in dates. The hundreds of Drury were more than ordinarily peaceable, and notwithstanding the stars shone brightly, and there was a new moon, the narrowness of White Horse Yard, in which the shop was situated, kept the houses in partial gloom. Following the watchman to his box, and waiting till that functionary had comfortably composed himself to sleep in his nightcap, Jack stole to the scene of action; he knew that he should be uninterrupted for half an hour at least; the coast was clear, all was dark and still. In the pavement, in front of Mr. Baines's shop, was a grating of wooden rails, forming a sort of area, which conducted to a cellar underneath the shop, from whence access could be obtained to any other part of the house. Jack's heart beat quickly as he surveyed it, and, stooping down, he was about to commence operations, when, just at that moment, the well-known chimes of St. Clement's announced the half hour after midnight, by playing the solemn and beautiful melody of the Hundred and fourth psalm,

" My Soul, praise the Lord!" As the sounds, borne on the night breeze, caught his ear, Jack started, and paused for a few moments irresolute: he remembered the words he had so often heard sung to that tune :—

> " With glory adorn'd,
> His people shall sing
> To God, who their beds
> With safety does shield."

He was about to abandon his sinful purpose when

the sounds died away in the listening silence.—
The thoughts of losing his pretty Bess, and the
prospect of securing her for ever, flashed across
his mind ; his guardian Angel deserted him, and
he resumed his intentions.   With a chisel, the
handle of which he muffled, and a muffled mallet,
he proceeded softly and cautiously to loosen the
wooden bars ;   he dexterously drew out the nails,
and, as he was remarkably strong in the wrist, and
skilful in the apt application of his tools, he had
in ten minutes, without any disturbance, removed
the bars, and obtained entrance into the house. Cautiously making his way up the cellar stairs, he
found the back door of the shop locked : to shoot
back the bolt, with one so skilful as himself, was
but the work of a moment.   A small skeleton key,
a keepsake from Mr. Blueskin, on which Jack
set great store, effected this last operation without
noise or violence.   Producing a light from a phos-
phorus box, he now proceeded to take stock of the
shop.   In the till, the lock of which soon yielded
to his ingenuity, he found about seventeen pounds
in money, which he was not long in conveying to
a place of greater security : he then ransacked the
stores and selected a variety of the choicest stuffs,
and best cloths as presents to the gang.   Having
loaded himself with as much as he could conveniently carry, he began to retrace his steps :
shooting the bolts of the locks back again, he
made his way through the cellar, leaving every-

thing in appearance exactly as he had found it The wooden bars he replaced, and nailed down again in the most workmanlike manner, so that no one could perceive they had been removed; and long before one o'clock, he by the aid of a latch key had made his way, undiscovered, to his truckle bed in the garret of Mr. Wood. This was Jack Sheppard's *first burglary*.

CHAPTER XIII.

JACK A ROMONER.

REBELLION IN THE CAMP.—THE GIPSY MARRIAGE.—THE LION AND LIONESS.

DAY had scarcely begun to dawn after the commission of the burglary at Mr. Baines's, when Jack arose: he had merely thrown himself across the bed, and was not over refreshed with his short and broken slumber. Dressing himself with unusual care, he proceeded to arrange and pack up his booty: placing a roll of fustian in his box, which he found inconvenient to carry with him, he made a compact parcel of the other articles, which he slung over his shoulders in the form of a knapsack; then, without having aroused his fellow apprentice, Griffith Thomas, he stole gently down stairs, and quitted his master's house, as it subsequently turned out, for *ever!*

It was not without some feeling of hesitation and regret that Jack closed the door of the house where he had passed the years of his boyhood, though he had formed no intention of not returning; an emotion of compunction stole over him;

P

he remembered Mr. Wood's simple hearted good-nature and honesty of purpose, more than counter-balancing his national choler and occasional iras-cibility—but the die was cast. Endeavouring to persuade himself that he was ashamed of having given way to such weakness, he assumed an air of bravado, and with a more determined step than the occasion seemed to require, swaggered down the Strand, and made the best of his way to the Mint. He found Mr. Blueskin up and ready to receive him: their eyes met on his entrance; a glance passed between them, which explained at once all that had occurred.

" Tip us your bunch of fives, Jack," said Mr. Blueskin, exultingly ; " I see it's all right my trump—the wench shall be yours before the day's out ; I'll carry the swag for you. Well, I always said you'd turn out a good one —I told the governor so long ago—and he was quite of my opinion ; —but what have you got here ?" said he, eagerly undoing the parcel. " Stuffs—cloths !" and here his eyes glistened with the most unctuous expression of gratification. " Why, what dealer in rags ken, have you been speaking to since I saw you last night ?—but no matter, I don't want to know—it's quite sufficient the trick's done. I sup-pose these are not the whole of the assets, are they ? You have got some *rag* of another sort as well, haven't you ? We shan't have to take these to a fence and smash them for browns, shall we ?

There's our old friend, Levy Lawrence, hard by, you know."

" No, no !" said Jack, with a knowing air, " you don't find me such a soft as that ;—look here, my boy !" and he produced a capacious leathern purse, which he had fully lined with the piece-broker's floating capital.

" Well, this is plummy !" said Mr. Blueskin, giving, at the same time, an extraordinary skip ; —" fork us your famble again, Jack—why, there must be a matter of twenty quid there :—a fig for old Zara—Black Martin will soon give that young lobster, your rival, orders to march—yes, yes, he'll have his furlough in no time, be billetted on another town in a twinkling :—why, hang me if I don't lend him a ticket of leave with my own particular pedestal;*—if you don't make the dimber morts and dells' eyes twinkle to-day, why, there's no corn in Egypt, that's all ;—but come along, come along."

Hurrying Jack from the cockloft he honoured with his residence, and spurring themselves on with sundry drams on the road, the pair reached the gipsy camp before the community had assembled to breakfast. Their early arrival created some surprise, but more pleasure. As Blueskin had prognosticated, Bess had, the evening before, returned to the camp, under the convoy of Poll Maggot ; she had been followed by the young soldier, who, not expecting their quarters would have been

* Feet.

beat up so soon, did not then happen to be on guard. Bess flew into Jack's arms; and while they were exchanging those endearments, which can always be better imagined than described, Mr. Blueskin requested a private audience with the gipsy regent, Black Martin.

This illustrious personage having conducted his friend Indigo, as he familiarly termed Mr. Blake, to a snug retreat, under cover of some donkey-carts, a conference was immediately opened. No sooner had Jack's plenipotentiary expressed his friend's wishes, and the means he possessed to carry out their accomplishment. than Black Martin instantly declared himself a rebel—damned his sovereign, Zara, for a hard-hearted old hag, and said. that in five minutes the whole camp should be in a state of mutiny. He proved as good as his word.

Assembling the tribe, he briefly explained to them Jack's views and resources, having previously instructed Mr. Blueskin to be prepared with the subsidies. Jack's parcel was opened, the cloths and stuffs were distributed, and the gang at once declared themselves a commonwealth. Never was a monarchy so easily overturned, nor treason more triumphant: in spite of the ordinances of Queen Zara, it was settled Jack's marriage should take place that very day. The patrico of the crew was summoned, and ordered to hold himself in readiness for the solemnities, an order to which that reverend person expressed his perfect acquiescence.

" Fortunately," said he, " one of our forest ponies died last night : there is nothing, therefore, to forbid the banns ; it is a special license.

A very few moments sufficed to prevail on the blushing Bess to consent to this arrangement : she knew it was her only chance of escape from the hateful union with another about to be forced on her, and easily yielded to Jack's impassioned solicitations. At this juncture her suitor. the soldier, appearing without being aware of the mine about to spring up under his feet, Black Martin beckoned him towards him.

" We have just been holding a court-martial, my friend," said that chief; "finding your presence here contrary to our articles of war, we have resolved that you shall be drummed out of the regiment without military honours : in fact, friend lobster, it is very plain to us you are a spy in our camp; you have been quartered here by mistake, and must be sent to the right-about as soon as possible."

Before the astonished soldier had time to inquire into the cause of this sudden alteration in the sentiments of the gang, he was seized by a couple of sturdy gentlemen, following the profession of tinkers, who, turning his coat inside out, and clapping an old saucepan on his head, by way of helmet, seated him on a donkey, with his face towards the tail; and in this state they conducted him, with much drumming and

hallooing, beyond the boundaries of their encampment, warning him that martial law was proclaimed, and that, if he ever presumed to appear
again in their territories, he would have to run the
gauntlet of the whole gang, without any further
notice.   It was in vain the discomfited soldier
threatened these rebellious subjects with the vengeance of their queen : they boldly declared they
had thrown off their allegiance, and dethroned her
in favour of her *protégée*, Bess, to whom they
vowed the utmost loyalty and affection—as long
as Jack's money lasted. Finding all remonstrances
perfectly useless, the defeated son of Mars retired,
to convey to her tawney Majesty, the tidings of
the insurrection.

Having thus got rid of the enemy, without his
baggage, as Mr. Blueskin facetiously remarked,
the tribe returned to that part of their retreat
which formed their state place of assembly.   It
was not the dingle before described, but a smooth
space, carpeted with verdant turf, and surrounded
on all sides with umbrageous trees and gently
rising hills, forming a species of amphitheatre.
A select orchestra had been instituted by some
feathered vocalists in a clump of trees on one side,
which overhung a small pool or tiny lake, formed
by the waters of two or three rippling streams,
which welled down from the neighbouring hills,
and met there, as in a basin, or reservoir.   That
most loving bishop, St. Valentine himself, could

not have desired a more hymeneal morning. The soft and vernal sward seemed teeming with vegetation; wild flowers sprang up at every turn; the air was that warm and balmy air which invites, while it predisposes to abandonment, producing a pleasing listlessness peculiarly amatory and favourable to the saffron-robed deity. It was before the little sylvan lake we have mentioned, as being backed by the clump of overspreading trees in which the forest choristers were accustomed to hold their concerts, that the morning repast which was to usher in the day's festivities was spread. Black Martin had given orders, in consequence of Jack's *largesse*, that the stores of the tribe should be thrown open for general use.

"Our granaries and wine-presses shall be made public," he said, "on this auspicious occasion." A variety of delicacies were therefore speedily brought forward for the gipsy breakfast, consisting of a cold game pie, which had been baked in a turf oven, some savoury smoked bacon, hot home-made bread, oaten cakes of peculiar sweetness, done on the ashes, butter and milk, a piece of new cheese, and a jug of clouted cream, abstracted from the dairy of a neighbouring farmhouse: to these were added for those who chose it, a keg of cider and a flask of strong spirits, tasting very potently of the peat, and called mountain dew, to take off the rawness of the morning air.

It was by the side of the pellucid waters before-mentioned, which were as cool and refreshing with their gurgling sounds, to the ear as they were to the eye, that Jack and Bess threw themselves. We cannot as honest chroniclers undertake to state positively whether they indulged in any of the good cheer so liberally provided, or whether, as on a former occasion, their appetites were satisfied with the lighter food of love; in fact, we do think they scarcely knew themselves,—Jack was so much employed in gazing into the blue depths of Bess's eyes, in which he discovered the faces of certain cherubs, bearing a strong infantine resemblance to himself; and Bess, we believe, was similarly occupied on her part: the birds seemed to enjoy the treat as much as the greater bipeds, and merrily carolled away in every possible variety of note; never was a happier set congregated together. They were only aroused from their morning repast by a very warm intimation from the sun, that the day had arrived at the maturity of noon, and the appearance of the patrico in his pontificals to make preparations for the ensuing nuptial ceremony. This primate of the canting and palming crew was arrayed for the occasion in a long canonical sort of robe, tied round with a wisp of straw by way of girdle; his long white beard had been carefully combed out with the teeth of an old garden rake, and a sort of mitre with asses' ears was on his head. " You have come well, reverend patrico," said Black Martin, as he saw him advancing; " we have dallied too long : it is time, brother Romoners, that we should install our new ally, Jack, into our ancient and honourable fraternity, by uniting him, according to our rites, with our pretty Bess, in virtue of which he will be entitled to the protection and privileges of our tribe. Let the altar be prepared forthwith : go some one to the next brook down in the valley, and form a rush ring for the bride; turn the beasts out to pasture on the common ; let them freely brouse where they will : we pronounce this a holiday for all, and excommunicate work of every description." A loud hurrah followed the delivery of this resolution.

The remains of the breakfast were immediately removed, in obedience to Black Martin's injunctions. The worshipful patrico set about preparing the altar, which was formed by the body of the dead pony he had alluded to, placed transversely on the turf, with its head towards the east ; the ceremony of marriage between members of the canting and palming crew being always performed over some dead animal—a horse for preference, which may have given rise to the common taunt of singing psalms over a dead horse. Poll Maggot, and two or three other brown matrons, volunteered their services as *bridesmaids* to Bess ; whilst Mr. Blueskin undertook to wait upon Jack. In a short time all was ready for the ceremony, and Jack and Bess, with their attendants, were led in grand procession to the upper part of the space, where the venerable patrico, with his ministering assistants, awaited them. Jack and Bess, placing themselves on either side of the dead pony, with the patrico in the centre, that reverend person's nose being immediately over the tail of the defunct animal, the whole of the tribe, with Black Martin at their head, formed themselves into a semicircle around them; and the patrico taking a tattered book in one hand whilst he held a glass of what he called "divine spirit" in the other, proceeded to perform the marriage rites, the form of which ran as follows:—

Romonce Marriage Ritual.

" Brothers, sisters, who together
  Here, in spite of wind and weather,
  Meet—a ranting roaring crew,—
  That nothing better have to do,
  Having first join'd hands and kiss'd
  To your autem bawler* list."

Here the males and females, with the exception of Jack and Bess, who were restrained by the barrier between them, having mutually saluted each other, the patrico kneeling down, and reverently paying homage at his altar, by pressing his lips to the latter end of the moribund beast that formed it, the whole crew joined hands, and the service continued.

* Parson, or patrico

"Why we've met here, if you'd know,
Thus propounds your patrico :—
Sheppard Jack, and Edgeworth Bess,
Wishing neither, nothing less—
Denizen of Romeville he,
She a dell of Romonee,—
Cannot longer live alone,
But would be one flesh and bone, —
Ride one donkey, share one tent,
Each on fun and frolic bent.
Sheppard Jack vows he must wive,
Or incontinently live.
Edgeworth Bess says she must pair,
Or of harming beck * beware.
Both are young and form'd for sport,
Ben cove strong and dimber mort.
The hour is meet, and fit the spot,
    Say subjects then of Romonee,
Shall we make one this twain or not,
    On payment of the autem fee ?"

Here a loud shout of " *Rumrib Noozlem !*" the
gipsy phrase for " marry them," almost deafened
the air, which was increased to vociferation, as Mr.
Blueskin, by Jack's direction, distributed a large
handful of the piece-broker's coin amongst them.
Order was for a few moments totally destroyed by
a general scramble, in which the august patrico
unfortunately got more kicks than halfpence. The
authority of Black Martin, however, at length restored decorum ; and the patrico, addressing himself to our hero and Bess more immediately, went
on with the service :—

* Constable or beadle.

" Here, as none the bands forbid,
  That you may do as Adam did,
Both must nimbly jump across
  This dead beast we'll call a horse ;
And till he starts alive again,
  None shall presume to part you twain.
That mystic ceremony done,
  You are now for ever one."

Here Bess and Jack, by desire of their attendants, exchanged sides, by each lightly jumping over the body of the dead animal, over whom, turning round, they joined in a conjugal embrace, to the great gratification of the crew, who hailed their union with loud and prolonged shouts, increased as before by Jack's largesse from the piece-broker's till, distributed by his trusty almoner, Mr. Blueskin. It now only remained, the hymeneal beast evincing no disposition to divorce the happy pair by coming to life again, for the patrico to pronounce the bridal benediction usual on the marriage of a ben cove and dimber dell, which he immediately did in these words, draining the glass of spirits he held in his hand with much apparent fervour :—

Bridal Benediction.

" By this glass of most pure spirit,
  The which within you may inherit,
  And by this mystic ring of rush,
    I now pronounce the autem tie,
  That you are free of every bush,
    And licensed 'neath one hedge to lie—

> Drink of one can, eat of one meal,
> In consort beg, in union steal,
> And peck and booze with kinchen store*
> Your marriage bless till all is o'er."

The patrico threw the glass into the air over his left shoulder for luck, presented the rush ring to the bride, and shut his book, the altar was removed, and the newly-wedded pair, conducted by their attendants, were led round to receive the congratulations of the whole assembly, among whom Black Martin was foremost. Mr. Blueskin nearly emptied Jack's treasury in a last distribution of his coin to the shouting crew, leaving our hero very little wherewith to meet the expenses of the conjugal state. The ceremony of installing Jack a member of the tribe, and entitling him to all the privileges of Romanee, followed that of marriage, and was conducted with much state and solemnity. We have not room to particularize it ; suffice, Jack received the freedom of the gang, which was impressed on his wrist by an old sybil of their number, with an indelible liquid, in some uncouth characters, which, he was informed, presented to the eye of the initiated the name of Pharaoh. The exhibition of this mystic signature was to secure in all cases the utmost assistance from any member of the gang he might chance to meet, to whom it might be shown. Whatever was his peril, by that token he would command protection and assistance:

---

* Meat and drink, and lots of children.

thus did Jack become a ROMONER, a high degree in the profession of vagabondism.

It may here be proper to mention that, during the time the marriage ceremony was being performed, a person had suddenly appeared from one of the clumps of trees surrounding the space, who, unobserved by Blueskin, Jack, and Bess, remained for some time a silent spectator of all that passed. The few members of the gang whose attention he attracted seemed awed from all remark by a single look :—he departed as suddenly and mysteriously as he had appeared. This person was Jonathan Wild.

It was settled that a tent should be raised for the especial accommodation of the newly-married couple in a convenient nook of overhanging hazles, where, on a fragrant couch of some new-mown hay, the birds singing their epithalamium in the leafy shades around them, they could forget the cares of the world, and think only of love and rapture. These arrangements made, revelry became the order of the day.

Jack and Bess, with Mr. Blueskin as their prime minister, were elected, by acclamation, king and queen of the festivities. While Mr. Blueskin went to announce that every one might do as he pleased, the lovers retired from the heat of the sun to commune with each other, beneath a convenient canopy that had been formed by throwing a piece of canvas across the lower branches of a couple of trees. Here they sat on a soft turf throne—recreation became general. The tribe divided themselves into little knots : some smoked and drank; some played at cards; others recounted stories of the former power of their race ; while others sang songs commemorating the history of JOHNNY FAW, one of their kings, and his adventures with Earl Casillis's lady, when he " cast the glamour o'er her." In this blissful state of things they were, when the attention of all was roused by the sudden appearance of Fox, the long-headed cur before mentioned, who came eagerly tearing into the enclosure, barking with a vehemence betokening something extraordinary.

Black Martin was the first to start up.

" By the damnable waters of the Red Sea," said that chief, " this bodes no good: I know that cur's bark well; a surprise is at hand—it may be the HARMING BECK : we must be on our guard ;—to your cudgels, lads !"

The whole of the crew were on their feet in an instant, and eagerly seized their sticks.

Surely no traps, on account of the speak last night," muttered Blueskin to Jack, coolly cocking a pistol which he drew from his bosom.

Jack turned pale at this anticipation of discovery. Poor Bess, greatly alarmed, clung closely to him. All at once Fox ceased his barking and crouched down at Black Martin's feet ; and suspense and expectation were put an end to by the appearance of Zara and the soldier, followed by half a dozen gipsies of peculiar height and ferocity of appearance, armed to the teeth with knife and pistol, as was evident when they threw open their long rough coats. Zara's black eyes flashed fire, the lightning of a dark night, as she indignantly surveyed the astonished group before her.

" What is this I see ?" she cried in a terrible voice ; " has my power then been set at nought— my orders disregarded ? Dog !" and here, before he could be aware of it, she felled Black Martin to the earth, with one blow of her powerful arm, and as suddenly drawing a knife from her girdle, would have plunged it in his heart, had she not been vigorously withheld by Mr. Blueskin, who, seeing the peril of the chief, by his sinewy grasp afforded him time to recover his legs. The daring promptness of their queen, and her meditated vengeance on their leader, struck terror to the souls of her rebellious subjects ; they instantly dropped their cudgels, which they had raised in attitudes of defence, and bent low before her, in token of submission and allegiance.

" Ah ! yield, ye rebel miscreants !" she cried, exultingly ; " why, this is well, but you shall not escape: look for our heaviest ban." The gang slunk back abashed. " For you, Black Martin, traitor that you are, we thrust you out from our community, remove you from our caste : no more you are minister and chief—away ;" Black Martin sullenly withdrew, not daring to brave an increase of anger by further disobedience. "But for this guilty pair," she continued, pointing to Jack and Bess, who still remained together closely united— "Yes, I will thwart the Fates in their despite, mar the prediction, though it be with blood: better it be by my hand than another's—there will be less of agony and shame. Norman—Bernard! seize that reckless girl!" Two of the six before-mentioned gipsies stepped forward. "Gaspard and Luke, remove that ill-starred fool, her paramour, who'd rush upon his fate." Her orders were instantly obeyed; Jack and the affrighted Bess were seized, and torn from each other's arms. Blueskin raised his pistol in defence of his friend, but it was immediately struck from his hand by the soldier; and he himself was seized by the two remaining gipsies. "Now hear my final orders." cried the queen. "Lyon," addressing the soldier, "bridegroom of my adoption, hasten to your affianced — this night she shall be your's—remove those bold intruders, trusty friends—convey them through the bye-ways to whence they came, whilst we strike tent, pannier our beasts, and in some distant quarter remove all trace of route and hope of rescue.—Away, your queen will be your leader!" In spite of Jack's imprecations, Blueskin's struggles, and Bess's heart-rending entreaties, the two former were instantly dragged one way, and the latter, under the direction of Rupert Lyon,) for such it

Q

appeared was the soldier's name, and the lioness Zara,) was dragged another. The encampment was struck, their moveables packed, the beasts caught and panniered, and long before Jack and Blue-skin were released from custody by their swarthy guards, in a lonely cross lane near Camberwell, all vestige of the gipsies had effectually disappeared from the neighbourhood of Norwood.

CHAPTER XIV.

JACK SHEPPARD SETS UP IN BUSINESS.

THE ROBBERY DISCOVERED.—SUBORNING THE EVIDENCE.—
A MOTHER'S LOVE.

"DAMN that queen Zara for a cantankerous old
hag," growled out Mr. Blueskin, on the departure
of their escort, after a few moments' silence; "did
ever any one come near such an incarnate devil."
Jack groaned in bitterness of spirit: he was heart-
sick with hope deferred; disappointment had struck
him to the very core: to lose his lovely prize in
the very moment of possession, was a thought of
desperation; to make the matter worse, Blueskin,
with the benevolent intention of condoling in his
misfortune, only added to his tortures. "A pretty
business we have made of it," said that cerulean
gentleman—" lost our blunt and our baggage,
too."—Jack groaned more deeply.—" I would'nt
so much have minded if it had been only one
of them," continued Blueskin; " but body and
breeches! oh, damn it!" Jack groaned again.
"Curse that Black Martin for a cowardly hound."
resumed his companion, whiffing a short pipe,

which he had managed to light, by means of a phosphorous box, that he always carried about him. " I'm almost sorry now, that I didn't let the witch knife him, as she wanted to do : to think that he should have turned tail after all, and that scurvy gang, when I had given them every dump we had, and such a prime cargo of cloths and stuffs!" Jack was roused almost to madness.

" Shall we not go back ?" said he, violently.

" What would be the good of that ?" coolly asked Mr. Blueskin, " we shouldn't find them if we did ; they are all off on the grand hop, long before this time. Didn't you twig what a roundabout way those gentlemen who handed us so politely along, brought us, on purpose to give their pals time ?—no, no, we must e'en stump it to town, and see how the land lies there. We must let Mr. Wild know what has passed—there must be no working under the rose with him ; for though he's a very civil, pleasant-spoken gentleman, he'd think no more of getting a fellow scragged, than I would of twisting the throat of a barn-door pecker—by the bye, said he, if there isn't a fine fat speckled hen, grubbing up the worms by the hedge-side there— well reminded, we shall want something for supper." The next minute the poor hen, with its neck tied in a knot, was safely deposited in Mr. Blueskin's coat pocket, leaving a brood of half-fledged young ones to deplore her untimely end.

It was quite dusk when the twain arrived in town, which Jack was not sorry for, as he wished to learn what had passed in his absence before any one saw him. Making their way unobserved to the back parlour of Mr. Nightingal, which they easily effected by diving up the sinister passage to the White Lion, we have before mentioned, they learnt from that gentleman, as well as the snatches of song with which he interlarded his information would permit, that Griffith Thomas, who it seemed had turned out to have been *not* quite so great a fool as he appeared to be, and had been awake while Jack supposed him sleeping, had seen the roll of fustian in Jack's box, and informed his master of it, who, on hearing of the robbery in the house of his customer, Mr. Baines, had suspected what was really the fact, that his runaway apprentice, Jack, was concerned in it, and hastened to Mr. Baines to give him information, when he found that gentleman busily employed in taking into custody a poor widow woman, who rented his back garret, being convinced, as he said, that no one but some one in the house could have perpetrated the robbery, there being no marks of violence; besides which there was the damning proof of the widow not having a thing in the world, which, as the piece-broker remarked, was positive evidence she possessed the property. Nevertheless, Mr. Baines thought, that in a case of such serious loss, there was nothing like having two strings to his bow; so he got the widow locked up, and caused a warrant to be issued for the apprehension of Jack.   A council of war was immediately held on this intelligence; and it was settled, by the advice of Mr. Nightingal, that, as there was only the fustian to bring in evidence against him, Jack should, in the middle of the night, enter Mr. Wood's house, making his way from the roof of the White Lion, over the tiles of the intervening houses, to the garret of the carpenter—get in at the window and bring away, if it could be found, the unfortunate fustian that had thus become a witness against him.

"And if to this," said Mr. Blueskin, "you could only manage to rob yourself, Jack, and bring your own things away, why, you'll prove a thief of thieves."

"It shall be done," said Jack, becoming bold by the repeated bumpers of brandy he had taken to drown his chagrin for the loss of Bess—"it shall be done: as soon as St. Peter's witness sounds the first morning call on his clarion, I'll catterwaul it along the gutters, and bring off the booty."

"Bravo, bravo!" said Blueskin; "you must make the cloth a *piece* offering to Mr. Wild; as you won't be able to go back to Old Chips after this, you'll have nobody else to look to now, you know."

"True, true," answered Jack, "that's to be thought of; though if I do manage to bring off the stuff, I am not going to put up so quietly with their nonsense as you may think : a plan has just occurred to me—but, mum—we'll talk of that to-morrow : if I am to be a thief, I won't be a half-and-half one—I'll be a bold one or nothing."

" Well said," again roared Mr. Blueskin, giving Jack a hearty slap on the back in token of appro-bation ; " but I always prognosticated it."

More brandy was ordered in upon these mutual assurances ; and as soon as the cock announced the first faint approach of day, and all the other cocks around the neighbourhood had answered the chal-lenge, and telegraphed it to their respective dis-tricts in token of their watchfulness. Jack stole from Mr. Nightingal's cockloft, and, with all the dex-terity of a tom-cat, made his way over the tiles to Mr. Wood's garret, obtained an entrance without arousing Griffith Thomas, and, after ascertaining that young gentleman really was asleep, by apply-ing the flame of the candle to his nasal organ, dis-covered that the roll of fustian was still where he had deposited it, and bore it triumphantly off, with a few favourite articles, back to the White Lion, retracing his steps by the same way that he had come.

It was lucky Griffith Thomas really was asleep, for Jack's determination was, if discovered by him, to have stood on no scruples to have secured his si-lence. The fustian was conveyed, the first thing, to Mr. Wild, as a trifling offering from Jack, in proof of his allegiance, previous to entering regu-larly into his service. It may be mentioned that, among other things really belonging to Jack, which he had brought away with the fustian from the garret of Mr. Wood, was the pair of pistols he had purchased with the retaining guinea he had received from Mr. Wild, on their first introduction to each other. As Jack handled these ill-omened weapons, the vein of daring and adventure which lay dormant in his bosom was fully aroused; he felt himself the hero he afterwards proved.

" Yes," said he, " enterprise shall be my guiding star, resolution my companion. If fate will make me a highwayman, it shall not be said that she has fixed on one either unfit for, or unworthy of, the distinction she would assign him." He here cocked his pistols with an air of determination, and began singing a slang song in praise of taking the road, which had the reputation of having been a great favourite with the prince of highwaymen, the celebrated Captain Hind :—

> " Of all gallants to frisk a gull,
>   My blessing on the bridal cull;
>   So ranting, roaring, wild, and free,
>   On road or plain there's none like he," &c. &c.

It was broad day-light ere Jack, on quitting the case* of Mr. Nightingal, arrived at the Attic residence of Mr. Blueskin, in the Mint, where he proposed to rest during the short period till morning, and then boldly to visit Mr. Baines, having secured the only evidence against him, and, by means of

* Flash house.

bullying, deter that gentleman from taking any further steps for his apprehension. Accordingly, at nine o'clock, after partaking of a regular Mint breakfast, consisting of red herrings and onions, with a copious accompaniment of early purl—a mixture of warmed gin and beer—he repaired to the shop of the piece-broker, where his presence excited no small surprise.

" Your servant, Sir," said he, " I understand you have had your house robbed since I was here last ; and that you have chosen to say, just because I made all your fastenings so secure that it was impossible for any one to break into your shop, that you think I had some hand in the business ; now I have only got this to say, I am a poor lad, 'tis true, but I am not going to have my character taken away. Touch my honour, touch my life ; my reputation's my bread ; and unless there's a public apology immediately made to me in the " Daily Post," for the defamation so unjustly heaped on me, why, my attorney shall bring an action against you for libel, that's all. People are not going to have their lives sworn away for nothing. My integrity is well known ; I could be trusted with thousands ; and if you injure my credit, you'll have to pay swingeing damages for it, I can tell you that." The poor piece-broker was electrified at this audacity : he could not deny the fact of Jack's having made the fastenings of the shop extra secure ; and had nothing more to bring against him than the circumstance that had been communicated by Mr. Wood, of some fustian having been found in his (Jack's) box. The ruinous consequences of an action for false imprisonment flashed across him, and he was on the point (being naturally a very timid man) of expressing his conviction of Jack's innocence, and begging pardon for his suspicions, when Mr. Wood suddenly entered, apparently greatly inflamed with choler, his face looking as crumpled and as red as a pickling cabbage. He started at seeing Jack; the rubicundity of his visage assumed a purple hue.

" Tog—fillain—thief !" said he, seizing Jack by the throat, " put I have caught you, Saint Tavit pe plessit."

" What have you got to say against me ?" said Jack, who had for a moment been thrown off his guard, but instantly recovered his effrontery. " What are you collaring me for ?"

" Passion of hur heart, hear this !" roared Mr. Wood; " are you not my apprentice, look you? have you not proke into my carrets, look you, like a thief in the night ; have you not roppet me, look you ?"

" No !" said Jack, sternly ; " so take your fingers from my throat, or it may be worse for you."

" Not roppet me !" spluttered out the Welshman, almost strangling with rising rage, " not roppet me ! Cot's poty, have you not proken open your pox, and taken away honest Mr. Paine's fustian, pesites going off with your own pistols, which I had left there, for they are wilful ploot-thirsty weapons—mercies on hur, and often times kill a poty pefore he is aware of it—not like your gentlemanly peaceful swords, that never kill any poty, put when you want them to to it, which was the reason hur tid not choose to mettle with your firearms, look you.—To you not call all that ropperies and treasons ?"

" No, I don't," said Jack, impudently; " surely a man has a right to do what he likes with his own ! I only took what belonged to myself—the fustian was my own, and so were the pops,—and now what have you got to say to that, old mouse-trap ?"

" Mousetraps ! Oh ! Saint Finifret, and all the eleven thousand firgins, tit ever any one hear the likes of this ;—here is plasphemies and sacrileges and scitions, look you."

" We had better let him go, neighbour," whispered Mr. Baines to the exasperated Welshman, " we may get into trouble ; you see what a desperate young dog he is, and we have no evidence."

What might have been the effect of this advice to Mr. Wood we are not able to say, for just at this moment Mr. Daniel Nibblo, the constable in whose hands the warrant for Jack's apprehension had been placed, entered the shop for the purpose of making some enquiries as to his haunts.

Mr. Nibblo was a short thickset man, with a

flat hard-looking face, in the middle of which was placed rather a large nose, carbuncled with a profusion of grog blossoms ; his eyes were small, but piercing, and seemed to lie in wait in his head ready to spring out on any one he wanted ; his frame was bony and sinewy : he was dressed in a plain brown coat with stiff skirts, and waistcoat and breeches to match ; high shoes with large silver buckles ; a round bob-wig and cocked-hat ; he bore in his hand a cudgel with a nob at the top of it, of about the diameter of a two-penny loaf. He had commenced life as a Qui-tam attorney, but becoming broken down by malpractices, had sunk into a bailiff's follower, from which situation his ferret like qualities and wolfish ferocity had raised him to the rank of constable ; to use his own words, he had left the civil for the criminal service. He was particularly fond of interlarding his discourse with a variety of dog-latin law phrases, which he rendered still more mongrel by invariably, through ignorance, misapplying and mispronouncing ; they served, he said, to give a weight to his conversation, and produced a wholesome awe in the multitude. His quick and practised glance informed him at once of all that was passing ; and in a moment he had released Jack from the grasp of Mr. Wood, and to his great surprise and terror had accommodated him with a pair of ruffles to his wristbands, as he termed it, by very securely handcuffing him.

Jack began to repent of his gratuitous boldness; and both Mr. Wood and Mr. Baines commenced explanations, which were abruptly cut short by the myrmidon of justice.

" It is all very well, gentlemen," exclaimed this worthy ; " but you must permit me to say, *ex officio*, the affair is now in the hands of justice—it is too late for you to withdraw—the law must take its course—I am responsible to the public. Were I to release this daring offender, as you seem to wish, I should be compounding felony, liable to be caught in *fragrante delicktoe*, and that is an enormity which shall never be winked at by me."

After much conversation, during which Jack vehemently protested his innocence, asserting that the fustian which had been seen by Mr. Wood in his box, and which he had that morning sold to a member of the Jewish persuasion, in order to enable him to purchase a new chest of tools, had been given to him the week before by his mother, the inflexible Mr. Nibblo consented that Jack should accompany him and Mr. Baines to Mrs. Sheppard's in Spitalfields, in order, as he said, to prove an alibi, by ascertaining from her whether the suspicious fustian had been given by her to Jack, or not,—Jack having declared the Hebrew unknown, to whom he had disposed of it. Mr. Wood, whose really good heart had been much moved at seeing Jack in the custody of the officer, expressed his readiness, if Jack could really prove his innocence, and would promise amendment for the future, to take him back again into his employment, and pass over what had occurred.

It was with a beating heart Jack repaired with the constable and Mr. Baines to the house of his mother ; he had not visited her for some months, and felt he had no right, from his neglect, to expect a very cordial reception. She was at home when they entered her shop, and, though surprised to see him accompanied by two strangers, immediately ran to embrace him.

" My dear, dear Jack !" she exclaimed, " how is it that I have not seen you so many months ?— what has occasioned your absence—and why are you here now ?

" Hey-day !" cried Mr. Nibblo, " how is this. young fellow ?—Why, you said just now you saw your mother only last week—and here, she says, she has not seen you for some months : this is what we call in the courts, *nulle testificandumb.*"

Mrs. Sheppard stood motionless ; the words of the constable, particularly his dog-latin, to which she attached some dreadful meaning, together with a glance at the handcuffs, which she now saw for the first time, perfectly petrified her.

" Gracious heavens !" she exclaimed, " what does all this mean ? My poor, poor boy ?"

" Nothing, mother !" cried Jack, eagerly anxious to put her on her guard, " the gentlemen only want you to confirm that it is true you really did give me that piece of fustian which you brought me last week to make a working-jacket and trowsers of, because somebody says I stole it from this here gentleman, when you know you gave—"

" Silence, silence !" angrily roared Mr. Nibblo, " here's contempt of court, prisoner—why you are putting the words into the witness's mouth :— take care, ma'am, take care, or you may make yourself *party cepts crimini* in this affair—you both stand on very ticklish ground : all I want to know, and I speak *quod warranto*, is, whether you did *bona fide* give this youth a piece of cloth called fustian—to wit, last week, *anno domino* in the present year ;—now remember, ma'am, you are on your adjudicator, so take time to consider."

The poor woman became dreadfully pale. Jack fixed a keen and anxious glance upon her : she trembled—she hesitated : there was a moment's silence—the constable looked sternly judicial— poor Mr. Baines looked more like a culprit than a prosecutor. Mrs. Sheppard met her son's meaning glance. True love never wholly departs from the object that possessed it : the affection felt for the father revives in his widow with double force and purity as she gazes on their offspring : she sees the father's image in the son ; and even when nature has not blessed their mutual passion with this sacred succour in deprivation, faithful memory

will still invest inanimate objects with the thoughts
and feelings of other days. The vacant chair, the
favourite book, the accustomed room, will all re-
call, as they are gazed upon, images of the departed loved one—will all awaken emotions of
tenderness that may seem to have been dead in
the heart for years, but which their vision, as by
a magic spell, recalls at once into life and action.
So it was with Mrs. Sheppard : she forgot, as she
wistfully looked upon Jack, all his neglect and
wilfulness ; she remembered only his present peril,
saw only the tenderly cherished son of the father
she had loved with so ardent and sincere a passion;
and at all hazards—ay, even to the peril of her
soul—such is the love of a mother—determined to
screen and save him.

" Yes," she exclaimed, with an effort of desperation, " he has spoken the truth—I did give
him the fustian—it was last week. When I spoke
of his long absence, do you not know that to a
fond mother a week appears an age—a day a
year ?"

Mr. Baines looked convinced—not so Mr. Nibblo.

" Hum !" cried that sceptical person, incredu-
lously ; " not being a mother, ma'am, I cannot
say any thing about days being years; all I can
say is, any year that has only four-and-twenty
hours in it must certainly be an *anus miraculus*,
as a certain learned Gent. of my acquaintance
used to say. But now to speak *de factor*, my

good woman—recollect you are upon your *asse-verantum*, your *allocater*, as I said before; if you really did give the fustian in question to the prisoner in custody, you can have no objection to state from whom you got it yourself."

"Oh, no, no," said the trembling woman, exchanging anxious glances with her son, "it was from a—a—weaver."

"Ha! and his locality?" said Mr. Nibblo; "you must state that; in what bailiwick? where is his *vennew*?"

"Sir?" said Mrs. Sheppard.

"I mean, where does he live; my good madam," answered Mr. Nibblo, with a forensic air.

"In—in Spitalfields, Sir," faltered Mrs. Sheppard.

"Umph! Spitalfields is a wide place, ma'am," returned the constable; "perhaps you can favour us by saying what street, what number?"

Jack was in a paroxyism of suspense. "I do not quite recollect," said the perplexed and agonised woman.

"Umph! You don't exactly recollect!—very good—just what I thought," drily returned the man of warrants; "then perhaps, ma'am, you'll be so good as to accompany Mr. Baines, the prosecutor, and refresh your memory by pointing out to him the identical house of the aforesaid weaver, that he may ascertain the truth in *improper purse-owner (propria personæ)*; and I, in the meantime, will remain in *custodiam* here with the prisoner. You can permit your man to step out for a pot of ale, and let me have whatever you have in the cupboard—I am not particular. I have departed from the strict duty of my office, in allowing your son this indulgence; he ought to have been committed at once; the sessions are just on, and ——"

" You shall have all you require, Sir," said Mrs. Sheppard, gratefully, " there is a bottle of wine, which I had stored up for the birthday of— of—" here looking at her son, she burst into tears, in which she was accompanied, from at least one eye, by Mr. Baines, who was at that moment seized with a sudden desire to blow his nose, which he did with great vehemence, whisking his handkerchief about in a singularly loose manner.

" Forgive me, Sir," said the poor widow, at length recovering herself; " but my heart is so full. There is a small case bottle of spirits; here is bread, butter, cheese, and you shall speedily be supplied with some ham and beef, and ale: only name what you want, Sir—you are welcome to all we have; and I thank you for your kindness to my poor Jack."

" What you have named will be quite sufficient, my good woman," answered Mr. Nibblo, complacently; " you need not get any thing else; I can manage with them."

The viands were produced, and Mrs. Sheppard,

with a lingering step, departed to point out the
weaver from whom she had bought the fustian to
Mr. Baines.   To describe the streets they went
down, the turnings they came up, the many unsa-
tisfactory inquiries that were made, would unne-
cessarily occupy the reader's time; suffice it, Mrs.
Sheppard walked Mr. Baines nearly off his legs,
who, beginning to be heartily tired of the business,
and finding that whenever they left off they were just
as wise as when they had first begun, compassion-
ately told the widow he was quite satisfied, and
had no doubt she knew the street and house perfectly well, if she could only recollect them ; and,
moreover, that he had no question that there was
the identical weaver she mentioned, if they could
only find him; that he would make it all right with
Mr. Nibblo, and was sorry he had caused her any
annoyance.   He then, with some difficulty, forced
a dram on the poor woman, to recruit her exhausted
spirits, and with no difficulty at all persuaded himself to follow her example.   Returning to her home,
they found Mr. Nibblo very contentedly emptying the bottle of wine, with the assistance of Jack,
whom he had graciously permitted to bear him
company ; the ale and spirits had been discussed
some time previously.

"It's all right, Mr. Nibblo," said the considerate Mr. Baines.

"Oh, it's all right, is it?" answered the constable.

" Yes, the street is there," said Mr. Baines; " the weaver does live in the house—I am quite satisfied."

" Oh, what you've seen him then ?"

" Why—not exactly," hesitated Mr. Baines; " he was not at home, as it were; but it's all right."

" Very well; then I have nothing else to do but to take this young gentleman's *habeas corpus* to St. Giles's roundhouse, lock him up there for the night, and to-morrow morning convey him before Mr. Justice Parry, who no doubt, as it's *all right*, will declare it a case of *noll prosecute*, and give him his *committimus* and discharge him immediately."

There was an irony in the tone with which these words were delivered by the constable, an air of malicious satisfaction in his manner, that did not escape the quick apprehension of Mrs. Sheppard. Woman is ever more ready in the understanding the language of looks than man; she has a more present prescience of the meaning unconsciously conveyed by tone and gesture, than has the proud lord of the creation who claims such an intellectual supremacy over her;—she saw at once Jack's fate was sealed, that her falsehood was known, that she had become the suborner and accomplice of crime, had borne false witness and forfeited her fair name, only to end in her own detection, and render her son's guilt still more black—she gave a piercing shriek as the constable rose to convey her son to prison, and sunk senseless on the floor. Jack felt no inclination to stay and witness further the remorse and agony that had been his work.

" Let us go," he cried, " to the roundhouse. God bless you, mother," and he imprinted a kiss on her cold and senseless cheek. " You will take care of her ma'am," said he to a neighbour the foreman had summoned to her assistance; " tell her to keep up her spirits, that I will soon see her again, and that there will be no occasion to trouble herself any more about this plaguy fustian; and now, Sir, if you are for a walk to St. Giles's," addressing the constable, " I'm your man—so on with you."

" After you, Sir; or you may give me your arm, which you like—any thing to make things agreeable—verdict, guilty," muttered the constable aside—" *nimingi contradictum.*"

With these words he grasped Jack's arm, and, followed by the stultified Mr. Baines, made his way from the widow's house in Spitalfields to the round-house in St. Giles's.

CHAPTER XV.

JACK A PRISON-BREAKER.

ESCAPE FROM ST. GILES'S ROUNDHOUSE.—THE LOST ONE FOUND.—LOVE IN A COTTAGE.

On arriving at St. Giles's roundhouse, Mr. Baines having quitted them at St. Clement's Church, not very much satisfied with the day's adventures, to report progress to Mr. Wood, the authoritative rap of Mr. Nibblo soon caused the door of that edifice to be unbarred by Jack's old acquaintance, Mr. Hannibal Guffin. The parochial functionary started as he saw our hero, and stared, as the saying is, with both his eyes.

"Your servant, Mr. Guffin," said Mr. Nibblo. "These comes greeting," delivering the warrant and Jack into the beadle's hands; " yes, know all men by these presents," he continued—" but, lord bless me, how you stare! have you ever seen this young hell-bird before?"

"Why, I don't exactly know," equivocated the beadle, wisely considering that he had nothing to boast of in his acquaintance with him.

"I think we *have* met," said Jack.

" Well, I have something in my head that almost convinces me that I have seen you before,"
observed the beadle.

" Ay, ay," returned Jack, " that's safe; you
need not cudgel your brains any further at present."

" Oh! well, if you are old acquaintances," said
Mr. Nibblo, " no occasion for any other introduction. You can tuck him up comfortably for the
night, can't you Guffin?—and to-morrow morning
I'll come and procure him an audience with Justice
Parry—you'll see what the charge is—a small affair of fustian—just enter it in your books, and
then I'll say bye-bye to you;—but stop, I must
not forget my ruffles."

Here he was about to remove the handcuffs from
Jack, when he was restrained by the beadle's exclaiming, with a look of great alarm—

" For Heaven's sake, what are you about?—
why, you surely would not let this young hang-dog
loose upon me, would you?"

" Why not?" inquired Mr. Nibblo; " you can
easily give him a rap on the pipkin if he's ob-
stropolous, can't you?"

" Ah! but two may play at that," said Mr·
Guffin, with much feeling; " no, no, safe bind,
safe find; we had better let him remain as he is.
I'll be answerable for your handcuffs; and what's
more, if you'll only be so good as to give me a hand
up with him to the top room, and help me to fasten

him in for the night, there is a jug of water there, and it's quite light—I'll——"

" What, friend Guffin?" asked Nibblo.

" Why, I'll stand a dram of the best—ay, two for that matter.

" Agreed," cried Nibblo. " Now, young fellow, tumble up : here's a writ *fieri facies* against you : you must go under the screw."

" I am afraid you are putting yourself to a great deal of very unnecessary trouble and expense, Mr. Guffin," cried Jack, significantly. " Do any of your lodgers ever bolt the moon?"

" Why, I don't know," growled out Mr. Guffin ; " but there'll be a moon out presently, so you can try, if you like."

" Why, that's true, so I can ; there *will* be *one out*, as you say. I should advise you, Mr. Nibblo, as a friend, to take a deposit for your hand-cuffs."

" I'm not afraid," laughed Nibblo ; you won't swallow them."

" Why, not exactly," said Jack. " Pray, Mr. Guffin, hadn't you a young woman here in your custody, some time ago? She took French leave, I understand : have you seen anything of her lately?"

" No," growled Guffin, who didn't like these inquiries of Jack.

" Then I have," replied the other ; " she sends her love to you ; and says that the *twelve* gentlemen who came and took her away forgot to pay you for her lodging; and that, if you would give me the particulars of your charge, I am to settle it with you."

"Go to the devil with you!" said the beadle, surlily; "do you think I carry my accounts in my head?"

"If you'll just take the trouble to search your nob for the score—dot and carry one, eh, Mr. Guffin?"

The beadle writhed with stifled rage.

"Come, come, my chick!" said Nibblo, who began to be impatient for his drams, let's have no more of this chaff; walk your chalks to your sky-parlour. I'll give you a leg up."

Jack was here conducted to the top room of the roundhouse (which consisted of two stories), Mr. Guffin considering he would be the most out of the way there; and after securely locking and bolting him in, the pair of congenial worthies retraced their steps down stairs again. No sooner was Jack left alone, than he took a survey of his new lodging. It was a square room; and by the light which was admitted through a small loop-hole, with an iron grating not large enough to admit of any one forcing their bodies through it, he perceived the only furniture of the room was an old feather-bed, with a dirty blanket on a crazy truckle, and a high-backed leather-bottomed chair, on which there was a jug with some water. Sitting down on the bed, he began to muse on the events

of the day, his present prospects, and what was
likely to be his future fate. The image of his
beloved Bess recurred to his mind, with all her
bridal beauty; he soon lost all thoughts of himself in speculating on what might be *her* hapless
destiny. At that very moment she might be falling a victim to the lawless violence—the brutal
lust of her hateful persecutor, the soldier, and he
not there to save or die for her. The idea was
agony. " And what restrains me ?" said he:
" what hinders that I should scour the earth to
seek and succour her ?"—These senseless walls!
Ah !" he continued in a tone of triumph and
contempt, as a thought suddenly flashed across
his brain—" Ah ! shall I then suffer my free will
to be controlled by a few bars and bricks? I,
that have life and action ? shall animate spirit
yield up the mastery to the mute resistance of
these inanimate walls? No! the same sense, and
being that made them what they are, were shamed
for ever, could they not un-make them. About it
then.—Yes ! up, Jack, up ! the day shall be your
own !"

Jack's heart bounded at the idea : every sinew
seemed to brace itself for the attempt: he was
all animation, all buoyancy; his energies his senses,
all hurried to his aid; one eagle glance below,
above, around the room, and his resolution was
taken—his plan was laid. It would have been easy
for him to have removed a plank of the floor-

ing, and to have penetrated through the ceiling to the room below, but he did not know who might be its tenant. The walls were massive: to have made an aperture in them would have occupied too much time: the roof presented the best point of attack. Although hands were made before tools, Jack knew that, for his work, they were but of small use without them. To disengage one of his very slender hands from the handcuffs was, though a very painful not a very difficult task; all his limbs and joints were singularly flexible and pliant. Unfortunately, on searching his pockets, he found nothing to aid his purpose but an old razor; but with this he set to work. His first step was, with this razor to cut a stretcher, or bar, from the back of the chair, one end of which he formed into a sharp point; then drawing the feather-bed into the middle of the room, and placing it so that it might receive without noise, all that might fall from the ceiling, he mounted the chair and commenced operations. With the sharp point of the bar he soon managed to unloose a considerable quantity of the lime and mortar; he then dislodged several of the laths, and began to remove the tiles by poking at them with his bar. He had made, in this manner, a very formidable orifice, when, unfortunately, one of the tiles rolling off the roof, which was rather slanting, fell on the head of a worthy clergyman, who was at that moment passing the front of the watchhouse, in deep meditation on some spiritual

observations for his next Sunday's sermon. However this gentleman might have wished his thoughts
to have been assisted by *inspiration from above*,
that which was afforded by the falling of the tile
was by no means agreeable to him.   Turning
sharply round, and looking up, in the confusion of
his ideas, occasioned by the concussion of his cra-
nium with the missile, he began to bellow out
" fire, murder, and robbery."

This alarm was distinctly heard by Jack, who
was aware that to avoid immediate detection,
he had not a minute to lose.   Making a plunge
through the aperture he had effected in the raf-
ters, he, with a sort of harlequin's leap, gained
the roof—not however, without removing a great
quantity of tiles and rubbish in so doing.   It was
nine o'clock in the evening : the cries of the reverend clergyman, who happened to be Mr. Top-
ping, the rector of St. Giles's, soon brought a
great mob around him ; a thousand questions were
asked in a breath.

" What is it ?—Where is it ?—Who is it ?"
inquired different individuals.

" Murder !—fire !—thieves !" answered the reverend gentleman, " the prisoners are escaping."

" Where ? where ?" demanded a myriad of
voices.

Jack saw that, to effect his escape, he must
create a diverson. Mr. Guffin, the beadle, had
now joined the group outside.   Mustering all his

strength, Jack, holding on by the coping-stone, pulled up a great part of the roof, and immediately precipitated it down on the heads of the astonished and affrighted mob below; then sliding down a considerable way, by a leaden pipe affixed to the back part of the building, he cautiously dropped into the neighbouring church-yard, and making his way over the church-wall on one side, while Mr. Guffin had proceeded up stairs to the scene of his late captivity, joined the mob, most of whom were half blinded with the dust, by a circuitous route, and greatly added to their mystification, and his own diversion, by hallooing out—" There he goes—I see him—that's his head behind the chimney—no, it's only a tom-cat—Ah! there he is, escaping down that street — stop him, stop him !''

The mob immediately gave chase at full speed, and while they ran down one street, Jack very safely and coolly walked off down another.

Jack's first object, on thus regaining his liberty, was to seek the sanctum sanctorum of Mr. Nightingal, which, to avoid observation, he reached by a circuitous route : he found that notable publican and singer very desperately engaged in chanting the well-known canticle of " Mad Tom," roaring with much wildness as he issued from his cellar,—

> " Forth from my dark and dismal cell,
> Or from the black abyss of hell,
> Mad Tom is come.''

"Dear me, Mr. Nightingal," said our hero, much surprised by this singular greeting, "how wild you look; is any thing the matter? has any thing happened?"

"Matter! matter enough," gloomily answered Mr. Nightingal, "a great deal too much has happened;" here he resumed his song—

> "Fears and cares oppress my soul."

"What! haven't you heard the news, youngster? Your pal is lumbered."

"Who? Blueskin?" quickly asked Jack."

"Yes, Blueskin," said Mr. Nightingal, with a sigh; for in Blueskin he had lost one of his best and most constant customers; "He was nibbled this afternoon, upon old Blackerby's warrant, and is now in rumbo."* Here again he began singing—

> "Come, Vulcan, with tools and with tackle,
> And knock off my troublesome shackle.'

But that's past praying for, I fear; however, he made a very pretty wrestle for it when he was taken—didn't surrender until he had got a very handsome crack on the sconce. There's one comfort, Mr. Wild's gone to him with the doctor;" and here again he hummed—

> "To see if he can cure his distemper'd brain.'

"There must have been some plaguy nosing † somewhere; somebody's been giving tongue.

* Newgate.   † Giving information.

'Hark! I hear Actæon's hounds.'

But what the devil!" he exclaimed, breaking suddenly from his subject, " how is it I see you here? why, I thought you had been laid up in lavender by Dan Nibblo? Old Wood said you were."

" And Old Wood said right," replied Jack, who, was very sorry to hear of his friend's misfortune. " But having and keeping are two very different things. Help me to take off this other ruffle," said he, alluding to the handcuffs ; " I had only time to disengage myself from one; they belong to old Nibblo ; but I shall make a present of them to Mr. Wild."

Nightingal released him from the ornament.

" Blueskin being taken, I must make myself scarce, I suppose," said Jack ; no doubt the cry is up —the hounds are out."

" Yes," said Mr. Nightingal, singing with a very ill grace—

" Ringwood, Rockwood, Jowler, Bowman,
    All the chase do follow."

Jack waited to hear no more, but took a hasty leave of Mr. Nightingal, crossed the water, and very soon arrived at the Mint. Obtaining admission into the late lodgings of his friend Mr. Blueskin, he packed up the articles he had left there in the morning, loaded the pistols he had bought with Mr. Wild's money, and, depositing them in his bosom, set out to seek his fortune wherever chance might lead him.

Hurrying along he knew not whither, Jack, soon after quitting the Mint, and darting down some obscure and ill-tenanted streets, found himself in the middle of St. George's Fields. These fields, now covered with rows of well built houses, and intersected with broad and secure roads, were, at that time, the dissolute haunts of the very refuse of the metropolis. Considered as the property of the public, they were freely used for the erection of booths, and as the standing place of caravans, shows of wild beasts, &c., in their progress to and from the different country fairs. Their stunted herbage was the common pasturage of the coster-mongers' donkies, higglers' worn-out ponies and prads, and of other destitute animals : they were unfenced, untended, and only divided from each other by some stagnant ditches, with here and there a straggling tree, partaking, by its blight and dismemberment, of the general desolation of the spot. The only house of entertainment that skirted this haunt was a low pot-house, known by the name of " The Dog and Duck," the secure resort of minor thieves and hedge prostitutes, who congregated there in great numbers nightly, spending their ill-gotten gains in obscene revelry, singing, dancing, drinking, and fighting, for the diversions commonly ended in a general brawl : these wretches were usually joined by a few bloods upon town, who came there to unbend, as they called it; in other words, to gratify a vulgar taste and an innate love of blackguardism with impunity. In after days this place became a very notorious house of entertainment: the gardens were fitted up as tea-gardens—an orchestra was erected for concerts, and it was, sixty years since, the principal scene of the exploits of the Toms and Jerrys of that day. The ostensible reason with many for visiting this place was to drink the waters of a certain mineral spring, which were said to cure every disorder, but, in reality, to indulge in waters of a much stronger description, that were more frequently the cause of every *disorder*.

The site of this resort of infamy was part of the ground on which the present New Bedlam is erected, as is evident from a stone still to be seen, on which is carved the figure of a dog holding a duck in his mouth, inserted in one of the walls of that institution by the proprietor of the original premises, the late Mr. Hedger, the father of the present chairman of the Surrey Sessions, as a grateful memorial of a fabric from which he had derived the greater part of his fortune. Strange retribution, that the place which had once been the scene of riot and infamy, should now re-echo only to the ravings of madness and despair!

On Sundays, St. George's Fields were frequented by a select variety of bird-catchers, boxers dog-fanciers, badger-drawers, bull-baiters, foot-ball-players, and vagabonds of every description.

As Jack unconsciously made his dreary and dirty way over them, he chanced to pass " The Dog and Duck." The sounds of riot attracted his attention; he heard music, both vocal and instrumental, and, feeling his mouth parched by excitement, in addition to being extremely tired with the exertion he had gone through during the last few hours, he stepped in to procure at once some rest and some refreshment. Calling for liquor, an ill-looking tapster showed him into a large room at the back of the house, in which, sitting on benches at various small tables in different parts of the room, were assembled together, drinking, smoking, and carousing in every possible manner, from eighty to one hundred persons of both sexes.

This room served as a sort of concert room, somewhat similar to the saloons of the present day, there being a temporary orchestra at one end of it, in which two or three wretched fiddlers were congregated, and where, from time to time, different strolling singers appeared to entertain the company; the songs, as in the case of many of the public-house saloons of our own time, were chiefly of the most vulgar and immoral description, written by the mongrel minstrels of Grub-street and the Seven Dials—wretched scribblers that had no object beyond that of procuring a passing dinner. The first part of the concert was about to close, as Jack

entered, with a favourite chaunt of that period—
‘ The Last Lay of the Fancy Snaffler,’ supposed
to have been originally written, and sung by its
hero, the celebrated amatory highwayman, Claude
du Val himself, whose adventures have before been
noticed. This choice and much relished morceau
was sung, in a slashing, ranting manner, by a dis-
sipated, but rather good-looking and somewhat
showily dressed young fellow, who had formerly
been employed as under cook in the kitchen of a
well-known wealthy Foreign nobleman, but who,
fancying he possessed, to use his own expression,
stew-pan-dous vocal powers, had shewn the various
spits and *dredging*-boxes a fair pair of heels one
fine morning, and boldly set up on his own account
as counter-tenor—his voice being esteemed to be
very fine—the *Count*, or Count Ketchup, as the
singer was generally called, from the dignity of his
late master, was a prodigious favourite with the
visiters of the Dog and Duck, he gave his song with
an air of confidence and recklessness that was most
uproariously applauded and encored. This ‘ pious
chanson’ ran to the following effect :—

The Lay of the Highwayman; or, Love and the Road.

Hurrah ! hurrah ! for the moonlight hour,
  The pleasures of plunder and beauty,
When stars shine bright, and eyes look light,
  And to rifle becomes a duty.

To rule o'er the highway, shall still be my plan,
   The lord of the heath and the common;
With sword and with pistol I'll vanquish each man,
   With gallantry conquer each woman.
Hurrah! then, hurrah, for the moonlight hour,
   The pleasures of plunder and beauty,
When stars shine bright, and eyes look light,
   And to rifle becomes a duty.

Two-fold will I conquer, by fear, and by love,
   My pistols shall beat Cupid's darts;
So courteous, so gallant, so killing, I'll prove,
   I'll steal, with their purses, all hearts.
Though while I affright, I delight will the fair,
   So polite on the road, still I'll be,
My pistol I'll cock, with so gallant an air,
   They'll rejoice to be rifled by me.
Hurrah! then, hurrah, for the moonlight hour, &c.

There shall not be a gallant in Park or in Mall,
   Though the beaux of the town you run o'er,
That shall cost the dear creatures so much as Du Val:
   Or, for whom, they will all give up more.
With lute and with dance, song and saraband gay,
   All hearts, and all eyes, I'll delight,
In the ring, and the concert, I'll conquer by day,
   On the heath, and the highway by night.
Hurrah! then, hurrah, for the moonlight hour, &c.

In the tavern, while seated at ease o'er my wine,
   I'll the day pass away with a friend,
And at eve, at the mask and the play when I shine,
   Who will think 'tis *their* money I spend?
With nobles, at gaming-house, great as a lord,
   I'll cheat with an air *à la mode*,
To the losers still proving 'tis fair with my sword,
   And, at night, wind up all with the road.
Hurrah! then, hurrah, for the moonlight hour, &c.

Be it mine on life's road, still to riffe the fair,
    What pleasure like plundering beauty,
What conquest on earth can with woman compare,
    Her smile, man's most glorious booty.
How sweetly the charmers will tremble and quiver,
    Young and old, maiden, widow, and wife,
When softly I breathe the words—' Stand and deliver!'
    And murmur—" Your money, or life!"
Hurrah! then, hurrah, for the moonlight hour, &c.

With a compliment 'tis that their jewels I'll take,
    With a bow will I vanish from sight,
My crape I'll but wear, for each dear creature's sake,
    'Twould grieve me to murder them quite.
And when my time comes, and I go to the tree,
    Bewept by the loves and the dears,
As I've lived on their smiles, so my solace 'twill be,
    To die 'mid their sighs and their tears.
Hurrah! then, hurrah, for the moonlight hour,
    The pleasures of plunder and beauty,
When stars shine bright, and eyes look light,
    And to rifle becomes a duty.

Previously to the commencement of the Count's
song, Jack had taken his seat on a back bench affixed to the wall, and which ran regularly round
the best part of the room, all the moveable seats
and tables being occupied. When the performance of Count Ketchup's song had closed the first
part of the concert, the audience replenished their
glasses, and smoking and talking became general;
and in the universal buz and hum that ensued,
Jack was some minutes ere he discovered that immediately before him, though with his back towards him, there was sitting on a bench, in company with another person, at one of the tables, no

less a personage than Mr. Jonathan Wild. Jack's attention was first attracted by the mention of Mr. Wild's name in a conversation that was going on between the two.

" How is it, Mr. Wild," said Jonathan's companion, who, it appeared, was one Mr. Shickery, a pettyfogging Fleet attorney, or sixpenny lawyer, as they were called, who procured straw bail for insolvent tradesmen, and was Old Bailey solicitor to some of the more thriving pickpockets, engaging witnesses for them when wanted, having in addition, an extensive practice in similar lines of respectability,—" How is it, Sir, that I meet you here—beating up for recruits, eh ?"

" You have hit it, Mr. Shickery," returned the great man ; " some of my best troops have just been clapped under hatches. Splitting has been the order of the day among them. Bob Wilkinson, who was nabbed and sent to the *Whit* * by Justice Hewitt, for being concerned in making cold meat of Peter Martin, the Chelsea pensioner, and some other little jobs, has peached Milksop, Lincoln, and Lock ; Lock has been laid hold of by Justice Blackerby, and has *sneezed* from a larger *nose* than t'other ; and to-day, my boy Blueskin has been collared, and he has informed against Bill Blewitt, Dick Okey, Jack Junks or Levi, as we call him, and Matt Flood, besides others, of a round dozen of *speaks* in which they

* *Newgate*, from Whittington, its original founder.

have been concerned. Bob Wilkinson must ride
the three-legged mare, for I never pardon murder: there's two or three others must mount the
nubbing cheat too; as for the rest, as they don't
quite weigh their weight yet, I must manage to
get them off—now this will thin my ranks a little,
so, as I must keep up my troops to the full com-
plement, I've come here to see who I can enlist."

" I believe you can't come to a better place,"
returned Mr. Shickery.

" Why, no," said Jonathan, " I generally get
some volunteers here ; I have had most of my best
men from this part of the country, Mr. Shickery,
—there was Will Maggot came from here."

" Oh, what, the spice Toby Cheesemonger?" said
Mr. Shickery.

" The same," returned Jonathan. " I need not
tell you, Mr. Shickery," he continued, " that the
Mint is the place where tradesmen, who have lived
a little too fast, generally retire to when the game
begins to be up : they usually take a few broad
pieces with them, and, as long as the coin lasts
live like fighting cocks ; but when the *gelt's* gone,
and it gets low-water mark with them, then's my
time—they are glad to do anything then."

" By the bye, speaking of Will Maggot, Mr.
Wild, would it be impertinent to ask what is become of that blade ?"

" Oh, the scoundrel !" replied Mr. Wild, " you
know what I did for that rogue, Mr. Shickery, or

if you don't I'll tell you : finding he could not get bread to his *cheese* by his business, the dog came over here ; as he was an active clean-limbed young fellow, I administered to his necessities, and finally concluded by proposing the road to him, as an honourable way of raising the wind : I furnished him with dog's meat* and ammunition † ; in short, from being a rotten cheesemonger, I made a complete gentleman of the snaffle‡ of him, contenting myself with only taking four fifths in the pound of his gains."

" And very liberal, too," said Mr. Shickery, who did not usually leave his clients quite so much.

" So I thought," said Wild ; " but see the ingratitude of man, Mr. Shickery. After I had put bread in his mouth, the villain became discontented, and deserted : for a long time I could obtain no trace of him ; but one day a gentleman coming to my office to inquire after some *tattlers* that had been *fobbed* on the Oxford Road, by a single *bridle cull*, and not being able to find, on referring to my books, (for you know I'm very particular, Mr. Shickery, in noting down my orders), that any gentleman under my command had been on that road for at least three weeks before, a suspicion crossed my mind that it must be my cheesemonger. A few inquiries satisfied me I was right ; so, arming myself at all points, off I set to Oxford in search of him. I peeped into all the stables on

* A horse.   † Pistols.   ‡ Highwayman.

the road, examined the horses, drank with the
ostlers and chamberlains, and inquired what company frequented their different houses; but without success, till, within a short distance of Oxford,
I met with the Oxford stage, the coachman of
which told me that they had just been stopped
and robbed by a single toby man, not a quarter of a mile from the spot, and bade me be
upon my guard. From the description he gave
me I had no doubt it was my gentleman, so I
clapped spurs to my horse and gallopped in the
direction Coachee had pointed out. On arriving at the scene of action that had been, I halted,
like an experienced general, and fell to considering what a man of any discipline would do after
such an incident in order to puzzle and beguile
his pursuers, in case any hue and cry should be
raised to take him : looking around me, I presently found a bye-lane on my left hand, and
rightly considered, that my cheesemonger, being a
man of some conduct, must have struck down that
lane after he had finished his adventure. Accordingly, I took the same course, doubled my speed,
and, after a short gallop, came in sight of a man
in a great coat, well mounted. I judged I had
come to the end of my inquiry : I therefore slack-
ened my pace that I might prepare for battle.
My gentleman, hearing the tramp of a horse looked
back, but, seeing only one man, did not think that
it bore the appearance of a pursuit, and therefore

never moved a step the faster. I must tell you I was at such a distance that he could not recognize my sweet phiz—I was as thickly stuck around with pistols as the man in the almanack is with darts, all ready cocked and primed, but hid from observation by my riding coat. As I approached nearer to him, however, Will cast another look back, and immediately twigged who was his touter*, upon which, without more ado, he faces about manfully enough, and guessing my business, boldly bade me stand off, for that he had done with me. I, however, hadn't done with *him*; still I thought the fox's was my game, so I set to wheedling him, told him I meant no harm, that I was there by chance, and begged we might be better friends than ever we had been. I had my hand all this time on a pistol, but it being under my coat my man of cheese could not perceive it; so I kept on wheedling and wheedling, and drawing closer and closer, till, at length arriving within a distance, where I had a sure and fair aim, I suddenly drew it forth, let fly at him full in the face, and then, rapidly drawing my hanger, with one blow felled him to his horse's feet, where he lay weltering in his gore.

"Having obtained this signal victory over my valiant knight of the butter-tub, you may be sure I was not long in looking after my plunder. Rifling his pockets, I found fifty odd guineas there

* A person on the watch.

together with some movables of value, of which having taken livery and seisin, according to the law of arms, I went to the next town, leading the horse of the slain as a trophy of my prowess. Inquiring for the first justice of the peace, I surrendered myself, telling his worship, I had killed a highwayman, and giving a direction where I had left the body, his worship sent and had it conveyed to the town-hall, when it was known by some stage-coachmen and others, to be the carcase of the *mit-e-y* highwayman that had infested the roads for some time past. Having signified to his worship that I was Jonathan Wild, the famous thief-taker, I was released on my own recognizances, and returned to town loaded with my plunder—and that's the way I'll serve all scoundrel's that would desert from their allegiance, and rob me of my just revenues."

" Quite right, Mr. Wild," returned Mr. Shickery—" quite right." Jack's ear eagerly drank in this recital ; he plainly saw, by the cool manner in which Jonathan narrated this exploit, that he was a man of too much determination to be wantonly trifled with. Jonathan had ordered in a fresh measure of gin—the ' *royal liquor*,' as it was then called ; and, while over this, he and his worthy friend Mr. Shickery were arranging the plan of a little bit of perjury, against the ensuing sessions, a nymph from one of the neighbouring lanes volunteered a *pas seul* to the company, which she performed with rather a scantier quantity of drapery than is even allowed at the Italian Opera House. It is needless to say, it produced thunders of applause, and a very considerable shower of browns.

At this moment Jonathan's attention was attracted by the entrance of a gentleman at the lower end of the room, who strutted down, dressed in the very height cf the fashion—a laced cocked-hat, a peruke which fell in ringlets about his neck, a brocaded waistcoat, a laced coat, with large moulded metal buttons, bearing on their surface the device of an anchor, and a great profusion of mock jewellery, consisting of chains, brooches, and rings. He held a gilt-headed ebony cane in his hand, and wore a pair of false mustachios, to give him a foreign and *distingué* appearance.

" Ah, ah !" said Jonathan, as he fixed his eye upon him, " there is one of my men, Mr. Shickery, the fellow little thinks I am here; he is the very chap I wanted to meet."

" What, that fine gentleman ?" ʼsaid Mr. Shickery; " why, he seems quite a beau."

" Ay, ay, thanks to the tailor," answered Jonathan; " that blade is one of my *spruce prigs*, as I call them. I shall show you some sport with him, in a minute or two: he has been keeping out of my way for some time; he must give an account of himself. I picked him up in a booth at Southwark fair. The *cull* was one of the Grub-street scribblers, and gained a wretched living by cutting down old plays, and making drolls of them. The drolls of ' Hero and Leander,' and the ' Siege of Troy,' performed at Kit Bullock's booth at Bartholomew fair, were among his productions.* The fellow was fond of aping the gentleman, and thrusting himself among his betters; of course, his literary talents did not furnish him sufficient to enable him to do this without assistance; so, scraping an acquaintance with him, as he was acting the gallant in one of the boxes of the booth, I enlisted him into my corps. As he was not exactly fitted to become one of my dragoons ——"

* Nearly one of the last of these drolls, which, by the bye, a collection was published by Francis Kirkman, a bookseller, a volume of rare occurrence, was written by Elkanah Settle, the last of the City poets laureat, it was called, " St. George for England," and was founded on our national legend of St. George and the Dragon, but must not be mistaken for the equestrian extravaganza on the same subject, and of nearly the same name, brought out, some few seasons since, at Drury Lane, by Ducrow, as a substitute for the Christmas pantomime—that droll was merely an attempted improvement and extension of its elder brother.

Poor Elkana performed the part of the Dragon in this droll of St. George, at a booth at Barthomew fair, in a green leather case of his own invention. A ludicrous circumstance attending this performance, obtained him a brothership in that noble foundation the Charter House. In this calm and dignified retreat he died, February the 12th, 1724, aged seventy-six. A posthumous play of his, still extant in print, was represented by the scholars of the Charter House, November the 6th, 173?. The scene was laid in the Vaticum; the characters being, the Devil disguised as a Pilgrim, and two Jesuits. It very curiously marks the feverish apprehensions entertained by the existing Government to the claims of the Pretender at that period.

" Your dragoons !" interrupted Mr. Shickery;
" what are they, Mr. Wild?"

" Why, they are the second division of my
troops. My *cavalry*, or toby men, that only take
the road on horseback, are the first. My dragoons
are gentlemen that serve both on horse and foot—
bold, manly fellows, that I generally send forth
doubly armed; they either take the air on the
wide common, well mounted, and nobly attack the
stage-coach, in the face of open day, or else lie in
ambuscade on foot, or wait *perdue* in some dry
ditch to surprise the heedless traveller. I count
these among my best men, because they have two
strings to their bow. Then there's my *mill-ken
coves*, or *cracksmen*, gentlemen that speak to a
case, and are not afraid to break open houses. I've
got a young fellow of this class just coming out;
he promises to be a rare one; his name's Jack
Sheppard; he'll be a great man or hanged before
he's one-and-twenty, or my name ain't Jonathan
Wild." Jack modestly drew back at this flattering
mention of himself. Mr. Wild continued—" My
fourth division, the spruce prigs, of which this
fellow is one, are a class of gentry of some address
and behaviour. I reserve them to send to court on
birth-nights; also to balls, ridottos, plays, and as-
semblies, for which purpose I furnish them, as you
see by that pattern, with laced coats, brocaded
waistcoats, fine periwigs; and sometimes provide
them with handsome equipages, such as chariots,

chairs, footmen in liveries, a *valet-de-chambre*—
the servants being all thieves like their masters.
That fellow, Jacky Planxty, as he's called from
his love of a dance—he's fond of cutting a caper,
and, but for his chicken heart, might soon dance
upon nothing,—he is an adroit hand enough. At
the last instalment at Windsor, the dog had the
address to possess himself of the Duchess of Marlborough's diamond buckle: she applied to me for
its recovery, but only offering twenty guineas, I
frankly told her the thing was impossible;—'Why,
madam,' said I, ' it cost the gentleman who took
it forty for his coach, and other expenses, to Windsor. You shall see now how I'll frighten him. He
some time ago, with some other rogues like himself (for there's a society of them), robbed and
greatly disfigured a *French* gentleman, and never
gave me any share of the profits, for which I'll
now bring him to book." With these words Jonathan made his way to where the beau was standing, and tapping him on the shoulder, presently
returned with him, he looking very pale and confused. Making him sit down, Jonathan, with many
menaces, began to question him where he had
passed the last two months.

The beau, in a very great fright, begged Jonathan to forgive him, urging he'd been in gaol, in
Lincolnshire, where he went to entrap a lady of
fortune; but that, miscarrying in his design, he
had *spoke* with a silver tankard and some spoons,

for which he was committed; "however," he said,
" I managed so well with Nimble Dick, who appeared as my servant, that nothing was found upon
me—so the pimps discharged me on my trial for
want of evidence; but," continued he, " I am now
on a capital lay, Mr. Wild, if you'll only let me
go, I am sure of getting a gold watch, and, upon
my honour, I'll bring you some money to morrow,
besides standing a bottle to-night, with the money
I have got from Mr. Pinkethman for a new droll
' Pyramus and Thisbe.'"

What the result of this intercession might have
been Jack was not suffered to know, for just then
a quarrel having taken place between a sailor and
a drunken blood, who had seduced a black lady,
the exclusive possession of whose charms had been
guaranteed for sundry broad pieces paid by the
tar, a general fight soon became the consequence
—the lights were all put out—the tables overturned—the fiddlers' heads broken—the glasses smash-
ed, and a scene of confusion created which beggars
all description; in the midst of which Jack managed, undetected by Mr. Wild, without waiting
for the second part of the concert, to vacate the
premises, and make good his retreat.

It was now fast approaching to midnight: the
sky, which had all the evening looked lurid and
unsettled, now became overcast with large masses
of black clouds; the atmosphere, which had been
particularly heavy and oppressive, changed its tem-

perature, and became dankly chill. A sullen silence brooded all around. Jack, seeing that a storm was fast approaching, pushed his way briskly onwards to procure a shelter for the night. Quitting St. George's Fields, and crossing a spot called the Mall, a much frequented rural walk at that time, he entered upon some marshes forming part of Lower Lambeth; they were both lonely and disagreeable, little frequented by day, and still less by night: the progress across them was rendered more difficult by a quantity of plashy pools and clumps of dwarf osiers.

It was whilst traversing this desolate rout that a low gust of wind arose; the stars were obscured from sight by hurrying masses of dark clouds; and the moon had sunk in the heavens: it now became so intensely dark that Jack could not distinguish his path, but blindly made his way with the greatest difficulty. The gust of wind we have mentioned gradually died in a series of low moans and fitful sobbings, or soughings, as the Scotch expressively term them. The silence became still more ominous; some large drops of rain then fell, at distant intervals, with a force and plash that caused an indistinct terror from being of rare occurrence. The elements were in this uncertain state when, all at once, there was a vivid flash of lightning, which completely lit up the whole scene, making the darkness more terrible, by making it perfectly visible. It was instantly followed by a report, as from a

T

cannon, which was caused by the falling of a thunderbolt ; this seemed to be the signal for a general conflict of the elements. A storm arose, such as is but seldom experienced in favoured England.

It will be remembered that the month was August. The storm was one that might be called a harvest storm. It is remarkable, but true, that the genius of the tempest usually rages more violently in summer than even in winter. The rain began to descend in torrents, falling literally in sheets of water ; the wind blew a perfect hurricane ; and, between every pause, flashes of blue forked lightning, and re-bellowing claps of thunder, loud and long-continued, seemed to awaken, to assert their supremacy.

Jack was very soon drenched to the skin, but he stoutly pushed onwards, till, emerging from the marshes, he found himself near the antiquated Manor House, Vauxhall. The Gardens, which were at that season a place of great entertainment and resort, had been closed for some hours, the performances invariably ending by eight o'clock. Jack looked round in vain for some place of safety and shelter, and heartily wished himself in Mr. Wood's little back garret again.

The storm did not at all abate its rigour, nor did he slacken his pace ; he pushed on till the appearance of a cluster of nine noble elms, now bending and shrieking in the blast, informed him he was in the little sylvan spot which, from their vicinity to it, bore then, as it still does now, the name of " Nine Elms." There was no public-house there in those days: two or three gentle-mens' seats, and about the same number of rude cottages, all closely barred up, seeming, from their stillness and the absence of any sort of light, as if they were the mansions of the dead, formed its only residences.

Hurrying down the little lane that runs through it, and crossing an intermixture of fields and mar-ket gardens, Jack now found himself on a wide common, which from its contiguity to the Thames, that then burst upon his view, roaring and writh-ing in the storm like a lashed monster, he imme-diately knew to be that of Battersea.

" Surely this common must lead to some human habitation," he exclaimed ; " at all events, I have no alternative but to cross it." Again the tempest raged with redoubled wildness, and again he in-creased his speed, when he was stopped by sud-denly encountering a party of six or eight gaunt-looking men, whose approach he had not, in the darkness, observed.

" Halloa, youngster !" cried out one of them, in a harsh loud voice ; " what are you doing out at this hour ? I must take the liberty of searching you, my kinchen cove ; you can be after no good."

Here he began to address a few words to his companions in Romanee, which Jack partially un-derstood, expressing his conviction that, as he was so wet, the best thing they could do would be to strip Jack to the skin, and accommodate him with a lodging in a neighbouring ditch.

From their pattering Romanee, Jack immediately knew they were gipsies; and as any attempts at resistance against such odds in number and strength would have been the height of madness, as also would have been any appeal to their compassion, he bethought him of an expedient which, as it ultimately proved, served his purpose.

" What, brother Romaners !" he exclaimed, " why, you surely wouldn't go to harm a ben cove* like me in the darkmans†, would you ?—see here, my dimber dambers, I am one of yourselves, free of every common from Romeville to Lesser Egypt—I bear the seal of Pharaoh, my hearts," holding his wrist out to let them ascertain by the glare of the lightning that he was speaking the truth;" and I charge you in the name of Queen Zara, and under pain of the curse of the Red Sea, to let me pass unmolested, and afford me aid and succour, by telling me where I may procure a shelter from the storm."

" Ah, a Romanee brother ! under what chief were you naturalized ?"

" Duke Martin, the black," returned Jack.

" Ah ! the Earl of Hungary," replied the gipsy, " we must allow the cull pass to free, brothers— the gipsy must not break faith—a true Romaner

* Good fellow.   † Night.

always respects the *seal*. Pass on, boy; keep by the bank; never mind the biting, cutting blast from the river, nor the chilling dashings of the spray, and a short quarter of a mile hence, upon the common, you will find a house where, if it's shelter you are seeking, you may chance obtain it. It is rather a queerish place, certainly, but any port in a storm, as the shipmen say. It is called the *Red* House, not for its colour, for age has turned it black enough for that matter, but because it was the last place in which Ikey Samuels, the Jew pedlar, was seen alive, when he was returning from Chertsey fair with the produce of his wares; he was found in a ditch a short distance from the house, with his throat cut and his pockets turned inside out, the morning after he had put up there. Old Luke Royster, the landlord, swore that he knew nothing about it; that the poor sheeny had left his house the night before in safety, and as there was no evidence, why, of course, the matter dropped. If Luke should ride rusty, and refuse to let you in, you can give him the pass word, " Corn in Egypt," and that will give you admittance whoever may be there; perhaps there may be some knights of the post there—their pops have been heard about these quarters lately. If you should fall into any of their hands, you have only to show them the seal, that will be sufficient — thought may go free then. And now, ben darkmans to you, son of the tribe."

" Ben darkmans to you, my Romanee coves,"
said Jack, " and thank ye, brothers — zounds, it
comes down faster than ever, I've staid pattering
here too long," and away he dashed again.

" A pretty chick, that," said a gipsy, as he and
his companions resumed their walk to town.

They were soon out of sight of each other.

The stunted willows that skirted the common
nearest the river moaned and bent to the blast as
Jack made his way under them. He was not long
in arriving at the house to which he had been
directed by the gipsies. It was a rude, uncouth
structure, the work of different periods, built entirely of wood. It may be proper to mention here,
that though standing nearly on the same site, this
was not the Red House that is now so much the
resort of our cockney and other shots. It has long
been swept away, and the present structure erected in its place, with its frontage of glaring red,
expressly to give a colour to the former's question-
able name—" The Red House."   Pigeons are still
plucked in the modern structure, as in the old one;
but the shooting practised, though perhaps not less
sanguinary, is of a more allowable and innocent
description.

Lights were visible through the crevices of some
of the crazy boards, for the house was closely shut
up, and between the gusts of the storm Jack heard
a murmur of voices within. He knocked long and
loud at the door, but no one answered ; for some

time he continued his application, and at length a gruff voice within was heard, demanding—

"Who's there?—What do you want?"

"I'm a traveller," answered Jack. shivering with cold. "I want shelter and refreshment."

"Then you can't have them," answered the voice; "we are all gone to bed."

Drenched and shivering as he was, Jack thought it would be folly to stand on further parley, so he resolved to give the pass word at once.

"What, won't you let me in?" he exclaimed; "You need not be afraid—'*I have corn in Egypt.* You'll let me in now, I suppose."

"Oh! that's another matter," resumed the voice; "wait a minute, and I'll open the door."

Some bolts were withdrawn, the chain unfastened, a rusty lock turned, and Jack was once more under cover.

"Come in," said Mr. Royster, for it was the worthy landlord himself. "You must be quick, and let me give you what you want at once, for I've a private party in the ale-room—some gemmen that are met there on particular business, and wouldn't like to be disturbed. You won't want to stay here till the morning, will you?"

"I have no other resource," said Jack; "I am completely worn out with walking, and you hear the storm is raging as furiously as ever. You may give me a shake down any where—I am not at all particular."

" I am sure I don't know where I can put you," answered the host, looking somewhat perplexed. " Stop ! now I think of it, there is the little lumber room, at the top of the house; it stands on the flats, where the gemmen goes up to take views of the beautiful prospects, and smoke their pipes in the fine weather—my observatory, as I calls it. You must hold hard on by the floor, if the wind should happen to carry your nest away, which I shouldn't wonder at, for it's a gimcrack place."

" It will do capitally," said Jack, " I'll warrant me. Now then, just give me a hunk of bread and cheese, and a double dram of strong waters to keep out the cold, and I don't care how soon you show me to my straw."

" Step this way, then," said Mr. Royster; " you shall be accommodated in a breath; but if you had not had that pass from Romanee, the devil a bit you'd have got in here, I can tell you that."

Taking Jack into a little side bar, Mr. Royster soon produced a loaf, and part of a Dutch cheese, with a curious globular-shaped bottle, formed of thick black glass, filled with Hollands of extraordinary strength. Jack fell to immediately, and worked away in such right good earnest, as very soon nearly to clear all before him.

Loud and imperious cries of " landlord—landlord—Luke Royster !" issuing from the ale parlour, Mr. Royster hurried Jack up some crazy stairs to the lumber room he had spoken of at the top of the house. It was a wretched shed, which seemed scarcely able to hold itself together: there was a small window at one side, formed by a bull's-eye pane of glass, to admit the day-light, and a door in the front leading out to the roof of the general building, which was flat, and afforded to occasional guests and visiters convenient prospects of the surrounding country. As Jack afterwards discovered, access was obtained to this roof from the bowling-green and skittle-ground at the back of the house, by means of a small wooden spiral staircase, which, but for being accommodated with a hand-rail, would have seemed very much like a ladder. In this select retreat, amid a profusion of old baskets, broken chairs, and other lumber, there was, fortunately for our hero, a truss of straw and two or three bundles of hay. Bidding Jack not to be surprised if he was disturbed by any noise in the night, Mr. Royster, shaking down the straw and arranging the bundles of hay, so as to form a sort of bed, wished Jack good night, and returned down stairs to attend on his particular guests in the ale parlour. He was no sooner gone than Jack threw himself down on the straw, and, fatigued as he was, despite the tumult of the tempest, immediately fell into a sound sleep, in which we will for the present chapter leave him.

CHAPTER XVI.

JACK A BENEDICT.

THE PRIZE REGAINED.—RURAL FELICITY.—THE ASP AMONG THE FLOWERS.

How long Jack slept he knew not: he was awakened by a sense of restlessness, which is not unusual after great fatigue, when we start after a short slumber, feeling as if we were even too tired to sleep. He rolled from one side of his humble couch to the other, turned and turned about, and endeavoured, in vain, to recompose himself to rest; there was a thrilling of weariness in every limb, amounting almost to pain, that effectually prevented him. The storm had completely died away —the wind was hushed, as were the pealings of thunder and the peltings of the rain—he could distinctly hear the voices of the guests below, intermingled every now and then with loud guffaws of laughter, announcing they were still engaged in their revelries.

Finding sleep impracticable, Jack arose and shook himself: his limbs were a little stiff from his exertions and the drenching he had experienced;

his clothes, however, from the heat of his body, had completely dried on his back, and the glow, occasioned by the copious drams of strong Hollands that he had taken, seemed to offer a guarantee against any evil consequences. A bright flood of light streaming through the pane of glass we have before mentioned, induced Jack to unfasten the door of his cabin that opened on the roof of the general building.

A change, as if wrought by enchantment, presented itself on his doing this : the clouds, having discharged themselves of their stormy elements, had left the sky perfectly clear and serene : the moon had again risen, and as if to re-assert her empire in the heavens after the late conflict, beamed with even a broader, fairer refulgence than usual, pouring a rich galaxy of silvery pearls upon the living waters of the Thames, which derived additional brilliancy from their ever-changing and sparkling motion. The common itself was bathed in liquid light, from the reflection of the moon on its dank verdure—all was calm and pellucid beauty.

Jack, who afterwards proved himself a bit of a poet, though perhaps not of the very first order, could not help being struck with the splendour of the scene :—his glance wandered across the Thames. On the opposite bank to the left, stood the noble gardens and sacred halls of Chelsea Hospital, founded by that luxurious monarch, Charles the Second, at the instance of the fine free-hearted Nell Gwynne. As Jack viewed this honoured retreat of the veteran brave, he could not help thinking how much superior was that queen of frail ones to the many frail queens, of which history records such sad and degrading memorials. He had remained gazing for some time, lost in various reflections, when he was aroused from his reverie by the distant splash of oars, and, looking forward, distinctly saw a boat making its way from that part of the opposite shore towards the right, then known by the name of the Five Fields, Chelsea, a place notorious for having been the scene of frequent robberies and murders; it rowing directly towards him, he observed it more minutely. A tall female, closely muffled up, stood in the stern of the boat, seemingly attending to another female figure, which, enveloped in white, appeared to be crouching down at her feet. Three or four men, in the uniform of foot-soldiers, were seated in the other part of the boat not occupied by the rowers. As they neared towards a parcel of rude white stones, which had been fixed in the water as a sort of landing-place nearest that part of the bank which led to the Red House, Jack, not willing to be regarded as a spy, concealed himself behind some boarding supporting the lower part of a high flag-staff erected on the flats, for the purpose of colours being hoisted on the occasion of rowing-matches, &c.

It was not long before the party gained the shore, and began to hail the place of their destination, as it turned out to be.

" Ahoy ! Ahoy, there ! Red House—landlord—Master Royster—Luke—bear a hand—make her fast there, Charley ! Now come—look sharp there—are you going to keep us here for ever ?"

The door of the Red House was immediately opened, and Mr. Royster appeared, bearing a light, followed by a gentlemanlike-looking portly person in black, and some others.

" Why, what the devil has detained you, friends, till this time ?" inquired Mr. Royster.

" Why, the storm to be sure," answered a voice from the boat ; " who the plague would have thought of crossing the water in such a hurly-burly as we have had ? But, come, lend us a hand."

The party now began to issue from the boat, the tall muffled female supporting the one we have noticed as being enveloped in a white mantle, whose deep sobbings were perfectly audible. The soldiers followed ; Jack thought he recognised the face of one of them, but in the confused light, occasioned by the flickering of the candle borne by Royster, and the gleams of the moon, he could not, at the moment, recollect where he had seen it. Making their way to the house the door was soon closed upon them, and Jack returned to his shed, in some surprise at the scene he had just witnessed.

He could not conceive what could be the purpose of a visit at such an hour. A thousand strange conjectures stole across his mind : he felt a secret prescience that some strange adventure was about to occur in which his interference might be required ; and, without any fear for the consequences, his first step was to look at his pistols, the product of Mr. Wild's gratuity. On examining them, he found the priming had sustained no injury from his drenching : he therefore cocked them ready for action. There was a great murmur of voices below ; he distinctly heard much hurrying of footsteps backwards and forwards, and slamming of doors ; but nothing occurred particularly to command his notice till he heard a door open at the back of the house leading into the yard, and immediately beneath distinguished a low muttering of voices, one of which sounded strangely familiar to him : its hollow tones could not possibly be mistaken for any other than those of Zara, the gipsy queen, the mysterious person who seemed to exercise so strange an influence over the destinies of his lost bride, poor Bess.

Greatly excited, and resolved, at all hazards, to gratify his curiosity, Jack immediately stole out of the door of his fragile nest, and, stretching himself full length on the flat roof at that part that commanded a view of the back of the premises, the moon then shining in all her lambent majesty, discovered to him two persons engaged in close and earnest conversation ; he immediately recognised in one the well-known figure of Zara, now divested of the mantle that had shrouded her, for it was she whom he had seen in the boat. The other, a male, was a portly but somewhat shorter person, dressed in black, wearing the air of a respectable attorney, or some other professional character ; he appeared to have been speaking with some apprehension, for Zara was endeavouring to assure him.

" Make your mind easy, Squire," said the sibyl, " I have noted well the planets—the wench's die is cast. From the conjunction at her birth disgrace and guilt were threatened her ; I read a felon's fate within her horoscope ; that I this night have snatched her from ; the baleful influence of adverse stars may be averted if we foresee it timely : the camp and the canteen, and not the lofty hall and gay assembly, as in thy solitude thou'st feared, shall be her portion. I snatched her at her birth from rank and fortune, moved by an artful villain—that bold, bad man——"

" Hush ! mention not his name," shudderingly interrupted her companion, " it chills my blood to hear it."

" I have no pleasure in mentioning it," bitterly answered the gipsy ; " but, as I said, I snatched her at her birth from rank and fortune : it was a wicked deed, yet not mine all the guilt, and I have made some expiation. I snatch her now from infamy and crime, the prison and the scaffold ; and though the lot to which I have consigned her is humble, it is honest—what would'st thou more, Squire, to calm thy fears? Hast thou not seen her wedded with thine own eyes scarce twelve hours since, and to the soldier, Rupert Lyon? Is he not now with her, surrounded by his comrades? Will not their nuptials here be consummated?—Can she escape?—for shame—for shame."

" Well, well—I will be satisfied," said her companion, who did not, however, appear over and above convinced with her arguments. " You have kept faith with me—done all that you promised. You say the soldier departs to morrow with his regiment?"

" Ay, for America," cried Zara, exultingly?"

" And bears her with him?"

" Thanks to his officer's permission; your gold, Squire, purchased that; fear not, she'll ne'er return! I am to join them in the morning to see their embarkation, and give the dower to Rupert you promised with his bride. I'd not stay now. Poor Bess!—the wench is squeamish; her bridal night may be a rough one. Where do you go from hence, Squire,—to Edgeware?"

" No, no, not there; never have I visited it since that fatal night; I shall return to Hampstead."

" I'll see you on the road. There is a ferry just below; the boatman knows me, and will get up to take us over: a back gate here leads to a path directly in our line ; we need not return to the house to say farewell. Luke Royster has my orders, and morning's dawn will see me here again. Come, Squire, cheer up—this way. Why, what a heavy step !"

" My heart is heavier than my steps, good, Zara," said her companion, in a tone of much deep sadness. " I know not how it is, but though that which has passed within these few hours makes me secure for ever, I could fain wish that it had never passed. That terrible storm ! it seemed to wake in reprobation. The very elements recoiled at what was doing. Heaven grant we do not fatally repent it !"

" Faint heart !" indignantly sneered Zara. " Why, Squire, I deemed you more a man. You will think otherwise to morrow. Rouse up ! this way—this way !"

She drew him almost unconsciously after her ; their echoing footsteps died away in the distance, and Jack, who had listened with an intensity almost painful, to every word that had fallen from them, withdrew again to his shed, his senses in a perfect whirl of astonishment, indignation, and alarm. A thousand plans presented themselves to him for the rescue of his beloved Bess from the power of her ravisher—for that it was she and the soldier, that had accompanied Zara in the boat, and were then below, there could be no doubt. Ere he had time, however, to resolve upon any thing, a loud shriek which reached his ear, and which he instantly recognised as the voice of his bride, determined him. Drawing forth his pistols, and rushing out of the room with the fury of a hunted tiger, he with one bound dashed down the stairs, and bursting into the ale parlour, from whence the cry proceeded, saw his beloved Bess struggling in the rude embraces of the ruffian Rupert. He instantly discharged his pistol. The villain let go his hold, but Bess was immediately seized by his companions; the discharge of a second pistol soon, however, set the poor girl at liberty again. With a shriek of joy she flew towards him. Holding her with one hand, and seizing the poker with the other, Jack made his way towards the door, which in the consternation excited by the fire-arms, he gained ere they had power to intercept him. Upsetting a table, the better to cover his retreat, and extinguishing the candles which happened to be upon it, in their fall, leaving the room in total darkness, he locked the door on the outside, and rushing out at the front, made his way, with Bess in his arms, to the little stone jetty, or landing-place, where he had seen the boat moored that brought the party there. Safely depositing his fair burden within it, he unloosed it from its fastenings, hastily seized an oar, and pushing the boat from the bank was soon in the middle of the river. The tide was favourable, and with but little exertion the lovers rapidly drifted down towards Putney.

They had floated completely out of reach when they saw the party they had left emerging from the house, and witnessed the rage and disappointment manifested by them at their escape. By the lights hurrying to and fro, it was plain the baffled party was searching for the boat, which they had evidently missed. There being now no immediate danger of being overtaken, Jack had time, as they floated silently down the stream, to devote a few moments to his beloved. We will pass over the tender endearments they exchanged on thus unexpectedly regaining possession of each other; nothing is so rapturous in reality, and so mawkish in detail, as the caresses of lovers. Love is a wholly selfish feeling, not to be participated in, or calculated to excite any sympathy, except when unsuccessful, by any but the parties personally concerned. Bess's history was soon told. She had been hurried from place to place, she knew not whither; this, however, she did know—that, in spite of her entreaties, her prayers, her tears, the haughty Zara, urged by a stranger she had never seen till that time, had but a few hours before caused her to be united, almost through violence, to the hateful soldier, by the aid of a Fleet parson; that then she had been conveyed to a canteen in the neighbourhood of Chelsea, where the soldier had remained drinking with some of his boisterous companions, till the subsiding of the storm allowed the whole party to cross the Thames to the Red

House, from whence Jack had so providentially rescued her.

Jack's relation, in his turn, was suited to circumstances. His search for her, and his being forced to seek shelter in the Red House, accounted for every thing. Holding a council of war, Jack rightly considered the enemy's first step would be to cross the water in search of them ; he therefore wisely determined, in order that his foes might take nothing by their motion, not to cross the water at all, but to keep close in shore, on the Surrey side. After floating down the river some time, and passing the ferry at Chelsea Reach he saw a very convenient creek, running considerably into the bank, into which he found he could push his boat, and by means of the sedge, the high flags and rushes, and the overhanging osiers, remain perfectly concealed. In this creek, then, he moored his little bark, and waited the progress of events, that he might better shape his future course. They had not continued there long, when the sound of voices adown the bank, in the distance, and the glaring of lights, announced that their pursuers were advancing in the direction towards them.

" Lie close, Bess," whispered Jack ; " doff your bonnet, lass, that your white streamers may not discover us, and nestle to me, love—closer, closer, dear."

Bess required no second bidding.

"Ah! they stop at the ferry," cried Jack, exultingly, "Just as I thought; they want to cross, and have come here for a boat. Ah! that splashing of oars—'tis the ferry-boat, returning in the very nick—hark, they hail it."

"Ahoy—ahoy, there, ferryman—quick—quick! you are out early, old man!"

"Surely you can have had no passengers at this hour?" inquired one amongst the party, whom Bess recognised, by the voice, to be the soldier.

"Ay, but I have, though," returned the ferry-man; "I have just taken a *couple* over; plague on them for rousing me out of my night-cap in this manner, though they paid well: if they were for any love passage, which I should hardly think they were, I wish they had stopped till it was fairly morning."

"'Tis they," ejaculated the soldier, eagerly; "that jade, Bess, and the scoundrel that took her off, and obliged me with a bullet in the fleshy part of my arm—he must be a very devil incarnate—that fellow, no doubt, has cut the boat adrift, and come here to gain time."

"He's got seventeen shillings to pay for broken glass and china," growled out Luke Royster, "if ever I catch him, I can tell him that. Do you know which way they took after you landed them, boatman?"

"Oh, yes! they took the King's Road, and, I dare say, are at Knightsbridge by this time. I heard them talk of making their way to Hampstead."

" They must get into town first," returned the soldier; " we may overtake them in the Five Fields."

" Ay, ay, and knock his brains out if you choose, there's nobody to prevent it there—it's a nice place that," muttered Mr. Royster.

" We must follow them instantly, boatman," cried the soldier, " so tack about—now, my lads, jump in, we have not a moment to lose—over's the word."

" I shall require double fare such an unseasonable hour as this."

" We'll not quarrel about the money, boatman," answered the soldier, " you shall have treble fare, only take us over quickly."

" That's another thing," said the boatman, feathering his oars; " now then, my masters, just dress the boat a bit to keep her steady, and you shall fly."

The old ferryman was almost as good as his word—he half performed a miracle; in three minutes the whole party were nearly across the river.

" Nothing can be more plummy than this, Bess," said Jack, in high spirits, as he saw them depart; " they are on a wrong scent: it's the old hag, Zara, and the mysterious cove that was with her, that the old fellow carried over; they are safe to follow them to town; and, while they are gone, 'now's our time. I've, in my hurry, left my luggage behind me at that infernal Red House, and, if I mistake not, so have you, lass. Now, it won't do exactly for us to commence matrimony without a rag to our backs, or a stiver in our pockets, so I shall just take the liberty, while the party are engaged in their wild goose chase, and the worthy landlord is absent, to return to the crib we've just left, and help myself to my own. We never could have a better opportunity. There can only be the slavey in charge of the premises (for, you see, they have got the tapster with them), and, no doubt, she's asleep fast enough, though if she shouldn't be, or should happen to wake, I can soon manage her. You lie close here, and in twenty minutes I'll return with our little property, and something else to make us comfortable into the bargain."

" Dear Jack," cried Bess, who half trembled at the risk he was about to run, " be cautious for my sake, dearest."

" Never fear, wench !" cried Jack; " but let me feed my bull-dogs before I go," coolly beginning to re-load his pistols. " There, now all's right, so off I go." With a hearty smack, Jack departed, and once more made his way to the Red House.

All was perfectly quiet as he approached it; there was no light visible, no sound audible. Entering the garden through the gate at the back, which the gipsy had left open, he crossed the bowl-ing-green and skittle-ground, and softly ascended the spiral staircase we have before noticed, which ran up by the side of the house, and led to the flats on the roof. He found the door of the lum-ber-room was, as he had left it, open to his pur-pose; he immediately entered and secured his bundle, from which he took a dark lantern, which he illumined with his friend Mr. Blueskin's phos-phorus box, and began cautiously to descend the stairs in the interior of the house.

Making his way without any interruption to the little ale parlour, the locality of the late conflict, and which presented a sad scene of confusion, he soon secured Bess's little bundle, and also took possession of the soldier's side-arms, consisting of his bayonet, cartouche-box, &c., which had been incautiously left there, well aware that their loss would subject the back of the son of Mars, on the following day, to an exemplary scratching of the Cat at the halberts. From the ale parlour Jack proceeded to the bar, where he found the maid-servant, sitting in an arm-chair, in a most blissful state of somnolency, and making such a noise with her own nose, as effectually to prevent her being disturbed by any other noise less vehement.

In the bar Jack helped himself to several " in-considerable trifles," particularly the loose coin in Mr. Royster's till, amounting to about three pounds, in silver, copper, and gold, a very fine knuckle of ham, a choice bag of biscuits, a bottle of ale, and another of curious old brandy, all of which he carefully stowed in his capacious pockets. He was then about departing, when all at once his eye rested upon the well-known wallet of queen Zara, which was deposited on one of the shelves of the bar, as it would appear, for greater safety. Jack remembered the few words that had dropped from the gipsy in the garden, respecting Bess's portion.

" There can be no harm in my taking this," he thought ; " 'twill only be my right—what I'm entitled to by law, by virtue of my wife—so, with your leave," he exclaimed, and immediately secured it, to bear company with the other property. Leaving the bar, and softly opening, and carefully closing after him the back door, he was, in five minutes more, safe in the arms of Bess.

Their mutual joy at the result of the expedition may be easily imagined, especially when, on examining the wallet, they found it contained, along with a variety of other articles, twenty guineas in gold, the fortune intended to have been given with Bess to the soldier.

" As he is not at his post, I must be his substitute," cried Jack, pocketing the cash ; " but now, Bess, for a little refreshment ; you must needs stand in want of something, and, to confess the truth, so do I, and then we'll about ship and away."

Making a hasty, but extremely relishing repast

off the ham and biscuits, which they washed down
with the ale, and a small portion of the brandy to
keep the cold off their stomachs, Jack committed
the soldier's accoutrements to the custody of Old
Father Thames, to whom also he confided the care
of the boat, which he sent adrift without oars or
rudder, and then, taking Bess under his arm,
pushed on in the direction of Richmond, stopping
to rest some time in the ruins of an old mill which
they passed in their progress through Kew. As
they now took their time, it was broad day when
they arrived at Richmond, and they found no difficulty in procuring some breakfast at the " Three
Pigeons," a small public-house in a bye street, in
that side the town nearest the river: here, the
place appearing private and convenient, they resolved to put up and spend a few days of their
honey-moon. To avoid discovery, they kept themselves to themselves as much as possible, content
with their own company, and wishing nothing else.

Who shall tell their delightful evening walks in
the park, and on the hill of that beautiful town,
so completely justifying, by its rich mound, and
sheeny splendour, both its ancient and modern appellation. In Richmond, then, did the lovers
continue some time—" the world forgetting, by
the world forgot," till a visible diminution in their
little treasury warned Jack it was time to look out
for squalls, and he beat about him to find if he
could not procure some honest employment in his

own trade of a carpenter, and provide a lodging which should be at once more economical and comfortable, than that afforded by the " Three Pigeons." Love and a cottage occurred to them both—to Bess poetically, to Jack practically. She only saw, in the perspective, roses and eglantine, sunshine and smiling cherubs, the cooing dove, the gurgling brooks, the shepherd's pipe, innocence and happiness. Jack thought of the savoury rasher on the coals, the barrel of ale, brown bread, and a pipe at evening with a neighbour, some noisy urchins, plenty and content. Both were equally satisfied with the prospect. Not deeming it exactly prudent to settle on that side the Thames, Jack crossed the water and accidentally falling in with a master carpenter in the little town of Fulham, to whom he represented he had served his time with a person in Smithfield, he was engaged by him as a journeyman.

A very neat cottage, situated in the midst of gardens, happening just then to be unoccupied in the pleasant neighbouring village of Parson's Green, Jack, under the name of Edgeworth, immediately became its tenant. Although, instead of doves, it was only visited by some chirping sparrows, and a dirty puddle ran by the side of it instead of a purling brook, Bess managed to be satisfied with it. Jack's expectations being more *realizable*, he was, of course, satisfied. How long their unmixed happiness might have continued, if it had not been for a circumstance which shortly afterwards occurred, it might have been hard to say : but, alas ! " the course of true love never *did* run smooth, and love in a cottage—except it happen to be a cottage *ornée*—was never known to continue unalloyed for more than a month, and that month the honeymoon, at least as far as our experience has permitted us to ascertain.   An event soon occurred, that blighted all their hopes, marred all their joys, and o'erturned all their plans : but it is of too much importance in this history not to form the subject of a separate chapter.   We shall therefore leave our unsuspecting lovers to enjoy their last meal of bread and cheese and kisses, in the uncloyed felicity of their rural retreat, and screw up our courage to the narration of the many stirring and exciting incidents that will rapidly follow.

CHAPTER XVII.

LOVE LAUGHS AT LOCKSMITHS.

A NEW FOE WITH AN OLD FACE.—CAPTURE OF EDGEWORTH BESS.—JACK'S ASTONISHING ESCAPE FROM THE NEW PRISON.

On the day of the untoward occurrence to which we have alluded in our last chapter, Jack had, early in the morning, left his beloved Bess, and repaired, according to custom, to the shop of his new master, Mr. Timbs, for so that gentleman was called. He found Mr. Timbs in unusual good spirits.

"We shall have a visiter, Edgeworth," said he; "a brother chip — yes, my old fellow apprentice, whom I have not seen for these twenty years, and whom I had quite lost sight of. Having, through a friend, heard of my settling in this town, he has written me a letter, signifying his intention of coming and spending the day with me, to talk over old times, and be once more boys again, as we used to be—rather old boys, to be sure; but no matter for that, it's no consequence how old every other part may be, if the heart be young.

My limbs may be fifty, but my heart is still only fifteen; therefore I'm resolved to be merry, and enjoy myself to-day, if I never do so again; and you, Edgeworth, shall enjoy yourself too. Yes, yes! my old friend and fellow-apprentice knows how to value a good workman, and will not refuse to take a glass with you, though he was never any great things of a workman himself. Poor fellow! we are not all gifted alike. Therefore you will hold yourself in readiness, Mr. Edgeworth."

Jack expressed his willingness and gratitude. Mr. Timbs left him finishing some little jobs whilst he went to the stage office to await his old fellow-apprentice's arrival.

Merrily whistling away in the lightness of his heart, and sending the shavings flying in all directions, Jack thought no more of this intimation till it was recalled to his remembrance by the brisk re-entrance of Mr. Timbs, exclaiming with much glee—

" This way, my dear Owen, this way—here we are, all snug and comfortable—this is an unexpected pleasure, 'faith!"

" Owen!" said Jack, the name strangely tingling in his ears, " why, surely it can't be——"

Ere he could finish the doubt it was at once removed—his old master, Mr. Wood, stood before him!

" Mercys of Cot! who is this, look you?" screamed out the astonished Welshman, on seeing Jack.

" My journeyman, Edgeworth," answered the good-natured Mr. Timbs, " and a very clever fellow he is, too, I can assure you."

" He is one fery great rascal ! look you, Roger Timbs," roared the ancient Briton. " Journeyman ! he is my apprentice, look you—and what nonsense is this you talk apout ?—Etgeworth !— Etgeworth !—the fillain's name is Sheppart, though Cot help me, he has peen more of the wolf than the sheppart : put hur will have justice—to not let him go, he is one rogue, one runaway ; he has proken into houses, proken out of prisons, look you —help, help, goot peoples, in Cot's name, in the King's name," *seizing Jack's collar*, " hur charges you all to aid and assist, look you."

Mr. Timbs was petrified by this sudden movement of his friend ; and so, to confess the truth, was Jack ; but the enraged Cambrian's outcry, having collected together a considerable number of spectators, our hero was soon secured ; and, on Mr. Wood's information of his being one of the most notorious villains breathing, was conveyed to the Fulham cage, which just then happened to be empty. The constable of Fulham, having some parish business which required his attendance before their worships at Westminster, was on the very point of setting out for town, therefore, after a somewhat wordy recapitulation by Mr. Wood of Jack's various offences, it was settled that the constable should convey him to London at once ; Mr.

Wood declaring, " he should not pe aple to eat a pit till he hat seen the fillain hanged." Jack was, of course, allowed no time to take leave of poor Bess. who did not discover what had taken place till some hours afterwards, when, almost heart-broken, she determined to follow and search him out.

Arriving in London, it being too late to take Jack before the chamberlain that day, he was conveyed to the house of Mr. Justice Newton, who, after a short inquiry, committed him to St. Ann's roundhouse, preparatory to a further examination in the evening. How poor Bess got to town, and by what means she traced Jack out, it is not exactly necessary to detail. It will be remembered that she had only been united to the object of her choice and love a few short months, that she was eighteen, was a woman ! What wonder, then, that she arrived at St. Ann's roundhouse nearly as soon as Jack himself ? It so happened, that Mr. Hannibal Guffin, the parish functionary of St. Giles's, was passing St. Ann's " Donjon Keep" at the very moment the constable of Fulham was conveying Jack to its custody, and recognizing his former prisoner, he stept in to renew his acquaintance with him, and put his brother in authority, the keeper of St. Ann's, upon his guard.

Jack saluted him in the most courteous manner as he saw him enter, affectionately inquiring after his health, and hoping he had sustained no cold the last evening they had met from the thorough draught which had been admitted through the roof the judicial domicile.

"By the bye, Mr. Guffin," said Jack, "you don't happen to have the bill for the repairs of the building in your pocket, do you? I should be sorry to put the parish to any expense; and as I was the cause of making the repairs necessary, I should be most happy to hand over the cash."

Mr. Guffin grinned, on what has been figuratively termed the wrong side of the mouth, at this bantering of Jack, and not caring to answer him, proceeded to relate to his cotemporary in office the manner in which Jack had withdrawn himself from his society when introduced by Mr. Nibblo —hinting at the necessity of not trusting him out of sight, and the propriety of supplying certain ornaments to his person in the way of chains, &c. It was while engaged on this interesting topic, that poor Bess made her appearance: she was, by far too beautiful for any one that had once seen her to forget her. Mr! Guffin instantly knew her again.

"Ah, ah, madam!" said he; "I've caught you once more, have I? You don't get away this time! Lay hold of her, Mr. Clinch," addressing the St. Ann's worthy; "don't let her escape; she's a desperate offender."

Poor Bess gave a scream of alarm, and Jack, aroused to a pitch of madness as he saw her rudely seized by the Fulham constable and the *par nobile fratrum*, Messrs. Guffin and Clinch, caught up a

x

quart pewter measure, and instantly commenced a vigorous symphony on the heads of the congenial trio, and, but for the intervention of two or three of those ancient and superannuated persons, the watch, who had accompanied Jack and the constable from Justice Newton's, would very likely have got clear off a second time with his beloved; as it was, Jack was overpowered by numbers, and obliged to yield to the persuasion of the weighty arguments furnished by their long staves. Bess was taken into custody as an accomplice, and was furthermore detained on the former charge of being concerned in the robbery of the plate composing the memorable May-day garland; also, with having escaped from the roundhouse. She in vain protested her innocence, and that she had only come to see her dear husband, for so she called Jack. The guardians of the peace had been too much damaged, and were too much incensed, to listen to any thing.

All the manacles and fetters in the place were then routed out to secure so daring and desperate an offender as Jack, and he was speedily decorated with a complete set of double irons, including fetters, handcuffs, &c. This was the first time Jack had ever been in irons, and they did not sit so easy on him as they did on many after occasions. He was then thrust, with Bess, into a strong dungeon at the back of the building. Bess had, however, picked up, unperceived the spike of a halbert that had been broken off in the scuffle, with which Jack speedily disenged himself from his *insignia*, as he termed the darbies, and then proceeded to 'perforate the wall of the cell. What might have occurred if the sagacious Mr. Clinch had not happened to be listening at the door at the time, by which means the point of the instrument was very near opening a communication with his brains, through a hole in his skull, it is impossible to say. The astonishment at seeing Jack free from his chains may be imagined.

It was now deemed dangerous to tarry any longer, and accordingly the whole *posse comitatus*, it drawing towards evening, proceeded, in much awful state, to the mansion of the Justice. Here they found Mr. Wood, Mr. Bains, and David Lloyd, the milkman (who had heard of the capture of Bess), and Mr. Nibblo, awaiting them.

The various charges were gone into. Mr. Wood's was heard the first; but after much spluttering, it appearing to the worthy justice that Jack, being then an inmate of the house, had only entered his bed-room at night through the window instead of the door, and that the property he had carried away had been only brought there by himself, and was, for the greater part, his own, the charge of housebreaking and robbery, in this case, was dismissed, for, as the worthy magistrate remarked, there was no law to punish a man for robbing himself; and though it was to have been wished Jack had entered his bed-room by the more usual means of access afforded by the door, yet his coming in by the window could not be construed into burglary, seeing that he was then authorised in the use and possession of the premises; that as for his " showing his indentures a fair pair of heels," that was a subject of consideration for the chamberlain, and not for him, Justice Newton.

The choleric Welshman was much displeased with this decision, and was spluttering forth some most incoherent remonstrances, when Jack requested some one would do him the favour to hand him the tongs, that he might lay hold of the mouse's tail that was then, he affirmed, sticking in Mr. Wood's throat, and would inevitably choke him if not pulled out.

Mr. Bains's charge was more successful, as was also that of David Lloyd against poor Bess; and when to these was added Mr. Guffin's evidence of Jack's daring rescue of Bess, and his own subsequent escape from St. Giles's roundhouse, and Mr. Clinch's testimony of his violence and hardihood in that of St. Ann, the worthy justice felt no hesitation in issuing his warrant for the direct committal of the two prisoners for trial to the New Prison, Clerkenwell; his wig having been perfectly raised from his head with astonishment at Jack's audacity and fearlessness.

It was late in the evening when the lovers arrived at the gate of the New Prison, to which place they were conveyed under a strong escort. In the absence of Captain Geary, the governor, they were received by the head turnkey, Mr. Shackle, who, in consequence of Jack's character having been sent along with him by Justice Newton, resolved to accommodate his two prisoners, whom he considered man and wife, with a lodging in the strongest part of the prison, called, from that circumstance, the Newgate Ward; in addition to which he furnished Jack with a pair of double links and heavy bazils of about fifty pounds weight. Tired out with the events of the day, Jack and Bess, on being locked in till the next morning, threw themselves down on their straw bed, and without deigning to taste of the little loaf of coarse brown bread and jug of water that had been provided and left for them, endeavoured to seek forgetfulnes of their sorrows in sleep. Jack, who never took any thing very much to heart, was soon buried in a profound slumber, and Bess very shortly after sobbed herself into a short repose. The next day, the news of Jack's committal having been made public, numbers of persons, who had heard of his rescue of Bess, his daring escape from St. Giles's round-house, his violent attack on the authorities of St. Ann, and his near evasion from their custody, came to see him. Jack was all life and spirits, dancing, singing, joking; he made a great boast of always carrying his own music with him wherever he went, and asked several of his visiters if they wanted to purchase any *old iron*, telling them he had just set up in the marine store line; that he had a stock *on hand*, which he was willing to dispose of, and would leave at the house of any person who might be inclined to purchase it.

Mr. Shackle, the head turnkey, was particularly tickled by Jack's sallies, declaring that he was a comical dog, and would be sure to make a great noise in the world in time; he did not fail, however, to keep a sharp look out upon our hero, narrowly watching every person that approached him, and suffering no conversation to pass that he was not privy to. Amongst other persons who came, as they said, to gratify their curiosity, Jack perceived one he thought he knew; he was, however, very much surprised at the individual sedulously keeping at a very respectable distance from him, and avoiding all communication with him. It must be Black Martin, he thought; there can be no mistake in those swarthy features; yet, why does he not recognise me? Ah! that glance of intelligence between him and Bess. There's something in the wind! Let me draw off Shackle's attention. Here he began to tell the gaoler a droll story, suited to that worthy's peculiar taste, which he had heard recounted by Blueskin, during the recital of which Bess found an opportunity of exchanging a shake of the hand with Black Martin—for it was he. Jack waited with the utmost impatience for the departure of the visiters. No sooner were their backs turned,

under the convoy of Mr. Shackle, who attended
upon them to let them out, than he rushed eagerly
towards Bess ———

"Now, lass," he exclaimed, " I saw Black Martin—what lay have you been upon ?—there's corn
in Egypt—is there not !"

" There is, dear Jack," exclaimed Bess, delight-
edly, at the same time displaying a small file, a
couple of gimlets, and a chisel.

" Bravo !" cried Jack ; " by the Lord we'll have
a merry evening of it; 'twill be the last one we
shall pass here, so we may as well enjoy ourselves,
girl.   Hide the implements—put them in your bosom, with them, hope, confidence, and courage, we
can't have a better chest of tools—yes, 'tis Whit-
Sunday, I think ; it shall be a holiday for us.
Hush ! here Shackle returns."

" Well, Mr. Shackle," Jack continued, gaily,
as the gaoler re-entered, " really I begin to find
these lodgings of yours exceedingly snug and comfortable—no rent nor taxes to pay, no fear of fire
—so well waited upon too—secured against thieves
—such attention—then such an airy situation, so
well guarded—really, if one could only now and
then be favoured with the company of such a pleasant fellow as yourself to a bowl of punch, I would
not tell my name to put up at any other tavern."

" Why, as to that, Jack," returned Mr. Shackle,
" we are new acquaintances as yet, not but what
we shall be old friends enough by and by, I dare

say. You seem a pleasant rogue, and it's my
foible to be seduced by good company; therefore when a lad of spirit, as you seem to be, is
willing to spend his money like a gentleman, and
wishes to bestow a bowl on me, I am not the man
to refuse him such an indulgence; so, if you have
a broad piece you do not exactly know what to
do with, give it to me, and as soon as I've supplied all the other inmates, that do us the honour to
put up here, with their bread and water, and have
locked them up comfortably for the night, I'll order
in a double crown bowl of the best, and we'll see
if we can't do honour to it. Your good lady, here,
can doubtlessly assist us; we shall have plenty of
time before the governor goes his last rounds."

" Admirably arranged," cried Jack, in high spirits; " my Bess shall lip you out some of her
primest chaunts, she warbles like a canary."

" That's your sort," said Mr. Shackle; " I'll be
back in the turning of a key."

" And you shall find us in the right key,"
laughed Jack; " Bess sings none the worse for a
few bars accompaniment, I can tell you that."

" No, no; caged birds often carol the sweetest,"
replied Shackle, departing to perform his promise.

" For heaven's sake, dear Jack, what is it you
mean to do?" asked Bess, as the sound of the turnkey's footsteps died away in the distance.

" Do!" cried Jack; " I mean to do this fellow
Shackle, and undo the doors of our prison?"

" With so many bolts and bars, and with those fetters ?"

" Psha ! love laughs at locksmiths," said Jack ; " Venus was always more than a match for Vulcan ; I tell you, wench, we shall change our lodgings to-night, I am going to bolt the moon."

The explanation of this very enigmatical piece of intelligence was cut short by the re-entrance of Mr. Shackle, who had performed his office of chamberlain to the various guests under his care with more dispatch than usual.

" Well, Jack, my fine fellow," said he, " here I am, and Scraggs will not be long before he brings us the punch."

" Take a seat, Mr. Shackle," said Jack, arranging one of the bundles of straw that had helped to form his bed, for the cell was totally devoid of furniture ; " make yourself quite at home ; excuse my being in déshabille—I have not had time to change my things yet," shaking his fetters.

" Oh, certainly," said Shackle ; " there's nothing like being free and easy, all the world over."

" You are right," returned Jack, tastefully arranging the remainder of the straw, part to serve as a table, and the other part as a sofa, for himself and Bess, " free and easy *is* the word, certainly."

Here Scraggs entered with the punch, which to do Shackle justice, it must be confessed was composed of the best materials. After Scraggs, at Jack's request, had tossed off a full glass by way of hansel, drinking to their better acquaintance, the party sat down to enjoy themselves, Jack observing he had no doubt they *should* be better acquainted before long. As we have observed, Jack was in high spirits; he did every thing he could to make himself agreeable, cracked a thousand jokes, and told a number of capital stories, which, having a turn for low comedy, he did with much humour; he also sung a great number of flash and other songs, most of which he had heard at Mr. Nightingal's nocturnal concerts, to the turnkey's great delight. One of these, which pleased that gentleman more particularly than any of the others, was the following, which Jack sung with a rustic simplicity, both of look and manner, that would almost have made a bystander swear that he had never been within fifty miles of the metropolis in his life, but had spent all his days in village alehouses, and his nights in thickets and preserves.

The Poacher's Song.

1.

"All among the green leaves,
   'Tis there our craft we ply,
In the pleasant season of the year,
   When there are none to spy;
And to the ale-house after,
   With store of game we creep,
Where we with song and laughter
   Our merry counsel keep.

Chorus.
All among the green leaves, &c.

2.

"All among the green leaves,
   'Tis there we win our gold;
We set our snares, for pheasants, hares,
   By law still uncontroll'd.
In the pleasant season of the year,
   A very merry gang,
The squire may stare, the parson swear,
   And the magistrate go hang.
      All among the green leaves, &c.

3.

"All among the green leaves,
   'Tis there we have our home;
And when the moon is shining boys,
   How fearlessly we roam!
The keepers may be watching us,
   But not a jot care we;
For we are merry poachers,
   And we'll merry poachers be.
      All among the green leaves, &c.

Mr. Shackle having expressed a desire to be favoured with a copy of this song, Jack grasped his hand with much warmth of friendship, and energetically assured him, that before the next four and twenty hours were over his head, he himself would furnish him with *a copy* of it. In addition to these pleasantries, Jack, with every fresh glass, proposed some choice toast; but as most of these toasts, according to the taste of the times, had a double meaning, and as we are not exactly sure which meaning our readers might choose to take, we must be excused from repeating any of them here. Bess, in her turn, was by no means backward in contributing, as the saying is, to the harmony and conviviality of the evening; she sang a variety of gipsy songs in a singularly wild and beautiful manner. Among these were several that were traditionally supposed to have been handed down by the tribe in their original emigration from the east, when forsaking the doctrines of Bramah, and driven without *caste* from their own burning plains, they reached Egypt, and dispersing themselves throughout Europe, became the wandering race they now are. One of these, describing the life of that portion of them that sought refuge on the Indian ocean, and led a piratical life, sailing from isle to isle, ran thus :—

Song of the Sea Gipsies.

1.

" From isle to isle o'er the Southern sea,
    We merry gipsies roam ;
After the sun still sailing free,
    The ocean our bounding home.
Ever we live on the dancing wave,
    Our tent is the spreading sail ;
No land can claim us as its slave,
    Our freedom's in the gale.

    Sea-gipsies we, from year to year,
        One livelong summer prove ;
    Sailing from all that's bleak and drear,
        To welcome joy and love.

2.

" And ever as o'er the waves we rove,
    The wandering sea bark's fate
We read in the stars that shine above,
    What calms, what tempests wait !

Under a rock, the storm we mock,
   And fearless brave the breeze ;
And all that's stray on our ocean way,
   By right of prize we seize.

     Sea-gipsies we, from year to year,
       One livelong summer prove ;
     Sailing from all that's bleak and drear,
       To welcome joy and love."

Mr. Shackle was so charmed by this last chaunt, that, with Jack's permission he could not avoid expressing his admiration by gallantly imprinting a kiss on the lips of the fair songstress. The bowl being now drained, and it approaching near the time for the governor and his officers to make their last round of the prison for the night, the head turnkey left the lovers, not, however, before he had assured them he had found in their society much pleasure, and heartily wished they might often pay him a visit, when he would endeavour to make every thing comfortable for them short of letting them go, but that he was too fond of their company for that. Jack assured him he should never want him to do that, and, with much interchange of good wishes, they parted.

Hastily disposing of the straw in its usual order, they laid down to await the governor's coming : it was not long before the prison bell sounded the hour of ten, and the distant noise of bolts, locks, and bars fastening and unfastening announced his approach. Whether any circumstanee had aroused his suspicion or not, he was very particular in examining Jack's irons, the grating that formed the window of his cell, and the fastenings of the door. Jack assured him that every thing was quite right, and expressed his gratitude at the kind care he evinced in their behalf, fearing he should never have it in his power to re-pay it as he ought. The governor bade him keep his irony to himself, and retired, as Jack said, rather grumpily. No sooner was he gone, and out of hearing, than Jack, bidding Bess join him in the old duet of " Beggars and Ballad Singers," purposely made such a noise as to attract the attention of one of the watchmen outside of the prison, who immediately repaired to the governor, just then returned from his rounds, and disposing himself to the enjoyment of a hot chicken and a nightcap of mulled Madeira, choicely spiced. To him he reported what was going on. Heartily cursing the interruption, and growling at every step he went, the governor once more repaired to Jack's cell, where he found Jack and Bess exercising their lungs with such good will, as almost to stun him. Again examining Jack's irons and the cell very carefully, and finding all was right, the governor ventured to remonstrate with Jack on his want of good manners in raising such a disturbance when they were all going to rest.

" Lord love your heart, Captain !" said Jack, " why, you would'nt be so werry cruel as to wish us to be here without enjoying ourselves, would

you ? We didn't come here for *good manners,*
you know; did we Bess?" and here again they
both began singing——

"There's a difference between a beggar and a queen,
    And I'll tell you the reason why;
  A queen she cannot swagger, nor get drunk like a beggar,
    Nor be half so happy as I."

"Besides," continued Jack, "it's Whit-Sunday,
you know, governor, and every body takes a little
pleasure then : it's **a poor heart wot never rejoices.**"
There was no answering this; so the governor
only shrugged up his shoulders, and departed,
leaving Jack and Bess to sing till they were tired,
when, as he sagaciously said, he had no doubt they
would leave off.

No sooner was he fairly gone the second time
than Jack, still singing as before, took the file,
and commenced, in earnest, releasing himself from
his irons. He worked away with such right good
will, that in rather less than half an hour he
had completely divested himself of those somewhat
troublesome ornaments to his person, and throwing
them down in the straw, he, in the joy of his heart,
again began singing, adapting his words to his
situation——

"I am a wild and a rambling boy,
  My lodging's in the isle of Troy;
  A rambling boy as all shall see,
  For I'll soon be at liber-tee."

Following up his successful operations, Jack now made a dent in the wall, by which he ascended to the grated aperture above, forming the window of the cell. Here, with incredible labour, he managed to take out, first, a large oaken bar, above nine inches thick, then one of the iron bars; Bess all this time playing in her turn the part of vocalist by way of accompaniment, which she did by extemporizing the following rather appropriate romance ballad, the words of which it will be observed singularly apply to the scene and situation.—

The Rover.*

My love he is a rover, all in the forest free
And he loves to hunt the wild deer, under the greenwood tree,
But the cruel keepers caught him, for no squire or knight is he,
And they've bound him fast in prison strong to sigh. Ah!
    woe is me!
Sing on, sing on, thou little bird, I'll sing as blithe as thee
When my sweet love is free again, under the greenwood tree.

Poor bird! thou too art in a cage, and 'gainst the bars so
    strong
I see thee vent thy little rage, but they shall yield ere long.
Thy prison wires break one by one, and merry may'st thou
    sing,
The grates unclosed, thy freedom's won, and thou may'st speed
    thy wing;
And I will sing as blithe a strain, thou little bird, as thee,
When my sweet love is free again, under the Greenwood tree.

* This song, set in a singularly beautiful and striking manner, strongly illustrative of the wild and originally touching pathos of the old English melody, by that talented composer Sidney Nelson, is published by Messrs. George, and may be had of all Music-sellers.

Having accomplished the removal of these impe-pediments, Jack now looked out, but found his ardour somewhat damped on discovering that they had to descend a height of at least four-and-twenty feet before they could reach the ground ; but difficulties only served to increase his resolution. Immediately descending into his cell, he took the sheet and blanket which had been furnished him, and tying them strongly together, fastened one end of the blanket round Bess's waist, who expressed her willingness to brave every danger for the sake of her dear Jack. With these he managed to raise her up to the window, then passing her through the cavity he had effected by the removal of the bars, he cautiously commenced lowering her outside, into the yard below.

" Steady, lass, steady !" he exclaimed, as she swayed from side to side.

" Hush, Jack, or we are lost !" suddenly whispered Bess, seeing a watchman turn round the corner of the yard. Jack paused, Bess remaining suspended midway in the air. At length the watchman's voice calling " Half past eleven, all safe !" dying away in the distance, convinced them he had departed, and Jack completed Bess's descent. He then fastened his end of the sheet to the remaining bars of the window, and soon let himself down, humming as he went,——

" Now all the world shall plainly see,
Jack Sheppard is at liber-tee."

Y

But what was his disappointment when, arrived at
the bottom himself, he found that he had only got
out of one prison into another ; or, to use his own
expressive words, " out of the frying-pan into the
fire ?"

" Why, it's wheel within wheel here, wench !"
said he. " Confound me if we haven't let ourselves down into the yard of Clerkenwell Bridewell. I recollect, now, it joins the prison. What's
to be done? I should like to know ! We are
worse off than ever, girl ! That wall's between
twenty and thirty feet high, at least. How the
devil are we to manage to get to the top of it?
We must either scale or climb it."

" I'm sure I don't know, Jack," said the confiding Bess. " I'll do any thing, dearest, you tell
me, to get out of this horrid place."

" Well, well, girl ; we'll never say die till
we're dead, at all events," said Jack ; " let me
see," he continued, reconnoitring, and making a
circuit of the yard. " Ah ! I have it ; here's the
great gate ; we can manage it capitally."

We have said Black Martin had, along with the
other tools, given Bess two gimblets ; fixing these
in the gate at proper distances, Jack made them
serve as steps, and by their help, and the assistance afforded by the locks and bolts of the gate,
he managed to ascend to the top of the wall ; once
reaching this, the sheet and blanket soon enabled
him to raise Bess to the same elevation. Forcing

off some spikes of the *chevaux-de-frise*, and fastening the blanket and sheet to it, as he had before done to the bars of his window, as the clock of Clerkenwell Church ushered in the morning of Whit-Monday, May the 25th, 1719, they had both safely gained the outside of the Bridewell, and were once more at liberty.

CHAPTER XVIII.

JACK IN BUSINESS.

PARTNERSHIP WITH BLUESKIN.—JONATHAN WILD'S LEVEE. —JACK'S WAREHOUSE AT THE HORSE-FERRY.

It was a fine clear moonlight morning, when Jack and Bess took their departure from the New Prison, one of those mild balmy mornings that peculiarly belong to May, which exist in an atmosphere of their own, make a world of their own. have thoughts and feelings wholly belonging to themselves, a delightful calm, a refreshing vigour, a juvenility and inspiration, which thousands of us pass through the world, and depart from it, without ever having once, except by accident, become acquainted with, restrained by those formidable giants, sloth and custom. Thrice happy are the birds, the flowers, the breezes, and the much bepitied portion of the labouring classes, whose avocations force them out by daybreak, that they enjoy the purest portion of nature's existence.

Jack felt new life as he inhaled the odours of awakening morn. If such young hearts as his own, and that of his beloved Bess, could have grown younger, this was the scene, the hour in which they would have done so. One moment for counsel, and Jack's course was decided.

" Whitsunday Eve," exclaimed Jack, " there will have been late revellers at Nightingal's: late, or early as the hour is, the odds are they will not yet have retired—we shall get admittance there— the Hundreds of Drury is our port then, girl—ay, to Wych Street, to Wych Street.

London, that mighty heart of England, was now lulled into temporary repose: its arteries slumbered gently, calmly. Jack and Bess made their way through the silent and almost deserted streets without any interruption. Jack felt a twitch, whether of his mind or body he did not stay to ascertain, as he passed the familiar and tranquil dwelling of his old master Mr. Wood, where he had spent so many happy, because guilt-less hours. Gliding up the murky passage, that led to the White Lion, a low murmur of voices, and some glimmerings of light between the shut-ters, soon showed Jack he had been right in his conjectures: he gave the well-known signal, the door was soon opened, and Mr. Nightingal stood before them.

" What! Jack—Jack Sheppard, my rum cull! and your doxy too! You here at this time of the morning !" here he began singing according to his usual custom—

> " To-morrow is St. Valentine's day,
>   All in the morn be time,
>   And I a maid at your window
>   To be your Valentine."

But what the devil! I thought you were in Clerkenwell quod-ken : but come in—here's plenty that will be glad enough to see you—gad ! this will be a rare surprise—walk in, young madam," addressing Bess, and here he resumed singing as he fastened the door—

> " Then up he rose and donn'd his clothes,
>   And oped the chamber door ;
>   Let in a maid, that out a maid
>   Never departed more."

Proceeding to the little back parlour, which the reader is already acquainted with, Jack was at once astonished and delighted at finding there his old pal and school-fellow, Blueskin, Mr. Jonathan Wild, Black Martin, and several other equally respectable gentlemen, including Mr. Wild's satellites, Mr. Quilt Arnold, Esquire, and the Patriarch.

" Done you all, by Pharaoh !" roared out Black Martin, exultingly, as he saw Jack enter, " I was certain he would be here."

" A bite by G—!" said Mr. Blueskin, " what a sap I was not to bar the bubble !"

" No bubble at all," returned Black Martin, "I merely conveyed my old acquaintance Bess there, two or three tools in the Quod-Ken, and I was certain with their assistance, the night wouldn't pass over without Jack being at liberty, and I naturally thought this would be the first place he would come to. I have fairly won my wager— glasses round—so bring them in, Ned—they can never come in a better moment."

> "I am gone, sir, but anon, sir,
> I'll be with you in a trice—
> Like the old vice," &c.

sung Mr. Nightingal, disappearing.

It is almost needless to say that the reception of Jack and Bess was of the most cordial and enthusiastic nature; the recognition of Mr. Blueskin, in particular, was more than usually hearty and joyous. Black Martin's winnings being brought in by Mr. Nightingal, Jack recounted the details of his escape, much to the astonishment and commendation of all present. The encomiums bestowed by Mr. Wild were indeed most flattering, as were those of his two satellites, Mr. Quilt Arnold, Esquire, and the patriarch; the latter declared, upon " his conschance, that he should not have thought so much of Jack's getting away by himself, but that hish bringing Besh with him exceeded any thing in the way of escape he ever remembered in all hish prishen experiensh."

In answer to some surprise expressed by Jack at Mr. Blueskin's liberation from Newgate, that gentleman informed him that, giving some evidence which led to the conviction of Oakey, Levy, and Flood, he had not only expected his pardon, but had also claimed part of the reward offered by government; but these the Court had refused on the ground of his not being a voluntary witness, also on account of the desperate resistance he had made when he was taken, and had ordered him to be sent to the Compter, where, in default of his consenting to be transported for seven years, he was to find security for his good behaviour before he could be discharged; that Mr. Wild had acted like a father to him, had paid for the cure of the crack in his sconce, which he received when he was apprehended, and had allowed him a small sum weekly to furnish him his little comforts, for which he vowed eternal gratitude, declaring he would lay down his life any time to serve Mr. Wild.

Here Mr. Quilt Arnold, Esquire, hemmed very significantly, and the patriarch indulged in a long grin of sardonic commentary. Mr. Wild coolly remarked that he might one day put him to the proof, while Mr. Nightingal nearly choked himself in draining his glass of brandy and water, part of it going the wrong way.

Blueskin resumed : — he had been fortunate enough to procure two of that class of respectables, known as poor, frozen-out, gardeners, to come forward in his behalf, who, by representing themselves to the Court as eminent market horticulturists, were allowed by Sir John Fryer to become security for his (Blueskin's) good behaviour for seven years.

" So you sees, Mister Blake, you musht pe a

very goot poy," remarked the patriarch, " it wash a very goot joke when Old Vigsby axed you how long it vould pe pefore you cumd afore the Court again, old Habeas Corpus, the keeper of Voot Street, answering three sessions—I says two—ha, ha, ha !"

All the company laughed amazingly at this sally of the Hebrew ; and the clear blue daylight beginning to steal into the room over the shutters, making the yellow flare of the mutton fats, as Mr. Blueskin termed the candles, look extremely unhealthy and disagreeable, a proposition was made for a general move. It was settled that, as no doubt a hot pursuit would be set on foot when Jack's escape with Bess should be discovered in the morning, that Mr. Blueskin should provide them, *pro tempore*, with a secure lodging in the Mint until Jack's future operations should be finally determined upon ; the company therefore broke up, Mr. Wild remarking, he supposed he should see Jack soon, and Mr. Nightingal closing the door on the whole party while humming the beginning of the fine old Bacchanalian—

" When Bibo thought fit from the world *to retreat*," &c.

Shaking hands with the usual parting benedictions, the revellers disappeared in different quarters with a celerity very remarkable, vanishing like so many evil spirits at the first crowing of the cock—Mr. Wild and his satellites one way, Black Martin and

his associates another, and Mr. Blueskin, Jack,
and Bess to the Strand ferry, where, making free
with a boat, they helped themselves to a cast across
the Thames to the opposite bankside. The pure
morning air from the river was quite refreshing
and invigorating, after the heated and fatiguing
atmosphere of Mr. Nightingal's back parlour, im-
pregnated as it was with the fumes of brandy and
tobacco, and the effluvia from the rancid fat of his
tallows. They gained the sanctuary of the Mint
long before any of its denizens were stirring, but
Mr. Blueskin being an old inhabitant soon procured them admission through its closed and
guarded entrances. Knocking up an intimate, the
proprietor of a select lodging-house in this sacred
retreat, especially devoted to the accommodation of
" single men and their wives," as the Portsmouth
landladies are accustomed to notify during war
time. Jack and Bess entered on the occupation of
a remarkably airy garret, upon very easy terms.

Promising to see Jack and Bess about noon, to
breakfast, for it was now fairly morning, Mr. Blueskin left them, and, worn out with the bustle of
the last twenty-four hours, the lovers threw themselves into each other's arms, and were soon locked
in a profound and reviving slumber.

It was quite the middle of the day before they
were awakened by Mr. Blueskin, when a cabinet
council was held over a beef-steak, rendered *pi-
quante* by some savoury onions, and washed down

with two or three mugs of strong porter, which that azure-hued worthy Mr. Blueskin, whom Jack styled on this occasion " a heavenly-faced fellow," had provided for their breakfast. It argues no disrelish, on the part of Mr. Blake, when we remark he looked blue at this compliment.

" You are in for it now, Jack," said he ; " it's no fault of yours, but you can't be honest if you would ; you must live, and so must pretty Bess here : the only thing you have got to do now is to endeavour, since the world *will* make you a thief, to prove a good one."

" I will, I will ! " cried Jack, emphatically, taking heart by emptying three parts of the contents of one of the mugs we have alluded to.

" You must not go rashly to work," said the prudent Mr. Blake, observing Jack's determinanation : situated as you are now, you will require some protection—only Jonathan Wild can render you secure. By the bye, to-night he holds a levee of all his subjects, at which you must be presented. I am first knobstick in waiting, and will do the formalities for you. You can then, having a market open to you where you can always dispose of your goods to advantage, commence business in a regular and proper manner ; and, if you like it, hang me if you sha'n't go into partnership with me."

" Done !" said Jack ; " 'tis a bargain—' Sheppard and Blueskin, Cracksmen and Divers, wholesale, retail, and for tranportation. Kens milled on the shortest notice. Cly-faking performed with skill and expedition. Goods carefully removed on the most reasonable terms.' Ha, ha, ha! Nothing can be better—ours will be an admirable firm."

It was agreed this compact should be celebrated by what Mr. Blueskin called " a tightening," or, according to Jack's vocabulary, " a blow out—that nosebags extraordinary should be provided"—all which figures of speech typified, they were to have a jovial entertainment. The Mint furnished a number of delicacies, particularly baked sheeps' heads, pigs' trotters, pickled herrings, black puddings, fried skait, &c., &c., and every species of liquor at that time in vogue. We will not run the risk of making the reader's mouth water, by dwelling on the various epicurean luxuries provided by the good taste and zeal of Mr. Blueskin ; suffice it to remark, the party was, as Jack said, " as merry as sand-boys." While he and Mr. Blueskin smoked and drank, Bess sung some of her choicest ditties ; and the afternoon passing rapidly away, the hour of Mr. Wild's levee soon approached. Accordingly, leaving Bess to take care of the premises till their return, the newly joined partners repaired to Mr. Wild's residence in the Old Bailey. Arriving here, they were received by Mr. Quilt Arnold, *Esquire*, and the Patriarch, who informed Mr. Blueskin that he was quite in time; that " Mr. Vild's leewy wouldn't commence for some time." Blueskin remarking that he must leave Jack, to go and robe for the ceremonies, the Patriarch volunteered to take our hero under his protection, till it should be time for his presentation; he accordingly conducted him into a little back room, or sort of counting-house, in which there was a desk, and a pane of glass inserted in the wall commanding through a reflector similar to those used by the *incurious* Dutch, a distinct view of all that was passing in the front office.

While waiting here, Jack saw a great number of persons successively arrive, consisting of men, women, and boys, apparently, from the great diversity in their dress, of many different classes. They were all of them received by Mr. Quilt Arnold, *Esquire*, who, after much individual greeting, ushered them, by the back stairs, to some upper apartment. Jack could not help feeling some expectation and curiosity. At length the Patriarch came to say that the leewy vas hopened, and that Jack might follow him up stairs, and take his turn to be presented.

Jack immediately obeyed the summons. The Patriarch conducted him to a spacious back room on the first floor, at the door of which, inside, stood Mr. Blueskin, by virtue of his office as first knobstick in waiting: he was rather ludicrously attired: he wore a counsellor's old gown over his own clothes: was strongly armed with two or three brace of pistols and a hanger; and had on his head a bag wig and cocked hat : he held a sort of official wand in his right hand.

As Jonathan happened to be very particularly engaged at the moment Jack entered, our hero had time to look about, and survey at his leisure the singular scene which presented itself. At the back of the room, which was crowded with Jonathan's subjects, sat that great man himself, in a large arm-chair, before a table, on which were various articles of booty, writing materials, pistols, proclamations, &c.; behind him stood his gentleman-usher, Mr. Quilt Arnold, *Esquire;* and around the room, on either side, were congregated his numerous forces, divided into their several classes. To the right were his cavalry, or high toby men before-mentioned—gentlemen who took the air by moonlight, well mounted and armed. They were dashing looking fellows, with cocked hats, laced coats, and formidable weapons; and bore, most of them, watches, pocket-books, portmanteaus, and other articles of plunder. On the other side were the dragoons, also before noticed—gentlemen who served occasionally on horse or foot : their plunder was much of the same description. There were then the mill-kens, or housebreakers,—ruffianly-looking fellows,—few of them without some parcels of plate, silver candlesticks, tea-pots, and the like. Near them were some fellows in the attire of gipsies and countrymen, who attended to make their different reports from the various fairs they had lately visited. Some nymphs of the *pavé* next attracted Jack's attention; these mostly had handkerchiefs, snuff-boxes, and other light articles. In addition to them, there were the spruce prigs, and other minor thieves, who might be classed as sharpshooters; and a whole battalion of young recruits, consisting of boys from ten to fifteen years old.

Jonathan was consulting with Mr. Toothandegg, a very dexterous artist, whom he kept constantly in his pay, respecting the re-setting of some diamonds in a necklace that one of his ladies had picked up at a masquerade, a night or two previously, together with other alterations necessary to be effected in some similar articles of jewellery just brought in. They were interrupted by the entrance of a rough-looking fellow in a naval dress, having very much the appearance of a smuggler, who was announced by Mr. Blueskin, as Captain Roger Johnson.

" You are welcome, Captain," said Jonathan; what news of my good sloop, ' The Hawk ?' and how do our friends at Ostend ?"

" All's well, Governor," said Roger; " I duly landed your last cargo, and saw it safely deposited in the warehouses of your factor, Dick Norman: he has sent you advices from Bruges and Ghent respecting the watches and the goldsmith's notes I took him in our last voyage; I shipped in a cargo of Hollands previously to my return: 'The Hawk' is now laying safely off the mouth of the river;

and I mean, wind and tide permitting, to run my cargo this very night."

" Bravo !" exclaimed Jonathan rubbing his hands with satisfaction ; "if ever I should have a squadron, Roger, I'll appoint you its admiral ; I must have a private conference with you, by and bye. Mr. Toothandegg, you have my complete instructions touching the removal of the crests, and substitution of the ciphers on that family plate. Gentlemen of the road, addressing the toby-men,— "you too have had my directions as to your several courses, and I have fully accounted with you for the product of your last excursions. Ladies,"—addressing the nymphs.—" I have always peculiar satisfaction in receiving any thing from your hands—convinced that nobody can regret parting with their property to such charmers."

It may be mentioned that Jonathan was a devoted admirer of the sex, and was then living with his *fifth* wife !

" As for you, gentlemen,"—addressing the gipsies and those in the garb of countrymen,—" your next place of destination must be Barnet Fair, whither I shall accompany you myself: my presence will inspire confidence in the multitude; they will not imagine there can be any danger where I am, and will therefore fall the easier victims. You Tom Dunn, may tell Bernard Tuckey, when you see him, that I will afford him a secure asylum in my own house. I will suffer no one to be hanged

who keeps his faith with me, and fairly accounts for his plunder. Rob the world as you will,—you shall do it with impunity,—but you must not rob me; that is death without benefit of clergy. You know I strictly keep my faith with you. When did Jonathan Wild ever forfeit his word?"

"Never, never!" exclaimed the whole assembly simultaneously.

"You are right, my children," returned Jonathan; "when hundreds of pounds' reward have been offered for many of you, and you have put yourselves in my power, on my giving my word for your safety, did I ever betray you?"

"No, no!" exclaimed one and all; "no, never!"

"I have saved many of you when the halter was fairly round your necks; have kept prosecutors out of the way, suborned witnesses, and supplied evidence. Whenever I have let the law take its course, and furnished the knubbing cheat with another victim, I have been urged to it by treachery and disobedience. It was necessary to my power—to your safety,—was inevitable for the existence and welfare of the paternal government, under which you have so long flourished."

"Hear! hear! hear!" was re-echoed round the room.

"You all acknowledge me your king, then, rogues," exclaimed Jonathan.

"We do! we do!" was the general answer.

"You will obey my laws?"

Every one bowed in token of homage, and an universal shout was raised of "Long live Jonathan Wild!"

"Enough, enough, my children; I am satisfied," returned Jonathan, with an air of fatherly dignity;—"but stay,"—his eagle eye fixing upon Jack,—methinks I see one here you must all be acquainted with—a new comrade."

Here Mr. Blueskin announced our hero with all due formality. At the name of Jack Sheppard, every eye was fixed upon our hero: the news of his daring exploits in St. Giles's roundhouse, and his wonderful escapes from the New Prison, had been bruited abroad, and he was regarded with singular interest and curiosity; all the young prigs, in particular, looked upon him with much admiration. A regular introduction to all Jonathan's subjects here took place; the sign of fellowship was given; Jack received a lieutenant's commission among Jonathan's dragoons, with permission to leave for the cavalry whenever so inclined. His name was formally entered in Jonathan's army list,—for so was the book called in which the different gangs were registered, — and a particular district and company were about to be allotted to him, when Jack, gratefully acknowledging the favour that had been shown him, requested permission to serve for a time as an engineer, or mill-ken cove,—in other words, as a house-breaker, his genius having a decided bias for laying siege to and storming the fortresses of his Majesty George the First's lieges : his request was most graciously complied with ; and the different parties present, having regularly given in their reports, and deposited their various articles of plunder with Jonathan, who dispatched them to his several warehouses, were allowed, after they had received their pay, being about one fourth the value of the booty they had brought, and had their further orders delivered to them, to kiss hands and leave his presence.

Jack could not help being struck with admiration at the statesman-like manner in which Jonathan conducted all these transactions. His subjects, while they appeared to place the most unbounded confidence in him, evidently feared him ; indeed there was an air of cool determination discernible in the midst of all Wild's bland assurances of protection, while they *continued to deserve it*, that was well calculated to keep them true to their allegiance. The apartment in which he received them was also evidently fitted up for effect : in addition to the portraits of Captain John Hind, Mull'd Sack, and other eminent characters of the same class that decorated the walls, there were the last dying speech of Jack Hall ; two or three bills offering large rewards for the apprehension of criminals at that time actually in Jonathan's employ ; there were also more than one brace of pistols, some handcuffs, and other objects of a like nature, calculated to enforce respect ; nor were occasional glimpses wanted of Jonathan's sceptre, his silver headed constable's staff. When the room was cleared of all but the great man, Jack and Mr. Blueskin,—

"You see, my son," said the monarch, "the mannner in which I conduct my government. I receive you regularly into my service with much satisfaction, anticipating in you a valuable aux-iliary. You desire to begin business as cracks-man : 'tis well ; follow me to my magazine—my armoury—and select your own tools."

Here Jonathan conducted Jack down stairs, into an extensive apartment under ground, on the walls of which were arranged, in regular order, a large quantity of picklocks, files, saws, crowbars for forcing doors and windows, centrebits, knives, bludgeons, and almost every other article used in the exercise of the predatory profession.

These Jonathan made no scruple of showing to casual visiters, asserting he had taken them from the different desperadoes he had secured in the course of his vocation ; but his real motive in col-lecting them together, was for the purpose of fur-nishing his subjects, whenever they might require or stand in need of their assistance ; for he was too good a general ever to send his men on any expedition without their being properly armed.

After much judicious advice from Jonathan on the subject of Jack's future operations. the latter took his leave, and returned with Mr. Blueskin, to the fair Bess.

On the following day, Jack engaged a cottage, at the suggestion of Blueskin, in the neighbour-hood of Camberwell, which appeared to be admi-rably adapted for his views. It was situated in a bye place called Higglers' Green, on one side of the high road, at the bottom of a long narrow lane, called Windmill Lane, but better known by its more common appellation of Cut-throat Lane, from its having formerly been the scene of a murder. and other atrocities. Higglers' Green was a sort of muddy common, on which had been erected some eight or ten rude cottages, detached from each other, and in different situations, but most of them having communications, by means of back gardens and other contrivances. A low-roofed beer-house was situated in the centre of these dwellings, in which the few neighbours usually met for the purposes of riot and debauchery. Se-veral cross paths, much unfrequented, and diffi-cult of access, led from this little community to Lambeth, Kennington, and other adjacent parts, and afforded means of escape, if necessary. The in-habitants of the cottages were all persons of despe-rate character; and as no one could approach the spot without being perceived at a great distance, and there were always plenty of fierce dogs about to give the alarm, it formed a very secure place of retreat.

After domiciling himself here, Jack next, in conjunction with Blueskin, looked out for a place in which to deposit any plunder they might in future acquire; after some search, they found an old stable, situated by the water-side, near the Horseferry Road, Westminster. It had possibly been used originally for the accommodation of cattle repairing to the ferry, but had now fallen into neglect. As there was a ready passage across the river from this spot to Lambeth on the one hand, while Town was easily and privately reached through many of the bye-streets in the neighbourhood of the Abbey, Almonry, and other portions of Westminster, it appeared to be highly eligible for their purpose. Possession of it was soon secured, and thus provided and established, it was agreed that on the following day Jack and Blueskin should regularly commence business.

CHAPTER XIX.

THE PROGRESS OF BURGLARY.

A CRACKSMAN'S LIFE.—JONATHAN WILD'S CORRESPONDENCE.—JACK AS GOOD AS HIS MASTER.

THE first exploit performed in partnership by Jack and Mr. Blueskin, or Blueskin, as we shall hereafter more familiarly call him, regarding him now as an old acquaintance, was at the house of Mr. Carter, a mathematical instrument maker, near St. Clement's Church, with whose nephew and apprentice, Anthony Lamb, Blueskin had managed to scrape an acquaintance at one of the free-and-easies of the White Lion. A very wealthy master tailor by trade, one Mr. Barton, happening to be a lodger in Mr. Carter's house, Lamb was easily persuaded to give Jack and Blueskin admittance in the middle of the night for the purpose of paying him a visit. Lamb was too conscientious to be concerned in any robbery of his uncle and master; but, as he said, a tailor was nobody; he would not rob any man living, but the ninth part of one was quite a different thing. Accordingly, repairing to Mr. Nightingal's, Jack and Blueskin remained there drinking till the clock struck two, when, being well armed, and provided with all the necessary implements for their design, they cautiously made their way to Mr. Carter's house; here, giving a signal, which had been previously agreed upon, the door was softly opened by their confederate, Lamb. Pulling off their shoes, and leaving the street door a little ajar, for the more easily effecting their retreat, Lamb conducted them to Mr. Barton's chamber, and then slunk off to his garret. The door of this room being locked, Jack, with a dexterity perfectly marvellous, forced it without giving the slightest alarm, and then leaving Blueskin, who had a pistol ready cocked in his hand, on guard outside, with orders to fire if there should be any resistance, he lit a small dark lantern, and stepped silently into the apartment. The poor tailor, little dreaming of what was about to occur, was locked in a profound and pleasant slumber.

Jack lost no time in going to work; drawers were opened, cupboards forced, and boxes ransacked, with a celerity and silence absolutely magical. Once only was he disturbed in his operations —the tailor had nearly awakened himself by his own snoring; but changing his position by turning round to the wall, for his face had before been towards Jack, he was soon faster asleep than ever; this gave Jack an opportunity of making still shorter work of it. Searching the trunks and drawers, he discovered a variety of clothes made and unmade, which he dexterously packed up in two large parcels, and placed them in charge of Blueskin; he then picked the lock of an iron chest fixed in the wall, from which he took a number of Goldsmith's notes, guineas, broad pieces, bonds, and other securities, to the amount of more than two hundred pounds; this done, he put the tailor's rings, which were lying upon the wash-hand stand, upon his own fingers, gently drew the watch from under the pillow pressed by the unconscious sleeper's head, and, helping himself to a glass of ratafia from a private case bottle, which he found by the bedside, darkened his lantern, bowed politely to the sleeping *schneider*, and rejoined Blueskin without any interruption.

As had been settled, they stole down stairs with their booty, leaving the street-door open behind them. Anthony Lamb remaining in his garret, feeling all the while as innocent as if he had actually been the quadruped whose name he bore. It was not long before a neighbour of Mr. Carter, getting up earlier than usual, to request the attendance of an ancient priestess of Lucina, at the pressing instance of his good lady, then in the condition "all ladies wish to be who love their lords," finding the mathematical instrument maker's door open, and no one stirring in the house, suspected that all was not exactly on the square, and instantly gave the alarm. This awakened the poor tailor, who jumped out of bed in the greatest consternation, and soon found, by breaking his shins over the trunks, &c. that lay scattered about his room, what sort of visiters they were that had favoured him with their company.

The first step of Mr. Carter and his lodger was to run up to the garret of Anthony, to whom their suspicions were immediately directed by his known practice of keeping late hours, and frequenting houses of ill repute. They found Anthony apparently buried in a deep slumber. After much shaking and calling, he gave a loud yawn, and stretching forth one arm, by which he almost put out the tailor's right eye, suffered himself to be made acquainted with what had happened. They were, however, not to be deceived; a few close questions soon confused him; they charged him, point-blank, with being concerned in the robbery; and, on the entrance of a constable to take him into custody, he cried *peccavi*, and avowed his willingness to confess all.

Jack and Blueskin meanwhile hurried along the Strand with their booty. Passing through Parliament Street, they soon reached Westminster Abbey. As they stole by it, the deep shade of that venerable and sacred edifice—its dark masses seeming to frown upon them in the bright moonlight—cast a temporary gloom over Jack's mind that he would willingly have avoided. Shadows have oftentimes more of apprehension in them than realities; there was reprehension to Jack's conscience in that of the

holy building.   Passing the princely hall of the
Red King, and the irregular buildings of the House
of Commons, then lone and silent, as if they formed
part of a city of the dead, they made their way to
their stable, on the overhanging bank of the river
adjoining the ferry.   The waters seemed to sob
mournfully and reproachfully as the rising tide
bore them in troubled waves against the bank.

Jack essayed a little merriment to drown their
influence.

"A glorious booty, Blueskin," said he.

" Booty !" answered Blueskin ;   "nonsense—
only a little cabbage !   Where did you say you
would meet poor Tony to-morrow night, Jack ?"

" At the music-house, among the *bona robas*,"
answered Jack.

" You should have fixed Newgate, poor devil,
if you really wanted to meet him," laughed Blueskin ;   "for he'll be sure to be there."

" I fear so," said Jack, " You didn't let him
know where we hang out, did you ?"

" Not quite such a flat as that," returned Blueskin.   " Ha, ha, ha! poor Lamb is a lost mutton.
Well, he won't be the first lamb that's had its neck
placed in jeopardy by his *Sheppard*.

Here both the parties indulged in a hearty fit
of laughter.   Concealing their booty in the loft
among some hay placed there for the purpose,
they locked up their warehouse, and soon got a
lift from an early boatman to Lambeth, from

whence they made their way over the fields to Higglers' Green, where Bess was anxiously awaiting
their arrival.

As Blueskin had foretold, Lamb, on being taken
before a magistrate, made a full confession, but
was unable, from not knowing, to state where his
accomplices were to be found. He was, of course,
committed to Newgate, and being tried at the
next sessions, escaped the heavier penalty of the
law, through the kind intercession of his master
and the good nature of the suffering tailor, who
pitied his youth, and was only rewarded with
transportation.

The clothes, jewellery, bonds, &c. of Mr. Barton,
all but the actual money, were duly forwarded to
Jonathan, who as duly accounted for and made his
market of them.

The partners' next robbery was in the house of
Mrs. Cook, a linen-draper in Clare Market, which
they broke open and robbed of property to the
amount of sixty pounds. Poor Bess was innocently
made an accomplice in this robbery, Jack having
requested her to be in waiting in the neighbouring
street, and consigning to her custody a portion of
the valuable linen, silks, satins, and laces, which belonged to their booty. Jack then robbed in succession the house of a Mr. Phillips in Drury Lane,
where he ransacked the stock of Mrs. Kenrick,
who rented the shop, and also the mansion of Mr.
Charles, in Mayfair, which he beame acquainted

with through a Mr. Panton, a master-carpenter, who had employed him for a short time as journeyman, not knowing him, and had sent him to execute some repairs there. This mansion, which was situated in the Piccadilly end of Mayfair, Jack broke open, and took from it a quantity of silver spoons and forks; six gold rings, one set with a rich stone; four suits of apparel, a considerable quantity of linen, and seven pounds ten shillings in money.

It was very soon, as he said, all "Charley over the Water" with the money; but the other articles, after being first deposited in the stable, found their way to Mr. Wild, and were disposed of accordingly. Numerous other burglaries and robberies rapidly succeeded these; but to recount all Jack's daring and successful depredations would fill a volume; he did not always get clear off, however, but was successively made the inmate of every roundhouse within the bills of mortality, from which he as successively escaped. London was alarmed, and Westminster waxed pale; locks, bolts, and bars were at a premium; and the Fleet parsons found their business more than doubled by the number of single young women, who became afraid to sleep *alone* through fear of the redoubtable Jack Sheppard; his acquaintance was courted, so great grew his fame, by every prig and scamp throughout the metropolis. King of the key, lord of the lock, and baron of the bolt and bar, locksmiths and ironmongers were, under Jack's reign, in the ascendant.

During this period Jack lived with Bess in extreme happiness. Though unconscious of any participation in them, she was the cause of more than one half of his depredations : to his ardent love for her, his wish to furnish her with every comfort and every luxury she might desire, must be attributed at least one half of his robberies.

Living in a sort of fairy world of her own, enveloped as she was in love and felicity, knowing no privation, having no want ungratified, Bess troubled herself little as to the means by which her happiness was procured ; her whole soul was centred in Jack ; her faith was firm in his affections ; he was her idol, her all ; her confiding trust in him was that of the noble Arabian courser for its chief. " The lightning of the desert" would as soon have thought of scrutinizing the means of its beloved master, from whose hands its daily meals were received, as she those of Jack.

Jack's life rolled onwards regularly enough. When not engaged with Blueskin in the Mint, planning fresh projects of plunder, he would pass the day in the little beer-house we have before mentioned, at Higglers' Green, with some of his neighbours : these consisted of two or three bankrupt traders. who had run away from their bail, an outlawed attorney, some dealers in contraband goods, under the semblance of costermongers, a couple of smashers, or utterers of counterfeit coin, and three or four other persons who, having no

ostensible mode of getting their living, we must
charitably set down as living upon their wits, that
being a general description, affording a sufficiently
wide latitude to the imagination. Here the hours
were spent in drinking, smoking, playing at cards
and dominoes, arguing, singing, spelling over an
old " Daily Post," or listlessly gazing upon the
mingled groups of ragged children and donkies,
mongrel curs, grunting pigs, and noisy cocks
and hens, that idly sported and foraged over
the withered patch of common on which this little
community was established; the women, meanwhile, were engaged in cooking and washing, or
leaning over their palings gossipping with each
other. The scattered ash-heaps by the side of
the miserable cottages, the dirty pools of water
running before the doors, the neglected gardens,
with their few stalks of cabbages, straggling sun-
flowers running to seed, broken palings- and the
stunted dried-up herbage of the common itself,
with its wild thistles here and there, and the few
remains of almost leafless hedges, gave the whole
a barren, squalid, comfortless, and dissolute appearance. Yet, amidst all this contamination Bess
lived unsoiled; she mingled not with her neighbours; Jack was all and all to her. She found
sufficient employment for her time in attending
to their humble dwelling, which, within that circle
of poverty and shift, was a model of neatness and
comfort. When evening had set in, Jack would

sometimes take her, arrayed in her best costume, through a sequestered path across the fields, to " The Fountain Gardens," at Lambeth, a well-known place of amusement at that time—the precursor of Vauxhall. Here there was not much fear of detection, the gardens were only frequented by a certain class, of very uncertain calling, and no gaoler or constable caring to visit them, except upon positive information, and then not unaccompanied.

Here they were usually entertained with a song, recounting how a certain swain, named Damon, was conducted by an antediluvian personage, called Cupid, into a pleasant grove, where a certain nymph, 'yclept Chloe, was most conveniently lying asleep on a bank of roses, fanned by some obliging zephyrs—the month being always May—when, after many tender sighs, and an appropriate blush or two, the intervention of another old-fashioned deity, called Hymen, generally ended the business, amid the cooing of doves, the murmuring of brooks, and the warbling of nightingales, to the infinite satisfaction of all parties. Cakes and ale, and a general dance, were also among the attractions of this place, and a cool refreshing walk home in the moonlight, Bess leaning upon Jack's arm, and interchanging tender endearments with him, wound up the day pleasantly enough.

Thus passed away nearly a twelvemonth, till one afternoon, turning over some old things which had been condemned as lumber, Jack stumbled on the wallet of the gipsy Zara, which he had taken from the Red House, in which, as we have before mentioned, was a packet of somewhat dirty letters. Idleness, that often engages in employment which industry had never undertaken—or curiosity, or some other motive, led Jack to unfold one of these scrawls and examine it. Though no great scholar he could read aptly enough: the name of Jonathan Wild, subscribed to the letter, instantly insured its attentive perusal; to his great surprise Jack found it to run as follows:—

" Cripplegate, Feb. 20, 1702.

" QUEEN OF MY HEART,

" THOUGH I have resigned the cares of sove-reignty I shared with you, to which your love and favour raised me, despite my being alien to your blood and stranger to your race, the interests of the tribe are still as dear to me as ever. I know full well, my Zara, that though king consort, I am but your subject; and though you've vowed be-fore the Patrico to honour and obey me, your will should still be law to me; but the Squire, love, is imperative: 'tis not sufficient that the husband's blood yet stains his sword, and that the mother has miserably perished without the knowledge of her father's will—the child is still remaining; this he would have removed. Black Martin, with a chosen few I can depend upon, will be with you at night-fall, near the Witch Elm upon the Edgeworth road:

A A

the nurse must be inveigled from the cottage; during her absence some of the gang must fire it— it will be thought the infant perished in the flames —I like not murder. By these means, while we save life and soul, we shall retain a hold on our employer's gratitude; 'twill be a certain income to us. No doubt the woollen-draper has some clue, should we e'er need it, not that I think the Squire will prove ungrateful; but we'll make sure.

" Believe me thine, my queen,

" JONATHAN WILD."

This letter was directed to " Queen Zara, the encampment, Hornsey." Several other letters of a similar nature, all of them written by Jonathan, when holding the rank of king of the gipsies, accompanied this: they were all addressed to Zara, and chiefly related to the affairs of the tribe; then came a paper written in a delicate Italian hand: the writing, apparently much blotted with tears, seemed to be part of a letter; what remained of it ran thus:—

" Oh, my father! could you see your once-loved Elizabeth now, surely you would not longer retain your anger. As my little innocent Bess smiles on me, and reminds me of her ill-fated sire, the hapless victim of my cruel cousin, the thought will rise to me, that my fault—if fault it was—has been too terribly avenged. These lines may never reach you, my dear father. I feel that I am dying—

why should I live? The world is now a blank to me, for it was centred in my Arthur. Could I obtain your pardon, or failing that, your promise of protection to my child, I could yield life in peace. Should I fail, while yet I live, to reach you, to implore your blessing, there is a packet at the draper Kneebone's—that generous man to whom I owe so much—he's sworn he'll only deliver it to one who bears the signet-ring, so long an heir-loom in our family. I have described it to him. You may go safely there, my father. I have not compromised the honour of our house—no, he knows nothing, though in possession of the documents, that will efface the stain unjustly cast upon my fame, prove my child's rights, my Arthur's claims to our alliance. Farewell, my father! The pen is faltering in my hand—the light is fading from my eyes. These blinding tears—I may—I can no more. Bless—but if thou canst not—wilt not—oh! do not curse thy poor Elizabeth—smile one day kindly on her child, her pretty little Bess.—Farewell— farewell, my father!"

Though not exactly one of the melting mood, Jack felt somewhat touched at these lines; a suspicion instantly darted across his mind that the pretty little Bess alluded to in them, and the child mentioned in Jonathan Wild's correspondence, respecting whom there appeared so much mystery, must be one and the same—and that one no other than the partner of his fortunes, his own beloved

Bess : if so, it was plain some treachery had been played her. Rights were withheld from her, perhaps fortune, title. He remembered the mysterious conversation of the gipsy and the stranger in the garden of the Red House, on the memorable night when he rescued Bess from the power of the soldier, and he determined not to rest till he had fathomed the whole mystery, and had seen full justice done to her.

His first step was to question Bess herself touching all she knew of her early history : he did not think proper to make her acquainted with what he had discovered, nor hint to her his suspicions, intending to surprise her, when he had reduced doubt to a certainty, and perhaps restored her to rank and fortune. A thousand bright visions of the future crossed his mind : possessed of wealth, and blessed with the love of Bess, he pictured his retirement from the hazardous life he then led to some other land, where, safe from the fears of detection, and freed from the necessity of plunder, he might forget his past misdeeds, or at least, by future good, make expiation for them.

Bess could tell but little : her earliest remembrance was of wandering with the gang from place to place, while but a child. She knew no mother—had called no one father. Zara had brought her up, but more in fear than in love ; she had been shown some trinkets—had worn them, as belonging to her, on high days and holidays. All the tribe called her Bess, and some few Edgeworth Bess; but why she knew not, except that she'd once been told she came *from* Edgeworth; that they were sometimes visited by Jonathan, of whom all the gang appeared to stand in awe. She had heard that Jonathan had once been king of the gipsies,* by virtue of his marriage with Queen Zara, who had herself chosen him from all others, and publicly announced her choice to a general council of the whole tribe; but that though a provision had been made for him by the gang, as king-consort, and he had been allowed his own separate kettle and household, he had thought proper to abdicate, and had been divorced from Zara, at her own request, probably from her tawny majesty having found their union was not likely to be blessed with any progeny. Bess further stated that Wild was

---

* The notorious Charles Hitchen the city marshal, Jonathan's prototype in villainy, and precursor in his trade of discovering stolen goods, in a pamphlet entitled " The Regulator, or a Discovery of Thieves and Thief-takers, &c." before mentioned, published expressly to expose Jonathan Wild, has the following passage :—

" When king of the gipsies, Jonathan Wild executed the hidden and dark part of a stroller to all intents and purposes, until in Holborn, by order of the justice, his skittish and baboonish majesty was set in the stocks for the same."

Jonathan Wild in his pamphlet, in answer to this statement, giving an account of himself and the city marshal, does not deny the assertion of his having been king of the gipsies, but contents, himself with remarking, " That he need not mention Hitchen having been nearer the pillory than ever a certain person was to the stocks."

wont to notice her, and to give her presents, calling her his bank; and once had said, she was a mine of wealth to him. That Jonathan, and Zara—who was of a very violent temper—had some time since broken their friendship with each other, she understood, about herself, but knew not the particulars; that a strange gentleman, the one who saw her wedded to the soldier, was brought to her by Zara, and seemed much moved at seeing her, exhibiting extreme alarm and anguish; that Zara had suddenly shown the greatest desire to get her married to the soldier, Rupert Lion, whom she had introduced to her; but of the cause of all these circumstances she was perfectly ignorant. This was the sum of Bess's knowledge; it certainly was not much, but it served to confirm Jack's suspicions.

Jonathan Wild was the first party he made up his mind to apply to: as Jonathan derived more profits from his labours than from those of any other of the gang, he thought he would not refuse to give him the necessary information for restoring Bess to her rights, whatever they might be. From Zara, even had he known where to find her, he did not expect much. Having once decided on any thing, Jack was never very long in commencing proceedings.

Towards night, taking a bye-path which led him to Walworth, he made his way to the Mint, where he was joined by his friend Blueskin, who, on learning he was going to Jonathan Wild, volunteered to accompany him. On their way to the Old Bailey, Jack made Blueskin briefly acquainted with the errand that took him to the great man. Blueskin promised to stand by him back and edge. Requesting a private audience with Jonathan, through his gentleman usher, Mr. Quilt Arnold, *Esquire*, while Blueskin remained outside, Jack entered at once upon the business.

"I believe, governor," said he, "you'll allow that you hav'n't any gentleman under your command that works better for you than I do; I have cracked, known and unknown, no less than forty-three kens within the last six months; and you know what a very low per centage I have been contented with upon my booty."

"I have never denied your merits, Jack," patronizingly answered Jonathan, "nor shall you want my protection whenever it may be necessary. To do you justice, you are as clean a workman as any on town, and mill a crib with a neatness and expedition that do you the greatest credit. What do you require of me—any preferment?—Even to furnishing you with the best nag on the road—"

"It a'n't that, governor," interrupted Jack, "I want no reward of that kind, the long and the short of it is, little Edgeworth Bess is now Mrs. Sheppard."

"What! pretty Edgeworth Bess?" exclaimed Jonathan, "I wish you joy, Jack. Ah! you young chaps are nothing without a mistress. I am always delighted when I find any one of my clever fellows fond of the ladies—it shows they have a spirit; I never mind their having a dell, nay, nor two, for that matter, provided they don't trust them too far, for I have a failing that way myself, Jack. Do you want me to put her on my books? I have a vacancy among my court and opera ladies, now poor Sally Salisbury's gone—can she cut a pocket in a side box, or take a watch at the drawing-room?—I will provide her with a chair and liveries if she can: the jade will become a hoop and stomacher as well as the best."

"You are right in that last respect, governor, said Jack, " though you are rather on a wrong scent with the other: the fact is, if I'm informed properly, she need not want a chair nor liveries of any body, but can have them of her own, if she only had her rights; now you are just the man that know how she can obtain them, and won't refuse one of your best men the necessary information."

Jonathan started; a heavy cloud immediately settled on his brow. Jack, however continued—

" What's Bess's is mine, governor, and what's mine is my own; so I only ask for my own, and, connected as we are, I don't well see how you can refuse me.—I'll slum you the best ken there is in London next week, and charge nothing for the booty, if you'll only whiddle*—so now come and let's know all about it."

* Confess.

Jonathan had by this time, resumed his usual composure, and answered Jack in rather an under but very determined tone.

"Hark ye, Jack, where you have got your information from I neither know nor care, it is evident you can know but little, or you would not apply to me. I will deal openly with you. You are a good workman, a very good workman, and an honour to your profession, and I would do any thing in the way of business to serve you, or your doxy, but good will must have its bounds where honour is concerned. You know, while faith is kept with me, I never forfeit my word : 'tis true the wench has some rights, but what they are is my secret, and you must obtain it from some other quarter than me. I am faithfully and honourably paid for keeping it, and as long as I continue to be so, will not betray my employer to you, if there was not another rogue left unhung in England."

" And this is your determination is it ?" coolly inquired Jack."

" It is," said Wild, rather sternly, at the same time giving a stamp with his foot which immediately brought in his satellite, Mr. Quilt Arnold, *Esquire*. A glance of communication passed between them, and the minion instantly took a position behind his master. Jack took no notice of his entrance, but continued his conversation.

" Since that's your determination, now hear

mine, governor : the cove that wouldn't act jannock by his fancy girl, and be steel to the back bone in support of her rights, is a rank cur, and that's a title which shall never be borne by Jack Sheppard. 'Tis true you are a very great man, and I, perhaps, (glancing at his own somewhat slight figure) am rather a little one ; but if you were ten times greater than you are—if you were twenty Jonathan Wilds, and I only half a Jack Sheppard, I'd not suffer you, nor any other man living, to do the wrong thing to my *mort*, and so I tell you plainly."

" Dog !" cried Wild, furiously, firmly gripping at the same time a bludgeon he happened to have in his hand, " this to me—do you forget that you are talking to your master ?"

" No, I do not," returned our hero, putting his hand in his breeches pocket, " nor should you forget that you are talking to Jack Sheppard, and that Jack's as good as his master any day."

" Ah! defied !" roared Jonathan ; " seize him, Quilt."

The latter made the necessary movement—

" I won't trouble you," said Jack, knocking Quilt down with the butt-end of a pistol, which he drew from his breeches-pocket, and which was one of the brace he had purchased with Jonathan's first money. Jonathan immediately raised his bludgeon to fell Jack to the earth.

" You have not trapped me yet," coolly remarked Jack, observing his intention, at the same

time most retributively clapping the mouth of the pistol to Jonathan's head. At this moment Blueskin, who had apprehended some mischief, and who had been alarmed by the fall of Quilt Arnold, rushed in with another pistol, which he also presented at Jonathan, while, with a bludgeon in the other hand, he again prostrated Quilt Arnold, who was attempting to rise, clapping his foot upon his body to keep him down.

" Villain !" said Jonathan, gnashing his teeth with baffled rage, " you shall hang for this, if there's not another rogue left unhung in England ;" his favourite expression.

" Another word, Jonathan," said Jack, " and I'll blow your brains out. Drop that bludgeon ; not a word of alarm, for your life."

The thief-taker was for once taken by surprise, and stood aghast.

" Gag and bind that hound, Quilt Arnold, Blueskin, while I take care of his master."

Mr. Quilt Arnold, *Esquire*, was immediately accommodated by having his own neckcloth thrust half down his throat, and otherwise so secured as to prevent his uttering the slightest exclamation ; his arms and feet were then firmly bound with his own garters, which happened fortunately, according to the fashion of the day, to be very substantial ones. Jonathan was next waited upon ; searching his pockets, a strong pair of handcuffs, and a regular iron gag, made in the shape of a pear, which he usually carried about him, were soon found, and were directly devoted to his own especial service. A little investigation round the room discovered two or three strong ropes; with these Blueskin adroitly bound the Jupiter Tonans, Jonathan, and his satellite, back to back, in which enviable situation they left them, and departed, persuading the patriarch (who had remained down below, and knew nothing of what had been going on,) to accompany them a little way on the road, when they promised they would treat him with a dram; observing that his master and Mr. Quilt Arnold, *Esquire*, were in close consultation with each other, and would not wish to be disturbed for some time. Thus did Jack Sheppard quarrel with Jonathan Wild.

CHAPTER XX.

HOUSEBREAKING FOR LOVE.

A VISIT TO MR. KNEEBONE.—TURN LOVE OUT OF THE DOOR
AND HE'LL COME IN AT THE WINDOW.—SYMPTOMS OF
YELLOW STOCKINGS.

TAKING the patriarch to a house where they were
not likely to be directly sought for, in the event of
Jonathan's suddenly getting free, the partners soon
made that believing Hebrew very drunk, when
they left him wrapped in a deep slumber, which
promised to last some time; they then held a consultation as to the course they were to pursue; it
was decided that Jack should immediately leave
Higgler's Green, Jonathan being aware of his
" whereabout" there, and they well knew what
they had to expect from him. To this place they
therefore repaired at once, and packing up what
few articles there were that were moveable, and sell-
ing the rest for a small sum to the proprietor of
the beer house, the moneyed man of the community, to Bess's great astonishment they cut over
the fields to Lambeth that very same night, and,
crossing the ferry by the palace, soon gained their

stable, with which retreat they had not made any one acquainted, not even their employer, Wild. Here it was settled they should pass the night, and that Blueskin should, the next morning, search for a lodging in the adjacent neighbourhood of Tothill Fields, where there were many haunts in which they could securely conceal themselves. A very few words of explanation sufficed to satisfy Bess for their sudden removal.

The night had set in darkly and stormily, but they crept up to their little loft, which, as before stated, was well stored with hay, for the better concealing their booty. The convenient Blueskin, who, to do him justice, was an excellent caterer, having procured a capital country-made pork pie of ample dimensions, from a dairyman near Palace Yard, with a couple of bottles of ale, and another of usquebaugh—for so whiskey was at that time called. As the wind howled over the river, and rocked their fragile retreat to its foundation, and the waters moaned beneath them, and beat against the base of the building, they nestled themselves warmly and cosily among the hay, and enjoyed their humble repast with a relish and content that might have been envied by kings.

The angry blast and pattering hail-storm, though dreary enough to the benighted wanderer, often sound not unpleasant to the ears of those who can listen to them at ease, beneath the shelter of some snug, secure, and protecting roof. Chat-

ting, joking, laughing, the time passed away, and
the chimes of the Abbey had long proclaimed the
departure of midnight, ere Bess warbled both Jack
and Blueskin to sleep, with one of her gipsy ballads.

On the following morning, Blueskin got them
a lodging in that part of Tothill-fields, then called
the kennel, a part almost wholly occupied by dog-
fanciers, rat-catchers, and other dealers in animals,
most of them persons with very liberal ideas of
morality: here, all the dogs lost, stolen, or strayed,
throughout the metropolis, were sure to be heard
of on a proper application being made. Held
sacred by constables and others, it formed a very
fit place for our hero's concealment. Blueskin
betook himself to his mother's residence in Rosemary Lane, after agreeing with Jack that in
future they should carry on business solely on
their own account, without the intervention of any
agent.

No sooner had Blueskin left them, and they
had settled themselves as well as they could in
their new residence, than Jack's thoughts again
returned to the hope of discovering Bess's family,
and restoring her to her rights. It was plain that
from Jonathan Wild there was nothing to hope;
Jack, therefore, determined to visit Mr. Kneebone,
and endeavour to procure the packet, mentioned in
the fragment, written by the unfortunate lady that
had, no doubt, been the mother of his beloved Bess.

Jack had not seen this gentleman since he had quitted the service of Mr. Wood, and knew not how he should be received. He felt conscious he had acted ungratefully by him, and hesitated at the thoughts of facing him; but his love for Bess, his anxiety for her welfare, made him brave all. It was not until the dusk of the evening on the following day that he ventured out, for he well knew a strict search would be set on foot for him by Jonathan. Using all possible caution, he at length reached the dwelling of the single-hearted, generous woollen-draper.

His first step was to see Mrs. Partington. That worthy woman's instant impression, on seeing him, was that she beheld an apparition: accordingly she screamed, sank into a chair, and was about to go into a fit, when Jack begged her, for God's sake, not to expose him to danger, by alarming the neighbourhood, but to compose herself, and listen to him; that he was no ghost, but really and *bona fide* Jack Sheppard. This seemed to frighten her still more.

" Are you sure, Jack," said the good woman, that you've not come here to break us all open, and rifle us, and that you don't mean to commit a burglary on poor dear Mr. Kneebone, and cut the throats of the whole house? for you know what a terrible desperado you are. Dear me, you fairly make my back open and shut. Whenever I even think of you, I feel all gooseflesh. I'm all of a creep, and don't know whether I'm standing on my head or my heels."

Jack assured her the house was perfectly safe, and everybody in it, as far as he was concerned; that he had been forced, by bad treatment, to do what he had done; but that he was about to reform, and leave off his wicked course of life.

"Lord send it, Jack!" said the good woman; "it is never too late; and I'll give you my own great family Bible, with pleasure."

As this was a large folio volume, nearly as big as a side of bacon, Jack felt it would be a very troublesome companion to return home with, and therefore declined accepting it, till a better opportunity should present itself.

"I have merely come," said he, "to ask a few questions of my early benefactor, and kind friend, to whom I have behaved so ill—tell him how penitent I am."

"But are you sure, Jack, you are not come to steal any of the plate?" asked the simple minded dame; "are you sure you've got no house-breaking tools in your pocket?—Mercy on me, what is that?"

"Only a snuff-box," said Jack.

"Dear me, I thought it was a crow-bar! then you've not come to commit a highway robbery?"

"No, upon my word and say so," replied Jack.

"Well, I will believe you," returned Mrs. Partington, who never dreamt that any one could falsify such a solemn asseveration; "follow me up stairs to the parlour, and remain outside the door till you hear me cough, when you may come in."

Jack did as he was desired.

At the first intimation that he was in the house, the worthy woollen-draper was violently excited.

"What! that scoundrel, Jack Sheppard, here?" he exclaimed, "send for a constable, Mrs. Partington—reach me my blunderbuss—I'll hang him —I'll shoot him—I'll—I'll—"

You'll pardon him, Sir," said Mrs. Partington, persuasively: "the poor lad has been led astray by bad company; and 'evil communications,' you know, Sir—he has returned like the prodigal son."

"And you want me to be killed as the fatted calf!" exclaimed the incensed Mr. Kneebone. "No, no, Mrs. Partington, let him take himself off directly, while you go for the constable, and I ascertain that my blunderbuss is properly loaded. —I'll not see him, I tell you."

Jack did not think it necessary to wait Mrs. Partington's signal any longer; he therefore crept in.

"Indeed you wrong me, Sir!" he exclaimed, "I have been a great sinner, but I would not harm you; I implore you but to satisfy me on one point. You have a sacred charge, a packet— left you years since; I cannot produce the signet ring that should be presented by the person claiming it, but, I conjure you, let me see it—indeed you'll do no wrong : I implore you to let me have it—it vitally affects the fortunes of one of the truest, fondest, best—one with whose destiny my fate is indissolubly bound."

Feeling, which much oftener takes away the powers of expression than it bestows them, had, for once, made Jack eloquent ; and he was proceeding, in a strain of forcible and glowing language, to urge compliance with his request, when the sudden rising of Mr. Kneebone, in the height of indignation to which this monstrous proposition, as he thought, had carried him, as suddenly stopped our hero.

" Rascal !—Villain !—this is beyond all—get out of my house—get out of my sight, or I shall do you a mischief—I shall murder you, I shall !— Give you another person's property, indeed !— Where is my blunderbuss ?—where's the poker ? —Why don't you go for a constable, Mrs. Partington?—Here, help! help! neighbours!—Seize the villain !"

Finding the alarm really about to be given, and that there was no chance of Mr. Kneebone's listening to reason, Jack now thought it prudent to make off.

He returned to Bess with a heavy heart. He now felt, more forcibly than ever, the propriety of the resolution he had adopted not to make her acquainted with his suspicions and views till he had,

one way or the other, satisfied himself of what would
be the result.   By awakening no hopes he could
cause no disappointment : accounting for his absence in the ordinary way, Jack held a consultation
with himself what was best to be done—his last
hope had failed him.   As with Jonathan, it was
now clear he had nothing to expect by fair means
from Mr. Kneebone; that worthy man's prejudices
being too strong to admit of his listening to reason,
he determined to ask the advice of Blueskin, who
usually saw every thing in a very clear, straightforward way.   Towards evening, that trusty pal
returned from Rosemary Lane to look out for
squalls, as he said—in other words, to plan some
fresh robberies.   Taking him to an adjoining skittle-ground, Jack, between the pauses of the pins,
unbosomed himself, finishing by asking what, in
such a situation, was to be done?

" What !" quoth Blueskin, laying down the
wood he was at that moment about to handle, " Is
it possible you can ask such a question, Jack?
Well, that is a good one—why, man, if you can't
get the papers by fair means, you must get them
by foul—if he won't give them to you, you must
help yourself to them."

" What do you mean ?" said Jack.

" Why I mean, if you can't get them any other
way, you must prig them."

" What ! crack the ken ?"

" Identically !"

" Joe, Joe," said Jack, transported with the idea, which had not occurred to him before, " you must certainly be inspired—I'll do it this very night."

"Ay, ay, the sooner the better," laughingly cried Blueskin, " and I'll accompany you."

" But mark me," said Jack, seriously, " Mr. Kneebone was the friend of my boyhood—was my earliest benefactor: his property must be held sacred :—though, for my dear Bess's sake, I will break open his house and steal from it that which is her's by right, I would not take the value of a farthing from him to save me from the hangman : this must be a *speak* for love, Blueskin—you must content yourself with *nix-my-doll* for your share of the booty."

" Ay, ay," again laughed Blueskin, " we'll see all about that—only let us get in."

" You promise me, then ?"

" Nothing so sure," returned Blueskin—" that is, *over the left.*"

This last mental reservation of course was not intended for Jack's knowledge.

" It's decided on, then," said our hero ; " Blueskin, you're a true friend. Bess shall get us some beef-steaks and onions for supper : we'll then have a pipe and a bowl of rum-slim, and by the time we've finished, it will be time for us to go to work."

" Agreed," cried Blueskin, " nothing can be better arranged, my lad."

It was between one and two o'clock on a fine July morning when they set out to Mr. Kneebone's.

"Acquainted with every hole and corner of the house, the only assistance I shall require of you, Blueskin," said Jack, "is to remain outside, and watch that I am not surprised; I shall enter the ken from the back—we shall be less liable to observation that way."

"You have only to command, captain," said Blueskin, who had every reliance on Jack's superior skill in these matters, "and you'll find your faithful lieutenant, Blueskin, ready to fall in the ranks and obey your orders."

Arriving at the spot, no one being in sight, Jack placed Blueskin as sentinel, and, getting over the back wall of Mr. Kneebone's house, commenced cutting through a strong wooden bar that was placed over the cellar; it was speedily removed, so firm was his wrist, and so adroit was he in the application of his tools: Jack had then to shoot back the bolts of the cellar door, and force the lock; this he effected as noiselessly as expeditiously. From the cellar he stealthily made his way up stairs to the well-remembered bedroom of Mr. Kneebone: here his heart sunk within him. He remembered the many happy hours he had passed within the house, the many acts of kindness he'd received from Mr. Kneebone; and the thought that he was there. a confirmed burglar, to commit an

act of robbery, smote him with painful consciousness. He listened at the keyhole with deathlike
breathlessness—not a murmur was to be heard—all
was awfully silent : he softly turned the handle of
the door ; it opened to his touch—Mr. Kneebone,
unsuspecting and relying, had not even locked it.
He entered the room—the massive damask curtains,
thickly quilted, that depended from the top of the
huge four-post bedstead in which the good man slept,
were closely drawn around, the woollen-draper lay
reposing in a species of living tomb; only his equal
and tranquil breathing proclaimed the existence of
any other being than Jack within the apartment.
Cautiously lighting up his dark lantern by means
of his phosphorus box, Jack let the light become
visible only by the most imperceptible degrees : a
sudden glare might have awakened the sleeper,
though there was little danger of that, thanks to
the curtains; and then Jack well knew that, when
accustomed to it, the eye will repose as undis-
turbedly in the broadest light as in the deepest
gloom. The experiment was successful : no symptoms were evinced of the sleeper's consciousness of
any change.

There was a small escrutoire which usually
stood on a table in this room, in which Jack knew
Mr. Kneebone was accustomed to deposit his money
and other valuables ; in this repository Jack naturally thought he should find the precious packet
of which he had come in quest. He found the

escrutoire in its accustomed place : as he approached towards it he suddenly paused, alarmed
by a noise he thought he heard below, as if of
some one moving.   He knew there were only Mr.
Kneebone and Mrs. Partington in the house.—
Could he by any chance have disturbed that good
woman ?—He thought not : besides he recollected
she slept in an upper apartment, and the sounds
proceeded from below : he had, however, known
her at times to sleep in a small turn-up bedstead
in the front kitchen—she might have got up to
procure something : he thought he would suspend
operations for a while till she had retired again.
He listened, but not hearing any further noise,
all continuing profoundly still, he made up his
mind it must have been fancy, and again turned
toward the escrutoire.

It stood on the accustomed table which was
placed against the wainscot between two windows,
in the front of the room that looked into the street.
His first care was to see that the curtains of these
windows were drawn, that the unusual circumstance of a light being seen there, at that early
hour, might not attract the attention of the watchman.   As Jack raised the lantern for that purpose,
the light fell full upon a portrait which was hung
directly over the escrutoire—he started—it was
the portrait of his *mother !*

Although apparently taken in her girlish years,
he could not be deceived in it.   Who is there

that, passing with her his earliest years, has ever wholly forgotten his mother? The love of our manhood may be effaced from our memory by time and absence: the features that have haunted us night and day may become no longer familiar to us; but the love of our childhood, pure filial love, remains true through every change, and accompanies us even to our graves: though long severed from us by the tomb, the maternal face is one of those that still smiles kindly on us, as eternity opens upon our vision, robbing even death of its sting, and mortality of its victory.

She was dressed in a robe of simple white; a rose was in her bosom: the colours of the portrait had become mellowed by time, and it bore the appearance of gently fading; the fresh hue of the complexion had also deadened; the features had a wan and saddened air with them, heightened by the raven jet of the hair; the eye, which rather declined downwards than otherwise, appeared fixed on some object; and the painter had so contrived it that, from whatever point you looked at the picture, you could not help imagining that object to be yourself. As Jack met its glance, he fancied it regarded him with a look of melancholy reproach: he remained riveted to the spot for some moments, unable to turn his eyes from it. There is strange power in the eye—a world of hidden intelligence, that has only to be sought for with earnestness to be instantly discovered. The powerful fascination ascribed to the orb of vision, by which the deadly reptile transfixes its victim, is not wholly fabled: the lion's ferocity has been known to quail beneath the steady gaze of the surprised traveller.

Unreal as it was, Jack stood spell-bound and irresolute before that mournful glance. Ashamed of his weakness, he at length, by a desperate effort, wrested his attention from it. He turned to the escrutoire; the picklock trembled in his hand; still he saw his mother's restraining look. He shut his eyes—in vain; it was still there; it seemed to warn him. A world of fond remembrances flashed across him—her constant tenderness, her virtuous counsels. Again, in desperation, he essayed the escrutoire, prompted by his love for Bess; and again, as if impelled by some supernatural influence, was his attention attracted to the picture; the picklock fell from his hand. Fearing the noise it made might arouse the sleeper, he hastily extinguished the light, and resolved to abandon his intention. Cautiously hurrying from the room, he stood outside some moments to recover himself.

To account for the unexpected appearance of Mrs. Sheppard's portrait in Mr. Kneebone's bedroom, it must be remembered that, as we have before stated, she had been the early and only love of that gentleman. This memorial of his affection might at one time have caused pain, and added bitterness to disappointment in its contemplation; but it not unfrequently happens that objects, the sight of which gives at first the keenest anguish, become, by the intervention of time, the most precious and treasured : that very anguish subsiding by degrees into a softened melancholy, from which are often drawn feelings of calm and chastened tenderness that almost amount to pleasure.

Removed from the immediate influence of his mother's memory, which had so unexpectedly arrested his purpose, Jack became more collected, and began to retrace his steps down stairs : while doing this, it occurred to him that adjoining the shop, at the back, there was a small room, which was used by Mr. Kneebone as a sort of counting-house, in which to keep his books, bonds, and other valuable papers—there being a strong cupboard in the room, where they could be securely placed. " Perhaps," said he, " I may not wholly lose my labour yet;" for he felt ashamed to retreat without having at least made an effort to accomplish his purpose. " I should prove a traitor to my love, did I not make another attempt ; but, then, my mother's portrait! Ah! it was just so she used to look at me, when my boyish wilfulness, my youthful waywardness, would excite a moment's anger. No, no, it was not anger—'twas sorrow." Jack had never read Shakspeare, and knew not how strongly Nature was asserting the truth of that immortal bard.

" But, then, my poor Bess! Why," he continued, " may not the precious packet have been deposited, along with Mr. Kneebone's other papers of importance in this room ;—it were disgrace to depart before having ascertained this."

Repairing to the room, he was astonished to find the door of it wide open. This appeared to him to be an act of supererogatory carelessness, for which he could not account. The cupboard in question was also open, and the books appeared to be lying about in some confusion. Jack had no time, however, to waste in conjecture. After a minute search among a large bundle of papers, tied with red tape, and marked " Private," he at last found the precious packet. It was simply directed " To my Father."

He was about to raise it to his lips, when he distinctly heard the heavy steps of some one in the shop. Again hastily extinguishing the light, he remained in stifled apprehension ; placing himself so that he could not be perceived, yet could perceive all, he directed his attention towards the shop. The fanlight over the door in the passage, the only means by which the light from without was admitted, was so obscured by dust and filth, that the beams of the moon could hardly make their way through it. It was, indeed, " darkness visible ;" but, in this gloom, Jack distinctly saw a tall dark figure slowly leave the shop, and vanish down the stairs which he had so recently ascended.

Could it be some supernatural being, intent to

warn him? He had heard of apparitions and ghosts, and his thoughts immediately recurred to his very small and doubtful knowledge on that subject. The first serious reflections we turn, towards the shadowy beings of another world, are always very far from satisfactory. Bold as Jack was—and he was always ready, to use his own words, " to face either man or devil"—he felt he dared not, after what he had seen, descend into the cellar. There appeared to him no sense in following a preternatural appearance, for such he felt assured it was : he therefore made his way through the shop door into the street, taking heed, however, to fasten it carefully behind him, intending to replace the bar over the cellar, that his benefactor might not be a loser any further by his visit. Stealing round to the back of the premises, he found Blueskin, as he had left him, on guard.

" Ah, Blueskin!" he exclaimed, " how glad I am that I am once safely out of that house ! Do not laugh at me—but Heaven hath set its finger against my entering there. I have had supernatural warnings: the semblance of my mother—yes, her pictured form—has frowned in reprobation ; but that's not all—I've seen an apparition !" Blueskin laughed. " Do not ridicule me," continued Jack ; " 'twas in the shop. If e'er I saw one bearing mortal form, 'twas there I beheld it ; a figure somewhat taller than yourself, and stouter."

The mirth of Blueskin here became downright

obstreperous. " I beg your pardon, Jack," said he, becoming at last somewhat more rational, " but I really never could have thought you would have been such a precious muns ! however, we won't talk about that *now*. Come along, my boy ; let's be off as fast as we can ; there may be danger in remaining here another moment. I'm glad you're come. You've got the 'fakement,' I hope ?"

" I have," said Jack.

" That's all right, then ; this way."

Here he began to hurry Jack along at a very quick rate : Jack mechanically followed him. At length Blueskin stopped, apparently out of breath, and quite exhausted.

" For Heaven's sake ! Blueskin," said Jack, who had now completely aroused himself from his late gloomy mood, " what is the matter with you ? Why, you appear to have grown twice as lusty as you were, all of a sudden ; surely you have not got more than one coat on ?"

" One coat ! my prince of pals," cried Blue-skin,—" why, I've got fifty on : look here my trump,"—throwing open his waistcoat, and dis-closing an immense quantity of superfine cloth, closely rolled round his body — " one hundred yards at least."

" Good heavens !" said Jack, " surely you haven't been robbing Mr. Kneebone—my gene-rous patron, my kind, my constant friend ?"

" Indeed, but I have," returned Blueskin.

" What would you have thought of me, if I'd visited your friend and patron, as you call him, and had not been a customer; this cloth will fetch us twelve shillings a yard at the least, and Will Field's just the 'fence' that will buy it of us."

" What, then the apparition in the shop ——"

" Was myself," said Blueskin, laughing heartily: " I little thought I was putting you in such a fright. It struck me, instead of cooling my heels outside, that, while you were employed above, I might do a little business below."

" Then it was you who forced open the locks of the counting-house and cupboard?"

" To be sure it was, my boy," said Blueskin, in great glee; " but I didn't find much there; only a parcel of musty old books and papers. I'd a devilish sight better luck in the kitchen: see here—how very foolish it is of people to leave their silver spoons about!" Here he showed a quantity of plate. " I took a snack of cold beef and a mug of ale, that they mightn't say I was proud, and stood upon ceremony. There's one thing I'm bound to own, and that is, that their mustard's capital;—well, I do think mustard eats better with a silver gilt spoon from a pot to match. I admired the pattern of our friend the draper's so much, that I brought them away with me."

Jack groaned with vexation; this was what he had neither contemplated nor expected: he felt hurt and mortified at the thought that his kind

benefactor should suppose him capable of such base-
ness and ingratitude, and he well knew the first
suspicions would be directed to himself;—but the
deed was done, and it was useless to say any thing
further: he therefore contented himself with a salvo,
that it had been done without his knowledge and
against his wish.

Reaching their stable without any interruption,
the partners safely deposited their booty. While,
with the precious packet, Jack repaired to Bess,
Blueskin returned to Rosemary Lane, where he
expected he should find his friend, Will Field,
whom he had mentioned to Jack as being likely to
purchase the cloth and plate; they having no Jonathan Wild to apply to now.

" Be careful," said Jack, " and mind who you
trust; you know Jonathan has set his dogs at our
heels; and, though they are at fault at present, if
once he gets on the right scent, he'll never rest till
he's hunted down his game."

" The pursuit has certainly been hot about the
Mint," returned Blueskin; " but there's no fear of
Will Field,—he's one of the right sort."

" Well, well; of course, you know best, Blueskin," replied Jack; " I only give you the office.
Good bye, lad !"

" Good bye !" said Blueskin; " I shall just get
to the Lane as the Sheenies are turning out." The
partners then separated.

Jack's first step, on reaching his lodging, was to

examine the important packet. It was some time before he could find an opportunity of doing this unobserved. Breaking the seal with a trembling hand, after unfolding a number of blank envelopes, he came to two enclosures : one was a certificate of marriage, dated April, 1701, between Arthur Montalbert and Elizabeth Smith ; the other was a register of the baptism of Elizabeth, the infant daughter of Arthur and Elizabeth Montalbert, and was dated January, 1702. Not a line of any kind accompanied these documents, and Jack found himself nearly as far off as ever. 'Twas true he had discovered the family names of the unfortunate pair, and possessed the means of sub-stantiating the legitimacy of his beloved Bess ; for he was now more than ever convinced that she was the infant daughter mentioned in the register. But what likelihood was there that this would ever be necessary ? How was he to trace out the families of either of the ill-fated couple ? Smith was so common a name, and Montalbert had a foreign sound with it. Jack fell into a deep reverie, in which he remained till his reflections were dis-turbed by the sudden entrance of Bess. Hastily concealing the papers, with some confusion, Jack made an excuse for visiting the room of one of their fellow lodgers. Bess started ; a deep crim-son overspread her face, which gave place to a death-like paleness.

"You were reading something," she falteringly

exclaimed; " may not your Bess be made acquainted with it?"

" It was a letter from Blueskin," Jack replied,
with some hesitation, "upon business, with which
you had better remain unacquainted."

" And was the letter you were reading yesterday
from Blueskin, too?" anxiously inquired Bess,
fixing on him an earnest gaze.

" Yes, yes," Jack replied, rather pettishly, not
relishing this catechizing.

" I did not know that Blueskin wrote so delicate and beautiful a hand as that appeared to be,
from the slight glimpse I caught of it," returned
Bess, in a tone of mingled irony, reproach, and
sadness.

Jack hurried from the room, to avoid reply. As
he closed the door, the deep sobbings of Bess announced that she had yielded to a burst of grief,
for which he hardly knew how to account.

" Foolish wench!" he muttered; " surely she
can't be jealous : these women are all so unreason-
able. Well, well ; her satisfaction will be all the
greater when she finds out what really is the case,
and learns how groundless and unjust are her suspicions." Jack little knew that there is less danger
in an infant's playing with a naked sword, than in
a lover trifling with a woman's affection.

CHAPTER XXI.

———

JACK IN NEWGATE.

THE RECEIVER WORSE THAN THE THIEF.—THE BITERS BIT.—JACK'S CAPTURE.

On the following morning, Blueskin again visited Jack: he was accompanied by a stranger, whom he introduced as his friend, Will Field,—a clumsy set fellow, with a loose shuffling gait, a bony countenance, and hooked nose, and whose clothes hung upon him much in the fashion of an old coat on a scarecrow. Bess was evidently displeased with his appearance; though she returned his salute with civility, she instinctively shrank from him; in truth there was a wiliness of look about him, which, though it might have passed with the multitude as an indication of sincerity, would, to a physiognomist, have borne the appearance of deceit and cunning. Jack welcomed him cordially.

" You must not expect, Jack," said Blueskin, " to find, in my friend Field, here, a practical workman like yourself; all men have not nerves alike, nor abilities either, I may say. Will is rather diffident of his own powers, as far as work-

c c 2

ing for himself goes : but a better touter, whenever a customer's wanted for any swag, there is
not to be found in all Romeville.   There isn't a
Lock, or Fence, from Paddington to Whitechapel,
that he don't do business with ; and I should like
to see the Case that he's not free of. I've been
telling him of our little expedition the other night,
and he says he knows a cull that's in want of just
such a bale of goods as we've spoken to ; therefore
the sooner we let him see the cloth the better."

"I'll use you well, Joe, you may depend upon
it," said Mr. Field, " if it's only because I know
your mother ; though I say it myself, you'll find
me as honest a factor, and as prompt in payment,
ay, even as Jonathan Wild himself."

" Then we'll take you to the lumber ken at
once," said Blueskin ; " of course we are all on
honour."

" Oh, yes ; honour, certainly, " replied Mr.
Field, warmly : " don't I know your mother?"

" Well, this way, then," said Blueskin.

The trio repaired to the stable, into which,
Field, with some caution, was admitted : he expressed great satisfaction at the sight of the cloth,
and said that he would certainly take it off Blueskin's hands, if it was only because he knew his mother. Having measured the cloth, and ascertained
the weight of the plate, Field, with many expressions of good will, took his leave, announcing his
intention of returning the next morning with the

money, which, he said, would be at least eighty pounds. He had, previously to this, advised them to be very cautious not to suffer themselves to be seen about the stable any more than they could possibly help, that they might not excite suspicion, as he knew Jonathan's satellites, the Patriarch, and Mr. Quilt Arnold, *Esquire,* were searching for them in all quarters, and that he shouldn't like any thing to happen to Blueskin, because he *knew his mother.*

In the afternoon, Blueskin having an engagement with a young lady of his acquaintance, whom he had promised to treat with a bowl of wine, and a sight of the horse-riding at the Three Hats, Islington, Jack determined, in order still further to prosecute his inquiries for the restoration of Bess to her rights, to ferret out the gipsies, and try what he could learn from them on the subject. With some trouble, he discovered that a portion of them were encamped in a lane between Highgate and Holloway ; thither he determined to repair.

It was a lovely summer's afternoon when he set forth. Crossing St. James's Park, he made his way through the broad road of Tottenham Court, stopping to refresh himself at that well-known baiting house, the " Adam and Eve ;" when, crossing the fields on which now are built portions of St. Pancras, and Camden and Kentish Towns, avoiding the high road, he made his way, in the

shade of the pleasant hedge-rows, towards Highgate. The birds were singing above and around
him ; daisies sprang up beneath his feet ; the sun
shone out with a genial warmth, tempered by the
balmy breezes that wantoned gently across his
path. Highgate Hill at length appeared in sight.
Leisurely climbing its steep acclivity (it had no
tunnel then), and arriving at its summit, Jack rewarded himself for his toils with a cool tankard,
at the first house of entertainment that presented
itself. Declining the proffered honour of being
sworn on the Horns, he then, by dint of repeated
inquiries, made his way through a number of small
shady lanes, or bridal roads, till at length he came
to one, embowered among the trees, in a retired
spot between Highgate and Holloway. Impassi-
ble to vehicles of every kind, and having scarcely
room, in some places, for even a horseman to pass,
—to say nothing of the overhanging branches which
crossed each other from the old trees fringing the
high banks on either side, which rendered the traveller's keeping his saddle a matter of much un-
certainty,—this lane was but rarely traversed.

The curling blue smoke, ascending from the
wood fire over which was suspended, as usual, the
general stock-pot, served, as on former occasions,
to conduct Jack to the gipsy camp ; though even
had this banner been wanting, he would have been
at no loss—the sharp nose of Fox detecting his approach at a considerable distance. The welcoming

bark of this sagacious cur was soon followed by the hearty gratulations of all the tribe. A thousand inquiries were made after the health and condition of Bess; also, whether there were any signs of " Hans in kelder" yet, &c. Queen Zara was fortunately absent; therefore, after recruiting his strength with a leg of a barn-door rooster from the stock-pot, and some other little trifles, which he washed down with some draughts of the crystal stream, diluted with the gipsy brewage prepared from a receipt peculiar and only known to the gang,—and which was neither wine, beer, nor spirit, but an agreeable and exhilirating drink, or cordial compound, partaking of the qualities of all three,—he found plenty of opportunities for satisfying his purpose.

His first application was to the Prime Minister and Field Marshal, Black Martin, who had always manifested much friendship for him. This illustrious person perfectly recollected the circumstances which had led to Bess's introduction into the gang.

" It was in the little town of Edgeworth," he said, " that we set fire to the cottage of the old woman and bore away the child, then an infant, who, from that circumstance, was afterwards called Edgeworth Bess, and who is now your ' autem mort,' ben cove, Jack. Jonathan Wild, who was then king consort, planned the whole affair. What his reasons were, I could never learn; 'tis certain they were not plunder: the owner of the cottage was a poor woman, who had formerly been servant in some great family, and had taken in the child to nurse; we had a difficult matter to inveigle her out. When she returned at midnight, and found the cottage reduced to ashes, as she supposed through her negligence in leaving it, and understood from the neighbours that the child had perished in the flames (for such was the general supposition), she lost her wits, I'm told, and has been crazed ever since. Our queen brought up the kid herself; but who the kid really belonged to, and for what purpose she was kidnapped, has always been a mystery. If Poll Maggot was here now, Mahogany Poll, as her husband, poor Will Maggot, the spiced toby cheesemonger, used to call her—if she was here now, she might let you know a little more about it; but she set off with the lady's maid that's going to smuggle her this evening into a house of a person of quality in St. James's, where she's to tell the fortunes of all the female part of the family; that she can easily do, for she's wormed all their secrets out beforehand from Mrs. Abigail, who was sent here expressly to conduct her. I expect she'll make a good night's work of it; she'll be sure to pick up a few odd spoons and trinkets, and perhaps a watch or two; and they'll never dare say a word of the matter when it's discovered, lest they should be blamed for their own carelessness and credulity: besides which, no doubt the jade will be well paid."

" I must visit Edgeworth," said Jack, involuntarily, his attention not having been at all attracted by these last remarks of Black Martin,— " Yes, I must visit Edgeworth—I must see this poor mad creature, if she be still alive; I must learn what family she lived with—it will afford a clue; but who can I get to accompany me, and search her out?—who is there that can recognize her?"

" Why, the very ' mort' we are talking about," replied the Egpytian chief. " I'll tell you what I'll do, lad: where's your tent, that is, your ken?—Where do you hang out? Just give me the office, and I'll send the slut to you the day after to-morrow; she shall go with you to the very spot."

" You will!" said Jack, gratefully grasping the vagrant minister's hand; " do that, and I'll honour and bless you for ever; but secrecy— Bess must not know a single syllable of what's going on—she has no suspicion."

" Leave a gipsy alone," laughingly observed Black Martin; " Mahogany Poll will be as close as an oyster; nay, better than that, for when secrecy's the word, the jade wouldn't even open to the knife."

" Capital! Capital!" said Jack, in ecstacy;" I may depend then?"

"You may, you may; leave it all to the cook."

They rejoined the gang—the glass and toast went round, seasoned meanwhile with laugh and joke, and song, and it was not till the moon was riding high in the heavens, plating the foliage with her silver light, that Jack took his farewell, and retraced his steps homewards.

The lane was partially in gloom, owing to the thickness of the overhanging branches, and there was a deep stillness in the air only broken by the occasional hum of some insect, and the soft ripplings of a neighbouring brook; but when he emerged at the top of the lane into an open meadow, the flood of splendid light, in which he seemed all at once to be completely bathed, as it were, had its effect even on his every-day nature. It was a delicious walk home through those fields, so calm, so dreamy, so fresh, and Jack was almost sorry when arriving at length at St. James's Park, one of the obscure streets near the Abbey brought him into the neighbourhood of his own retreat. As he turned into Tothill-fields, the contrast betwixt its close, muggy, oppressive atmosphere, almost fetid with the rank odours of the number of animals pent up as if in another but less saving ark, and the mild reviving breath of nature that he had inhaled from field and flower during his walk home, struck him most forcibly; the presence of innocence in the one resort, and the feeling of guilt in the other, could not be mistaken. The abiding place of each was strongly marked out by their attributes—Jack's heart was softened, and he felt almost saddened at the silent lesson that was read him.

"Well, well!" he mentally ejaculated; "let me but restore Bess to her rights, let me but gain the means to seek some other country, and live beyond the reach and fear of want, and I will forswear my present course of life, and become honest. I could have wished to have done something for men to remember me by—there is no labour I would not undergo, no privation I would not endure, could I but achieve some deed that might render my name celebrated, and get me talked of hereafter. Yes, I feel that I am not without ambition, but I have shut out to myself all the paths of honourable enterprise.—What can I do to make my memory renowned?—Who, when I am gone, will cast a thought upon Jack Sheppard—the low-born burglar?—'tis madness thinking of its possibility."

Poor Jack! how little did he imagine that his adventures were to occupy the attention of succeeding generations; that he was to figure on every stage, the favourite hero of the play and the pantomime; that the novelist and romance writer would embalm his fame in their pages, and that the more than usual brevity of his mortal career would be compensated by a length of immortality in fiction, far exceeding that of many of the great-

est warriors, statesmen, and other worthies of his
age!

Jack found Bess sitting up for him; she was
thoughtful and pensive, but she essayed to look
cheerful, and to receive him with her wonted welcome : he saw she had been weeping, but he forbore to inquire the cause, rightly attributing it to
his absence; he contented himself with evincing
more than his usual tenderness towards her. They
arose the next morning with their accustomed good
humour. Jack spoke of a little excursion of pleasure to which he intended to treat Bess in the afternoon—a visit to Sadler's Wells, then a very favourite place of amusement : her countenance regained
its gaiety; she became once more all smiles, and returned Jack's caresses, when he left her, after breakfast, to accompany Blueskin, according to their
appointment with Field, with a fervour and sincerity that assured him of her continued and ardent
devotion.

Jack found Blueskin waiting for him at the
public-house where it was settled they were to meet.
Taking a morning draught, and playing a game of
skittles, they amused the time till the approach of
the hour of their appointment with Field, who was
to join them at the stable.—To the stable then they
repaired.

"Hallo, Jack!" said Blueskin, who was the first
to reach the door, "what's in the wind here?—a
screw loose, by all that's damnable! Why, here's

the jigger* open ; surely we couldn't have forgotten to have locked it after, us yesterday. No! here's somebody been playing booty.—Why, the ' Case' has been cracked !"

Jack rushed forward : the door had indeed been broken open.

" It must have been that infernal fellow that *knew your mother*, Blueskin," said Jack. " I thought, all along, there was something *cross* about the scoundrel ; pray Heaven he mayn't have turned snitch ! Let us look if the swag is safe."

Quick as thought they ascended to the loft ; the hay was there, but, as Blueskin remarked, " the cloth and plate had danced the hays, and vanished."

" Damnation ! I'll chive† that villain Field," said Blueskin. " Rob a pal ! it's death, without benefit of clergy. The world will very soon come to an end now, and the sooner the better ; for who'd wish to live in it ? When there's no honour left among thieves, it will be in vain to look for it any where else. But come, Jack, the sooner we cut our sticks, and leave this place, the better ; we can't be off too quickly. I've always heard the receiver was worse than the thief ; and now, dam'me, I know it. Rob a pal !—A fellow that nursed me when I was a child !"

" Yes, he said he *knew your mother*, Joe," said Jack, with a bitter sneer ; " that made him, I sup-

* Door. † Knife him, cut his throat.

pose, make so free with our property ; if you can't take a liberty with your friends, who can you do so with ?—But let's be off—this way."

Opening the outer door to quit the stable, to their utter surprise they encountered Jonathan Wild's satellite, Mr. Quilt Arnold, *Esquire*, who was apparently in attendance there to receive them.

" Good morning, gentlemen," said that worthy, bowing with ironical politeness ; Mr. Field's compliments, and he's sorry he cannot have the pleasure of waiting upon you this morning, touching that little affair of the broad-cloth, but he sent me instead, in hopes I shall do as well."

" Trapped, by G—," roared Blueskin, at the same instant felling Mr. Quilt Arnold to the earth.   " To the loft, Jack—the river ; it's our only chance of escape ; no doubt the fellow has got plenty of his companions at hand."

To the loft they accordingly flew like lightning, and opening a little door that looked upon the river, were about to precipitate themselves below, when they were stopped by the apparition of the patriarch, who was waiting, in a boat, with a couple of constables immediately beneath.

" How do you do, my dears," said the Israelite, with a grin. " You can jump down ; dere's no danger ; ve'll take care of you ; those that are porn to be hanged, will never be drowned, you knows."

Muttering execrations, they retraced their steps, on the chance that Quilt Arnold might be alone, but no sooner had they re-descended, when they were met by a body of constables, headed by Quilt Arnold, who had by this time regained his legs, and was brandishing a huge hanger. Blueskin instantly drew out a penknife, the only thing in the shape of an instrument of offence he had about him, and swore he would stab the first man that should stop him.

"Then I'm the first man," said Quilt, boldly; "and Mr. Jonathan Wild is not far behind me; and if you don't instantly drop that knife, I'll chop your arm off."

At the formidable name of Jonathan Wild, the weapon instantly fell from Blueskin's hand, and both he and Jack were immediately secured. Jonathan then made his appearance.

"Snug hiding place, this!" he exclaimed; "I am sorry to disturb you, but business is business, you know. Where are the bracelets, Quilt? we mustn't be less polite than they were to us the last time we had the pleasure of meeting—psha? those ruffles are a mile too large; dont you know that Jack has the power of distending the muscles of the wrist? You must hand him number one, those we use for the young prigs."

"I'll take care of number one, governor," said the satellite, with great glee, thrusting Jack's wrists into a very small pair of handcuffs.

A whistle from Jonathan here brought the patriarch to add to their number, who very officiously waited upon Blueskin. When the partners were both firmly secured, Jonathan gave the word—to the Strand ; and the whole party proceeded to make their way there.

Jack preserved a sullen silence, while Blueskin gave vent to his feelings in a variety of inward execrations. As they passed through the streets, Jonathan leading the way, followed by Quilt Arnold, the patriarch, and the two prisoners, and a whole posse of constables bringing up the rear, the report that the renowned Jack Sheppard was taken, arrested every one's steps, and so great was the crowd that gathered round to catch a glimpse of so dexterous and daring an offender, that it was with the utmost difficulty that they could force their way along. Jack would have taken advantage of this concourse, and attempted a rescue, but receiving the solemn assurance of the patriarch, that on the slightest movement indicative of such a design he would immediately shoot him through the head, Jack thought it prudent to forego such a resolution. Whether purposely or by accident, in going down the Strand, Jonathan took them past Mr. Kneebone's house.

" There's the ken," said he, pointing to it with malicious satisfaction.

" I beg you wouldn't mention it, Mr. Wild," said Blueskin, who now, for the first time since his capture, found his tongue. " I know very well I'm a box of cold meat,* I'm quite sure of that; all I care for is the bone-pickers† getting hold of me — I should not like to be made an ' atomy,' of at Surgeons' Hall, that I must say."

" Make your mind easy, Joe," blandly answered Jonathan ; " don't be afraid of the ivory-turners having any thing to do with you—I'll take care to prevent that, for I'll provide you with a wooden surtout‡ myself.

" The devil thank you and your surtout," muttered Blueskin to himself.

Jack did not dare raise his eyes to the house, fearing to encounter the reproachful glances of his early benefactor, and the good-natured Mrs. Partington; he, however, passed it with a bold and determined step. Reaching Fetter Lane, Jonathan conveyed his prisoners to the house of Justice Blackerby, to undergo an examination, for the purpose of getting them committed at once to Newgate.

As Jack had conjectured, the first witness that appeared against them was the acquaintance of Blueskin's mother, the infamous Field. He deposed, that having become acquainted with Blueskin, he had been as good as a stepfather to him.

"I think you said 'stepfather,' " fiercely growled Blueskin, who, if he could at that moment have

* A dead man.   † Surgeons.   ‡ Coffin.

turned his eye into a boarding pike, would most assuredly have run it through Mr. Field's body; " I think you said ' stepfather!'"

Field resumed : having known Blueskin's *mother*, he had, out of pure respect to *her*, consented to become an accomplice in the robbery of Mr. Kneebone's house. Here Jonathan groaned with conscientious horror, and Jack lifted up his hands and eyes, while Blueskin contented himself with doubling his fist, and shaking it very earnestly at the witness. Field continued—he had certainly assisted in stealing the cloth.

" He tells no lie there, at all events," muttered Blueskin, " although it was not exactly from Mr. Kneebone." As a proof of what he then affirmed, Field could, he said, produce a part of the cloth himself.

" He could produce the whole, if he chose," said Blueskin, unconsciously committing himself. " Damn me, if I'll ever have any thing to do with any scoundrel who knows my mother again !"

On Field's testimony, who was admitted King's evidence, Jonathan Wild giving bail for his appearance at the sessions, Jack and Blueskin were fully committed on the capital charge, and a warrant was instantly made out for their immediate removal to Newgate. Arriving at the Old Bailey, Jonathan had the prisoners conveyed to his own house, whilst he sent over to Newgate to prepare for their better reception. Introducing them into his armoury for greater security, and being left alone with them, he thus addressed Jack:—

" You seem down on your luck, Jack! I thought you had been a braver man; every one to his trade; this is but what you must have expected; you know I'm a man to be trusted; whatever I say I mean, and religiously observe. I told you, Jack Sheppard, I'd hang you, and I'll keep my word."

Jack smiled contemptuously. " You'll not hang me yet, Jonathan," he exclaimed; " I told you I'd make you restore my poor girl to her rights before I'd done with you, and I'll keep *my* word."

Jonathan gave a scornful laugh. At this moment a third prisoner was brought in by one of Jonathan's minor runners.

" Ah, ah! what, is that you, Simon Jacobs?" cried Jonathan, with evident satisfaction; " why, it never rains but it pours! But it's a pity the patriarch hadn't the pleasure of taking you—set a Jew to catch a Jew, you know."

" Yesh, set a thief to catch a thief, Mishter Vild;" said the discomfited Hebrew, gnashing his teeth.

Jonathan grinned awry. " You see what it is not to act fairly," said he; " but you needn't be very much afraid—I don't think you'll bring forty pounds this time. I wish this mad fool," pointing to Blueskin, " was in your case; I shall endeavour to bring you off as a single felon. As for you, Joe," he continued, addressing Blueskin, " your attachment to this rash cull, Sheppard, leaves me no alternative. You must die; but you shall not be anatomized ; and I will send you a good book or two."

" Damn his good books and his bad books too," muttered Joe, between his teeth ; " he's a charitable churchwarden, he is. We shall see who will die first."

Mr. Quilt Arnold, *Esquire,* now came in to announce that every thing was prepared for the prisoner's reception at the Royal Hotel, as he facetiously termed Newgate ; and that the keepers would be most happy to have the honour of being introduced to them. To Newgate then they went. They were met at the door by Mr. Austin, the head gaoler, who was attended on the occasion by his two under turnkeys, Messrs. Langley and Revel ; the trio warmly welcomed their visiters. Being conducted into the lodge, the usual process of ironing took place. Jack's fame necessarily rendered this a task of much circumspection. The heaviest fetlocks, bazils, and handcuffs the prison could furnish, were produced and fitted upon Jack, who manifested the utmost indifference.

" There," said Mr. Austin, after conveying Jack to a strong dungeon, in which he was stapled to the floor by a chain, fastened with a massive padlock, and communicating with his irons, sufficiently long to give him the range of the cell ; " there,

Jack, if you can get away from this place, why I give you leave, that's all."

" I'll take you at your word, my nibbs," said Jack, with a laugh; " but won't you let me have my pal with me ?"

" No, no ! too good a judge for that," said Mr. Austin ; " visiters of your distinction should always be accommodated with a private room—Mr. Blake's apartment is at the other end of the building."

" I think now, Jack," said Wild, coolly, as Mr. Revel brought in some straw and a blanket, with a pitcher of water and a brown Tommy, as the prisoners were accustomed to call the Newgate loaves ; " I think you've got all you want, and are quite comfortable, so I'll leave you."

" Oh yes ! Mr. Wild," said Revel ; " I promised Jack the first time he visited us, that, if ever he came to stop here I'd take care of him, and so I will—he'll be as snug as a bug in a rug here ; but we must leave him now, I've got to attend Mr. Blueskin — good bye for the present, Jack ; see you again by and by."

" Do not put yourself out of the way," said Jack, " any time will do—good day Mr. Wild, I'll give you a call the very first opportunity, depend on it."

" When you can, I've no doubt you will," drily returned Jonathan, " and I shall expect to see you, but not till then.   Now, Mr. Austin, I'm at your service. As Jack has not intimated his intention of paying his footing here, I must lay down the entrance money for him, I suppose."

"Which shall be expended in a half-guinea bowl of punch to drink his good health—Jack ain't used to the place yet; we shall, I dare say, be very good friends when he once is."

With these words Mr. Austin, his official, Revel, and Wild, departed, closing the ponderous door on our hero, and putting into effect all its massive machinery of locks, bolts and bars. Thus was Jack, for the first time, at that height of a felon's notoriety, a prisoner in Newgate.

CHAPTER XXII.

JACK IN NEWGATE.

JACK'S CONDEMNATION.—POLL MAGGOT.—THE ESCAPE FROM
THE LODGE.

THE first thing Jack did, after the departure of the
gaolers and Wild, was to examine, very minutely.
the state of his new lodgings ; the result was not
very satisfactory : the walls were all of massive
stone; there was no light but that which was admitted through a strong iron grating over the door,
which door opened into a passage that led to the
interior of the prison, where some of the turnkeys
were always sure to be found : his irons, though
strong and heavy, he did not take much into account.

" I must trust to chance and opportunity," Jack
exclaimed ; " Rome wasn't built in a day—there's
plenty of time for me to concert some plan of escape
between this and the arrival of the dead warrant.
That infernal villain, Field !—he did provide us
with a customer for our goods, certainly—*himself*,
the scoundrel ! Poor Bess !—what will be her

distress when she hears of my capture! Her
fears will magnify the danger a hundred fold.
Then how shall I manage to send her the intelligence?—Plaguy unlucky, that this should have
happened just at this time; had I but had an
opportunity of seeing the gipsy, Poll Maggot, and
of visiting Edgeworth with her, Fate might have
done its worst: I might, perhaps, have procured
intelligence, through Mahogany Poll, to have enabled my insuring Bess's future welfare—my own
I should not have cared about."

He was interrupted in his reflections by the re-
entrance of Mr. Revel, a rubicund-looking gentleman who not unhappily illustrated his name,
both in person and nature. Mr. Revel was fond
of enjoyment; he loved a cheerful glass, and had
a very pretty wife, though she was ultimately
carried off by one of his prisoners—whether from
love or revenge is not known. Revel was fond of
a joke, and delighted in a good song and a funny
story.

"Well, Captain Sheppard," said he, coming
in and shutting the door, "I thought we should
have the distinction of entertaining you at last.
You won't find Newgate such very bad quarters,
if you'll only take to it kindly."

"I desire nothing better," returned Jack; "is
there anything to be had here?"

"Everything but liberty," returned Mr. Revel,
"that is, if you've only plenty of money. I dare

say you didn't come here without being properly breeched—trust you for that."

" You may take your oath of it," said Jack, laughingly, at the same time chinking some broad pieces which he happened luckily to have in his pocket.

" That's your sort," said Mr. Revel, " it's no use coming empty-handed here ; we like gentlemen that do the handsome thing."

" I know it, my trump," said Jack ; and as a proof of it—what will you take to drink, Mr. Revel ?—only give it a name."

" Only *you* give it a name, Captain," said Mr. Revel ; " you can have anything ; for my own part, I am not at all particular, if it's only wine or punch ; to be sure I do give the preference to punch, but I can put up with wine."

" Punch, then, by all means," said Jack ; " a crown bowl to begin with. Here's a broad piece ; you can give my compliments to the other gentlemen of the key, and tell them to drink the change out of it to our better acquaintance."

" Bravo !" cried Revel, in high glee ; " well, if I have a failing, it's being fond of the company of a young fellow of spirit."

The punch was duly procured, and Jack was so droll over it, and ingratiated himself so much with Mr. Revel by his convivial qualities, that the social turnkey readily undertook to get a note conveyed for him to his good lady, Mrs. Sheppard,

—for so Jack thought proper to style Bess. In this note Jack informed Bess of what had happened, making, however, as light of it as possible; and, as she was liable to be apprehended on the charge of being concerned in the robbery of the plate of the May-day garland, as also for breaking out of the New Prison, he advised her to await the arrival of Poll Maggot, and only to visit the prison in company with her; desiring that Poll, the better to avert suspicion from Bess, might pass herself off as his wife. In the course of the next day this note was answered in person—both Bess and Poll came to visit Jack. Liberally feeing the turnkeys, greater indulgence was extended to them than to visiters in general; they were allowed to remain longer with Jack than was usual with one in his situation.

Bess did not appear to be at all pleased at Mahogany Poll's passing for Jack's wife, though the first burst of her grief, at witnessing the sad condition in which Jack was placed, restrained her from giving vent to the full force of her misgivings. It may be remarked, that though somewhat matronly, Poll Maggot was uncommonly comely, and might have awakened feelings of jealousy in a heart much less devoted than that of poor Bess. Comforting her as well as he could, Jack devised a thousand means of escape; but the sessions drew near without any thing being finally decided on.

In the meantime, Poll Maggot had contrived to have a private interview with Jack, and expressed her readiness and willingness to afford him all the assistance in her power, to enable him to obtain the much desired information respecting Bess ; although, as she said, Bess should not show her tantrums to her in the way she did.

This made Jack wish, more than ever to gain his liberty. His love of Bess was even stronger than his love of life ; but still no practicable means of escape presented itself.

At last the day fixed for Jack's trial arrived, and with his accomplice, Blueskin, he was placed at the bar. He had employed no counsel for he knew it was useless. Jonathan Wild was to have been one of the witnesses against them, but this was prevented by a circumstance which is too memorable to be passed over, and which might have saved the hangman some future trouble. Just before the trial, Wild desired to speak with Blueskin in the bail-dock, and while they were there, in order that Wild's testimony might not operate to the injury of Jack, Blueskin suddenly pulled out a clasped penknife, and drew it across Jonathan's throat ; the knife being somewhat blunt, and Blueskin being instantly secured, before he had time to make a second attempt, the wound, though it effectually prevented Wild appearing as a witness on the trial, and was of a very dangerous character, did not prove mortal, or the triple tree at Tyburn would have lost one of its most distinguished ornaments. Bitterly did Blueskin regret that he had not provided a knife sharp enough to have cut off his former patron's head at once.

"I shall deserve to be hanged," he said, "if it's only for that."

The testimony of Mr. Kneebone, and the perjury of Field, were, however, sufficient to make out a case against both the prisoners. The jury found them guilty without retiring, and sentence of death was immediately passed upon [them. Jack would have heard it with unconcern, but a piercing shriek from the gallery, which went to his very heart, for a moment unmanned him. It was Bess —she had fainted in the arms of Poll Maggot, and was carried, in a senseless state, out of the court.

The two principal witnesses had each excited strong, but very different, emotions, in the bosoms of the prisoners; the sight of Mr. Kneebone, although conscious he had been no party to the robbery intentionally, gave Jack the keenest reproach; he turned his eyes away at the mild testimony of his revered benefactor, who gave his evidence with a reluctance which fully evinced his sorrow.

Jack's stifled feelings almost choked him, and he would gladly, at that moment, have escaped by death the anguish of a contrition which he felt was unavailing.

Blueskin's sensitiveness was no less aroused by the appearance of Field, although he exhibited it in a very different way: he gnashed his teeth, and threatened him by every variety of violent gesture; in fact, it was with the utmost difficulty he was restrained from jumping over the bar, and throttling him in open court, while at the mention by the villain of a knowledge of Blueskin's mother, he became absolutely raving.

Immediately after their return to prison they were placed in the condemned hold. Hundreds of people of all ranks flocked daily to gratify their curiosity with the sight of the renowned house and prison breaker, and the emolument of the keepers, who exacted a liberal gratuity from every visiter, before they would afford the gratification so much desired, was more considerable than ever had been known even in the days of Claude Du Val himself.

Jack passed a merry time of it; he had been visited by nearly all his old acquaintance, including Mr. Wood, his fellow apprentice, Griffith Thomas, and even worthy Mr. Kneebone and Mrs. Partington. The honest Welshman freely forgave Jack, and treated him to a can of ale, though, as he said, he " fas a sad tog." To Mr. Kneebone, Jack made a full confession, and implored his pardon; his kind benefactor was affected to tears. He could give Jack no information respecting Bess's parents, further than that they had lodged in his house; they came as strangers; the lady had borne an infant girl during their residence with him; he had been present at the christening of it, and thought it possible, from a particular mark about its person, that though grown up to woman-hood, he might still recognize her. The young couple had staid with him till the tragical death of the gentleman, (who had fallen, it was alleged, in a duel at Rosamond's pond,) compelled the lady to leave him and retire into the country; pre-viously to doing this, she had placed in his hands the packet to obtain which Jack had forfeited his life. Mr. Kneebone had never seen the unfortunate lady nor her infant since that time; he fervently bestowed his blessing on Jack, and offered up his prayers to Heaven that the pardon of the Father of all good might be added to his, and that Jack might obtain that grace hereafter which he could not expect on earth. Jack was deeply moved; if a truly contrite heart could obtain remission for past offences, such was his at that moment. As for Mrs. Partington, she sobbed and prayed by turns; and the necessity of consoling her some-what restored Mr. Kneebone to composure.

At the earnest entreaty of Bess, whose agonized feelings were all this time wrought up to the highest pitch, heightened, as they were, by jealous misgivings of Poll, whose attentions were no less constant and anxious than her own, Jack had pe-titioned to have his sentence of death commuted to transportation; but he had been too daring and notorious an offender to allow of this grace being extended to him by the government. The court was at this time resident at Windsor, which caused a delay in signing the dead warrants, for the execution of the various malefactors, that was rather unusual. Taking advantage of this delay, Bess had provided Jack with some watch-spring saws, which no one knew better how to use than himself; but still nothing had been decided upon. At length the arrival of the dead warrant for the execution of two of the prisoners, put Jack seriously upon his mettle. It was followed, on Monday the 30th of August, by the warrant for his own execution on the Friday following. He now plainly saw there was not a moment to be lost, he therefore roused himself for action; he was doubly urged—the attempt to effect his liberty was at once for love and life. To break out of the condemned hold was impossible on many accounts, and he looked out for some other means: his fertile brain was not long in suggesting a plan, which, though bold in the extreme, appeared both practicable and easy.

In the lodge of Old Newgate, it may be proper to remark, there was a hatch with large iron spikes, that communicated with a dark passage, which conducted up a few steps to the condemned hold. Through this passage it was customary to allow prisoners, under sentence of death, to pass from the condemned hold, and speak to their friends inside the lodge over the hatch. During the bustle incidental to the knocking off the irons of the two unfortunate prisoners, who had been ordered for execution previously to the arrival of his own dead warrant, Jack managed, unobserved, to saw with his watch-springs through a great part of one of these spikes ; and on the evening of the day before that fixed for his own execution, after the visiters had nearly all departed, Bess and Poll as had been previously concerted, came, as they said, to take their last farewell of him. Revel and Langley the two turnkeys on duty, were relaxing themselves, after the fatigues of the day, in a little recess close to the entrance of the lodge, with a game at " All Fours." In this recess, every one who came in or went out of the lodge must necessarily pass them ; they therefore deemed themselves secure. In addition to this precaution, the lodge was attended by a demi-official officer of the prison, known by the name of Shuffling Sawney. This nondescript, for it would have been difficult to have defined him truly, was a mixture of rogue and fool, sharper and natural ; he had formerly been confined in Newgate for some petty larceny, when he had made himself so useful in cleaning out the wards, waiting on the turnkeys, and doing all the little odd jobs of the gaol, that when the term of his imprisonment expired, he was, at his own earnest request, still allowed to remain an inmate.

" I have no home but Newgate," he whined; " and if you turn me out, what is to become of me?—it is so natural to me!—Ain't you my fathers?"

" Well, well !" said Mr. Austin, moved, and, perhaps, a little flattered by the reluctance Sawney evinced to leave them. " We certainly do act like fathers to our customers, and as, perhaps, we may make you useful in whipping the juvenile offenders, ironing the capital ones, attending the pillory, running on the prisoners' errands, and waiting upon us, why, I think, we may manage to let you remain a hanger-on; but, mind, all will depend on your good behaviour; if you show the least compassion, feeling, or indulgence to any one, or are guilty of the slightest disobedience to our orders, however hard they may seem, that instant out you go: so you know your doom, Sawney."

Sawney was too cunning to subject himself to the punishment of being turned out of Newgate, and was therefore very guarded in his behaviour before any of the authorities of the prison. His predominant passion was a love of secret mischief, not unusual with those coming under the denomination of naturals, or idiots; this itching for mischief he would practise alike on friend and foe, if he could but do it with impunity; to get any one into a dilemma was his delight. As may be surmised from his *sobriquet*, he was from the north country, and was shrewdly suspected to have formerly belonged to the Tolbooth in " Auld Reekie." Jack had become a favourite with him, from the liberality with which he paid him for the various little offices he performed for him.

On this eventful evening, as we have said, Sawney was in attendance in the lodge, lurking and shambling about, as was usual with him. He saw Poll and Bess enter; they were closely muffled up in large hoods and scarves, and appeared, from holding their handkerchiefs to their eyes, to be weeping bitterly; Sawney fixed an oblique glance upon them with an expression of much sinister significance. To relieve themselves from his unusual scrutiny, they gave him a broad piece; he turned it over, and chuckled with malignant satisfaction; he saw at once there was something on foot; and the idea that the very men—his employers, his patrons—to whom he owed the means of shelter and subsistence, might get into trouble, gave him a feeling of much inward satisfaction. Placing himself at the back of Revel's chair, as if to watch the progress of the game, he stood immediately between the turnkeys, and Jack and his companions, a position which enabled him to observe, askance, what both parties were doing.

Jack's first step was to complete the sawing off the spike; this he did, favoured by the affected sobbing of Bess and Poll, and his own loud expressions of consolation to them.

" You'll lose your *Jack*, Governor, if you don't mind," malignantly drawled out Sawney to Re-vel, with marked emphasis, observing the move-ment, as that functionary was putting his knave in jeopardy, to secure him one point of the game ; " the queen will take him." ·

Poll had by this time removed the spike, and Jack, with the assistance of the faithful Blueskin on the one side the hatch, and the two women on the other, was forcing his slender form through the narrow aperture he'd made.

" Well; all fours is a fine game," said Sawney, drily, observing the movement ; a very fine game, Ah ! the deuce—that's low, Mr. Revel.

Jack was here muffling his irons with a towel, brought for the purpose, and disguising himself in a similar hood and scarf as that worn by Bess.

"Farewell, dear Jack," sobbed Bess, as if taking leave of him ; " I must tear myself away."

" That's high, Mr. Revel," said Sawney, as Langley laid down the ace.—" I'll let you out directly, *ladies;* this way."

With his handkerchief to his eyes, Jack passed the two turnkeys, made his way, with a profusion of sobs, through the lodge door, and was the next moment in the street. closely followed by Bess. Sawney returned.

" Having lost your *Jack*, Mr. Revel," said he, pointedly, " there's the game; you and Mr. Langley are quits."

" Well, I'll play you another game, Langley just to see who is conqueror," said Mr. Revel, " and then we'll lock up for the night."

" But not before you have let me out," said Poll, advancing.

" Halloo !" said Mr. Revel, surprised ; " why I thought the two women were gone !"

" And so did I," said Sawney, maliciously ; " let us see that this is really a woman !"

He was proceeding to an inspection rather more close than necessary, when a smart slap on the face from the gipsy, by arousing the risibility of the keepers, permitted her departure. A very few moments after, and the escape of Jack was discovered. The consternation and surprise of the gaolers must be conceived : in the first burst of their rage, they accused Sawney of aiding and abetting ; but he artfully exculpated himself by reminding them of the caution he had given Revel, that he would lose his Jack if he did not mind. The mixture of stupidity and simplicity he assumed succeeded ; and he was allowed to join in the general pursuit, which was immediately set on foot in all quarters. Gloating over the angry reproaches of the indignant Mr. Austin, and enjoying the downcast looks and mortified air of Revel and Langley, Sawney's participation in the search was confined to directing his steps to a neighbouring Geneva shop, where he regaled himself by means of part of the broad piece Bess had given him.

CHAPTER XXIII.

JACK IN CHICK LANE.

FIELD LANE, IN 1723.—THE OLD RED LION TAVERN.—
THE HIGHWAYMAN'S STIRRUP CUP.—TRAGEDY DICK.—
THE CLERKS OF ST. NICHOLAS.—MELO-DRAMA IN THE
OLDEN TIME.

JACK and Bess, immediately on leaving Newgate, got into a hackney-coach, and drove past Jonathan Wild's house to the Blackfriars' stairs, where they took water to Lambeth, and put up at the " White Horse," an obscure public-house, only frequented by watermen and fishermen, in an alley by the bank-side, where they felt themselves quite secure. Jack easily finding an opportunity of getting rid of his irons.

In the mean time the news of his escape was bruited forth in all directions. That he should have effected it before the very eyes of the keepers, was an act so daring and dexterous, that all London was astounded. It had been Jack's intention, had he been detected in passing through the lodge, to have seized upon some of the weapons that hung over the chimney-piece, and have fought his way to liberty.

Locating Bess for a while in the obscure and humble vicinity of the 'White Horse,' Jack himself, for greater security, determined, till the storm had somewhat blown over, to seek the protection afforded by the Old Red Lion Tavern, in Chick Lane, a notorious house of rendezvous at that period for highwaymen, burglars, footpads, coiners, smugglers, and desperadoes of every description. In this haunt he well knew he might remain with comparative impunity, for even though suspected of being harboured there, such was its retired situation, its numerous means of escape, in addition to the ferocious character of its inmates, that few headboroughs, constables, or other officers of justice, could have been found hardy enough to intrude upon its privacy; indeed, it had long, by tacit consent, been regarded both by officers and thieves, rather as a species of sanctuary for crime than any thing else. Accordingly, recrossing the Thames, and making his way by numerous street and alleys, crossing Covent Garden, down the Hundreds of Drury, through Clare Market, along Portugal Street, Lincoln's Inn, and *Fetter Lane*, (at which he snapped his fingers in defiance,) Jack leisurely walked down Shoe Lane to Holborn Hill. The veil of evening which had now set in, favoured his progress, and he passed unnoticed and unsuspected.

The reader must not form any idea of the different streets, &c., we have just named from their present appearance, they were then very different. Trees in London and its suburbs, were nearly as numerous as houses, and town and country were strangely mingled together.

At the bottom of Holborn Hill, Jack found, as he would have done now, the entrance to Field Lane,—but how different was it then in appearance and nature! At that time, Field Lane was a rural, respectable, and quiet retreat, inhabited chiefly by retired tradespeople, or persons of moderate income, wishing for repose and fresh air. Its vicinity to the then pleasant prominence of Saffron Hill, Turn-Mill Brook, where once stood the busy water corn mills of the Holy Brotherhood of St. John of Jerusalem, the secluded retirement of Chick Lane, the umbrageous walks of Coppice Row, and Clerkenwell Green glowing with rural beauty,—constituted Field Lane quite the country. Many of its houses displayed no mean pretensions to architectural skill in their construction.

The back gardens of those houses on the right hand city ward, each of which had its little arbour, or summer box, where the master of the mansion could smoke his pipe, whilst his lady took her tea—ran down to the very bank of the Fleet river, or ditch, which flowed on that side, parallel with the lane itself; the busy rippling of this stream in its rapid progress, from which it derived its name *Fleet*, and the occasional clear sparkling

glances of its running waters in the bright sunshine, and milder moonlight, conveyed soothing
and cheerful images to the weary sense.

Though the Fleet had long degenerated from
the dignity of a river to that of a ditch, and was
no longer fed by its three tributary streams, the
River Wells, Old Bourn, and Turn-mill Brook,
it was far from being the filthy, pestiferous nui-
sance into which it has of late years degenerated.
A spectator might still have imagined the probability of the recorded fact—that the uxorious Henry
the Eighth gallantly sailed in his royal barge up
the Fleet, along the present Farringdon Street, to
visit one of his six Queens, at his Palace of Bridewell, and that, at an earlier period, the Danish
fleet, under the command of the victorious Sweyn,
sailed down it after burning Southwark, and an-
chored in triumph near the spot now known as
Bagnigge Wells.*

* Stowe tells us that this river was of sufficient depth and
width for ten or twelve ships at once with merchandise to sail
down it. Another writer tells us the tide flowed as high as
Holborn Bridge. It is certain that anchors have been found
in the bed of the stream, as high up as Battle Bridge and Saint
Pancras. It was not till the year 1740, that the Creek which
flowed from the Thames, at the spot which is now the foot of
Blackfriars Bridge, to the bottom of Holborn Hill, was converted into a species of sewer, and covered over, making way
form the present Bridge Street and Farringdon Street ; the
ground thus obtained was leased to the City of London, and
the City constructed a market on the site of the present Farringdon Street, long since removed, but long known as Fleet

Slinking somewhat furtively under cover of the night, through the secluded and quiet lane, Jack found its staid inhabitants sitting smoking the pipe of peace at their several doors, and conversing in friendly proximity ; he boldly returned their hearty good nights to him, and soon reached in safety the entrance of Chick Lane. The denizens of Field Lane were perfectly aware of the vicinity of their equivocal neighbourhood, but in that very vicinity consisted their safety ; they knew they were regarded as sacred ; that both from policy and honour, their rights would be observed ; they therefore neither noticed nor meddled with the visiters and occupiers of the Old Red Lion, and the different doubtful haunts around it ; and were, themselves, consequently, neither noticed nor meddled with at any time, by those very worthy persons.*

Market, Fleet Street, the Fleet Prison, &c. &c., all derive their names from this once important river.

* "Evil communications corrupt good manners." Never was the truth of this proverb made more manifest than in the present condition of Field Lane. How has it fallen from its once high estate ! it is now one of the most filthy, dangerous, and disgraceful parts of our great metropolis, and its existence is a reproach both to the police and the community at large—Tothill Fields and St. Giles's, both fastly disappearing, were comparatively respectable—it is wholly inhabited by thieves and receivers of stolen goods, who display their wares with the most unblushing effrontery. On each side are a series of shops, or Jew fences, the fronts of which are, for the greater part, covered with pocket-handkerchiefs, every one known to

There was an air of solitude on entering Chick Lane at this time, a shade and silence that made

have been stolen; these are hung out as blinds to the unwary, but serve as signs to the initiated that, where they are exhibited, every other article of stolen property, as well as Bandana's, is dealt in, from a silver pencil-case to a service of plate, or from a vintner's apron to a bale of broad-cloth. It was, at one time, dangerous to pass down this place unless accompanied by a police officer. The inhabitants are, for the most part, off-shoots of the chosen people, and have a decided ancient and oriental cast of countenance and appearance—the flowing beard, dark mantle, keen eye, and capacious forehead, with the unusual guttural sounds heard now and then, would lead the passenger to suppose himself wandering in some low bazaar, in some popular suburb of the East, but a glance at the surrounding buildings instantly dispels the illusion. In addition to its contiguity to Chick Lane, a little beyond this choice retreat, is Saffron Hill, the back slums of which form the whereabout of the poor Italian boys who, with their laughing looks, and merry hurdy gurdies, make our streets vocal in summer, and carry sunshine and gladness into regions otherwise never cheered by a sweet sound or a pleasant smile. In the wretched purlieus of Saffron Hill these patient little beings, with their monkeys and white mice, huddled together, twenty or thirty in a room, under the severe surveillance of their mercenary taskmasters, fade away, uncomplaining and unlamented, except, perhaps, by their mute companions. Alas! that the children of the warm south, the land of melody and beauty, pregnant at every step with classical recollections, and replete with picturesque attractions, should be crowded together in such miserable abodes of filth and squalor—that those, only accustomed to breathe a language which is spoken music, and hear the harmonious strains of a Paisiello, and a Rossini, should be sent forth to grind such airs as " Nix my Dolly," " Jim Crow," and " Sich a Gittin up Stairs !" but what will not the prospect of gain effect ? Gold ! gold ! thou hast created more crime, and occasioned more misery than all thy vast amount themselves sensibly felt by the wayfaring wanderer, and curious visiter.

As we have said, it was evening at the time of Jack's approach, the deep shadow cast by the row of lath and plaster houses that led to the archway, opening to the inn-yard of the Old Red Lion Tavern, was deepening as night advanced, a flickering light was dimly discernible to Jack's vision, as he emerged into the lane, from towards the bottom of it where the old inn stood. Making a cautious halt, and concealing himself behind the stump of an old tree, which had been left standing on the right hand side of the lane, Jack could distinctly see issuing through the archway before mentioned,

can compensate. It is well for these little Lazzaroni, or Lazzioni, as the vulgar call them, that the inroad in that neighbourhood, of the new street, now cutting by the worthy subjects of King Lud, from Farringdon Street to Islington, will drive these wandering minstrels into some other region—a worse they cannot find—alas! that they should have been doomed to exchange the fragrant field, embowering lane, and breezy hill of their own sunny land, for the murky atmosphere of the Field Lane and Saffron Hill of our own overgrown Babylon! A school for the gratuitous instruction of these forlorn little wanderers has lately been opened, by subscription, at the instance of some benevolent individuals; the result, however, has not been so satisfactory as had been anticipated; in addition to the usual abuses, like the philanthropic interference with the blacks, the effects have been rather those of evil than of good.

Mr. Dickens has rendered Field Lane familiar and memorable, by making it the abiding place of the Jew FAGAN, in his masterly, but incongruous novel, "Oliver Twist;" but why insult the Emerald Isle by giving the infamous Israelite a purely Irish name—for such Fagan certainly is.

a number of individuals, each leading out a horse, with apparent circumspection, congregating together at the front of the old tavern, whose tall gable end made it impossible to mistake it; besides, this tavern was the last of the row of houses. The Fleet ditch, covered by an archway, crossing the lane, at this spot, and running under the side walls of the tavern itself, in its course to Bagnigge Wells, Battle Bridge, St. Pancras, Hampstead, &c., till it lost itself in Hertfordshire.

At this moment, the moon suddenly rising, rendered the whole scene perfectly visible in her broad beams. Ten or twelve individuals strongly armed, and whom it was not difficult, from their swaggering and dissolute air. to recognize as highwaymen, were severally mounting their ready steeds, by the assistance of the horse-block, then standing in front of the tavern; their feathers, at that time not wholly discontinued, swayed saucily in their gold laced cocked hats, and the silver hilts of their pistols, were daringly peeping out from their holsters.

Mr. Lines, the landlord of this same Red Lion, or 'Ranting Richard,' as he was more commonly called, was serving each of the gentlemen with a dram of strong waters, out of a long necked glass, from a curious squab looking green bottle, by way of stirrup cup, previously to their taking the road, or in other words, departing on their different predatory excursions, the whole of them, as they drained the glass, carolling, though in a somewhat under tone, a well known flash chaunt of that day, called the 'Highwayman's Stirrup Cup,' and which ran nearly as follows :—

The Highwayman's Stirrup Cup.

1.

The hour has come at last,
    Our prads are at the door,
And the traveller hurries fast
    Across the lonely moor ;
Our pistols are full cocked,
    And the crape is on our brows,
The churl his door hath locked,
    We no longer must carouse ;
But ere in the stirrup's ring,
    From the horse-block leaping up
Like true Toby Gloaks we spring,
    Let us drain the Stirrup Cup.
            Hurrah ! hurrah !

2.

Old Noll is whiddling bright,
    The dull world is asleep,
'Tis a high spiced Toby night,
    Let's in our saddles leap ;
May our road be free and clear,
    Bold each heart, and cool each brain,
May we find our booty near,
    With a clear coast back again !
But ere in the stirrup's ring,
    From the horse-block leaping up,
Like true Toby Gloaks we spring,
    Let us drain the Stirrup Cup.
            Hurrah ! hurrah !

3.

May our prads prove swift and sure,
 And no angry storm arise
Till our booty we secure—
 A well filled purse the prize !
May the glasses sparkle high,
 And the faggot brightly burn,
And beauty's warmest sigh
 Fondly welcome our return !
But ere in the stirrup's ring,
 From the horse-block leaping up,
Like true Toby Gloaks we spring,
 Let us drain the Stirrup Cup.
    Hurrah ! hurrah !

4.

With the sweetheart and the wife,
 Be ours the laugh and song,
A short and merry life ;
 Give fools the sad and long.
For the Dubsman we'll not care,
 Nor at Nubbing Cheat look grave,
So the blessing of the fair
 Still but reward the brave !
But ere in the stirrup's ring,
 From the horse-block leaping up,
Like true Toby Gloaks we spring,
 Let us drain the Stirrup Cup.
    Hurrah ! hurrah !

Finishing this choice ditty, the different gentlemen of the road, to use their own expression, stuck steel into their dogs' meat, and gallopping past the spot where Jack stood concealed, disappeared, making their way along Saffron Hill, and through Clerkenwell and Gray's Inn Lane, by the different outlets in that direction, in search of their booty, to the Great Northern and Western Roads.

They had no sooner departed, leaving the coast clear, than Jack, emerging from his hiding place, made his way to the desired hostel of Mr. Lines (Dick Lines), the ranting, ramping, roaring host of the Red Lion.

All had subsided into silence as Jack advanced towards the house. There was no unusual light or noise; no busy stir within; no congregated murmur to awaken suspicion, and draw attention to the place. Passing the archway which led to the inn yard, at the back of which stood a substantial homestead, called Chalk Farm, once respectable, from which extended a long range of stabling, capable of accommodating from thirty to forty horses, which were constantly kept ready saddled and bridled, in order to take the road whenever booty was in expectation, or to convey their owners beyond the reach of pursuit, should the search prove too hot, and circumstances render evasion necessary, Jack reached the entrance to the tavern: he found the door was shut, but giving a private signal, with which he had become acquainted at one of those congenial haunts of infamy, the White and Black Lions, it was speedily opened by Mr. Lines himself. This gentleman started back rather theatrically on seeing Jack, who was in person at least unknown to him; recovering himself, however, Mr. Lines proceeded at once to challenge the counter-sign.

" Who comes here ? Stand, and unfold your-self," said he ; " discuss—*white soup !*"

" Spoons and tankards," answered Jack, boldly.

" Good, good," cried Mr. Lines, complacently. " Brown gravy ?"

" Rings and brooches," returned Jack.

" Right, right, bully boy," answered Mr. Lines, patronizingly ; enter, and leave all to the cook."

With these words he ushered Jack in, carefully fastening the door behind them ; conducting Jack to a private room at the back of the bar.

" Now then," said he, " we are alone. One proof more, and then your sweet history. Name the nurse ?"

" The Fence."

" Christen the child ?"

" Mill Ken."

" Ah, ha ! Spell the pap-boat ?"

" C-r-u-c-i-b-l-e," said Jack.

" Right to a letter," returned Mr. Lines ; " now make the pap ?"

" First take some tatlers,* the handle of a toasting-fork,† with swag‡ of all sorts. sweat the whole carefully over a slow fire, strain, and pour out, cut into small bars, and serve up when cool."

" Rob me the Exchequer, Hal, and do it with unwashed hands," shouted Mr. Lines, smacking his fingers with much exultation—" done to a turn.

---

* Watches.   † Hilt of a sword, generally silver.
‡ Plate.

Now then, one last proof and I have done. How do you make the child *speak?*"

" Give it a crowbar and a centre-bit."

" Excellent! And how do you *silence* the child ?"

" Put a necklace round its squeeze."†

" This is conclusive," cried Mr. Lines, with great glee, " I want no more—to your history ; but first, what say you to a toothfull of my Lady Cooper's drops? The night blows coolly—'it is an eager and a nipping air.' "

Without exactly knowing who my Lady Cooper was, but shrewdly suspecting that her drops were very nearly akin to the celebrated eye-water of our general grandmother, Jack expressed his cordial assent to this proposal ; and Mr. Lines touching, with a tragedy air, a part of the wall on one side of the room in which they were standing, a sliding pannel flew back, to Jack's great surprise, and discovered a beaufet well filled with bottles of every description. Taking one of a very alchymical form, Mr. Lines poured out a glass of its contents—it took away Jack's breath—that worthy then tossed off two himself, without winking an eyelid.

" This is your right rosa solis," said he proudly, " none of your sack, ' villainous sack ; Faugh ! there's lime in't ;' but, come, recount to ' me the story of your life, and run it o'er, e'en from your

* Rob.   † A halter, a very *anodyne* sort of necklace.

F F

boyish days,' to the very moment I now bid you tell it; 'nothing extenuate, nor set down aught in malice.' If you have cracked one ken, and want the shelter of another, propound—If you have been cooling your heels in dark Cimerian deserts or find your 'whereabout' too hot to hold you, confess—'If there is blood upon your face,' make a clean breast of it—'Behold thy father's spirit'— 'this castle hath a sweet and pleasant scent.' "

The effluvia that rose from the adjacent Fleet Ditch at this moment rather belied the assertion.

" 'I will a round unvarnished tale deliver,' " frankly exclaimed Jack, falling in with his questioner's peculiar humour, and resolved to trust him implicitly.

Mr. Lines was delighted.

" Come to my arms, dear boy," said he, warmly embracing Jack.

Jack then briefly detailed to the worthy host, all the particulars with which the reader is already acquainted. Mr. Lines felt proud to have so celebrated a person as Jack Sheppard under his roof; it was indeed an honour.

" 'Thou art the very prince of cut-throats!' " said he, affectionately grasping Jack's hand ; " and 'I applaud thee unto the very echo, that doth applaud again'—'I love thee for the dangers thou hast past, thy hair breadth 'scapes, and perils in the imminent deadly breach'—''tis true, 'tis pity, and pity 'tis, 'tis true,'—but you are safe here, though

I must not conceal from you, that you are in the very heart of the enemy's camp."—

Jack started.

"Yes," continued Mr. Lines, part of this very house is rented, under the rose, by the great captain of the age himself, aye, Wild the great—King Jonathan the First of glorious memory."

"Damn him!" cried Jack, energetically.

"Hush! treason," cried Mr. Lines, that's flat rebellion; but I repeat again, here you will be safe, honour among thieves, bully boy. Though it is here that Mr. Wild deposits his choicest goods for greater security, it is but seldom he visits this place, and then only to attend to his live stock, recruit his forces, exhort the troops in his pay, to do their duty, and use greater diligence, and look about for subjects for a decent execution, as the sessions approach. I will protect you—I, Dick Lines, 'master of the Tiger'—'for I am one that has heard lions roar'—Basta! I have said it, 'Sessy my boy, let him go by.' You shall not perform as a principal 'actor upon the platform, betwixt eleven and twelve'—'Tom will throw his head at them;' but it may be as well that you should not appear here openly—I shall introduce you to the boys as the Arcadian, there are some rare gallants drinking here, lads of Cyprus, but thou shalt see them; again I bid thee welcome to the Red Lion."

Jack thankfully accepted of Mr. Lines proffered protection.

The Red Lion Tavern was of some antiquity, having been erected as far back as the year 1683, by a noted smuggler of that time, named McWelland, chief of a tribe of wandering gipsies. It was opened by him ostensibly as the Red Lion Tavern, but in reality to afford a sure asylum to convicted thieves and desperadoes of every description, and also to furnish a safe receptacle for stolen property, contraband goods, &c.

Under king Mc Welland's sway the Red Lion flourished till the commencement of the last century, when, about the year 1710, it fell into the hands of Mr. Lines, or as we have said, ranting Richard, so called from his practice of spouting portions of plays.—Mr. Lines was a gentleman of rare and varied qualities, all of them it is true, inclining more or less to the ingenious,—he was highly accomplished, and had seen much of the world; brought up as a joiner, he had early displayed much skill in mechanics, but his lively genius disdained to jog on in that way—plodding labour was irksome to him, he liked a short course with every thing—he soon showed his indentures a fair pair of heels, and under the auspices of Mr. Mouldygrub, a well known wandering patentee of that period, commenced stroller, and traversed almost every part of the country as actor, and mechanist, or property man; he did not to be sure, attain much eminence in the histrionic art. His principal and favorite part being that of Filch

in Mr. Gay's famous piece, 'The Beggars Opera.'
—Independently of this part, Mr. Lines never got
beyond the first murderer in Macbeth. The second
ruffian in Beaumont and Fletcher's 'Two Noble
Kinsmen,' and the third thief in Sir John Suck-
ling's 'Goblins.'

At last Mr. Lines was forced, on the *score* of too
intimate an acquaintance with sundry alehouses, to
retire from the stage; he then became successively
—poacher, smuggler, swindler, and other characters equally respectable; he liked the bye ways
no less than the *high ways* of life—the crooked
path was dear to him, he disdained the straight
road. Fortune smiled upon his little endeavours,
—he managed to escape the stocks, horsepond,
whipping-post, harming beck, and headborough,
and amassed sufficient money to enable him to
take the Red Lion Tavern, where he had contrived
to turn his knowledge of theatricals to account,
by constructing a variety of trap-doors, sliding
pannels, concealed entrances, draw bridges, &c.,—
till the interior of the Tavern was much more like
that of a theatre than any thing else; he dug
cellars, and erected staircases, &c. The Red Lion
was much more extensive than it seemed to be
from its outward appearance. Built upon no regular plan, its passages &c. were intricate, and
its apartments various. At the instance of Jonathan Wild, Mr. Lines had divided his Tavern
into two houses as it were, having a communica-

tion with each other.—The further half that stood
on the west bank of the Fleet, whose rapid stream
fell here with a deep fall under an archway that
crossed the lane, had been converted by Jonathan
into a sort of lock or fence, for the reception of
such select property as he did not care to have
about his premises in the Old Bailey. The side
windows of this part of the building looked into
the ditch, which was not then covered over. On
the opposite side of the bank of this ditch, was a
cadgers' lodging-house, or a penny dab dormitory,
much patronized by the Bamfield Moore Carews',
Billy Waters's, and little Jemmies of the days of
good Queen Anne, and our First George.

Jack could not help reflecting on the singula-
rity of the chance, which had led him thus unknowingly, to seek shelter under the very roof, as
it were, of his most redoubtable enemy,—the man
who was then scouring the town far and near to
take away his life; but Jack knew Mr. Lines was
'jannock'—indeed, this gentleman was shrewdly
suspected of having been concerned in as many tra-
gedies off the stage as on,—murdering, and helping
to murder other gentlemen besides the characters of
Messrs. Shakespeare, Massinger, &c. Then the
inmates of the Red Lion were exactly the very
last persons in the world who should betray him to
Jonathan, whom they feared more than they loved,
having a well grounded apprehension that they
themselves might one day fall victims to his cupi-

dity, resentment, or convenience, as circumstances might occur. How could Jonathan ever dream that he was affording Jack an asylum on his own premises, his country house as he was pleasantly used to term it! Jack therefore made himself quite easy.

" Let me now introduce you to the lads, my pippin, said Mr. Lines.

" Lads," said Jack, where are they, I dont see them."

" But you soon shall," said Mr. Lines, " ' I can call spirits from the vasty deep—behold !' " Here, throwing himself into a teapot attitude, he gave a mysterious knock on the wall at the back of the room.

" Enter !" loudly roared a hoarse voice from the interior.

Mr. Lines touched a concealed spring, a secret aperture in the wall opened, and discovered to Jack's astonished vision another apartment, in which from ten to twelve persons were enjoying themselves, smoking and drinking.

" ' How now ye secret black and midnight *dogs*, what is't ye do?' " roared out Mr. Lines, " 'Scoundrels that ye are, " how do you dare to trade and traffic on the heath.'

' In plunder and affairs of death,
    And I, the close contriver of all arms,
    Am never called to bear my part,
    Nor show the wonders of our art.' "

He pronounced these words with an earnestness, and emphasis, that would not have disgraced either Betterton or Booth.

"Oh, damn it, Dick," said one of the guests, "don't let us have any more spouting; we are not in Bartholomew fair now, though cursedly near it—let's have another dram of strong waters."

You must *all* have another dram of strong waters," replied Mr. Lines, impressively " to welcome a new comer, and drink his health. I have brought you a pall, boys, a brother, an Arcadian like yourselves, Giannotto Pastor," introducing Jack.—You are all Arcadians, you know. ' Arcades Omnes.' "

Dick affected at times to be a bit of a scholar, as well as a wag.—" But mind, it must be all on the square."—This gentleman is under a cloud just at present, has a bit of crape over his name, so if you know him, you mustn't know him.— You understand, a little account unsettled between him and Jonathan."

" Oh, damn Jonathan," growled all the gentlemen, in an under tone.

Then followed sundry ejaculations of " Bloodsucker," " Wolf," " Cur," " Hangdog," &c. &c.

" Hush !" said Mr. Lines, authoritatively, Mr. Wild is our Master; under his protection we all flourish, the ' king's name is a tower of strength, which they upon the adverse faction lack,' therefore it won't do openly to rebel against him, though it certainly is our duty to cheat him whenever we can, especially when it's to serve a trump in trouble, and such a trump as this is, eh?"

" Here Mr. Lines winked most significantly to all the company present.

" Aye, aye!" uproariously shouted the whole of them, returning Mr. Lines's wink.

Jack saw that though he was not openly recognized, he was well known. Sundry drams were immediately drank to Giannotto Pastor, and much precious blood, and many limbs were pledged, for his safety.

" Yes, yes," said Mr. Lines to our hero, " you'll be safe enough here; you'll see and hear a few queer things, to be sure, that may somewhat try your courage; but you must not be nice to a shade."

Jack answered confidently, that it was not a little that would frighten him.

" That remains to be proved," said Mr. Lines, significantly; " it will be so much the better if you are right; however, time will show—bolder hearts than yours have been cowed in the Red Lion."

" I have no fear," said Jack, laughingly.

The night turned out a stormy one; a fresh log was heaped on the fire. " We shall have no guests to-night," said Mr. Lines, " unless it be our High Toby friends, and they know how to let themselves in, so let me replenish your glasses, lads; and I beg to say for this once, tick *shall*, if necessary, be the order of the evening."

A loud hurrah! followed this welcome imformation, and moisture and smoke were presently in great demand: never had the 'element' in the memory of the Red Lion been known to flow so freely; liquid was at a premium, and the incense of the weed ascended—

" From the bowl of every pipe."

The conversation soon became general, and a thousand tales were told of the wonderful escapes that had been effected in consequence of Mr. Lines's ingenious mechanical skill in the formation of various trap-doors, sliding pannels, secret apertures, dark closets, subterranean retreats, &c.

" Don't you remember," said one, " how Bill Giblet, the slashing butcher, made his escape, thanks to the drawbridge on the roof of the ken, over the tops of the different cribs, to old Tough's, in Caroline Court, though the house was closely surrounded by Austin, and the whole of the squadron of the Whit? Poor Giblet! he paid a visit to the Elms* at last; but that was his own fault, he should never have left the Lion. To be sure it was lucky, when he bolted, that all the neighbours' cribs were occupied by ' *Family men*'—they knew what's what. Poor Giblet! he was the flower of Saffron Hill!"

* Tyburn.

Many similar adventures were recounted ; and time passed so quickly, that it struck twelve before they scarcely knew where they were.

" Ah, ha!" said Mr. Lines, starting, " ' the iron tongue of midnight sounds the hour of twelve. Now o'er one half the world—'"

" Oh, stow it, Dick, stow it," vociferated the whole of the company ; " we've heard that every night the last ten years !"

" Well, well," said Mr. Lines, " but you must not forget your Lauds, lads—duty before every thing else. Come, come, our midnight service, the chaunt of ' The Clerks of St. Nicholas.'"

Here three of the company immediately stood up, and turning the tails of their coats over their heads, so as to form a species of monkish cowl, and assuming a very evangelical air, they drawled out most puritanically, long metre of course, the following choice article, the others, led by Mr. Lines, all joining chorus :—

Chaunt of the Clerks of Saint Nicholas.

'Tis we are the Clerks of Saint Nicholas,
 Saint Nicholas' Clerks are we,
At the closing of day, on the lone highway,
 For the wandering traveller we pray,
And watch right pious-lie.
 For we are the Clerks of Saint Nicholas,
 Chanting our Ave Ma-rie,
With barkers and prancer,
Cheating the dancer,
 We gallop the high Tobie.

Oh, we are the Clerks of St. Nicholas,
    And patter so gnostic and free,
Our prayer to deliver
The sinner makes quiver,
    Nos libera miserere.
For we are the Clerks of St. Nicholas,
    Chanting our Ave Ma-rie,
With barkers and prancer,
Cheating the dancer,
    We gallop the high Tobie.

Oh, we are the Clerks of St. Nicholas,
    And to churls who would cling to their gold,
We but breathe on the heath a whisper of death,
    And their treasures we presently hold!
For we are the Clerks of Saint Nicholas,
    Chanting our Ave Ma-rie,
With barkers and prancer,
Cheating the dancer,
    We gallop the high Tobie.

This delectable morçeau was sung in a very ghostly, and pious manner with a most edifying snuffle. On its conclusion, two of the company, one rejoicing in the appellation of Cat's-eyes, from the peculiarly green hue of his optics, and the other in that of Four-toed-Timothy, from some presumed deficiency of his pediments, after giving the office to Mr. Lines, begged permission to retire, remarking they had work to do. They were severally followed at intervals by the rest of the company, until Jack and Mr. Lines were left alone.

" Now then Giannotti, my prince of cracksmen," said Mr. Lines, " we'll just have a parting dram, by way of night-cap, and then I'll show you to your snooze; talk of a bug in a rug! why you'll be ten times as snug."

Draining the parting dram, Jack followed Mr. Lines, who had taken a lamp to show him the way up a flight of stairs, which led to a capacious landing. In this landing were two retired recesses, not so prominent in appearance, however, as to attract attention, and they were passing by them to proceed up another flight of stairs when their steps were arrested by a deep groan.

" 'Angels and ministers of grace defend us!'" exclaimed Mr. Lines, starting back in apparent alarm, " what's that?"

Two ghostly looking figures closely enveloped in white sheets, here issued from the recesses and barred their progress. Jack's blood fairly curdled in his veins, at the appearance of these fearful apparitions.

" 'Art thou a spirit of health or goblin damned?'" enquired Mr. Lines.

" I'll be damned if we're either," answered one of the mysterious figures, with a very loud laugh, throwing off a sheet, and discovering Mr. Cat's-eyes, his companion at the same time throwing off his disguise, and presenting Four-toed Timothy.

" Didn't you know us?" this *is* a lark !"

" Funny dogs, funny dogs," said Mr. Lines, " but where did you get that whitening that you've been chalking your faces with, I didn't think there had been any in the house."

"No more there was," answered Cat's-eyes, "so we were obliged to rub our faces against our scores in the bar, and get some chalk that way."

Mr. Lines laughed the wrong side of his mouth —Cat's-eyes, and Timothy disappeared.

"These are convenient recesses enough, Giannotto," said Mr. Lines, recovering himself after a short pause. "You see they are sufficiently large to conceal one or two lads, so that if any unlucky wight should come upon them unawares, the lads would fell him like an ox, and he be none the wiser for it, though he may show his brains. Ha! ha!—but come, let's toddle up stairs; Lord bless you, this is nothing. Curse those fellows for rubbing out their scores though. Well I think they gave you a bit of a turn!—'The thief doth fear each bush an officer'—you'll be up to these snuggeries another time,—this way."

Mr. Lines now led Jack up to a room on the second floor, in which there was a large old four-post bedstead.

"You'll be all secure and undisturbed here, Giannotto," said he; "but stop, let me see that there is no one concealed any where."

Stooping down on all-fours, he speedily disappeared under the bed; Jack waited a few moments to see him emerge again, but he was disappointed, Mr. Lines did not appear. Jack waited a few moments' longer; then, beginning to feel uncomfortable, he determined to hazard being laughed at, and to call him.

" Hallo! Lines," said he; " Mr. Lines, Dick, where are you? Damn it, don't stay there; come, come, no larking; I hate practical jokes. Where are you? Come out."

No answer being returned, and knowing what a wag Mr. Lines was, Jack determined to follow him, and pull him out of his hiding place.

" Come come," said he, " you are not going to frighten me; I'm up to you; you had better come out; I'm coming after you; a joke's a joke, but confound such tricks as these."

Jack had all the talk to himself—he had no answer of any kind; so, stooping down on all-fours, he prepared to proceed under the bed.

" Where are you?' said he, his body disappearing half under the sacking.

" Here, my lad!" answered a voice behind him, with a laugh; and immediately Jack felt the tails of his coat turned up, and the *argumentum a posteriori* applied to the broad front presented by his nether extremity, with a force and good-will much more piquant than pleasant. Hastily turning round, getting up, and rising, he found himself, to his great surprise, facing Mr. Lines.— " Zounds, is it you?" said he, " how the devil did you come here? Why you must be Beel- zebub himself!"

" ' Die, prophet, in thy speech!" roared out Mr. Lines, applying something to Jack's breast which looked very like a dagger,—' for this, amongst the rest, was I ordained.' "

" Come, I say, none of that," said Jack, disconcerted ; " no lancets ; I don't want letting blood, I'm much obliged to you."

A loud laugh from Mr. Lines was the only reply; and Jack saw, to his mortification, that gentleman had merely threatened him by presenting a table-spoon to his bosom. A few words explained the mystery.

" Underneath that bed," said Mr. Lines, " is a trap door leading to the room beneath, through which a cove lately escaped, before the very eyes of the officers themselves, and one of them jumping after him, broke his leg. What a jolly lark ! lucky for you, I bolted the flap after me.—I had only to walk up stairs again, and come through that secret door there," pointing to one in the wall, that stood open, " and here I was to wait on you."

" Well, well, said Jack, rubbing the part affected, " I can only say as Marshal Turenne said under similar circumstances, when Stephen, the cook, mistook him, as he was leaning out of the window, for his comrade Thomas.—" It is an excellent joke, but I wish you had not hit quite so hard though."

" ' The hand of little employment hath the daintier sense,' " replied Mr. Lines, again laughing,

" but come, I'll now bid you good night ! ' May flights of angels choir thee to thy rest !" '

" Good night," said Jack.

Mr. Lines disappeared through the secret door, which he fastened after him, when Jack threw himself on the bed, and very soon after fell into a sound sleep.—This was Jack's first night in the Red Lion Tavern, Chick Lane.

CHAPTER XXIV.

———

JACK'S ESCAPE FROM THE RED LION.

PANTOMIME TRICKS.—SECRETS OF THE PRISON HOUSE.—
APPARITION OF JONATHAN.—A MISS AS GOOD AS A
MILE.

JACK had a refreshing sleep, though his slumbers
were several times disturbed during the night, by
the sudden clattering of horses' feet in the Inn-
yard, with voices of arrival, enquiry, and command, in the stabling behind the house ; and loud
peals of laughter, and other sounds of merriment
and revelry, from different inner apartments below.
Rightly setting down these inroads on his rest to
the high spiced Toby Gloak gentlemen, alluded to
by Mr. Lines, Jack very coolly turned a deaf ear
to them, and ultimately fell into a sound sleep,
from which he was not aroused till nearly ten
o'clock, when a loud shouting in his ear caused
him to start up from his pillow, and he beheld
Mr. Lines, standing by his bedside, holding a
shining tankard to his head, which, in his consternation, Jack took for a blunderbuss, Mr. Lines

bellowing out in a very theatrical tone—" Drink! Anthropophagian !"

A loud laugh, which proceeded from the facetious host, the sight of the open secret pannel, and a moment's reflection, restored Jack to his senses. This was another practical joke of Mr. Lines, who, finding his guest slept rather longer than he expected, took this dramatic way of arousing him. The tankard was filled with some highly spiced early purl, prepared by Mr. Lines's own hand. This Jack gratefully emptied, by way of a whet to his appetite.

" You mustn't, as I told you, be surprised at any thing you see here, Giannotto," said Mr. Lines, who had by this time fastened the secret pannel behind him. " There are more things in Heaven and earth, Horatio, than are dreamt of in your philosophy."

" No doubt, no doubt," answered Jack, who was very soon convinced of the truth of this assertion, for stooping to pick up his waistcoat, which had fallen down, he was much surprised at finding, when he raised himself up again, that Mr. Lines had vanished. It seemed the work of magic; but that gentleman had totally disappeared, and not through the secret opening, nor under the bed.

" Where the devil is he gone to, now ?" cried Jack, " and where's my unmentionables ?" finding his breeches had disappeared as well as his jocular host, " Why Lines, Mr. Lines, where the devil are you? Curse such practical jokes as these."

There was no answer—Jack called again. At length an unseen voice was heard, singing in reply the words of Hecate—

" My little airy spirit, come and see,
Come and see."

Jack stared round in amazement, when a part of the wall in one corner of the room, slowly moving, attracted his attention and fixed his gaze. The motion continuing, a screen was gradually displaced, corresponding in appearance with the rest of the wall, and discovering behind it a sharp angle, large enough to conceal a man, from which Mr. Lines emerged. Advancing towards Jack with a solemn step, somewhat like that conventionally used by the Ghost of Hamlet's father, or the statue of the Commandant in Don John, he held Jack's breeches in his hand, and presenting them, exclaimed in a hollow voice—" This handkerchief did an Egyptian to my mother give."

" I'm very glad to hear that," said Jack, " for it will enable you to give them to me."

Thankfully taking his nether garments, Jack soon made himself decent; and after taking a more particular survey, for his future guidance, of the concealed angle in the wall, the trap door under the bed, and the secret pannel, he followed his host to the parlour below, Mr. Lines promising after breakfast to show him the lions of the Red Lion.

In the parlour Jack met many of his companions of the previous night, together with such of the Bridle Culls, whose return had disturbed him whilst in bed, as were then stirring. They had, according to Mr. Lines's account, caroused till the third cock. There was Gold-laced Jemmy, so called from the quantity of binding of that material he displayed about his cocked hat, coat, waistcoat, &c. The Bit of Blood, a very dashing blade, Peter the Popper, the Barker, Bludgeon Bill, and many others.

Jack was duly introduced to these several worthies by Mr. Lines, who, with the air of a Polonius, acted as master of the ceremonies: he met with a very cordial reception from all. They recounted their different adventures: the *road* had been very *dark* and muddy with some, while with others it had been very light and pleasant, according as they had had a good booty or not.

After breakfast, on the old principle of 'short reckonings' making 'long friends,' a maxim most especially observed by the Gentlemen of the Road, Jack proceeded to settle with Mr. Lines for his bed and refreshments of the preceding evening.

" Two white tails and a half," said that gentleman, meaning a couple of good Queen Anne' shillings, and a tizzy, for the Prince of Denmark, her consort.   Jack handed out a broad piece.

" I have got no change," said Mr. Lines, " but I'll get you some made in a minute."

" What !" said Jack, " make change ?"

" ' Season your admiration' for awhile," laugh- ingly answered Mr. Lines: " I'll soon show you much greater wonders than that. Come, I promised to *chap*-erone you all over my house here, ' boxes, pit, and gallery, scenery, machinery, dresses, and decorations.'   I'll be as good as my word.   It's fit you should be made acquainted with a few of our dodges, so you shall see all from the cellar to the flies—Lord bless you, if there were a dozen traps surrounding the house, I've a trap for every one within.   Yes, ' my great revenge hath stomach for them all.'   Come, we will descend to my pit, the cellar, first.   You shall make your exit through our great grave-trap.   I have made it after the model of the one we had at Hogs' Norton. ' Down, down, to Hell, and say I sent thee thither !' "

Jack shuddered as Mr. Lines proceeded to pull up a large trap door, ingeniously cut in the floor, discovering a blank chasm beneath.   He was resolved, however, not to flinch at any thing; he, therefore, followed Mr. Lines down a ladder, which could be moved at pleasure, into a dismal dungeon-like looking vault, dug out of the solid earth, evidently for the purpose of concealment, and which extended under the whole of the basement; this vault, or cellar, was divided by brick walls into two or three dens or compartments. A strong glare of light flashing from one end attracted Jack's attention towards it; he turned and saw, with some surprise, several swarthy looking individuals busily engaged at a furnace, the fire of which was blazing in full play.

"Hallo! Teddy the Mole," cried Mr. Lines, advancing towards a Cyclop looking person, who was pouring some boiling metal out of a crucible into a mould. "What are you doing there? You must make us the change out of a broad piece here, some of your best workmanship—some that will smash well. You understand me?"

"Aye, aye," returned Teddy, with a loud laugh.

As Jack surveyed this gang of ruffians, black with smoke, and gazed on their gaunt forms, working in the very fire, as it were, in this dreary pandemonium, he for a moment almost imagined himself in company with the denizens of the infernal regions.

In the wall behind the forge, there was a sufficient opening through which the coiners could, on the slightest alarm, throw the whole of the implements of their nefarious trade into the Fleet ditch, which ran, as has been stated, immediately past the premises, and thus, by destroying every proof, effectually escape punishment.

There was much merriment among this gang of

miscreants at Mr. Lines' proposition to ring the changes on Jack with their bits of *queer*.*

Jack was duly introduced to this precious fraternity, and stood his footing out of a case bottle which Mr. Lines happened to have about his person.

At the back of the cellar, near the centre, Jack observed a gutter like aperture, debouching into the cellar itself; this he found was the termination of a shoot, descending from the top of the house for the conveyance of stolen goods, which will be noticed hereafter.

" Let me now, Giannotto," said Mr. Lines, "show you a short cut to liberty in case of need; but don't bolt the moon without paying your rent, my lad, mind that, though no fear. As you are going to be one of our lodgers, it is very proper that you should be familiar with a ready key of the street, so come this way.

Leaving Teddy the Mole and his companions, earnestly employed in multiplying her most gracious Majesty's countenance, Mr. Lines then conducted Jack into an inner cell, where he showed him a massive iron door strongly bolted inside, through which an offender might escape over the Fleet Ditch, and if his retreat was cut off, return, bolt himself in, and defy capture that way.

In another part of the wall there was also a secret aperture, through which a person might pass and escape by the means of a rolling plank over the

* Counterfeit coin.

Fleet ditch, the plank being kept ready for the purpose, to a corresponding aperture in a cellar of the opposite house on the other side. The dead bodies of incautious visiters that might be robbed and murdered in the tavern, might also, through the opening, be thrown into the ditch, where they would be rapidly carried away, the ditch by this means being made to bear more than the 'Large tribute of dead dogs,' for which Pope has so liberally given it credit.

Unclosing with difficulty the ponderous iron door we have mentioned, as opening on the banks of the ditch, Mr. Lines and Jack emerged into the fresh air. The effect was singular issuing from so charnel-like a vault into the bright daylight. On the other side of the ditch stood the house, already noticed, as being a species of low cadger lodging-house, where thimble-riggers, magsmen, duffers, and maunders, of every description, congregated to plan their various robberies on her Majesty's liege subjects, at the different fairs and races throughout the country, of which they kept an accurate list as they successively occurred.

In the unglazed window of this precious palace of poverty and fraud there sat, at the moment Jack appeared in sight, an old woman, the wrinkled skin of whose countenance was of a hue and texture varying between that of leather and parchment; she was earnestly employed in sewing some additional flounces on the holiday robe of her daughter and heiress, a well known Venus of the vicinity, who boasted that she had had as many fancy men lagged as she had fingers and toes—the old woman was apparently seated here to enjoy the odoriferous breezes rising from the styx-like stream running beneath. The whole scene was one worthy the pencil of an old Dutch or Flemish master—the elder Teniérs would have delighted in it. Exchanging a gracious nod of recognition with Mr. Lines, and bestowing a kind look of patronage on Jack, the beldame continued her work, which their sudden appearance had for a moment caused her to suspend.

Mr. Lines here pointed out to Jack the facility of escape over the ditch by the plank, and instructed him what steps to pursue to effect this object in an emergency; they afterwards returned to the cellar, where they fastened the iron door behind them, took a short leave of the coiners, whom they left at their laudable occupation, and re-ascending the ladder, were again very soon in the common room of the Red Lion again.

Mr. Lines now proceeded to show Jack some more of his ' machinery,' as he termed it ; in short, the house was more like a pantomimic one than any thing else, though pantomimes were then unknown, not having been introduced into England until after Jack's death, nearly one of the first having been that of which Jack was the hero—entitled 'Harlequin Prison-breaker.'

Ascending the stairs, Mr. Lines shewed Jack a landing place in which there were four distinct staircases, with as many means of escape, and another with a triple flight of stairs, by and from which, any one pursued, could get into the yard, and proceeding out of the gateway, reach the front of the house in safety. " I will now," said Mr. Lines, " make you free of Mr. Wild's portion of the premises."

Taking Jack, by means of a secret door, through a sort of party-wall, which, as before stated, divided the Tavern into two, he took him into a sort of shop, stored with miscellaneous property of every description. The shop, of course, was only a blind; behind the counter was a trap, through which persons pursued could reach the cellar beneath, already mentioned, in safety, and through which stolen property could be expeditiously stowed away; there were also many secret drawers in the flooring, for the preservation of booty. The upper apartments in this part of the building were replete with dark closets, concealed passages, and other contrivances for plunder, &c.

At the top of the house was Jonathan's chief depository, or 'sanctum sanctorum,' as he called it; or, in other words, the warehouse of his choicest property; in this room there was at one side a private outlet, through the wall, over the roofs of the adjacent houses, by which Saffron Hill might easily be gained, and pursuit set at defiance. At the back of this room was a recess, where, level with the floor which covered it, when not in use, was the mouth of a large shoot, similar to a pawn-broker's spout, descending the whole extent of the building, by which, in case of alarm, every thing could be safely conveyed into the cellar below; this was another of Mr. Lines's ingenious contrivances.

But for his separation from Bess, Jack would have lived a pleasant enough life here.

If the inmates of the Red Lion had but too generally a short life, they had at least a merry one; it was one continued round of enterprise, excitement, and enjoyment; no restraint, no care; there was, it is true, a little danger, and it might be some fear, but these only served to give a zest to the security, enjoyment, and abandonment that followed. Day, to others a season of labour, was to the inmates of the Red Lion a time of rest; it was usually slept away—whilst night, to half the world a period of repose—sombre, sober night was from its exclusiveness and quiet their season of adventure; then could they revel uncontrolled— then the lone highway had booty for them, they were indeed true 'minions of the moon,'—the sun ne'er shone upon their like. Nor was the society of the fairer portion of creation wanting to give a charm to their desperate revels; the unceremonious Aspasias of the neighbourhood made the Red Lion their head quarters; each of these nymphs of the pavé had *flopped* her particular affections on some select gentleman of the gang, to whom they sacrificed all others ; this was the love of the heart ; in every other case, theirs was merely one of the purse.

Fortunately, during Jack's stay, no incautious gallant was inveigled into the Red Lion by the sisterhood, there was therefore no tragedy performed at which his heart would have revolted— for murder invariably followed robbery in this horrid den.—No one was suffered to live to tell the tale ; this may account for the long impunity the place enjoyed. A blind fiddler and minstrel, residing in the locality, singing and dancing usually wound up the evening's entertainments. In these orgies it may be observed, Mr. Lines invariably proved himself a very ' diverting vagabond.'

Though every inmate of the Red Lion was perfectly aware of Jack's identity, no one ever hinted at his incognito, it was rigidly preserved.

Thus a fortnight passed away, and Jack, deeming that the heat of pursuit must now be over, was thinking of leaving his sanctuary, and retiring with Bess to some more congenial retreat ; when, one evening, as he was carelessly looking out of an upper front window of the Tavern, catching a feeling of calm and holiness from the mild moonlight that was floating around, bathing every object in its silver lymph with light and beauty, he casually observed three men approaching from the

Smithfield end of the lane ; he did not at first notice them particularly, but as they advanced nearer, a guardian flood of splendour, which suddenly seemed to beam from above, expressly for Jack's preservation, distinctly disclosed to him the well known features of Jonathan Wild, and those of that gentleman's two satellites, the Patriarch, and Mr. Quilt Arnold, *Esquire.*

" By Heavens, 'tis Wild !" cried Jack, in some alarm, " this means mischief ! let me seek Lines, what want they here, and at this hour ? no good, I fear—they can have but one object, but I will foil them yet."

Jack saw at once that they were well armed, nor was he himself less unprovided ; he therefore made up his mind, should issue be joined, for a desperate encounter, " I will sell my life dearly !", he exclaimed, " but where is Lines ?"

Hastily rushing down stairs, he fortunately encountered that worthy, the very first thing. A few hurried words explained all. Mr. Lines was evidently disconcerted at the intelligence.

" You must cut, Giannotto," said he, " Jonathan don't come here at this time of night for nothing, but which way ? ' Ah, there's the rub !' At this moment Jonathan was thundering at the door outside.

" ' The Devil damn him black,' tis he !" said Mr. Lines," ah ! he gives me an idea—What's the good of having friends if you don't make use of them?"

The knocking became louder.

" Quick, quick, Jack, there's not a moment to be lost," resumed Mr. Lines, " there's nobody in Wild's part of the premises, 'tis from thence you must escape; here any attempt may lead to detection—pass through the secret aperture into the shop, descend through the trap door behind the counter into the cellar, make your way through the opening in the wall, and across the Fleet ditch you will find the plank ready, then plunge through the cellar of Mother Cummins' Hotel, into Black-boy Alley, and from thence to Cow Cross. Once in Smithfield, you are safe.—They come! away— ' stand not on the order of your going, but go ;' ' farewell, remember me ? ' "

He pushed Jack hastily through the secret aperture and closed the door. It was but just in time, Jack heard the harsh voice of Jonathan muttering curses on Mr. Lines for keeping him waiting, the very moment afterwards—He soon stood alone in his greatest enemy's den. To raise the trap door behind the counter was the work of an instant, Jack was equally expeditious in descending to the cellar, and in passing through the aperture of the wall at the side; but he forgot in his haste to remove the ladder by which he descended—his enemies were at his heels, they followed close upon his track. Jack easily pushed the rolling plank across the noisome stream, reaching the end of the plank at the very moment his pursuers gained the beginning of it. What was to be done—there was but the ditch between them, and over it a passage. To escape seemed impossible, but one way presented itself—With the courage and strength of a lion, Jack seized hold of *his* end of the plank, while his two pursuers were yet upon it; with a violent effort he suddenly drew it half over to his own side, precipitating the patriarch, and Mr. Quilt Arnold, *Esquire*, up to their necks in the filthy stinking stream over which he had passed.

Escaped! escaped!" cried Jack.

To bound through the aperture in the cellar of Mother Cummins' Hotel, and gain Black-boy Alley, was but the effort of a moment, and in five minutes more, he had threaded Cow-cross, dived through Smithfield Bars, and bounding over the pens in the Market, darted up Long Lane, and gained the Barbican.

A shot from Jonathan's pistol, the report of which reached his ears and quickened his progress, as he closed the door of the Cadger's ken, testified that worthy's disappointed rage at losing his prey before his very eyes.

A scornful laugh from Jack expressed his contempt for the well intended compliment. Making his way over London Bridge, and through Southwark to Lambeth, Jack once more rejoined Bess. Her surprise and delight may well be imagined.

Thus finished Jacks' connexion with the Red Lion in Chick Lane, afterwards rendered so memorable as the "Old House" in West Street.*

* Of the Old Red Lion and its various apartments a faithful account has been given in the text above, the only correct one, it is believed, that has yet appeared; it has now ceased to exist. As it is well known, the commissioners for carrying out the improvements in this quarter, in the progress of forming the new street, from Farringdon Street to Islington, had occasion to remove many old houses, and amongst them the Old Red Lion tavern in Chick Lane. The name of Chick Lane, from its Newgate Calendar notoriety, had, long before, from being situated on the west bank of the Fleet Ditch, been changed to West Street—'worst' Street would have been the more suitable name.

Many strange discoveries were made in pulling down the old houses, Nos. 2 and 3, formerly the Old Red Lion tavern—discoveries which excited the greatest surprise and curiosity in all classes—the élite of the fashionable world, and even royalty itself, greedily flocked to feed their morbid appetites and wonder-seeking eyes, with the dismal vaults, dark closets, trap-doors, sliding pannels, secret recesses, and intricate passages which were laid open to them. In the subterranean cellars formed under the house, for the purpose of concealment, as described above, awful evidences of the diabolical nature of the building came to light.

In excavating the foundation of this den of infamy, the labourers dug up the skeletons of two men of rather large stature, both of whom had, no doubt, been robbed and murdered, from the circumstance of their being buried in a spot immediately over which had been a large trap-door. In another portion of this cellar, a skull and some human bones were also found, with the half of a butcher's steel, bearing the name of Benjamin Thurle, July 19, 1787, in silver letters and figures. This fellow was a butcher, who was executed the latter part of

H H

Here leaving the satellites to extricate themselves from their disagreeable position as well as

the last century, for murder ; he was of a notoriously bad character, and was, for a long time, concealed here.

Another portion of the cellar was walled up, so as to form a
species of living tomb, and in this horrid cell, one Jones, a
chimney-sweeper, a sort of minor Jack Sheppard, of escape notoriety in our own century, was, for many weeks, concealed
with impunity, setting the exertions of the police at defiance,
who repeatedly searched the cellar whilst he was hidden there,
but to no purpose. Jones was, at length, betrayed, through
the extorted confession of a confederate.

That Jonathan Wild ever made this house his residence is
extremely problematical, though an old rusty and almost worn-
out knife, the blade of which bore the name of Rippon, while
on the handle was stamped J. Wild, was found in one of the
rooms; it is of very peculiar make, and evidently of ancient
manufacture, notwithstanding which, some incredulous persons
have hinted their surmises that it was manufactured for the
occasion—be that as it may, that Jonathan had a fence here,
there can be no doubt.   Its contiguity to his own house in the
Old Bailey, and various other circumstances, rendered it a very
eligible depôt for him; it was not till the year 1740, that the
Old Red Lion Tavern was finally closed, as a house of entertainment, by order of Government, its real character being
well known.   Since then, until the summer of 1844, when the
commissioners obtained possession of it, by purchase, from its
owners; it has been used as a receptacle for stolen property,
and a lodging-house for abandoned characters of both sexes.

Of the nature of the dark transactions carried on under its
baneful roof, some idea may be formed from the fact of a sailor
having been thrown, *alive*, into the Ditch, which ran beneath
the walls, from the window of a room called " the Puff' and
Dart room," about seven years since, by an abandoned prostitute, named " Blue Eyed Mary," and two ruffians. her para-
mours, after having been stripped and robbed of all he had.

they could, and having deposited Jack safely in the arms of Bess, we will, with the reader's permission, end our chapter.

The stream carried him to the Thames, near Blackfriars Bridge, where his *corpse* was found. Blue Eyed Mary, and her companions, were subsequently transported for fourteen years for this offence.—Why were they not hanged?

The Old House, with its various rooms and contrivances, having been minutely described in the text, need not be further dwelt upon here. The change now being effected in converting this horrid haunt from one of the meanest to one of the most handsome parts of the metropolis will not be a little striking, but quite as great a metamorphosis had been wrought four centuries since. The whole of this filthy locality being then watered by various fertilizing streams, studded with magnificent palaces, noble monasteries, stately gardens, and many a retreat of sylvan beauty, and rural quiet.

CHAPTER XXV.

JACK A FUGITIVE.

JACK'S WANDERINGS.—VISIT TO EDGEWORTH.—JACK'S
RE-CAPTURE.

Having safely rejoined Bess, after his miraculous escape from the clutches of Jonathan Wild, at the Old Red Lion Tavern, Jack sought, by moving about with her from place to place, to ensure security in a ceaseless change of quarters; but the pursuit, at length, became so hot, that, by the advice of a friend named Page, the son of a respectable tradesman in Clare Market, with whom he had become acquainted while he was an apprentice to Mr. Wood, Jack left Bess with his mother in Spitalfields, and withdrew for a time to the quiet little village of Warnden, in Northamptonshire, where Page had some relations, and where it was not likely, from its distance from town, and the want of regular communication at that period, that Jack's name and exploits had ever been heard of. This journey the friends effected pleasantly enough, on foot, resting themselves, during the heat of the day at the different hedge alehouses by the road-side, and only travelling in the cool of the evening and the fore part of the morning; the nights they usually passed in some outhouse, or under some hayrick belonging to the different gentlemen's mansions on their road; there being much less suspicion, and much more charity then, than there is now. In this way they reached Warnden.

Page's relations were small farmers—honest simple people—who owned the land they lived on, the culture of which supplied them with every necessary of life, while its surplus produce furnished them with the few luxuries such unsophisticated natures required, for the entertainment of casual visiters. Their farm was neat and compact; its thickly thatched roof and substantial walls presented the very image of comfort. All around proclaimed plenty; a well-stored granary, orchard, kitchen-garden, piggery, poultry-yard, a range of bee-hives, with stacks of fodder for cattle, a small river running at the back, well stored with fish, a rabbit-warren, not a mile distant, and plenty of game in the neighbouring woods to be had for the shooting, on an understanding with the keepers, effectually shut out all fears of starvation.

The worthy people received their kinsman, Page, and his acquaintance, Jack, with a hearty welcome: the best they had was at their guests' command; in fact, it was one scene of eating and drinking while they stayed there. The first thing in the

morning there was home-made brown bread, but-
termilk and clouted cream from this hospitable
people's own dairy, broiled fish and game, new-laid
eggs, bacon of their own curing, and strong humming ale of their own brewing—these served for
breakfast. Then a walk over the ploughed fields,
or a turn at fishing and shooting, brought dinner
time, with its substantial geese, joints of pork, capons, puddings, and a variety of vegetables, doubly
delicious from being fresh gathered from the garden. In the afternoon, a bottle of home-made
wine would be produced, with fruits just gathered
from the orchard, some preserves, and a spiced
cake of the good dame's own making. At night, a
cold rook pie, some broiled mushrooms, cheese,
nuts, and cider, with a tumbler of spirits and water,
would complete the day's entertainment ; and Jack
and his friend would retire to rest in the snug
little tent bedsteads, with their white furniture and
clean home-spun sheets, fragrant with lavender, to
awaken the next morning to renewed enjoyment.

At first the various noises incidental to rural
life, the thousand twitterings of the birds at early
morn, the crowing, cackling, gobbling, quack-
ing, grunting, and lowing, of the poultry and
cattle, with the eternal cawing from a hard-by
rookery, sounded rather strangely to Jack's ears ;
but he soon got used to them. Page had given
a satisfactory reason for their staying some days

at the farm; the good unconscious people were easily satisfied, they never dreamt of guile.

It was the beginning of September, the most beautiful of the autumnal months, and here Jack might have revelled in unmixed enjoyment; but after the novelty of the first few days had passed, the very serenity and comfort he experienced began to cloy upon his senses—his thoughts yearned to Bess, and the recovery of her fortune. What wonder, then, that, after sojourning there about ten days, during which he thought the eagerness of pursuit after him must somewhat have abated, Jack should bid his kind entertainers farewell, and, with his friend Page, leave this scene of calm and pure delight, and once more retrace his steps to town. As ill-luck would have it, no sooner had Jack arrived in the metropolis, than, in crossing through Holborn, he passed a milk-cellar to which, only a few days before, his old acquaintance, David Lloyd, the Welshman, from whom the May-day plate had been stolen, had removed; Lloyd happened to be looking up at the time, and catching a glimpse of Jack, with all the sudden choler of his countrymen, he at once began to give the alarm for the purpose of having him secured. Jack's only chance was immediately to wrest the cellar door off its hinges and throw it down upon the pans of milk below; in the confusion which this step created, he made good his retreat.

Arriving, with Page, at the Cock and Pie, public

house, where they refreshed themselves, they sent for Bess, and as they well knew David Lloyd would make no secret of their being in London, they determined to set off for Finchley. Jack chose this retreat for two or three reasons: in the first place, it was out of the way; and in the next place he could make his way from it by some unfrequented cross roads to the gypsy encampment at Highgate. Jack did not find Bess in such good spirits at his return as he expected; she was thoughtful and pensive; there was evidently something on her mind; she did not appear to be at all satisfied at Jack's account of his absence; for the first time she pressed him to make their union legal; he could take her, she said, to the Fleet, where their marriage could be privately and securely performed. Jack desired nothing better than this, but the moment had not arrived; he satisfied her as well as he could. The next morning, without acquainting her with his intentions, he made his way to the gipsy encampment, where, as he expected, he found Poll Maggot. Zara had not yet returned. The gang welcomed him with their usual warmth, but he did not stay long to partake of their hospitality; his object was Edgeworth, now called Edgeware, as we before noticed, and to this quiet little town he at once repaired, accompanied by Poll.

Poll's first step was to seek out the poor house, a clean, though humble building, situated on a green; here she enquired if crazy Sally was alive.

An old woman, who was sitting basking in the sun, was pointed out to her as being the object of her search. Rather small of stature, and withered in her appearance, the precision with which her dress was arranged, the taste and good order displayed in it, would not have led any one to suspect the slightest aberration of intellect in its wearer, had not a lurking wildness in her eye, and the anxious haggard look that overspread her features, betrayed too evidently a mind diseased.

" Let *me* speak to her," said Poll to Jack ; " I know how to draw her out : you must be well acquainted with the tantrums of these mad creatures, if you want to get any thing out of them. Good morning, mother," she exclaimed, advancing towards the poor maniac ; " cross the gipsy's hand with a bit of silver, and I'll read you your fortune."

" Ah ! a gipsy," exclaimed the bewildered woman, a gleam of recollection suddenly darting across her brain, and lighting up her eyes with anger. " Begone, wretch !"

" Nay, but listen to me," said Poll, soothingly.

" Listen to you ! I did listen to you, listened but too well for my peace," said the maniac, with a shudder. " Had I never listened to you, never left my home, never deserted the sacred charge entrusted to me, I might not now be the lost crazed thing I am ; but my brain was scorched up with the fire that laid my cot in ashes, and destroyed the precious babe I swore to cherish. Her family have perished with her. No one to claim their wealth, to bear their honours. I was her murderer!—I that first lisped within her grandsire's halls. An alien now, foe to her race, possesses them! Tell me my fortune!—have you not told it me? —- ruin, degradation, madness, want. Away, witch, away!"

" Nay, nay," said Poll, " 'twas not your fault, 'twas accident."

" Thou liest! the villain Pargiter, the wily lawyer, the distant kinsman of the babe, 'twas he suborned you—he was her mother's enemy, her father's murderer—well may he revel in his proud manor house, 'tis with their wealth—had the old Baronet repented sooner—the proud Sir Tracy—"

" Sir Tracy *Smith!*" eagerly exclaimed Jack, recollecting that Smith was one of the names in the marriage certificate.

" Ay, Sir Tracy Smith," sharply returned the maniac, " the father of my young, my beautiful, my much wronged, and much loved mistress ; the grandsire of the murdered babe. That manor house of Frognall, it was his. Though now a viper warms him by its hearths, there is not one fairer to be found 'mongst all the pleasant dwelling places in those sweet shades of Hampstead, my native home."

" Mark you that, Jack," whispered Poll, who had all the shrewdness and quickness of the gipsy

tribe in extracting information from the most un-
guarded word, the most trifling circumstance.
"You hear—Sir Tracy Smith, of Frognall Manor House, Hampstead, your Bess's grandfather;
a distant kinsman, the lawyer, Pargiter. is in possession of her rights, is living in her halls. There
is but one thing more, and I'll soon fish that out.
'You said the old man's was a late repentance,
mother.'" Here she addressed the maniac in a distinct but low voice.

"Too late! too late!" shrieked the maniac.
"He made a will—he left his pardon and his
wealth, his lands, his houses, when they were in
the grave, ha! ha! ha! The villain has it in his
keeping; he dreams not that I know it—but I do
—ha! ha! ha!"

The wild shrieking laugh of the phrensied
woman, here brought some of the inmates of the
poor house to her side.

"You must away, strangers," said they, rather
angrily, to Jack and his companion: "you have
aroused her mood, it may be dangerous your
staying, leave us to manage her."

With these words they hurried their unhappy
charge into the house.

"We have got all we want," said Poll, exultingly, "and may depart satisfied; there's a *will*
you find—the villain has it."

"But how are we to get possession of it?" said
Jack.

" Psha! where there's a *will* there's a way,"
laughed the gipsy, " and Jack Sheppard is not
the Ben Cove to be long without any thing he
wants, when once he knows where, it is to be obtained."

Jack became thoughtful; they repaired to the
little public-house of the Eight Bells, where Jack
liberally refreshed Mrs. Maggot for her services.

" I must go to town to-night," he exclaimed, a
sudden thought occurring to him. "You will return
to the camp, Poll, and the next time we meet I
trust you will find Bess a lady, and Jack on the
eve of securing freedom and safety for life, when
he will show that he can be grateful to those, to
whose good services he will have been mainly indebted for blessings so unlooked for."

Say no more, dimber Jack," said Poll, " I only
hope all may turn out as you wish; it is not often
that I practise my art for myself, or any of those
belonging to me; I left it off when the cards deceived me respecting the fate of my 'autem ben
cove,' poor Will Maggot. They said he would not
perish by the hands of justice; perhaps he did
not—yet that villain Jonathan ! 'twas by his hand
he fell—but no more of this, for once I'll cast a
figure."

Here she drew various configurations with a
piece of chalk on the table, and after casting them
up backwards and forwards, tracing and retracing

them several times, with rather a puzzled air, she bade Jack go forth and prosper.

"You will succeed in your enterprise," she said, " and yet there is a something behind ; but as it is past my art to reveal it, we will hope for the best."

They parted, the gipsy for Highgate, and Jack for London. Jack determined, whatever might be the hazard, before deciding on any thing else, to see Jonathan Wild that very evening, and make him one last proposition. Repairing to Fleet Market, he made his way, about ten at night, up Breakneck Stairs, and through Green Arbour Court, (since celebrated as the residence of Goldsmith), to the back of Jonathan's house in the Old Bailey. Acquainted with a secret entrance that would conduct him to Jonathan's study, he waited till the whole household appeared to have retired to rest. He knew Jonathan delighted in bold measures, and would take no advantage of any confidence that was placed in his honour. Ascertaining by a light in the study window that Jonathan was there, Jack softly crept up the stairs, as softly turned the handle of the door, and in a moment the redoubtable housebreaker and the indomitable thieftaker stood before each other ! Jonathan started, and grasped a pistol. Jack coolly held one ready cocked in his hand, his finger on the trigger.

" I come on business, Jonathan," he exclaimed ; " I am under your roof, and throw myself on your good faith."

" I have never forfeited it yet, Jack," said Jonathan, surprised, but firmly, " say what you have
to say, you are safe within these walls, the price of
your blood is within my pocket, I leave it to others
to see judgment done on you."

"Well then, Jonathan," returned Jack, " I have
discovered the secret of Bess's parentage, I know
the villain who has her property ; help me to restore her to her rights, and name your own reward."

" Hark you, Jack," said Jonathan : " since we
last met, things have changed ; circumstances have
rendered it expedient for me to make myself heir
to the property ; I possess the means, and you
know Jonathan Wild too well to suppose that
when he is certain of the whole, he would forego
his security for the chance of obtaining a half."

" This is your fixed resolution?" said Jack.

" It is," answered Jonathan calmly.

" Very well, then I shall know what to do," said
Jack, with a determined air. " What law* do you
give me, Jonathan, from the time I leave your
house ?"

" Half an hour," said Jonathan.

" I have your word ?" said Jack.

" You have," replied Jonathan, " which I never
yet broke to a thief, though I may have done so to
an honest man.'

" I believe it," replied Jack ! " farewell, Jonathan."

" Farewell, Jack Sheppard," said the thieftaker.

* Time.

Jack left the house by the same way he had entered, perfectly unmolested by Jonathan, and through many circuitous turnings and windings, retraced his steps back to Finchley, having settled in his own mind, after he had seen Bess, to repair to Hampstead, and pay a visit to Mr. Pargiter at the manor-house, Frognall. Unfortunately for Jack, no sooner had he departed in the morning, than Bess, conjecturing his visit was to Poll Maggot, and stung by jealousy, resolved to follow and watch him; but Jack, by turning down a by cross-road, in a contrary direction to that which she thought he would have taken, unconsciously baffled all her endeavours to track him; she blindly rushed onwards, scarcely knowing whither she went or what she was doing. The frequent interviews of Jack with Poll Maggot, respecting which he had observed such mystery, his wish that Poll should appear as his wife at the prison, her joint anxiety to effect Jack's escape, his absence in the country, and evasion of Bess's request to legalise her union with him by marriage,—all convinced the poor girl that in Poll she had a favoured rival, who would, ere long, wholly deprive her of Jack's affections. She had, almost unwittingly, made her way to town, when fatigue forced her to stop, and she became aware of the hopelessness of her attempt to overtake him. She turned to retrace her steps; at this moment she was observed by the unlucky milkman, David Lloyd, who was passing at the opposite side of the way ; he instantly recognised her as the principal in the robbery of his plate, and as the reputed mistress of Sheppard. Burning with revenge for the late destruction of all his pans of milk, and for a pair of broken shins into the bargain, no less than for his former loss, he resolved to follow her at a distance, and dodge her to her hiding place.

" Where the female is," said he, " there will the dog fox be found."

" The Welsh, with all their choler, are at times patient and persevering ; he tracked her footsteps to Jack's retreat at Finchley, saw her safely housed, and was returning late home, when he again caught a glimpse of Jack on his road, though unperceived by him. This confirmed him, and, with a glad heart, he hastened to town to give the necessary information for Jack's seizure in the morning.

Bess's reception of Jack was any thing but cordial, and he could not avoid rallying her.

" What ! pouting, Bess ?" he exclaimed ; " in the sulks ?—this is not right. What have I done, that I should be received with such black looks ?"

" Ah, Jack," said she, " that, you best know. I only know that you have withdrawn your confidence from me, that you have secrets, and surely that is enough for one whose passion is as ardent and sincere as mine ; 'tis plain that you no longer love me ; you have taken another into your companionship—that odious Poll Maggot; you think it scarcely necessary to conceal it. Have you not passed her off as your wife? Then your fortnight's absence—your refusal to wed me! Ah! Jack, Jack, you cannot deceive me!"

Jack could not avoid a smile at the unfounded nature of her suspicions.

" Do not treat me with derision," she continued; that I cannot bear—have you not secret meetings with her ?"

" Suppose I should say I had, Bess," said Jack, good-naturedly, " it does not follow that there is any petticoat treason in it."

" Have you not been with her to-day ?" inquired Bess, with much bitter anguish.

" May be I have, and may be I haven't," answered Jack, laughingly. " Hark ye, lass, get this *Maggot* out of your head as soon as you can, make your mind easy, and give me one of your sweet smiles again, and I promise you, on the honour of a cracksman, that before four-and-twenty hours have passed over my head, you shall know all."

" There *is* a secret, then ?" eagerly asked Bess.

" Well, then, there is," said Jack.

" And one in which she is concerned ?"

" I'll not deny that, neither," said Jack ; " but come, put me a rasher on the coals, and get me a draught of something good to wash it down with, and let's forget all this till to-morrow. I tell you, Bess, girl, there's bright days in store for you yet; you have linked yourf ate with a burglar, a condemned one, but you might have done worse, wench—Jack will make you a lady still."

" No, no; no more plunder, no more crime; let us fly to some other country, far from the cruel men that seek your life, far from this treacherous Poll Maggot." Here again poor Bess sobbed deeply, though her manner was more subdued. " Let us live in obscurity, in innocence; I will work my fingers to the bone for you, dear Jack, if you will only remain the same true fond heart that first I knew you."

She sunk into his arms in a paroxysm of tender emotion. Jack kissed the tears from her cheeks, and ere they had retired to rest, managed, by sundry endearments and assurances, somewhat to recompose her. In the morning, Page called upon Jack early, pursuant to appointment, to accompany him to an acquaintance with whom they had some business; their way lay across Finchley Common. Sauntering along, closely engaged in conversation on their future operations, they had proceeded a considerable distance before Jack's quick and restless eye discovered any thing to excite suspicion; but all at once, at the very extremity of the common, before the door of a small alehouse at the outskirts, bearing the sign of the Fox and Hounds, the unusual appearance of a coach and four, with several persons, both mounted and on foot, convinced him they were betrayed.

"We are trapped, Will," said he fiercely; "the blood-hounds have got scent of us—by hell, there's that villain Austin! Ah! he sees us—he comes followed by the whole pack. Turn about, lad, into the footpath, their horses cannot follow us there—fool! that I should have left my pistols behind me—fly, fly, we must not be taken to-day —to-morrow, and I would care not to lose my liberty—quick, quick!"

Like lightning they darted into a by footpath, but Austin and the rest pressed hard upon them. Jack being lighter and more active than Page, soon outstripped him; and while Page fell into the keeper's hands, Jack had made his way into a farmer's stable by the road side, where he concealed himself under some straw. Page made no resistance, and was immediately secured; the search then became general for Jack, who might have got off but for a little girl espying one of his feet under the straw. The keepers on this discovery immediately threw themselves on him, and though he struggled violently, yet, unarmed, and overpowered by numbers, he was at last forced to yield, and once more became their prisoner; binding him hand and foot, they placed him in the coach, on the box of which was David Lloyd the milkman. Austin and Revel took their seats on each side of him, while Langley faced him with a brace of loaded pistols, ready to blow out his brains at the least attempt at escape. The party then formed themselves into a procession: first proceeded a body of mounted constables, strongly armed; then followed the coach and four, with numerous persons on the box, roof, and behind, waving their hats in token of triumph; these, it must be premised, were persons mostly connected with the gaol; the rear was brought up by other mounted and strongly armed constables, with a numerous body of persons on foot, mostly attracted by curiosity, though some few were so from sympathy. In this state the cortége proceeded to London, the whole having rather the appearance of the triumphal *entrée* of some great conqueror, than the capture of a common housebreaker. It was two o'clock in the afternoon ere they reached Newgate, so much was their way impeded by the crowds of persons the news of Jack's capture had congregated together.

Jack made an attempt to spring out of the keeper's arms as they were conveying him into the lodge; but they were too quick for him, and immediately conducted him to a strong room in the very centre of the prison, known by the name of the Castle, from its supposed impregnability. Here he was placed remote from all the other prisoners, where he was handcuffed, loaded with double irons, and fastened with an enormous padlock to a heavy staple in the floor; where the keepers for that time left him, it may reasonably be presumed, plunged in the most hopeless despair; but such was not the case, as will be seen in the following chapter.

CHAPTER THE LAST.

JACK'S END.

JACK'S WONDERFUL ESCAPE FROM THE CASTLE-ROOM.—ROBBERY OF MR. PARGITER.—THE PREDICTION FULFILLED.

IF Jack had been an object of curiosity before his escape from Newgate, his fame was now increased tenfold—hundreds flocked to see him; lords, ladies, authors, and artists, who, pitying the sad condition to which he was reduced, and admiring the good humour with which he detailed his various exploits, gave him considerable sums of money; and many would even have furnished him with tools for his deliverance, which he would have liked much better, but they were too closely watched; the money, in some measure, however, enabled him, to solace his sufferings. Bess had flown to him on the first news of his capture, as also had Poll, but the keepers, profiting by experience, refused them admittance. Jack was not at all daunted, difficulties only served to increase his ardour; his thoughts were wholly bent on devising plans for another escape; he had set his whole soul on visiting the lawyer, Pargiter, and effecting Bess's restoration to her rights ; in addition to this, there was an innate love of notoriety ; his biography had been printed, and his portrait published in all shapes ; to break a second time out of Newgate, while it served his love and saved his life, would crown his fame—would be an act worthy of his genius. It was something very like a noble ambition that fired him ; he felt there was nothing he dared not attempt, could not accomplish.

The proper opportunity at length presented itself : on Wednesday, October the 14th, the sessions were to begin at the Old Bailey. At this time Jack knew that the keepers would have so much to do in attending the court that it would leave them but little leisure to visit him ; he therefore thought this the proper period for his purpose. Accordingly next day, about two in the afternoon, when Mr. Austin, attended by Langley and Shuffling Sawney, brought him his dinner, and giving it to him asked him if he wanted any thing more, saying, if he did he must speak then, as they could not visit him again till next morning, Jack replied in the negative. The keepers then, as usual, very carefully examined his hand-cuffs, fet-locks, and other irons, and finding them secure, left him. No sooner were they gone than Jack set to work. He first, with great pain and exertion, worked off his handcuffs, and then, with a crooked nail, which he fortunately found upon the floor, opened the immense padlock that fastened his chains to the staple. He next twisted asunder a small link of the chain between his legs, and drawing up his fet-locks as high as he could, made them fast with his garters, so as to prevent their clinking. He then commenced attempting to get up the chimney, but he had not advanced far ere his progress was arrested by a large iron bar placed across the inside of it; this caused him to descend, and set to work on the outside. With a piece of his broken chain he speedily picked out some mortar, and removing a small stone or two about six feet from the ground, got out the iron bar, which was an inch square, and nearly a yard long, and was ultimately of great service to him; with this he soon made so large a breach that he effected a passage into a room above, called the Red Room. In this room he found another and much larger nail, which also turned out to be a very useful implement to him. The door of this place had not been opened for seven years; but in less than seven minutes, such was the undaunted resolution, and almost superhuman exertions of Jack, that he had wrenched off the lock, and got into the entry leading to the chapel of the prison, which fortunately was adjoining. Here he found a door bolted on the other side; but Jack defied stop, and set toil at nought; to break a hole through the wall, and force the bolt back, was the work of a moment. Arrived at the inside of the chapel, while the big drops of perspiration fastly coursed one another down his brows, the awful silence and solemn gloom of the sacred place cast a momentary chill upon his energies.   Sinner as he was, he involuntarily sank upon his knees, implored Heaven's pardon for the offences he had committed, expressed his deep repentence, and prayed for strength and fortitude to enable him to accomplish his escape, that he might live to sin no more.   He arose confirmed in spirit, and ready to oppose every obstacle that might present itself.   His communion with Heaven had been rude and brief, but it had yielded him confidence and solace.

Passing through the chapel door, he broke off one of the iron spikes, which he kept for future use, and then made his way through an entry between the chapel and the lower leads.   The door of this entry was very strong, and was fastened by a ponderous lock of unusual security.   In addition to this the night had now set in, and he was forced to work in the dark; but all these impediments proved as trifles to his perseverance and determination.   In half an hour, by the help of the great nail we have mentioned, the chapel spike, and the iron bar, Jack forced off the box of the lock and got open the door; this led to another door still more difficult, for it was not only locked, but firmly barred and bolted.   For a moment his heart sank, and his spirits failed him; but the thoughts of a shameful death at Tyburn, and Bess and poverty on one side, and on the other of Bess a lady, and he in ease and safety, renowned and admired, again recruited his flagging energies ; he paused a few moments for breath, and with fresh strength, desperately setting to work again, he wrenched the formidable fillet from the main post of the door, the box and staple came off with it, and the door flew open.

It was now eight o'clock, and there was no other obstructions to his proceedings, for Jack had only another door to open, which being bolted on the inside, was unclosed without difficulty.

As he placed his foot on the lower leads, with what a refreshing freedom did the breath of Heaven, from which he had been so long shut out, play o'er his throbbing temples ! what a bracing energy, a soothing calm did nature administer to his exhausted resolution, his spent and toil-worn faculties ! Jack stood for a few moments to inhale its influence, the felon's heart was softened, his spirit was rebuked spite of his bravado. He bent in reverence, almost unknowingly, yet still he owned Heaven's providence, and as he bent, breathed forth a brief " thank God! thank God !" Recovering himself, he now mounted a wall, and got upon the upper leads of the prison ; there was no moon, but the stars shone brightly ; he looked on the broad expanse before him, there was a softened hum murmuring around him, as if the mighty city was settling itself into repose ; he longed to commit himself to the protection of its thousand retreats, and his consideration naturally turned to the way by which he could descend with the greatest safety. After a careful inspection, he found the most convenient place on which he could alight would be the roof of a turner's house adjoining the prison, but the depth was too great to admit of his making a descent without something by which he could let himself down ; he therefore retraced his steps to his old abode, the Castle-room, having some difficulty in making his way over the heaps of rubbish he had created by his operations. Procuring the blanket with which he had been used to cover himself, he returned, and making it fast to the wall with the spike he had taken out of the chapel, he slid gently down on the turner's leads just as St. Sepulchre's clock was striking nine. It happened that the door of the turner's garret was open, through this he stole softly down two pair of stairs, when he heard some persons talking in one of the rooms. His irons by chance clinking, a female voice exclaimed, " Good Heavens ! what noise is that ?"—when a man answered, " Perhaps the dog or cat."

Somewhat alarmed, Jack, who was now completely worn out, retreated again to the garret, where he reposed himself for upwards of two hours, after which he crept down once more to the first floor where the company were met, and there heard a gentleman taking leave, and saw the maid light him down stairs. As soon as the maid returned to the company, Jack resolved to brave all hazards and depart. In stealing down the remaining flight of stairs, he stumbled against the parlour door; however, instantly recovering himself, he got into the street undisturbed.

By this time it was past twelve o'clock. Boldly passing the watch-house of St. Sepulchre, he bid the watchman good morning; then making his way down Snow Hill, and through Holborn, he turned into Gray's Inn Lane, from whence he went across the lonely fields on which now stand great part of Lamb's Conduit Street, Russell and Brunswick Squares, into the highway of Tottenham Court; in the fields on the other side of which now forming the sites of Charlotte Street, and Fitzroy Square then, a very out of the way, and very lonely place, he found a deserted ruined building that had formerly been used as a cow-house, in which he took shelter and slept soundly for three hours. Having his fetters still on, his legs were necessarily greatly bruised and swollen, he dreaded the approach of daylight lest he should be discovered. Examining the state of his pockets, he found he had nearly fifty shilllings about him; but he knew no one to whom he could send for assistance.

At seven in the morning it began to rain hard,

and continued to do so all day, so that no person appeared in the fields; and during this melancholy day he would, to use his own words, have given his right hand for 'a hammer, a chisel, and a punch.' Night coming on, and being pressed by hunger, he ventured to a little chandler's shop in Tottenham Court Road, where he got a supply of bread and cheese, small beer, and some other necessaries, hiding his irons with his long great coat. He asked the woman of the shop for a hammer; but she had no such thing; on which he retired again to the cow-house, where he slept that night and remained all the next day.

He would immediately have sought Bess, but he knew not where to find her; independently of which, he was certain a strict watch would be kept wherever she might happen to be residing.

At night he went again to the chandler's shop, supplied himself with more provisions, and again returned to his hiding-place. At six the next morning, which was Sunday, he began to beat the basils of his fetters with a large stone, in order to bring them to an oval form to slip his heels through. In the afternoon, the master of the cow-house by chance visiting the place, and seeing his irons, said, "For God's sake, who are you?"

Jack said that he was an unfortunate young fellow, who having had a *love-child* sworn to him, and not being able to give security to the parish for its support, had been sent to Bridewell, from whence he had just made his escape, and implored him, for Heaven's sake, not to betray him.

The owner of the shed, who was a married man, and of an easy good-natured disposition, said, that if that was all, he did not see that there was much harm in it; but that he didn't care how soon he was gone, for he didn't much like his looks: the man then went away. It was well for him that he did so, for Jack had resolved to make a desperate resistance rather than be taken.

Soon after his departure, a man in the garb of a mechanic crossing the fields, Jack called to him, and repeating the story of the love child, offered him twenty shillings to procure him a smith's hammer and a punch. The poor man, tempted by the reward, complied with his wishes, and assisted him in getting rid of his irons: by five in the evening he was once again unfettered.

Night coming on, Jack tied an old handkerchief round his head, tore his woollen cap in several places, and made a number of rents in his coat and stockings, so as to give him the appearance of being a beggar: in this disguise he sallied forth. To describe his various wanderings would fill a volume, and our limits are becoming but too circumscribed. Every where his exploits formed the subject of general conversation; some reviled him, and expressed their wish that they could retake him, but the major part pitied and admired him. He reposed that night in a beggar's lodging house, or night cellar, in St. Giles's, and slept soundly and sweetly on a wretched pallet, that would at other times have defied all rest.

The next day, Monday, he ventured, towards evening, to the Haymarket, and joined a crowd that were surrounding two ballad-singers, who were most lugubriously chanting forth a metrical narrative of his adventures and escapes. In one of these persons, to his great surprise, he recognised the vocal Mr. Nightingal, the landlord of the memorable White Lion. This *base* worthy had been turned out of his house, which had been shut up by order of the justices, and being deserted by Wild, was now in the greatest misery and destitution. To this person Jack resolved to disclose himself. Making him a private signal, Nightingal soon disengaged himself from his companion and the crowd, and privately joining Jack, humming *sotto voce*, part of Beaumont and Fletcher's well known lyric—

" Come sheppard! come away without delay,
    While the gentle time doth stay."

they made their way into an obscure public house in Rupert Street, the landlady of which Jack had heard express herself in a friendly manner towards him, as he had casually taken a dram there in the morning. Now then, warbled Mr. Nightingal singing part of Morley's Madrigal—

" Where art thou wanton, and I so sought thee ?"

" your history, captain, your history."

Jack told him all. Mr. Nightingal looked disconcerted, and only answered by humming with Michael Wise—

" Old Chiron thus preached to his pupil, Achilles,
I'll tell you, young gentleman, what the Fates' will is;

" You, my boy, must go;
The gods will have it so."

" Curse your singing," said Jack ; " there's no time for chirping, let us descend to plain prose."

Conferring together, Jack soon learnt from Mr. Nightingal that Jonathan Wild had been indefatigable in his search after him; as also, but with different views, had been Bess, who was at that time living in the old lodgings in Tothill Fields. Jack saw plainly, that, for his own safety, the sooner he could get out of the kingdom the better : he was glad he had learnt where to find Bess.

Nightingal rented a wretched garret in Newport Street, the occupation of which he freely offered. Jack's mind was soon made up. His first step was to procure some decent clothing, and send for his mother : he could not resolve on quitting England without taking a last farewell of her ; he therefore dispatched Nightingal to Spitalfields in search of her, appointing to join them at a public house in Maypole Alley, in the neighbourhood of Clare Market, the landlord of which he knew was friendly to him.

" That meeting over," said he, " I shall have to speak to a ken at Hampstead to-night—one in which Jonathan is interested ; and to-morrow, in company with the girl I love best, I shall quit England for ever."

" What, pretty Bess, eh ?"

" No, no ! she must know nothing of this as yet."

" Oh, oh ! I'm mum ; sly dog !" said Nightingal.

" Well, go thy way, since thou wilt go."

sung Mr. Nightingal.

" As for toggery you can have plenty.
    Lawn as white as driven snow,
    Cyprus black as e'er was crow."

" Yes, Jonathan Wild," continued Jack, " by that time I shall be in a way to clear off all old scores with you."

" I am delighted to hear that, said Mr. Nightingal, essaying to sing " The Nightingale, the organ of delight," but breaking down in the attempt ; " Jonathan is the most ungrateful of villains, and will die like a dog.

' The silver swan that living had no note,
    Dying ————' "

" Prithee peace," said Jack, " and away ; I need a short repose, and will seek it."

" Aye, aye," said Mr. Nightingal—

" I wander up and down, and fain would rest me."

" You know the snooze, so by-by."

> " Her eyes the glow-worm lend thee,
> The shooting stars attend thee,
> The little birds also ——"

Jack forced him off in a rage.

They parted; and while Nightingal repaired to Spitalfields, Jack, having the key of the garret, took a turn down Monmouth Street to look after some clothes. Passing a shop where there was only a young woman sitting, he thought this a favourable opportunity; accordingly, jumping over the hatch, and blowing out the candle, he so frightened the girl that she immediately fainted, and he had leisure to help himself to whatever he wanted, with which he made clear off before she recovered.

Changing his clothes in Nightingal's garret, he took a short rest, which somewhat revived him, and then repaired to the place of meeting. His appearance was so completely metamorphosed, that few would have recognised him. He had not long to wait for the arrival of his mother—the heart-broken woman was too anxious to see her son to delay a moment: their meeting was a touching one—almost too much even for the sensibility of Mr. Nightingal, who was obliged to have recourse to frequent libations of brandy to keep his spirits at all up.

Mrs. Sheppard now embraced her son a hundred times; but her joy at beholding him safe was more than counterbalanced by her fears for his security; she conjured him, as he valued her life, as well as his own, not to lose a moment in getting out of the reach of pursuit.

"Quit this fatal country," she exclaimed, "dear Jack! Quit the evil courses, the wretched associates, that have brought disgrace and ruin on you. My prayers, my blessings, shall attend you. You need not go without resources; here are the hard-earned savings of long years—my little all, put by for your poor sister's marriage portion,—but 'tis better thus; take it—take it, and Heaven protect and prosper you."

She placed a pocket-book within his hand; an affectionate struggle between them followed, but Jack could in no way be induced to touch a penny of it.

"He could do well without it," he said; "he did not want it—he soon should be in a situation to succour her."

With many tears and last fond looks the poor woman at length tore herself away; and it now getting somewhat late, Jack parted from Nightingal, agreeing to meet him at his lodgings on the following morning.

Leaving Nightingal, singing the old catch—

> " Orpheus, with his lute, made trees
> And the mountain tops that freeze,
> Bow themselves when he did sing."

Jack set about procuring the various articles for his expedition; these consisted of the usual house-breaking tools, a brace of pistols and ammunition, a stout hanger, a few yards of cord, a phosphorous box, and a dark lantern. To obtain all these was a matter of no difficulty in the dissolute environs of Clare Market, which were, at that time, the head-quarters of every species of villany. He pushed briskly forward to the gipsy encampment at High-gate, to procure the co-operation of the faithful Poll Maggot. The gang had retired to rest, but the barking of Fox soon aroused them. Poll sprang from her tent, and expressed her willing-ness to accompany Jack.

" Zara is absent on some of her night wander-ings," she said ; " we cannot, therefore, have a bet-ter opportunity."

It was near twelve o'clock, when, reaching the top of Hampstead Hill, they were about turning down the little lane leading to Frognall, where the mansion occupied by the villain Pargiter was situated ; the moon shone brightly—all was calm —most of the inhabitants of Hampstead had re-tired to rest ; only a twinkling taper here and there in some lattice casement announced the presence of man. As they turned to go down the lane,

Poll suddenly disappeared, and a tall gaunt figure crossed Jack's path and barred his steps; he started—it was the well remembered form of the gipsy Zara. She fixed on him a piercing glance; a cloud at this moment passed over the moon, and threw them both partially into shade.

" And it indeed is thou !" she exclaimed—" can nothing withstand the decrees of destiny? Will not the watchful eye, the stone wall, the bolt, the bar, the lock, the chain, the gyve, restrain the victim doomed by fate from rushing on his ruin? No, no! who shall hope it? — This I foresaw when light first dawned upon thee; but where is *she*, the partner of thy destiny? Ah! why is she not here to do her work? But she will not be long—here the gipsy cast her eyes earnestly upon the starry Heavens above her — there is her natal planet, Venus, fair as of wont, yet surely shining paler, sadder; and there is Saturn, baneful as ever. —Fly, fly! be warned while yet 'tis time—enter not the house—be warned, be warned, I say."

" Away, hag !" cried Jack, angry at the interruption, and accounting for her presence by the near neighbourhood of the spot to the encampment of the tribe, " away with your mummeries ! I am not to be fooled by them—off to your tent, I say—dare to dog my steps, or be a spy upon my actions, and, by hell, I'll brain you, witch !"

Here he fiercely presented a pistol to her head; the gipsy flinched not.

" Slave of fate, he rushes on his doom ; the warning is in vain, rash fool ! but destiny is all powerful."

Uttering these words in a sad and solemn tone, she strode slowly away, and soon was lost in an adjoining thicket.

Jack was a little unsettled by this encounter, but Poll rejoining him (she had fled unobserved on catching a glimpse of Zara), he soon regained his determination : he found the Manor-house— an old but noble building ; leaving Poll on guard at the door, he set to work. We have no space to detail the skill by which he gained admittance, and penetrated into the very bed-room of the lawyer Pargiter, the treacherous kinsman of poor Bess, whom he forced at the muzzle of the pistol, to deliver up all the papers requisite to substantiate her rights ; her grandfather's will, and a series of letters fully corroborating her identity, tracing her from her birth in the house of Mr. Kneebone to her abstraction from the cottage of Crazy Sally, her residence with the gipsy tribe —in short, every circumstance that was necessary to satisfy the most sceptical.

Strongly binding and gagging the affrighted lawyer, Jack now felt no hesitation in helping himself to whatever was in the house he thought might suit his purpose ; he dressed himself like a gentleman in a ruffled shirt and a genteel suit of black,

put on a light tye-wig of several guineas value,
clapped a silver-hilted sword by his side, slipped
his fingers into some valuable rings, put a gold
family watch in his fob, and, in addition to the
precious documents, lined his pockets with some
odd rouleaus of broad pieces, which he happened
to discover in an old escritoire,

" It will be all in the family," he exclaimed,
taking down the lawyer's dressed cocked hat ; and
now, looking more like a lord or duke than any
thing else, and having got all he wanted, he prepared to depart, So skilfully had his operations
been conducted, that he had not disturbed even a
single domestic. He found Poll Maggot as he had
left her, at the door on guard.

" Well, my ben cove," said she, " all plummy ?"

" Nothing can be better, my lass," answered
Jack, gallantly imprinting, in the joy of his heart,
a warm kiss upon her ripe lips.

" Ah, traitor !" shrieked a piercing voice, " I
can doubt no longer—seize him—'tis he — tear
him from her—Tyburn, rather than with her !"

'Twas Bess ! and ere Jack had time to recover
from his surprise, he was seized by Quilt Arnold,
the Patriarch, and a strong body of constables,
who rushed forward, headed by his implacable
enemy, Jonathan Wild himself.

" Bess, Bess !" said Jack, sadly, who saw at
once all that had occurred, " your fatal *jealousy*

has destroyed us both—and that at the moment, too, when I had secured your rights, and had obtained for you the means of rank and fortune."

"Yes, the prediction is 'fulfilled," said Zara, mournfully, as she emerged from some trees by the road side ; "Heiress of Sir Tracy, riches and rank have come too late. I fain would have averted this, but it could not be—the stars will work their destiny."

Our narrative draws to a close.—Why should we seek to linger over the unavailing remorse and despair of the luckless Bess !—Why should we dwell on the brutalizing details of Jack's execution at Tyburn, which soon after followed this, his last capture ? Jack did not die till he had secured Bess the possession of her ample fortune and estates, all which she would willing have resigned to have bought him but one hour of added life. Every effort that could be made to procure his pardon or escape was tried, but unavailingly; Jack's fame had become too notorious.

To account for Bess's luckless appearance with Jonathan Wild, at the very moment when Jack had effected all, it may be necessary to state that it was the unconscious work of Jack's old acquaintance, Nightingal. When Jack parted with him, his intellects had become somewhat muddled with repeated bumpers of brandy, which, as we have stated, he had taken to keep up his spirits; the fresh air, instead of restoring him, only added to the effect of the liquor. It was in this glorious state that he happened, unfortunately, to meet with poor Bess, to whom he could not avoid communicating that he had seen Jack — had just parted from him. Fired with jealousy, the sharpness of woman's wit soon drew from him the further intelligence that Jack would, the next day, leave the country in company with a favoured female, who, she had no doubt, would be Poll Maggot.

In answer to her eager inquiries where she could find Jack, Mr. Nightingal cunningly told her that was a secret; that Jack was going that night to crack the ken of an old acquaintance of Jonathan Wild's at Hampstead, which would make the fortunes of him and his doxy—

"It was a lover and his lass"

Hiccupped he.

" Hence away, ye syrens, leave me."

He knew no more, but staggered off, chanting the well known words :—

"Oh ! mistress, mine, where art thou roaming !
Oh ! stay and hear, your true love's coming,
That can sing both high and low."

Distracted, mad, scarce knowing what she did, and heedless of all consequences, so she but gratified her revenge, for such she mistakingly supposed her excess of love, Bess hurried to the residence of Jonathan Wild. He was alone. Almost incoherent with passion, she related to him the

story of her wrongs, her ill-requited love; she told him she would put him in possession of a secret that would preserve the property of one of his friends, if he would pledge himself to tear Jack from the arms of her rival. She did not wish his death, though she would rather see him hanged a hundred times than know him the property of another. Sad wretch! how falsely did she read her own heart! She knew, she said, Jonathan could get him transported, which would be bliss to her if it but tore him from Poll. Wild readily promised everything. When she mentioned the house of one in whom he was interested at Hampstead as her only clue, Jonathan was at no loss to divine, from Jack's late discovery and conversation, that he meditated a visit to Pargiter. Assembling his forces they accordingly instantly repaired thither. The fatal result has been stated.

On Monday, the 16th of November, the day of Jack's execution, he made one last attempt for life and liberty; it was more on Bess's account than his own. Having obtained a pen-knife, it was his design in his way along Holborn to have cut the ropes that bound him, and have sprung among the mob, most of whom he knew were favourable to him; to have darted down Little Turnstile, where his escort could not pursue him; but the plan was discovered, and, after a desperate resistance, the knife was taken from him, and he was secured.

A mourning coach, which contained the ill-fated

victim of unfounded jealousy, followed the sad procession. Jack's remains were deposited, the evening of his execution, in a humble grave, under the
protection of a regiment of guards, whose presence
the excitement of the multitude had rendered necessary, in the church-yard of St. Martin's-in-the-
Fields; but they were not destined to remain there
long.

In a retired part of Edgeworth church-yard,
there is a beautiful monument of white marble,
overhung by venerable yew trees. On one side of
this are inscribed the initials 𝔍. 𝔖 .with the date,
November 16. 1724. On the other side 𝔈. 𝔖.,
and the date of February 20., in the year following; a brief three months! In this tomb repose the ashes of the renowned house and prison
breaker, Jack Sheppard, and those of his unfortunate partner in love, the ill-fated Bess.

Of the other personages of this narrative, it may
be sufficient to say, the faithful Blueskin perished
a few days before his friend, and Jonathan Wild's
career did not continue more than a few months
afterwards: he had lived by treachery, he died
midst execrations, and his bones now moulder in a
doctor's surgery at Windsor, unblessed, even with
a grave. Such is the end of crime!

APPENDIX.

The Life and Actions of John Sheppard, written by himself during his confinement, comprising a Narrative of all his remarkable Robberies, surprising Escapes, &c. Printed by J. Applebee, Water Lane, London. 1724.

[THE genuineness of this confession, faithfully transcribed from a scarce copy in the British Museum, is evident, beyond all doubt, by the interpolations which occur throughout. The free and daring sentiments of Jack contrast too strongly with the pious reflections of the Ordinary, to allow them to be mistaken for a moment. We have, however, thought it as well to point out, in a few foot notes, the parts which Jack and the Ordinary appear to have taken alternately in this curious production.]

JACK'S CONFESSION.

As my unhappy life and actions have afforded much amusement to the world, and various pamphlets, papers, and pictures relating thereto, have gone abroad, most, or all, of them misrepresenting my affairs, 'tis necessary that I should say something for myself, and set certain intricate matters in a true light; every subject, how unfortunate or unworthy soever, having the liberty of publishing his case, and it will be no small satisfaction to me to think that I have thoroughly purged my conscience before I leave the world, and made reparation to the many persons injured by me, as far as is in my poor power.*

If my birth, parentage, or education, will prove of service or satisfaction to mankind, I was born in Stepney parish, the year Queen Anne came to the crown; my father, a carpenter by trade, and an honest industrious man by character, and my mother bore and deserved the same. She being left a widow in the early part of my life, continued the business, and kept

---

* This pious prohemium is evidently by the Ordinary, not by Jack.

myself, with another unfortunate son and daughter, at Mr. Garrett's school, near St. Helen's, in Bishopsgate parish, till Mr. Kneebone, a woollen-draper, in the Strand, an acquaintance, regarding the slender circumstances of our family, took me under his care, and improved me in my writing and accompts, himself setting me copies with his own hand; and he, being desirous to settle me to a trade, and to make my mother easy in that, agreed with Mr. Owen Wood, a carpenter in Drury Lane, to take me apprentice for seven years, upon condition that Mr. Kneebone should procure Mr. Wood to be employed in performing the carpenter's work, &c., at a house at Hampstead, which he did accordingly, and upon that, and upon no other consideration, was I bound to Mr. Wood.*

We went on together for about six years, there happening in that time, what is too common with most families in low life, as frequent quarrels and bickerings. I am far from presuming to say that I was one of the best of servants, but, I believe, if less liberty had been allowed me then, I should scarce have had so much sorrow and confinement after. My master and mistress, with their children, were strict observers of the sabbath, but 'tis too well known in the neighbourhood that I had too great a loose given to my evil inclinations, and spent the Lord's day as I thought convenient.† It has been said, in print, that I did beat and bruise my said master, Mr. Wood, in a most barbarous and shameful manner, at Mr. Brett's, the Sun alehouse, at Islington, and that I damned my mistress's blood, and beat her to the ground, &c. These stories have been greatly *improved* to my disadvantage. Mr. Wood cannot but remember how hard I wrought for him that day at Islington, what refreshment was offered to my fellow servant and myself; the cause of that unhappy quarrel is still fresh in my memory; and, as for that of my mistress, when Elizabeth Lyon and her husband, a soldier, were quarrelling together in Mr. Wood's yard, I bid them begone, and threw a small lath at Lyon, which might have fallen on my mistress, but she received no harm as I know of, and if she did, I am sorry for it.

After all, I may justly lay the blame of my temporal, and (without God's great mercies) my eternal ruin on Joseph Hind, a button-mould-maker, who formerly kept the Black Lyon alehouse in Drury Lane; the frequenting of this wicked house brought me acquainted with Elizabeth Lyon, and with a train of vices, that before I was altogether a stranger to. Hind is now

* This is evidently a correct and straightforward detail of the facts.
† A side wind by the Reverend Wagstaff.

a lamentable instance of God's divine vengeance, he being a wretched object about the streets ; and I am still far more miserable than he.*

It has been said, in the History of my Life, that the first robbery that ever I committed was in the house of Mr. Bains, a piece-broker in White Horse Yard; to my sorrow and shame, I must acknowledge my guilt of a felony before that, which was my stealing two silver spoons from the Rummer tavern, at Charing Cross, when I was doing a job there for my master, for which I ask pardon of God, and the persons who were wrongfully charged and injured by that my crime.†

Unhappy wretch! I was now commenced thief, and soon after house-breaker : growing gradually wicked, 'twas about the latter end of July, 1723, that I was sent by my master to do a job at the house of Mr. Bains aforesaid, I there stole a roll of fustian containing twenty-four yards, from amongst many others, and Mr. Bains not missing it had consequently no suspicion. I offered it for sale, among the young lads in our neighbourhood, at 12d. per yard, but meeting with no purchasers I concealed the fustian in my trunk.

On the 1st of August following, I wrought at Mr. Bains's shop, and that night, at about twelve of the clock, I came and took up the wooden bars over the cellar window, so entered and came up into the house, and took away goods to the value of fourteen pounds, besides seven pounds in money out of the till; then nailed down the bars again and went off.

The next day I came to the house to finish the shutters for their shop, when Mr. Bains and his wife were in great trouble for their loss, saying to me they suspected a woman, their lodger, had let the rogues in, for that they were assured the house had not been broken ; the poor people little dreaming they were telling their story to the thief, I condoling with them, and pretending great sorrow for their misfortune. Not long afterwards, my fellow-prentice, Thomas, acquainted Mr. Wood that he had observed a quantity of fustian in my trunk. My master and I had broke measures, and I being absent from home, and hearing Thomas had tattled, in the night time I broke through a neighbour's house, and into my master's, and so carried off the fustian, to prevent the consequence of that discovery. Mr. Wood, rightly concluding I had stolen it from Mr. Bains, sent him word of what had happened, who upon overlooking his goods soon found his loss, and threatened to prosecute me for the robbery. I thought it was advisable to meet the danger, and therefore went to Mr. Bains, bullied and menaced him, and bid him be careful how he sullied my reputation, lest he might be brought to repent of it. But this was not sufficient to avert the danger. Mr. Bains resolving to proceed upon the circumstances he was already furnished with, I thought of another expedient, and acknowledged that I had a piece of fustian which my mother had bought for me, in Spitalfields, of a weaver; and she, poor woman, willing to screen her wicked son, confirmed the story, and was a whole day together with Mr. Bains in Spitalfields to find out the pretended weaver. In the end, I was forced to send back about nineteen yards of the fustian to Mr. Bains, and then the storm blew over. I related all these particulars to Mr. Bains, when he came to see me in the castle room, as well to wipe off the suspicion from the poor innocent woman, Mr. Bains's lodger, as for his own satisfaction.

I abruptly quitted Mr. Wood's service almost a year before the expiration of my apprenticeship; I went to Fulham, and there wrought as a journeyman to a master-carpenter, telling the man that I had served out my apprenticeship in Smithfield. Elizabeth Lyon cohabiting with me as my wife, I kept her in a lodging at Parson's Green; but Mr. Wood's brother, being an inhabitant in the town, discovered me, and my master, with Justice Newton's warrant, brought me to London, and confined me in St. Clement's Round-house, all night. The next day I was carried to Guildhall, to have gone before the Chamberlain, but he having left, I agreed with Mr. Wood, and making matters easy got clear of him, and then fell to robbing almost every one that stood in my way. The robbery of Mr. Charles's house in May-Fair, I have confessed in a particular manner to Mr. Wagstaff, and to many others.

The robberies of Mr. Bains, Mr. Barton, and Mr. Kneebone, together with the robbery of Mr. Pargiter, and two others on the Hampstead Road, along with Joseph Blake, alias Blueskin, I did amply confess before Justice Blackerby; Mr. Bains and Mr. Kneebone being present, and did make all the reparation that was in my power, by telling them where the goods were sold, part whereof has been recovered by that means to the owners. I declare upon the word of a dying man, that Will Field was not concerned with Blueskin and myself in the breaking and robbing Mr. Kneebone's house, although he has sworn the same at our respective trials; and I have been informed, that by certain circumstances which Field swore to, Mr. Kneebone himself is of opinion, that he was not concerned in the fact. But he has done the work for his master, who in the end no doubt will reward him, as he has done all his other servants.* I wish Field may repent and amend his wicked life, for a greater villain there is not breathing. Blueskin and myself, after we had robbed Mr. Kneebone's house, lodged the goods in my warehouse, a little stable at Westminster Horse-Ferry, which I had there for such purposes. I was so cautious of suffering any one to be acquainted with it, that even Elizabeth Lyon was out of the secret; but hearing of a Lock, or Ferne, in Bishopgate Street, to dispose of the cloth to, Blueskin carried the pack, and I followed to guard him, and met the *chap* † at the alehouse; a small quantity we got off at a very low price, which was always not ours,‡ but is the constant fate of all other robbers; for I declare that when goods (the intrinsic value whereof has been £50) have been in our hands, I have never made more than ten pounds clear money; such a discount and disadvantage attends always the sale of such unlawful acquirements.§ Field lodging with Blueskin's mother in Rosemary-lane, we thus became acquainted, and being all of a piece, made no secret of Mr. Kneebone's robbery; we told him the manner of it, the booty, &c., and withal carried him down to the warehouse, which the next time we visited, we found broken open, the cloth gone, and only a wrapper or two of no value; we concluded, as it appeared after, that Field had played at *rob-thief* with us; for he produced some of Mr. Kneebone's cloth at my trial, of which he became possessed by no other means than those I have related. I must add this to what relates to Mr. Kneebone's robbery, that I was nearly a fortnight, by intervals, in cutting the two oaken bars that went over the back part of his house in Little Drury-lane. I heartily ask his pardon for injuring my kind patron and benefactor in that manner, and desire his prayers to God for the forgiveness of that, as of all my other enormous crimes.||

I have been at times confined in all the round-houses belonging to the respective parishes within the liberty of West-

* Jack evidently alludes here to Jonathan Wild.
† Dealer.
‡ Jack's meaning is rather obscure here—nor has the reverend Ordinary elucidated it. Jack possibly meant that, small as the sum was that was generally given by receivers of stolen goods, the thief did not always get the whole of it.
§ "Handy Dandy, which is the justice and which the thief?" Jack's regret is here adroitly improved and turned to pious account by the reverend Ordinary.
|| Wagstaff, without doubt.

minster; Elizabeth Lyon has been a prisoner in many of them also; I have sometimes procured her liberty, and she at others has done her utmost to obtain mine; and at other times she has again betrayed me into the hands of justice. When I was formerly in St. Ann's round-house, she brought me the spike of a halbert, with the help whereof I did break open the same, but was discovered before I could get off, and was put into the dungeon of the place, fettered and manacled; and that was the first time that I had any irons put upon me. I, in return, rescued her from St. Giles's round-house soon after, but the manner of my own escape from St. Giles's round-house may be worthy of notice.

Having in confederacy with my brother Thomas, a sea-faring person, and Elizabeth Lyon, committed several robberies about Clare-market, and Thomas being in Newgate for them, impeached me and Lyon; and the prosecutors being in close pursuit of us, I kept up as much as possible; 'till being one day at the Queen's Head ale-house, in King-street, Westminster, an acquaintance called Sykes, (alias Hell and Fury), a chairman desired me to go thence to an alehouse at the Seven Dials, saying he knew two *hubs** that we might make a penny of at skittles; we being good players, I went with him; a third person he soon procured, and said the fourth should not be long wanting, and truly he proved to be a constable of St. Giles's parish. In short Sykes charged him with me, saying I stood impeached of several robberies.

Justice Parry sent me to St. Giles's Round-house for that night, with orders to the constable to bring me before him the next morning for further examination. I had nothing but an old razor in my pocket, and was confined in the upper part of the place, being two stories from the ground; with my razor I cut out the stretcher of my chair, and began to make a breach in the roof, laying the feather bed under it to prevent any noise by the falling of the rubbish on the floor. It being about nine at night, people were passing and re-passing in the street, and a tile or brick happening to fall, struck a man on the head, who raised the whole place; the people calling aloud that the prisoners were breaking out of the Round-house. I found there was no time then to be lost, therefore, made a bold push through the breach, throwing a whole load of bricks, tiles, &c. upon the people in the street; and before the beadle and assistance came up I had dropped into the church-yard, and got over the lower end of the wall, and came amidst the crowd

* Two well conditioned Flats.

who were staring up, some crying—"there's his head; there he goes behind the chimney, &c." I was well enough diverted with the adventure, and then went off about my business.*

The method by which I escaped from the New Prison, and the Condemned Hold of Newgate, have been printed in so many books and papers that it would be ridiculous to repeat them; only it must be remembered that my escaping from New Prison, and carrying with me Elizabeth Lyon over the wall of Bridewell-yard, was not so wonderful as has been reported, because Captain Geary and his servants cannot but know, that by opening the great gate I got Lyon upon the top of the wall without the help of a scaling ladder, otherwise it must have been impracticable to have procured her redemption. She indeed rewarded me well for it, in betraying me to Jonathan Wild so soon after. I wish she may reform her life. A more wicked, deceitful and lascivious woman there is not living in England. She has proved my bane, God forgive her,—I do, and die in charity with all the rest of mankind

Blueskin has atoned for his offences. I am now following, being just on the brink of eternity, much unprepared to appear before the face of an angry God!!† Blueskin had been a much older offender than myself, having been guilty of numberless robberies, and had formerly convicted four of his accomplices, who were put to death. He was concerned with me in the three robberies on the Hampstead Road, besides that of Mr. Kneebone, and one other. Though he was an able-bodied man, and capable of any crime, even murder, he was never master of a courage or conduct suitable to our enterprises; and I am of opinion, that neither of us had so soon met our fate, if he would have suffered himself to have been directed by me; he always wanted resolution when our affairs required it most. The last summer, I hired two horses for us at an inn in Piccadilly, and being armed with pistols, &c., we went upon Enfield Chase, where a coach passed us with two footmen and four young ladies, who had with them their gold watches, tweezer cases, and other things of value; I declared immediately for attacking them, but Blueskin's courage dropt him, saying that he would first refresh his horse and then follow, but he designedly delayed till we had quite lost the coach, and hopes of the booty. In short, he was a worthless com-

* Evidently Jack, by the relish with which it is detailed.
† Ordinary again. There is the true Newgate slang in these reflections.

panion, a sorry thief, and nothing but the cutting of Jonathan Wild's throat, could have made him so considerable.*

I have often lamented the scandalous practice of thief-catching, as it is called, and the publick manner of offering rewards for stolen goods, in defiance of two several Acts of Parliament ; the thief-catchers living sumptuously, and keeping publick offices of intelligence. These, who forfeit their lives every day they breathe, and deserve the gallows as richly as any of the thieves, send us their representatives to Tyburn once a month : thus, they hang by proxy, while we do it fairly in person.†

I never corresponded with any of them. I was, indeed, twice at a thief-catcher's *Levee,* and must confess the man treated me civilly; he complimented me on my successes, said he heard that I had both a hand and head admirably well turned to business, and that I and my friends *should be always welcome to him ;* but caring not for his acquaintance, I never troubled him, nor had we any dealings together.

As my last escape from *Newgate* out of the strong-room, called the *Castle,* has made a greater noise in the world than any other action of my life, I shall relate every minute circumstance thereof, as far as I am able to remember; and thereby satisfy the curious, and do justice to the innocent. After I had been made a public spectacle of for many successive days —with my legs chain'd together—loaded with heavy irons, and stapled down to the floor, I thought it was not altogether impracticable to escape, if I could but be furnished with proper implements; but as every person that came near me was carefully watched, there was no possibility of any such assistance; till one day, in the absence of my jailors, being looking about the floor, I spy'd a small nail within reach, and with that, after a little practice, I found the great horse-padlock that went from the chain to the staple in the floor might be unlocked, which I did afterwards at pleasure, and was frequently about the room, and have several times slept on the barracks, when my keepers imagined I had not been out of my chair. But being unable to pass up the chimney, and void of tools, I remained but where I was, till being detected in these practices by the keepers, who surpriz'd me one day before I could fix myself to the staple in the manner in which they had left

* Nobody can mistake these being Jack's own sentiments and reflections ; he here shows himself in his true character.

† A palpable hit at Wild, partly by the Ordinary and partly by Jack. Public good awakening the remarks of the one, and private revenge calling forth the expressions of the other.

me, I showed Mr. Pitt, Mr. Rouse, and Mr. Parry, my art, and before their faces unlocked the padlock with the nail; and though people have made such an outcry about it, there is scarce a smith in London but what may easily do the same thing. However, this called for a further security of me, and till now I had remained without handcuffs, and a jolly pair was provided for me. *Mr. Kneebone* was present when they were put on. I with tears begged his intercession to the keepers to preserve me from those dreadful manacles, telling him my heart was broken, and that I should be much more miserable than before. Mr. Kneebone could not refrain from shedding tears, and did use his good offices with the keepers to keep me from them, but all to no purpose; on they went, though at the same time I despised them, and well knew that with my teeth only I could take them off at pleasure; but this was to lull them into a firm belief that they had effectually frustrated all attempts to escape for the future. I was still far from despairing. The turnkey and *Mr. Kneebone* had not been gone down stairs an hour, ere I made an experiment and got off my handcuffs, and before they visited me again I put them on, and industriously rubb'd and fretted the skin on my wrists, making them very bloody, as thinking (if such a thing was possible to be done) to move the turnkey to compassion, but rather to confirm them in their opinion; but though this had no effect upon them, it wrought much upon the spectators, and drew down from them not only much pity, but quantities of *silver and copper*. But I wanted a still more useful *metal*, a crow, a chisel, a file, and a saw or two, those weapons being more useful to me than all the Mines of *Mexico;* but there was no expecting any such utensils in my circumstances.

Wednesday, the 14th of *October*, the *Sessions* beginning, I found there was not a moment to be lost, and the affair of Jonathan Wild's throat, with the business at the *Old Bailey*, having sufficiently engaged the attention of the keepers, I thought then was the time to bustle. *Thursday* the 15th, at about two in the afternoon, Austin, my old attendant, came to bring my necessaries, and brought up four persons, viz. the Keeper of *Clerkenwell Bridewell*, the Clerk of *Westminster Gate-House*, and two others. Austin, as it was his usual custom, examined the irons and hand-cuffs, and found them all safe and firm, and then left me—and he may remember that I asked him to come again to me the same evening—but I neither expected nor desired company; and happy was it for the poor

man that he did not interfere, while I had the large iron bar
in my hand, though I once had a design to have barricaded
him, or any other from coming into the room while I was at
work; but, then, considering that such a project would be useless, I let fall that resolution.

As near as can be remembered, just before three in the
afternoon, I went to work, taking off my hand-cuffs; next, with
main strength, I twisted a small iron link of the chain between
my legs asunder; the above pieces proved extremely useful to
me in my design; the fet-locks I drew up to the calves of my
legs, taking off before that my stockings, and, with my garters, made them firm to my body, to prevent them shaking.
I then proceeded to make a hole in the chimney of the castle,
about three feet wide and six feet high from the floor, and, with
the help of the broken links aforesaid, wrenched an iron bar
out of the chimney, of about two feet and a half in length, and
an inch square, a most notable impediment.   I immediately
entered the *Red Room*, directly over the Castle, where some of
the Preston rebels had been kept a long time agone; and, as
the keeper says, the door had not been unlocked for seven
years; but I intended not to be seven years in opening it,
though they had; I went to work upon the nut of the lock,
and with little difficulty got it off, and made the door fly before
me; in this room I found a large nail, which proved of great
use in my further progress.   The door of the entry between the
Red Room and the *Chapel* proved a hard task, it being a labo-
rious piece of work, for here I was forced to break away the
wall, and dislodge the bolt which was fastened on the other
side.   This occasioned much noise, and I was very fearful of
being heard by the master-side (debtors).   Being got into the
chapel, I climbed over the iron spikes, and with ease broke one
of them off for my further purposes, and opened the door on
the inside.   The door going out of the chapel to the leads, I
stripped the nut from off the lock, as I had done before from
that of the *Red Room*, and then got into the entry between the
chapel and the leads, and came to another strong door, which
being fastened by a very strong lock, there I had like to have
stopped, and it being full dark, my spirits began to fail me, as
greatly doubting of succeeding; but, cheering up, I wrought
on with great diligence, and in less than half an hour, with the
main help of the nail from the *Red Room*, and the spike from
the chapel, wrenched the box off, and so made the doorway
stumble.

A little farther in my passage another stout door stood in m

way; and this was a difficulty with a witness, being guarded
with more bolts, bars, and locks, than any I had hitherto met
with; I had by this time great encouragement, as hoping to
be rewarded for all this toil and labour. The clock at St. Sepulchre's was now going the eighth hour, and this proved a
very useful hint to me soon after. I went first upon the box
and the nut, but found it labour in vain, and then proceeded to
attack the fillet of the door! this succeeded beyond my expectation, for the box of the lock came off with it from the main
post. I found that my work was near finished, and that my
fate soon would be determined.

I was got to a door, opening to the lower leads, which being
only bolted on the inside, I opened it with ease, and there clam-
bered from the top of it to the higher leads, and went over the
wall. I saw the streets were lighted, the shops being still
open, and, therefore, began to consider what was necessary to
be further done, as knowing that the smallest accident would
spoil the whole workmanship, I was doubtful on which of the
houses I should alight. I found I must go back for the blanket, which had been my covering a-nights in the Castle, which
I accordingly did, and endeavoured to fasten my stockings
and that together, to lessen my descent, but wanted necessaries to do so, and was therefore forced to make use of the
blanket alone. I fixed the same with the chapel spike into the
wall of Newgate, and dropt from it on the turner's leads, a
house adjoining to the prison; 'twas then about nine of the
clock, and the shops not yet shut in. It fortunately happened
that the garret door on the leads was open. I stole softly
down about two pair of stairs, and then heard company talking
in a room, the door open; my irons gave a small clink, which
made a woman cry, " *Lord! what noise was that?*" A man
replied--" *Perhaps the dog or cat,*" so it went off. I returned
up to the garret, and laid myself down, being terribly fatigued,
and continued there for about two hours, and then crept down
once more to the room where the company were, and heard a
gentleman taking his leave, being very importunate to be gone,
saying he had disappointed friends by not going home sooner.
In about three-quarters more the gentleman took leave and
went, being lighted down stairs by the maid, who when she returned shut the chamber door; I then resolved at all hazards
to follow, and slipt down stairs, but made a stumble against a
chamber door; I was instantly in the entry, and out at the
street door, which I was so unmannerly as not to shut after
me. I was once more, contrary to my expectations, and that
of all mankind, a free man.

I passed directly by *St. Sepulchre's* watch-house, bidding them *good-morrow*, it being after twelve, and down *Snow-hill*, up *Holborn*, leaving *St. Andrew's* Watch on my left, and then again passed the Watch-house at *Holborn Bars*, and made down *Grays-in-lane* into the fields, and at two in the morning, came to *Tottenham*,* and there got into an old house in the fields where cows had some time been kept, and laid me down to rest, and slept well for three hours. My legs were swelled and bruised intolerably, which gave me great uneasiness; and having my fetters still on, I dreaded the approach of the day, fearing that I should be discovered. I began to examine my pockets, and found myself master of between forty and fifty shillings. I had no friend in the world that I could send to or trust with my condition. About seven on *Friday* morning it began raining, and continued so the whole day, insomuch that not one creature was to be seen in the fields. I would freely have parted with my right hand for a hammer, a chisel and a punch. I kept snug in my retreat till the evening, when after dark I ventured into *Tottenham*, and got to a little blind chandler's shop, and there furnished myself with cheese, bread, small beer, and other necessaries, hiding my irons with a great coat as much as possible. I asked the woman for a hammer, but there was none to be had ; so I went very quietly back to my dormitory, and rested pretty well that night, and continued there all *Saturday*. At night I went again to the chandler's shop, and got provisions, and slept till about six the next day, which being *Sunday*, I began with a stone to batter the *basils* of my fetters, in order to beat them into a large oval, and then to slip my heels through. In the afternoon, the master of the shed or house came in, and seeing my irons, asked me—"*for God's sake who are you ?*" I told him an unfortunate young man, who had been sent to *Bridewell* about a bastard child, as not being able to give security to the parish, and had made my escape. The man replied "*If that was the case, it was a small fault indeed, for he had been guilty of the same thing himself formerly ;*" and withal said—"*however he did not much like my looks, and cared not how soon I was gone.*"

After he was gone observing a poor looking man like a joiner, I made up to him, and repeated the same story, assuring him that twenty shillings should be at his service, if he could furnish me with a smith's hammer and a punch. The man

* Tottenham *West*, now called Tottenham Court Road, and *not* Tottenham near Edmonton.

proved a shoemaker by trade, but, willing to obtain the reward, immediately borrowed the tools of a blacksmith, his neighbour, and likewise gave me great assistance, and before five that evening I had entirely got rid of those troublesome companions, my fetters, which I gave to the fellow, besides his twenty shillings, if he thought fit to make use of them.

That night I came to a cellar at *Charing Cross*, and refreshed very comfortably with roast veal, &c., where about a dozen people were all discoursing about *Sheppard*, and nothing else was talked on whilst I staid amongst them. I had tyed a handkerchief about my head, tore my woollen cap in many places, as likewise my coat and stockings, and looked exactly like what I designed to represent, a beggar fellow.

The next day I took shelter at an alehouse of little or no trade in *Rupert Street*, near *Piccadilly*. The woman and I discoursed much about Sheppard. I assured her it was impossible for him to escape out of the kingdom, and that the keepers would have him again in a few days. The woman wished that a curse might fall on those who should betray him. I continued there till the evening, when I stept into the *Haymarket*, and mixt with a crowd around two ballad singers, the subject being about Sheppard, and I remember the company were very merry about the matter.

On *Tuesday*, I hired a garret for my lodgings at a poor house in *Newport-market*, and sent for a *sober young woman*, who for a long time past had been the real mistress of my affections, who came to me, and rendered all the assistance she was capable of affording. I made her the messenger to my mother, who lodged in *Clare-street*. *She* likewise visited me in a day or two after, begging on her bended knees of me to make the best of my way out of the kingdom, which I faithfully promised; but I cannot say it was in my intention heartily to do so.

I was often times in *Spittle Fields, Drury Lane, Lewkiner's Lane, Parker's Lane, St. Thomas's Street, &c.*, those having been the chief scenes of my rambles and pleasures.*

I had once formed a design to have opened a shop or two in *Monmouth Street* for some necessaries, but let that drop;† and came to a resolution of breaking the house of the two Mr. *Rawlins'* brothers and *Pawnbrokers* in *Drury Lane*, which I

---

* It was during this period, doubtless, that among the places he has enumerated here, Jack visited Chick Lane, so familiar to every one lately, under the name of West Street.

† Very cool this intention of Jack. The Ordinary missed a fine peg here.

accordingly put in execution, and succeeded; they both hearing me rifling their goods as they lay in bed together in the next room.   And though there were none others there to assist me, I pretended there were, by loudly giving out directions for shooting the first person through the head that presumed to stir—which effectually quieted them, while I carried off my booty;* with part whereof, on the fatal *Saturday* following, being the 31st of October, I made an extraordinary appearance: and from a *carpenter* and *butcher* was now transformed into a perfect gentleman; and in company with my sweetheart aforesaid, and another young woman her acquaintance, went into the city, and were very merry together at a public house not far from the place of my old confinement.† At four that same afternoon we all passed under *Newgate* in a hackney coach, the window drawn up, and in the evening sent for my mother to the *Shears* alehouse in *Maypole Alley*, near *Clare Market*, and with her drank three quarterns of brandy, and after leaving her I drank in one place or other about that neighbourhood all the evening, till the evil hour of twelve, having been seen and known by many of my acquaintances; all of them cautioning of me, and wondering at my presumption to appear in that manner.   At length my senses were quite overcome with the quantity and variety of liquors I had all the day been drinking of, which paved the way for my fate to meet me; and when apprehended, I do protest I was altogether incapable of resistance, and scarce knew what they were doing to me, and had had but two second-hand pistols scarce worth carrying about me.‡

A clear and ample account have I now given of the most material transactions of my life, and do hope the same will prove a warning to all young men.

There nothing now remains. But I return my hearty thanks

---

* This circumstance, as well as many others, prove Jack had no small talents for Comedy—the idea of the two brothers frightened out of their lives, remaining quietly trembling in their beds, whilst their property is being carried off is ludicrous enough.

† There can be little doubt this was the Old Red Lion Tavern, though, from prudential reasons, at that time, the name is not mentioned.

‡ It is quite clear Jack intended to have made a desperate resistance to any attempt to take him; had he not stupified himself he would doubtless have stood on no repairs. From the commencement of the account of his last escape from the Castle, up to this period, Jack's statement appears to be scrupulously faithful and ungarbled, and is intensely interesting. The concluding remarks—expressions of resignation, thanks to the clergy, flourish about Jack's mother, &c. &c., would all appear to have been furnished by our friend Wagstaff; they, however, terminate the confession appropriately enough, and with this admission we will leave it.

to the Reverend Dr. *Bennet*, the Reverend Mr. *Purney*, the Reverend Mr. *Wagstaff*, the Reverend Mr. *Hawkins*, the Reverend Mr. *Flood*, and the Reverend Mr. *Edwards*, for their charitable visits and assistance to me; as also my thanks to those worthy gentlemen who so generously contributed towards my support in prison.

I hope none will be so cruel as to reflect on my poor distressed mother, the unhappy parent of two miserable wretches, myself and brother; the last gone to *America* for his crimes, and myself going to the grave for mine; the weight of which misfortune is sufficient surely to satisfy the malice of her enemies.

I beseech the infinite Divine Being of Beings to pardon my numberless and enormous crimes, and to have mercy on my poor departing soul.

JOHN SHEPPARD.

Middle Stone Room, in Newgate.
November, 10, 1724.

POSTSCRIPT.

After I had escaped from the *Castle*, concluding that *Blueskin* would have certainly been decreed for death, I did fully resolve and purpose to have gone and *cut down the gallows* the night before his execution.*

JACK'S LAST CAPTURE.

The two following curious accounts of Jack's last capture, he himself being unable to furnish it, are copied, *verbatim et literatim*, from the *Daily Journal* and *Daily Post*, of Monday, November 2, 1724, now in possession of the writer of the foregoing work. The appearance of these daily papers, each a small folio leaf of two pages, contrast strangely with that of the voluminous double *Times* of our own age, which contains, at least, fifty times as much matter as did the journals of 1724. To get through a morning paper now, the reader must have a

---

* How kind and friendly of Jack! It is extraordinary that the Reverend Wagstaff should have suffered this declaration to appear.

capacity of, at least, fifty *quid nunc* power, compared to that necessary for the perusal of a journal by the newsmongers of one hundred and twenty years since.

THE DAILY JOURNAL.

Monday, November 2, 1724.

" On Saturday night last, the famous John Sheppard was apprehended and taken in the manner following :—At between eleven and twelve of the clock he came to the shop of one Nicks, a butcher in Drury Lane, and, having agreed for three ribs of beef, he desired Nicks to go with him to Mrs. Campbell's, a *chandler's shop*, a door or two further, intending to treat him with a dram of *brandy*, and to pay him for the same ; Nicks went accordingly, and whilst they were drinking, an ale-house boy, belonging to Mr. Bradford, who keeps the Rose and Crown against the house, came in to ask for pots, and, seeing Sheppard, went and acquainted his master, who, being a headborough, took to his assistance the watch, and seized Sheppard in the brandy shop, who was dressed in a handsome suit of black clothes, a diamond ring, and a cornelian ring on his finger, and a light tye perriwig of about seven pounds value, three other plain gold rings in his pocket, two tortoise-shell snuff-boxes, a tortoise-shell watch, and five guineas and two half-guineas, and two loaded pistols in his pockets ; Mr. Eyles, a constable, was sent for, who, together with the headborough aforesaid, watch, &c., put him into a hackney coach, and conveyed him to Newgate ; several thousands of people being assembled in Holborn, as he was in the coach, he called out " murder, help, for God's sake, rogues, I am murdered, and am in the hands of blood-hounds, help, for Christ's sake," &c. Being brought to Newgate, he owned that, on Friday morning last, he did break open the shop of Mr. Rawlins, a pawnbroker, at the Four Balls in Drury Lane, and took from thence a suit of black cloth clothes, a light tye perriwig, and a bob perriwig, a gold watch, and a tortoiseshell watch, two tortoiseshell snuff-boxes, a silver hilted sword, a night-gown, and other goods, to the value of about sixty pounds. He is now put into an apartment called the Middle Stone Room, adjoining to the Castle, and is loaded with three hundred weight of irons.

THE DAILY POST.

" *Monday, November 2, 1724.*

" John Sheppard, the famous thief, house-breaker, and gaol-breaker, who, being under sentence of death, had made his escape out of Newgate two several times, in a very surprising and wonderful manner, was re-taken on Saturday night last, about twelve, and brought back thither before one next morning, where sufficient care is taken to secure him for the remainder of his time, he being confined in a very strong apartment, doubly ironed on both legs, handcufft, and chained down to the ground with a chain running through his irons, which is fastened on each side of him, and, we hear, a watch will be kept upon him besides. He was apprehended in the following manner :—A boy belonging to Mr. Bradford, a headborough in Drury Lane, saw him at a butcher's shop, near Newtoner's Lane, cheapening some ribs of beef, and meeting with an acquaintance of his, of the Hundreds of Drury, commonly called Moll Frisky,* he went to treat her with a dram at a chandler's shop adjoining ; in the mean time the boy, who knew him perfectly well, told his master what he had seen, who, getting some persons to his assistance, apprehended him. When he was searched, they found a pair of pistols about him ready charged. He was equipped every way like a gentleman, having on a wig worth about seven guineas, a diamond ring on his finger, a watch and snuff-box in his pocket, and some gold, being also dressed in a suit of black, having furnished himself therewith on Friday morning last, by breaking open a pawn-broker's shop in Drury Lane, and taking from thence most of the said goods, and divers others, to the value, as we are told, of about sixty pounds. When he was brought back to the goal he was very drunk, carried himself insolently, and defied the keepers to hold him, with all their irons, art, and skill."

---

* Probably the " *sober* young woman" that Jack mentions had for a long time been the mistress of his affections, and whom he sent to after his last escape, as this young person had passed the afternoon in his company, according to his own account, on the day of his apprehension.—*Vide his Confession.*

JACK'S EXECUTION.

[The following account of Sheppard's execution appeared in the papers of the day.]

" On Monday morning, about nine of the clock, the famous John Sheppard was carried up from the condemned hold to the chapel in Newgate, where having heard prayers, and received the holy sacrament, he was brought down again to the press yard, between ten and eleven, when Mr. Watson came, in the name of the sheriffs, to demand his body; Mr. Perry and Mr. Reuse, after taking the proper receipt, delivered the same; Mr. Watson told the prisoner that he must put him on a pair of handcuffs for his security; he vehemently resisted the same, flying into the greatest passion, and endeavoured to beat the officers; upon searching him, they found a penknife concealed about his clothes, with which it is apprehended he designed to have cut the ropes and attempt to escape out of the cart. Never was such a concourse of people ever seen in Holborn, and the place leading to Tyburn. An undertaker, with a hearse, followed him thither, in order, as we are told, to bring back the corpse to be interred in St. Sepulchre's church-yard: but the populace, having a notion that it was designed to convey him to the surgeons, carried off the body upon their shoulders to an ale-house in Long Acre, and the undertaker and his men got off with great difficulty. The violence of the multitude continued so outrageous that it was thought necessary, about eight o'clock at night, to send a detachment of the Guards from the Savoy to Long Acre to disperse them, at whose approach they thought fit to retire.

" Before Sheppard's death, he sent for Mr. Applebee, a printer, into the cart, and, in view of several thousands of people, delivered to him a printed pamphlet, entitled, ' *A Narrative of all his Robberies and Escapes,*' " being the Confession made to Mr. Wagstaff, the Ordinary, when under sentence in Newgate.

* This, doubtless, was a bit of a gag got up between Applebee and Jack, to serve by way of a *pilot paragraph* to the publication of the Work in question, of which we have given a correct transcript. It was certainly a striking advertisement to the work, and no doubt materially enhanced its sale.

JONATHAN WILD.

The skeleton of Jonathan Wild, enclosed in a glass case, is still to be seen by the curious in such delectable sights, in the museum of a Mr. Fowler, a surgeon, of Church Street, Windsor; it is in tolerable preservation. From a phrenological examination of the skull by a pupil of Gall and Spurzheim, ignorant of the history of its subject, all those astute qualities for which Jonathan was so remarkable, were found to be distinctly developed in the different craniological organs. This should teach persons the folly of treating too lightly any new discovery, either in nature or art, however improbable it may appear on the first blush. The ridicule passed on the system of Gall and Spurzheim, when first made public, cannot but be remembered, yet the infallibility of phrenology is now as firmly established, and generally admitted, as that of any other science, let self-sufficient *bump*-kins say what they will. Jonathan Wild did not long survive his victim, Jack Sheppard; he was hanged at Tyburn, on Monday, the 24th May, 1725, for being accessary to a robbery which he planned, and caused to be committed, whilst in prison for another very trifling offence. As might have been expected, he met his fate in the most dastardly manner, after vainly attempting, by a recapitulation of the many lives he had caused to be sacrificed to offended justice, to preserve his own.

Some idea may be formed of the plausible and unsuspicious manner in which Jonathan was used to carry on his trade, by the following advertisement, which appeared in the *Daily Post*, the very same day that it contained the account of Jack Sheppard's last capture.

ADVERTISEMENT.

Lost, the 1st of October, a black shagreen pocket-book, edged with silver, with some notes of hand. The said book was lost in the Strand, near the Fountain Tavern, about seven or eight o'clock at night. If any person will bring the aforesaid book to Mr. Jonathan Wild, in the Old Bailey, he shall have a guinea reward.—Monday, November 2, 1724.

[When the reader is informed that, in the year 1724, the Fountain Tavern was one of the most notorious brothels in the Strand, it will require no great stretch of imagination to conceive that the black shagreen pocket-book, containing some notes of hand, and lost at the time of evening prayers, between the chapel hours of seven and eight in the evening, had been abstracted by some adroit nymph of the pavé in Jonathan's service, from the person of some gentleman of repute and character that might not exactly wish to be known, and that the said shagreen pocket-book, edged with silver, with its notes of hand, might actually have been, at the time of advertising a reward for it, in the identical breeches pocket of the praise-worthy and truly disinterested Mr. Jonathan. The thing is quite clear, but who would have thought it?]

EXECUTION OF BLUESKIN.

, [In Gent's *York Journal*, No. 1, Monday, November the 16th, to November the 23d, 1724, the following paragraph, no doubt extracted from some London newspaper of the period, occurs—] " The corpse of Blueskin, lately executed at Tyburn, was interred at a burying-ground belonging to Saint Andrew's, Holborn, being attended by a great mob to the grave."

[It was a pity Jack had not been at liberty to have carried into effect his friendly intention of cutting down the gallows on the evening previous to the day fixed for Blueskin's execution, who must have looked very *blue* indeed when the dead warrant came down, as it is termed, for his exit.]

J. LEIGHTON, PRINTER, JOHNSON'S COURT, FLEET STREET.

LIST OF PLATES

DIRECTIONS TO THE BINDER.

www.ingramcontent.com/pod-product-compliance
Lightning Source LLC
Chambersburg PA
CBHW080942020726
47505CB00009B/2121